EPISODE II

ATTACK OF THE CLONES™

STAR WARS

EPISODE II

ATTACK OF THE CLONES™

R. A. SALVATORE

BASED ON THE STORY BY
GEORGE LUCAS

AND THE SCREENPLAY BY
GEORGE LUCAS
AND
JONATHAN HALES

CC 7424
26.⁰⁰
AF
6/02

LUCAS
BOOKS

DEL REY BALLANTINE BOOKS
NEW YORK

A Del Rey® Book
Published by The Ballantine Publishing Group

Copyright © 2002 by Lucasfilm Ltd. & ® or ™ where indicated.
All Rights Reserved. Used Under Authorization.

All rights reserved under International and Pan-American Copyright Conventions.
Published in the United States by The Ballantine Publishing Group, a division
of Random House, Inc., New York, and simultaneously in Canada by
Random House of Canada Limited, Toronto.

Del Rey is a registered trademark and the Del Rey colophon is a trademark
of Random House, Inc.

www.starwars.com
www.starwarskids.com
www.delreydigital.com

Library of Congress Catalog Card Number: 2002101521

ISBN 0-345-42881-1

Manufactured in the United States of America

First Edition: April 2002

10 9 8 7 6 5 4 3 2 1

A LONG TIME AGO IN A GALAXY FAR, FAR AWAY....

EPISODE II

ATTACK OF THE CLONES™

PRELUDE

His mind absorbed the scene before him, so quiet and calm and . . . normal.

It was the life he had always wanted, a gathering of family and friends—he knew that they were just that, though the only one he recognized was his dear mother.

This was the way it was supposed to be. The warmth and the love, the laughter and the quiet times. This was how he had always dreamed it would be, how he had always prayed it would be. The warm, inviting smiles. The pleasant conversation. The gentle pats on shoulders.

But most of all there was the smile of his beloved mother, so happy now, no more a slave. When she looked at him, he saw all of that and more, saw how proud she was of him, how joyful her life had become.

She moved before him, her face beaming, her hand reaching out for him to gently stroke his face. Her smile brightened, then widened some more.

Too much more.

For a moment, he thought the exaggeration a product of love beyond normal bounds, but the smile continued to grow, his mother's face stretching and contorting weirdly.

She seemed to be moving in slow motion then. They all did, slowing as if their limbs had become heavy.

No, not heavy, he realized, his warm feelings turning suddenly hot. It was as if these friends and his mother were becoming rigid and stiff, as if they were becoming something less than living and breathing humans. He stared back at that caricature of a smile, the twisted face, and recognized the pain behind it, a crystalline agony.

He tried to call out to her, to ask her what she needed him to do, ask her how he could help.

Her face twisted even more, blood running from her eyes. Her skin crystalized, becoming almost translucent, almost like glass.

Glass! She was glass! The light glistened off her crystalline highlights, the blood ran fast over her smooth surface. And her expression, a look of resignation and apology, a look that said she had failed him and that he had failed her, drove a sharp point straight into the helpless onlooker's heart.

He tried to reach out for her, tried to save her.

Cracks began to appear in the glass. He heard the crunching sounds as they elongated.

He cried out repeatedly, reached for her desperately. Then he thought of the Force, and sent his thoughts there with all his willpower, reaching for her with all his energy.

But then, she shattered.

The Jedi Padawan jumped to a sitting position in his cot on the starship, his eyes popping open wide, sweat on his forehead and his breath coming in gasps.

A dream. It was all a dream.

He told himself that repeatedly as he tried to settle back down on the cot. It was all a dream.

Or was it?

He could see things, after all, before they happened.

"Ansion!" came a call from the front of the ship, the familiar voice of his Master.

He knew that he had to shake the dream away, had to focus on the events at hand, the latest assignment beside his Master, but that was easier said than done.

For he saw her again, his mother, her body going rigid, crystallizing, then exploding into a million shattered shards.

He looked up ahead, envisioning his Master at the controls, wondering if he should tell all to the Jedi, wondering if the Jedi would be able to help him. But that thought washed away as soon as it had crossed his mind. His Master, Obi-Wan Kenobi, would not be able to help. They were too involved in other things, in his training, in minor assignments like the border dispute that had brought them so far out from Coruscant.

The Padawan wanted to get back to Coruscant, as soon as possible. He needed guidance now, but not the kind he was getting from Obi-Wan.

He needed to speak with Chancellor Palpatine again, to hear the man's reassuring words. Palpatine had taken a great interest in him over the last ten years, making sure that he always got a chance to speak with him whenever he and Obi-Wan were on Coruscant.

The Padawan took great comfort in that now, with the terrible dream so vivid in his thoughts. For the Chancellor, the wise leader of all the Republic, had promised him that his powers would soar to previously unknown heights, that he would become a power even among the powerful Jedi.

Perhaps that was the answer. Perhaps the mightiest of the Jedi, the mightiest of the mighty, could strengthen the fragile glass.

"Ansion," came the call again from the front. "Anakin, get up here!"

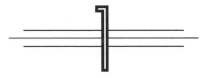

Shmi Skywalker Lars stood on the edge of the sand berm marking the perimeter of the moisture farm, one leg up higher, to the very top of the ridge, knee bent. With one hand on that knee for support, the middle-aged woman, her dark hair slightly graying, her face worn and tired, stared up at the many bright dots of starlight on this crisp Tatooine night. No sharp edges broke the landscape about her, just the smooth and rounded forms of windblown sand dunes on this planet of seemingly endless sands. Somewhere out in the distance a creature groaned, a plaintive sound that resonated deeply within Shmi this night.

This special night.

Her son Anakin, her dearest little Annie, turned twenty this night, a birthday Shmi observed each year, though she hadn't seen her beloved child in a decade. How different he must be! How grown, how strong, how wise in the ways of the Jedi by now! Shmi, who had lived all of her life in a small area of drab Tatooine, knew that she could hardly imagine the wonders her boy might have found out there among the stars, on planets so different from this, with colors more vivid and water that filled entire valleys.

A wistful smile widened on her still-pretty face as she remembered those days long ago, when she and her son had been slaves of the wretch Watto. Annie, with his mischief and his dreams, with his independent attitude and unsurpassed courage, used to so infuriate the Toydarian junk dealer. Despite the hardships of life as a slave, there had been good times, too, back then. Despite their meager food, their meager possessions, despite the constant complaining and ordering about by Watto, she had been with Annie, her beloved son.

"You should come in," came a quiet voice behind her.

Shmi's smile only widened, and she turned to see her stepson, Owen Lars, walking over to join her. He was a stocky and strong boy about Anakin's age, with short brown hair, a few bristles, and a wide face that could not hide anything that was within his heart.

Shmi tousled Owen's hair when he moved beside her, and he responded by draping an arm across her shoulders and kissing her on the cheek.

"No starship tonight, Mom?" Owen asked good-naturedly. He knew why Shmi had come out here, why she came out here so very often in the quiet night.

Shmi turned her hand over and gently stroked it down Owen's face, smiling. She loved this young man as she loved her own son, and he had been so good to her, so understanding of the hole that remained within her heart. Without jealousy, without judgment, Owen had accepted Shmi's pain and had always given her a shoulder to lean on.

"No starship this night," she replied, and she looked back

up at the starry canopy. "Anakin must be busy saving the galaxy or chasing smugglers and other outlaws. He has to do those things now, you know."

"Then I shall sleep more soundly from this night forward," Owen replied with a grin.

Though she was kidding, of course, Shmi did realize a bit of truth in her presumption about Anakin. He was a special child, something beyond the norm—even for a Jedi, she believed. Anakin had always stood taller than anyone else. Not physically—physically, as Shmi remembered him, he was just a smiling little boy, with curious eyes and sandy-blond hair. But Annie could do things, and so very well. Even though he was only a child at the time, he had raced Pods, defeating some of the very best racers on all of Tatooine. He was the first human ever to win one of the Podraces, and that when he was only nine years old! And in a racer that, Shmi remembered with an even wider smile, had been built with spare parts taken from Watto's junkyard.

But that was Anakin's way, because he was not like the other children, or even like other adults. Anakin could "see" things before they happened, as if he was so tuned to the world about him that he understood innately the logical conclusion to any course of events. He could often sense problems with his Podracer, for example, long before those problems manifested themselves in a catastrophic way. He had once told her that he could feel the upcoming obstacles in any course before he actually saw them. It was his special way, and that was why the Jedi who had come to Tatooine had recognized the unique nature of the boy and had freed him from Watto and taken him into their care and instruction.

"I had to let him go," Shmi said quietly. "I could not keep him with me, if that meant living the life of a slave."

"I know," Owen assured her.

"I could not have kept him with me even if we were not slaves," she went on, and she looked at Owen, as if her own words had surprised her. "Annie has so much to give to the galaxy. His gifts could not be contained by Tatooine. He belongs out there, flying across the stars, saving planets. He was born to be a Jedi, born to give so much more to so many more."

"That is why I sleep better at night," Owen reiterated, and when Shmi looked at him, she saw that his grin was wider than ever.

"Oh, you're teasing me!" she said, reaching out to swat her stepson on the shoulder. Owen merely shrugged.

Shmi's face went serious again. "Annie wanted to go," she went on, the same speech she had given Owen before, the same speech that she had silently repeated to herself every night for the last ten years. "His dream was to fly about the stars, to see every world in the whole galaxy, to do grand things. He was born a slave, but he was not born *to be* a slave. No, not my Annie.

"Not my Annie."

Owen squeezed her shoulder. "You did the right thing. If I was Anakin, I would be grateful to you. I'd understand that you did what was best for me. There is no greater love than that, Mom."

Shmi stroked his face again and even managed a wistful smile.

"Come on in, Mom," Owen said, taking her hand. "It's dangerous out here."

Shmi nodded and didn't resist at first as Owen started to

pull her along. She stopped suddenly, though, and stared hard at her stepson as he turned back to regard her. "It's more dangerous out there," she said, sucking in her breath, her voice breaking. Alarm evident in her expression, she looked back up at the wide and open sky. "What if he is hurt, Owen? Or dead?"

"It's better to die in pursuit of your dreams than to live a life without hope," Owen said, rather unconvincingly.

Shmi looked back at him, her smile returning. Owen, like his father, was about as grounded in simple pragmatism as any man could be. She understood that he had said that only for her benefit, and that made it all the more special.

She didn't resist anymore as Owen began to lead her along again, back to the humble abode of Cliegg Lars, her husband, Owen's father.

She had done the right thing concerning her son, Shmi told herself with every step. They had been slaves, with no prospects of finding their freedom other than the offer of the Jedi. How could she have kept Anakin here on Tatooine, when Jedi Knights were promising him all of his dreams?

Of course, at that time, Shmi had not known that she would meet Cliegg Lars that fateful day in Mos Espa, and that the moisture farmer would fall in love with her, buy her from Watto, and free her, and only then, once she was a free woman, ask her to marry him. Would she have let Anakin go if she had known the changes that would come into her life so soon after his departure?

Wouldn't her life be better now, more complete by far, if Anakin were beside her?

Shmi smiled as she thought about it. No, she realized, she would still have wanted Annie to go, even if she had foreseen the dramatic changes that would soon come into her life. Not for herself, but for Anakin. His place was out there. She knew that.

Shmi shook her head, overwhelmed by the enormity of it all, by the many winding turns in her life's path, in Anakin's path. Even in hindsight, she could not be sure that this present situation was not the best possible outcome, for both of them.

But still, there remained a deep and empty hole in her heart.

I can help with that," Beru said politely, moving to join Shmi, who was cooking dinner. Cliegg and Owen were out closing down the perimeter of the compound, securing the farm from the oncoming night—a night that promised a dust storm.

Smiling warmly, and glad that this young woman was soon to be a member of their family, Shmi handed a knife over to Beru. Owen hadn't said anything yet about marrying Beru, but Shmi could tell from the way the two looked at each other. It was only a matter of time, and not much time at that, if she knew her stepson. Owen was not an adventurous type, was as solid as the ground beneath them, but when he knew what he wanted, he went after it with single-minded purpose.

Beru was exactly that, and she obviously loved Owen as deeply as he loved her. She was well suited to be the wife of a moisture farmer, Shmi thought, watching her methodically go about her duties in the kitchen. She never shied from work, was very capable and diligent.

And she doesn't expect much, or need much to make her happy,

Shmi thought, for that, in truth, was the crux of it. Their existence here was simple and plain. There were few adventures, and none at all that were welcomed, for excitement out here usually meant that Tusken Raiders had been seen in the region, or that a gigantic sandstorm or some other potentially devastating weather phenomenon was blowing up.

The Lars family had only the simple things, mostly the company of each other, to keep them amused and content. For Cliegg, this had been the only way of life he had ever known, a lifestyle that went back several generations in the Lars family. Same thing for Owen. And while Beru had grown up in Mos Eisley, she seemed to fit right in.

Yes, Owen would marry her, Shmi knew, and what a happy day that would be!

The two men returned soon after, along with C-3PO, the protocol droid Anakin had built back in the days when he had Watto's junkyard to rummage through.

"Two more tangaroots for you, Mistress Shmi," the thin droid said, handing Shmi a pair of orange-and-green freshly picked vegetables. "I would have brought more, but I was told, and not in any civil way, that I must hurry."

Shmi looked to Cliegg, and he gave her a grin and a shrug. "Could've left him out there to get sandblasted clean, I suppose," he said. "Of course, some of the bigger rocks that are sure to be flying about might've taken out a circuit or two."

"Your pardon, Master Cliegg," C-3PO said. "I only meant—"

"We know what you meant, Threepio," Shmi assured the droid. She placed a comforting hand on his shoulder, then quickly pulled it away, thinking that a perfectly silly gesture to offer to a walking box of wires. Of course, C-3PO was much more than a box of wires to Shmi. Anakin had built the droid . . . almost.

When Anakin had left with the Jedi, 3PO had been perfectly functional, but uncovered, his wires exposed. Shmi had left him that way for a long time, fantasizing that Anakin would return to complete the job. Just before marrying Cliegg had Shmi finished the droid herself, adding the dull metal coverings. It had been quite a touching moment for Shmi, an admission of sorts that she was where she belonged and Anakin was where he belonged. The protocol droid could be quite annoying at times, but to Shmi, C-3PO remained a reminder of her son.

"Course, if there are Tuskens about, they'd likely have gotten him under wraps before the storm," Cliegg went on, obviously taking great pleasure in teasing the poor droid. "You're not afraid of Tusken Raiders, are you, Threepio?"

"There is nothing in my program to suggest such fear," 3PO replied, though he would have sounded more convincing if he hadn't been shaking as he spoke, and if his voice hadn't come out all squeaky and uneven.

"Enough," Shmi demanded of Cliegg. "Oh, poor Threepio," she said, patting the droid's shoulder again. "Go ahead, now. I've got more than enough help this evening." As she finished, she waved the droid away.

"You're just terrible to that poor droid," she remarked, moving beside her husband and playfully patting him across his broad shoulder.

"Well, if I can't have fun with him, I'll have to set my sights on someone else," the rarely mischievous Cliegg replied, narrowing his eyes and scanning the room. He finally settled a threatening gaze on Beru.

"Cliegg," Shmi was quick to warn.

"What?" he protested dramatically. "If she's thinking to come out and live here, then she had better learn to defend herself!"

"Dad!" Owen cried.

"Oh, don't fret about old Cliegg," Beru piped in, emphasizing the word *old*. "A fine wife I would make if I couldn't outduel that one in a war of words!"

"Aha! A challenge!" Cliegg roared.

"Not so much of one from where I'm sitting," Beru dryly returned, and she and Cliegg began exchanging some good-natured insults, with Owen chiming in every now and again.

Shmi hardly listened, too engaged in merely watching Beru. Yes, she would certainly fit in, and well, about the moisture farm. Her temperament was perfect. Solid, but playful when the situation allowed. Gruff Cliegg could verbally spar with the best of them, but Beru had to be counted among that elite lot. Shmi went back to her dinner preparations, her smile growing wider every time Beru hit Cliegg with a particularly nasty retort.

Intent on her work, Shmi never saw the missile coming, and when the overripe vegetable hit her on the side of the face, she let out a shriek.

Of course, that only made the other three in the room howl with laughter.

Shmi turned to see them sitting there, staring at her. From the embarrassed expression on Beru's face, and from the angle, with Beru sitting directly behind Cliegg, it seemed obvious to Shmi that Beru had launched the missile, aiming for Cliegg, but throwing a bit high.

"The girl listens when you tell her to stop," Cliegg Lars said, his sarcastic tone shattered by a burst of laughter that came right from his belly.

He stopped when Shmi smacked him with a piece of juicy fruit, splattering it across his shoulders.

A food fight began—measured, of course, and with more threats hurled than actual missiles.

When it ended, Shmi began the cleanup, the other three helping for a bit. "You two go and spend some time together without your troublemaking father," Shmi told Owen and Beru. "Cliegg started it, so Cliegg will help clean it up. Go on, now. I'll call you back when dinner's on the table."

Cliegg gave a little laugh.

"And if you mess up the next one, you're going to be hungry," Shmi told him, threateningly waving a spoon his way. "And lonely!"

"Whoa! Never that!" Cliegg said, holding his hands up in a sign of surrender.

With a wave of the spoon, Shmi further dismissed Owen and Beru, and the two went off happily.

"She'll make him a fine wife," Shmi said to Cliegg.

He walked up beside her and grabbed her about the waist, pulling her tight. "We Lars men fall in love with the best women."

Shmi looked back to see his warm and sincere smile, and she returned it in kind. This was the way it was supposed to be. Good honest work, a sense of true accomplishment, and enough free time for some fun, at least. This was the life Shmi had always wanted. This was perfect, almost.

A wistful look came over her face.

"Thinking of your boy again," Cliegg Lars stated, instead of asked.

Shmi looked at him, her expression a mixture of joy and sadness, a single dark cloud crossing a sunny blue sky. "Yes, but it's okay this time," she said. "He's safe, I know, and doing great things."

"But when we have such fun, you wish he could be here."

Shmi smiled again. "I do, and in all other times, as well. I wish Anakin had been here from the beginning, since you and I first met."

"Five years ago," Cliegg remarked.

"He would love you as I do, and he and Owen . . ." Her voice weakened and trailed away.

"You think that Anakin and Owen would be friends?" Cliegg asked. "Bah! Of course they would!"

"You've never even met my Annie!" Shmi scolded.

"They'd be the best of friends," Cliegg assured her, tightening his hug once again. "How could they not be, with you as that one's mother?"

Shmi accepted the compliment gracefully, looked back and gave Cliegg a deep and appreciative kiss. She was thinking of Owen, of the young man's flowering romance with the lovely Beru. How Shmi loved them both!

But that thought brought with it some level of discomfort. Shmi had often wondered if Owen had been part of the reason she had so readily agreed to marry Cliegg. She looked back at her husband, rubbing her hand over his broad shoulder. Yes, she loved him, and deeply, and she certainly couldn't deny her joy at finally being relieved of her slave bonds. But despite all of that, what part had the presence of Owen played in her decisions? It had been a question that had stayed with her all these years. Had there been a need in her heart that Owen had filled? A mother's need to cover the hole left by Anakin's departure?

In truth, the two boys were very different in temperament. Owen was solid and staid, the rock who would gladly take over the farm from Cliegg when the time came, as this moisture farm had been passed down in the Lars family from generation to generation. Owen was ready, and even thrilled, to be the logical and rightful heir to the place, more than able to accept the often difficult lifestyle in exchange for the pride and sense of honest accomplishment that came with running the place correctly.

But Annie . . .

Shmi nearly laughed aloud as she considered her impetuous and wanderlust-filled son put in a similar situation. She had no doubts that Anakin would give Cliegg the same fits he had always given Watto. Anakin's adventurous spirit would not be tamed by any sense of generational responsibility, Shmi knew. His need to leap out for adventure, to race the Pods, to fly among the stars, would not have been diminished, and it surely would have driven Cliegg crazy.

Now Shmi did giggle, picturing Cliegg turning red-faced with exasperation when Anakin had let his duties slide once again.

Cliegg hugged her all the tighter at the sound, obviously having no clue of the mental images fluttering through her brain.

Shmi melted into that hug, knowing that she was where she belonged, and taking comfort in the hope that Anakin, too, was where he truly belonged.

She wasn't wearing one of the grand gowns that had marked the station of her life for the last decade and more. Her hair was not done up in wondrous fashion, with some glittering accessory woven into the thick brown strands. And in that plainness, Padmé Amidala only appeared more beautiful and more shining.

The woman sitting beside her on the bench swing, so obviously a relation, was a bit older, a bit more matronly, perhaps, with clothes even more plain than Padmé's and with her hair a bit more out of place. But she was no less beautiful, shining with an inner glow equally strong.

"Did you finish your meetings with Queen Jamillia?" Sola asked. It was obvious from her tone that the meetings to which she had referred were not high on her personal wish list.

Padmé looked over at her, then looked back to the playhouse where Sola's daughters, Ryoo and Pooja, were in the midst of a wild game of tag.

"It was one meeting," Padmé explained. "The Queen had some information to pass along."

"About the Military Creation Act," Sola stated.

Padmé didn't bother to confirm the obvious. The Military Creation Act now before the Senate was the most important piece of business in many years, one that held implications for the Republic even beyond those during the dark time when Padmé had been Queen and the Trade Federation had tried to conquer Naboo.

"The Republic is all in a tumult, but not to fear, for Senator Amidala will put it all aright," Sola said.

Padmé turned to her, somewhat surprised by the level of sarcasm in Sola's tone.

"That's what you do, right?" Sola innocently asked.

"It's what I try to do."

"It's *all* you try to do."

"What is that supposed to mean?" Padmé asked, her face twisting with puzzlement. "I am a Senator, after all."

"A Senator after a Queen, and probably with many more offices ahead of her," Sola said. She looked back at the playhouse and called for Ryoo and Pooja to ease up.

"You speak as if it's a bad thing," Padmé remarked.

Sola looked at her earnestly. "It's a great thing," she said. "If you're doing it all for the right reasons."

"And what is that supposed to mean?"

Sola shrugged, as if she wasn't quite sure. "I think you've convinced yourself that you're indispensable to the Republic," she said. "That they couldn't get along at all without you."

"Sis!"

"It's true," Sola insisted. "You give and give and give and give. Don't you ever want to take, just a little?"

Padmé's smile showed that Sola's words had caught her off guard. "Take what?"

Sola looked back to Ryoo and Pooja. "Look at them. I see the sparkle in your eyes when you watch my children. I know how much you love them."

"Of course I do!"

"Wouldn't you like to have children of your own?" Sola asked. "A family of your own?"

Padmé sat up straight, her eyes going wide. "I . . ." she started, and stopped, several times. "I'm working right now for something I deeply believe in. For something that's important."

"And after this is settled, after the Military Creation Act is far behind you, you'll find something else to deeply believe in, something else that's really important. Something that concerns the Republic and the government more than it really concerns you."

"How can you say that?"

"Because it's true, and you know it's true. When are you going to do something just for yourself?"

"I am."

"You know what I mean."

Padmé gave a little laugh and a shake of her head, and turned back to Ryoo and Pooja. "Is everyone to be defined by their children?" she asked.

"Of course not," Sola replied. "It's not that at all. Or not just that. I'm talking about something bigger, Sis. You spend all of your time worrying about the problems of other people, of this planet's dispute with that planet, or whether this trade guild is acting fairly toward that system. All of your energy is being thrown out there to try to make the lives of everyone else better."

"What's wrong with that?"

"What about *your* life?" Sola asked in all seriousness. "What about Padmé Amidala? Have you even thought about what might make your life better? Most people who have been in public service as long as you have would have retired by now. I know you get satisfaction in helping other people. That's pretty obvious. But what about something deeper for you? What about love, Sis? And yes, what about having kids? Have you even thought about it? Have you even wondered what it might be like for you to settle down and concern yourself with those things that will make your own life fuller?"

Padmé wanted to retort that her life didn't need to be any fuller, but she found herself holding back the words. Somehow they seemed hollow to her at that particular moment, watching her nieces romping about the backyard of the house, now jumping all about poor R2-D2, Padmé's astromech droid.

For the first time in many days, Padmé's thoughts roamed free of her responsibilities, free of the important vote she would have to cast in the Senate in less than a month. Somehow, the words *Military Creation Act* couldn't filter through the whimsical song that Ryoo and Pooja were then making up about R2-D2.

*   *   *

"Too close," Owen remarked gravely to Cliegg, the two of them walking the perimeter of the moisture farm, checking the security. The call of a bantha, the large and shaggy beasts often ridden by Tuskens, had interrupted their conversation.

They both knew it was unlikely that a bantha would be roaming wild about this region, for there was little grazing area anywhere near the desolate moisture farm. But they had heard the call, and could identify it without doubt, and they suspected that potential enemies were near.

"What is driving them so close to the farms?" Owen asked.

"It's been too long since we've organized anything against them," Cliegg replied gruffly. "We let the beasts run free, and they're forgetting the lessons we taught them in the past." He looked hard at Owen's skeptical expression. "You have to go out there and teach the Tuskens their manners every now and again."

Owen just stood there, having no response.

"See how long it's been?" Cliegg said with a snort. "You don't even remember the last time we went out and chased off the Tuskens! There's the problem, right there!"

The bantha lowed again.

Cliegg gave a growl in the general direction of the sound, waved his hand, and walked off toward the house. "You keep Beru close for a bit," he instructed. "The both of you stay within the perimeter, and keep a blaster at your side."

Owen nodded and dutifully followed as Cliegg stalked into the house. Right before the pair reached the door, the bantha lowed again.

It didn't seem so far away.

"What's the matter?" Shmi asked the moment Cliegg entered the house.

Her husband stopped, and managed to paste on a bit of a

comforting smile. "Just the sand," he said. "Covered some sensors, and I'm getting tired of digging them out." He smiled even wider and walked to the side of the room, heading for the refresher.

"Cliegg . . ." Shmi called suspiciously, stopping him.

Owen came through the door then, and Beru looked at him. "What is it?" she asked, unconsciously echoing Shmi.

"Nothing, nothing at all," Owen replied, but as he crossed the room, Beru stepped before him and took him by the arms, forcing him to look at her directly, into an expression too serious to be dismissed.

"Just signs of a sandstorm," Cliegg lied. "Far off, and probably nothing."

"But already enough to bury some sensors on the perimeter?" Shmi asked.

Owen looked at her curiously, then heard Cliegg clear his throat. He looked to his father, who nodded slightly, then turned back to Shmi and agreed. "The first winds, but I don't think it will be as strong as Dad believes."

"Are you both going to stand there lying to us?" Beru snapped suddenly, stealing the words from Shmi's mouth.

"What did you see, Cliegg?" Shmi demanded.

"Nothing," he answered with conviction.

"Then what did you hear?" Shmi pressed, recognizing her husband's semantic dodge clearly enough.

"I heard a bantha, nothing more," Cliegg admitted.

"And you think it was a Tusken mount," Shmi stated. "How far?"

"Who can tell, in the night, and with the wind shifting? Could've been kilometers."

"Or?"

Cliegg walked back across the room to stand right before his wife. "What do you want from me, love?" he asked, taking her in a firm hug. "I heard a bantha. I don't know if there was a Tusken attached."

"But there have been more signs of the Raiders about," Owen admitted. "The Dorrs found a pile of bantha poodoo half covering one of their perimeter sensors."

"It may be just that there's a few banthas running loose in the area, probably half starved and looking for some food," Cliegg offered.

"Or it might be that the Tuskens are growing bolder, are coming right down to the edges of the farms, and are even beginning to test the security," Shmi said. Almost prophetically, just as she finished, the alarms went off, indicating a breach about the perimeter sensor line.

Owen and Cliegg grabbed their blaster rifles and rushed out of the house, Shmi and Beru close behind.

"You stay here!" Cliegg instructed the two women. "Or go get a weapon, at least!" He glanced about, indicated a vantage point to Owen, and motioned for his son to take up a defensive position and cover him.

Then he rushed across the compound, blaster rifle in hand, zigzagging his way, staying low and scanning for any movement, knowing that if he saw a form that resembled either Tusken or bantha, he'd shoot first and investigate after.

But it didn't come to that. Cliegg and Owen searched the whole of the perimeter, scanned the area and rechecked the alarms, and found no sign of intruders.

All four stayed on edge the remainder of that night, though, each of them keeping a weapon close at hand, and sleeping only in shifts.

The next day, out by the eastern rim, Owen found the source of the alarm: a footprint along a patch of sturdier ground near the edge of the farm. It wasn't the large round depression a bantha would make, but the indentation one might expect from a foot wrapped in soft material, much like a Tusken would wear.

"We should speak with the Dorrs and all the others," Cliegg said when Owen showed the print to him. "Get a group together and chase the animals back into the open desert."

"The banthas?"

"Them, too," Cliegg snarled. He spat upon the ground, as steely-eyed and angry as Owen had ever seen him.

Senator Padmé Amidala felt strangely uneasy in her office, in the same complex as, but unattached to, the royal palace of Queen Jamillia. Her desk was covered in holodisks and all the other usual clutter of her station. At the front of it, a holo played through the numbers, a soldier on one scale, a flag of truce on the other, tallying the predicted votes for the meeting on Coruscant. The hologram depiction of those scales seemed almost perfectly balanced.

Padmé knew that the vote would be close, with the Senate almost evenly divided over whether the Republic should create a formal army. It galled her to think that so many of her colleagues would be voting based on personal gain—everything from potential contracts to supply the army for their home systems to direct payoffs from some of the commerce guilds—rather than on what was best for the Republic.

In her heart, Padmé remained steadfast that she had to work

to defeat the creation of this army. The Republic was built on tolerance. It was a vast network of tens of thousands of systems, and even more species, each with a distinct perspective. The only element they shared was tolerance—tolerance of one another. The creation of an army might prove unsettling, even threatening, to so many of those systems and species, beings far removed from the great city-planet of Coruscant.

A commotion outside drew Padmé to the window, and she looked down upon the complex courtyard to see a group of men jostling and fighting as the Naboo security forces rushed in to control the situation.

There came a sharp rap on the door to her office, and as she turned back that way, the portal slid open and Captain Panaka strode in.

"Just checking, Senator," said the man who had served as her personal bodyguard when she was Queen. Tall and dark-skinned, he had a steely gaze and an athletic physique only accentuated by the cut of his brown leather jerkin, blue shirt, and pants, and the mere sight of Panaka filled Padmé with comfort. He was in his forties now, but still looked as if he could outfight any man on Naboo.

"Shouldn't you be seeing to the security of Queen Jamillia?" Padmé asked.

Panaka nodded. "She is well protected, I assure you."

"From?" Padmé prompted, nodding toward the window and the continuing disturbance beyond.

"Spice miners," Panaka explained. "Contract issues. Nothing to concern you, Senator. Actually, I was on my way here to speak with you about security for your return trip to Coruscant."

"That is weeks away."

Panaka looked to the window. "Which gives us more time to properly prepare."

Padmé knew better than to argue with the stubborn man. Since she would be flying an official starship of the Naboo fleet, Panaka had the right, if not the responsibility, to get involved. And in truth, his concern pleased her, although she'd never admit it to him.

A shout outside and renewed fighting drew her attention briefly, making her wince. Another problem. There was always a problem, somewhere. Padmé had to wonder if that was just the nature of people, to create some excitement when all seemed well. Given that unsettling thought, Sola's words came back to her, along with images of Ryoo and Pooja. How she loved those two carefree little sprites!

"Senator?" Panaka said, drawing her out of her private contemplations.

"Yes?"

"We should discuss the security procedures."

It pained Padmé to let go of the images of her nieces at that moment, but she nodded and forced herself back into her responsible mode. Captain Panaka had said that they had to discuss security, and so Padmé Amidala had to discuss security.

The Lars family was being serenaded through yet another night by the lowing of many banthas. None of the four had any doubt that Tuskens were out there, not far from the farm, perhaps even then watching its lights.

"They're wild beasts, and we should have gotten the Mos Eisley authorities to exterminate them like the vermin they are. Them and the stinking Jawas!"

Shmi sighed and put her hand on her husband's tense fore-arm. "The Jawas have helped us," she reminded him gently.

"Then not the Jawas!" Cliegg roared back, and Shmi jumped. Taking note of Shmi's horrified expression, Cliegg calmed at once. "I'm sorry. Not the Jawas, then. But the Tuskens. They kill and steal whenever and wherever they can. No good comes of them!"

"If they try to come in here, there'll be less of them to chase back out into the desert," Owen offered, and Cliegg gave him an appreciative nod.

They tried to finish their dinner, but every time a bantha sounded, they all tensed, hands shifting from utensils to readied blasters.

"Listen," Shmi said suddenly, and they all went perfectly quiet, straining their ears. All was quiet outside; no banthas were lowing.

"Perhaps they were just moving by," Shmi offered when she was certain the others had caught on. "Heading back out into the open desert where they belong."

"We'll go out to the Dorrs' in the morning," Cliegg said to Owen. "We'll get all the farmers organized, and maybe get a call in to Mos Eisley, as well." He looked to Shmi and nodded. "Just to make sure."

"In the morning," Owen agreed.

At dawn the next day, Owen and Cliegg started out from the compound before they had even eaten a good breakfast, for Shmi had gone out ahead of them, as she did most mornings, to pick some mushrooms at the vaporators.

They expected to pass her on their way out to the Dorrs' farm but instead found her footprints, surrounded by the im-prints of many others, the soft boots of the Tuskens.

Cliegg Lars, as strong and tough a man as the region had ever known, fell to his knees and wept.

"We have to go after her, Dad," came a suddenly solid and unwavering voice.

Cliegg looked up and back to see Owen standing there, a man indeed and no more a boy, his expression grim and determined.

"She is alive and we cannot leave her to them," Owen said with a strange, almost supernatural calm.

Cliegg wiped away the last of his tears and stared hard at his son, then nodded grimly. "Spread the word to the neighboring farms."

There they are!" Sholh Dorr cried, pointing straight ahead, while keeping his speeder bike at full throttle.

The twenty-nine others saw the target, the rising dust of a line of walking banthas. With a communal roar, the outraged farmers pressed on, determined to exact revenge, determined to rescue Shmi, if she was still alive among this band of Tusken Raiders.

Amidst the roar of engines and cries of revenge, they swept down the descending wash, closing fast on the banthas, eager for battle.

Cliegg pumped his head, growling all the while, as if pleading with his speederbike to accelerate even more. He swerved in from the left flank, cutting into the center of the formation, then lowered his head and opened the speederbike up, trying to catch the lead riders. All he wanted was to be in the thick of it, to get his strong arms about a Tusken throat.

The banthas were clearly in sight, then, along with their robed riders.

Another cry went up, one of revenge.

One that fast turned to horror.

The leading edge of the farmer army plowed headlong into a wire cleverly strung across the field, at neck height to a man riding a speeder bike.

Cliegg's own cry also became one of horror as he watched the decapitation of several his friends and neighbors, as he watched others thrown to the ground. Purely on instinct, knowing he couldn't stop his speeder in time, Cliegg leapt up, planting one foot on the seat, then leapt again.

Then he felt a flash of pain, and he was spinning head over heels. He landed hard on the rocky ground, skidding briefly.

All the world about him became a blur, a frenzy of sudden activity. He saw the boots of his fellow farmers, heard Owen crying out to him, though it seemed as if his son's voice was far, far away.

He saw the wrapped leather of a Tusken boot, the sand-colored robes, and with a rage that could not be denied by his disorientation, Cliegg grabbed the leg as the Tusken ran past.

He looked up and raised his arms to block as the Tusken brought its staff slamming down at him. Accepting the pain, not even feeling it through his rage, Cliegg shoved forward and wrapped both his arms around the Tusken's legs, tugging the creature down to the ground before him. He crawled over it, his strong hands battering it, then finding the hold he wanted.

Cries of pain, from farmers and Tuskens alike, were all about him, but Cliegg hardly heard them. His hands remained firmly about the Tusken's throat. He choked with all his considerable strength; he lifted the Tusken's head up and bashed it back down, over and over again, and continued to choke and to batter long after the Tusken stopped resisting.

"Dad!"

That cry alone brought Cliegg from his rage. He dropped the Tusken Raider back to the ground and turned about, to see Owen in close battle with another of the Raiders.

Cliegg spun about and started to rise, putting one leg under him, coming up fast . . .

. . . And then he fell hard, his balance inexplicably gone. Confused, he looked down expecting that another Tusken had tripped him up. But then he saw that it was his own body that had failed him.

Only then did Cliegg Lars realize that he had lost his leg.

Blood pooled all about the ground, pouring from the severed limb. Eyes wide with horror, Cliegg grabbed at his leg.

He called for Owen. He called desperately for Shmi.

A speeder bike whipped past him, a farmer fleeing the massacre, but the man did not slow.

Cliegg tried to call out, but there was no voice to be found past the lump in his throat, the realization that he had failed and that all was lost.

Then a second speeder came by him, this one stopping fast. Reflexively, Cliegg grabbed at it, and before he could even begin to pull himself up at all, it sped away, dragging him along.

"Hold on, Dad!" Owen, the driver, cried to him.

Cliegg did. With the same stubbornness that had sustained him through all the difficult times at the moisture farm, the same gritty determination that had allowed him to conquer the harsh wild land of Tatooine, Cliegg Lars held on. For all his life, and with Tuskens in fast pursuit, Cliegg Lars held on.

And for Shmi, for the only chance she had of any rescue, Cliegg Lars held on.

Back up the slope, Owen stopped the speeder and leapt off,

grabbing at his father's torn leg. He tied it off as well as he could with the few moments he had, then helped Cliegg, who was fast slipping from consciousness, to lie over the back of the speeder.

Then Owen sped away, throttle flat out. He knew that he had to get his father home, and quickly. The vicious wound had to be cleaned and sealed.

It occurred to Owen that only a single pair of speeders were to be seen fleeing the massacre ahead of him, and that through all the commotion behind, he didn't hear the hum of a single speeder engine.

Forcing despair away, finding the same grounded determination that sustained Cliegg, Owen didn't think of the many lost friends, didn't think of his father's plight, didn't think of anything except the course to his necessary destination.

"This is not good news," Captain Panaka remarked, after delivering the blow to Senator Amidala.

"We've suspected all along that Count Dooku and his separatists would court the Trade Federation and the various commercial guilds," Padmé replied, trying to put a good face on it all. Panaka had just come in with Captain Typho, his nephew, with the report that the Trade Federation had thrown in with the separatist movement that now threatened to tear the Republic apart.

"Viceroy Gunray is an opportunist," she continued. "He will do anything that he believes will benefit him financially. His loyalties end at his purse. Count Dooku must be offering him favorable trade agreements, free run to produce goods without regard to the conditions of the workers or the effect on the environment. Viceroy Gunray has left more than one planet as a barren dead ball, floating in space. Or perhaps Count Dooku is offering the Trade Federation absolute control of lucrative markets, without competition."

"I'm more concerned with the implications to you, Senator," Panaka remarked, drawing a curious stare from Padmé.

"The separatists have shown themselves not to be above violence," he explained. "There have been assassination attempts across the Republic."

"But wouldn't Count Dooku and the separatists consider Senator Amidala almost an ally at this time?" Captain Typho interjected, and both Panaka and Padmé looked at the usually quiet man in surprise.

Padmé's look quickly turned into a stare; there was an angry edge to her fair features. "I am no friend to any who would dissolve the Republic, Captain," she insisted, her tone leaving no room for debate—and of course, there would be no debating that point. In the few years she had been a Senator, Amidala had shown herself to be among the most loyal and powerful supporters of the Republic, a legislator determined to improve the system, but to do so within the framework of the Republic's constitution. Senator Amidala fervently believed that the real beauty of the governing system was its built-in abilities, even demands, for self-improvement.

"Agreed, Senator," Typho said with a bow. He was shorter than his uncle but powerfully built, muscles filling the blue sleeves of his uniform, his chest solid under the brown leather tunic. He wore a black leather patch over his left eye, which he had lost in the battle with that same Trade Federation a decade before. Typho had been just a teenager then, but had shown himself well, and made his uncle Panaka proud. "And no offense meant. But on this issue concerning the creation of an army of the Republic, you have remained firmly in the court of negotiation over force. Would not the separatists agree with your vote?"

When Padmé put her initial outrage aside and considered the point, she had to agree.

"Count Dooku has thrown in with Nute Gunray, say the reports," Panaka cut in, his tone flat and determined. "That mere fact demands that we tighten security about Senator Amidala."

"Please do not speak about me as though I am not here," she scolded, but Panaka didn't blink.

"In matters of security, Senator, you *are* not here," he replied. "At least, your voice is not. My nephew reports to me, and his responsibilities on this matter cannot be undermined. Take all precautions."

With that, he bowed curtly and walked away, and Padmé suppressed her immediate desire to rebuke him. He was right, and she was better off because he dared to point it out. She looked back at Captain Typho.

"We will be vigilant, Senator."

"I have my duty, and that duty demands that I soon return to Coruscant," she said.

"And I have my duty," Typho assured her, and like Panaka, he offered a bow and walked away.

Padmé Amidala watched him go, then gave a great sigh, remembering Sola's words to her and wondering honestly if she would ever find the opportunity to follow her sister's advice— advice that she was finding strangely tempting at that particular moment. She realized then that she hadn't seen Sola, or the kids, or her parents, in nearly two weeks, not since that afternoon in the backyard with Ryoo and Pooja.

Time did seem to be slipping past her.

*   *   *

"It won't move fast enough to catch up to the Tuskens!" Cliegg Lars bellowed in protest as his son and future daughter-in-law helped him into a hoverchair that Owen had fashioned. He seemed oblivious to the pain of his wound, where his right leg had been sheared off at midthigh.

"The Tuskens are long gone, Dad," Owen Lars said quietly, and he put his hand on Cliegg's broad shoulder, trying to calm him. "If you won't use a mechno-leg, this powerchair will have to do."

"You'll not be making me into a half-droid, that's for sure," Cliegg retorted. "This little buggy will do fine."

"We'll get more men together," he said, his voice rising frantically, his hand instinctively moving down to the stump of his leg. "You get to Mos Eisley and see what support they'll offer. Send Beru to the farms."

"They've no more to offer," Owen replied honestly. He moved close to the chair and bent low, looking Cliegg square in the face. "All the farms will be years in recovering from the ambush. So many families have been shattered from the attack, and even more from the rescue attempt."

"How can you talk like that with your mother out there?" Cliegg Lars roared, his frustration boiling over—and all the more so because in his heart, he knew that Owen was speaking truthfully.

Owen took a deep breath, but did not back down from that imposing look. "We have to be realistic, Dad. It's been two weeks since they took her," he said grimly, leaving the implications unspoken. Implications that Cliegg Lars, who knew the dreaded Tuskens well, surely understood.

All of a sudden, Cliegg's broad shoulders slumped in defeat, and his fiery gaze softened as his eyes turned toward the ground. "She's gone," the wounded man whispered. "Really gone."

Behind him, Beru Whitesun started to cry.

Beside him, Owen fought back his own tears and stood calm and tall, the firm foundation determined above all to hold them together during this devastating time.

4

The four starships skimmed past the great skyscrapers of Coruscant, weaving in and out of the huge amber structures, arti-
ficial stalagmites rising higher and higher over the years, and
now obscuring the natural formations of the planet unlike anywhere else in the known galaxy. Sunlight reflected off the many
mirrorlike windows of those massive structures, and gleamed
brilliantly off the chrome of the sleek ships. The larger starship, which resembled a flying silver boomerang, almost glowed,
smooth and flowing with huge and powerful engines set on
each of its arms, a third of the way to the wingtip. Alongside it
soared several Naboo starfighters, their graceful engines set out
on wings from the main hulls with their distinctive elongated
tails.

One of the starfighters led the procession, veering around
and about nearly every passing tower, running point for the second ship, the Naboo Royal Cruiser. Behind that larger craft came
two more fighters, running swift and close to the Royal Cruiser,
shielding her, pilots ready to instantly intercept any threat.

The lead fighter avoided the more heavily trafficked routes of the great city, where potential enemies might be flying within the cover of thousands of ordinary vehicles. Many knew that Senator Amidala of Naboo was returning to the Senate to cast her vote against the creation of an army to assist the overwhelmed Jedi in their dealings with the increasingly antagonistic separatist movement, and there were many factions that did not want such a vote to be cast. Amidala had made many enemies during her reign as Naboo's Queen, powerful enemies with great resources at their disposal, and with, perhaps, enough hatred for the beautiful young Senator to put some of those resources to work to her detriment.

In the lead fighter, Corporal Dolphe, who had distinguished himself greatly in the Naboo war against the Trade Federation, breathed a sigh of relief as the appointed landing platform came into sight, appearing secure and clear. Dolphe, a tough warrior who revered his Senator greatly, flew past the landing platform to the left, then cut a tight turn back to the right, encircling the great structure, the Senatorial Apartment Building, adjacent to the landing platform. He kept his fighter up and about as the other two fighters put down side by side on one end of the platform, the Royal Cruiser hovering nearby for just a moment, then gently landing.

Dolphe did another circuit, then, seeing no traffic at all in the vicinity, settled his fighter across the way from his companion craft. He didn't put it down all the way just yet, though, but remained ready to swivel about and strike hard at any attackers, if need be.

Opposite him, the other two fighter pilots threw back their respective canopies and climbed from their cockpits. One,

Captain Typho, recently appointed as Amidala's chief security officer by his uncle Panaka, pulled off his flight helmet and shook his head, running a hand over his short, woolly black hair and adjusting the black leather patch he wore over his left eye.

"We made it," Typho said as his fellow fighter pilot leapt down from a wing to stand beside him. "I guess I was wrong. There was no danger at all."

"There's always danger, Captain," the other responded in a distinctly female voice. "Sometimes we're just lucky enough to avoid it."

Typho started to respond, but paused and looked back toward the cruiser, where the ramp was already lowering to the platform. The plan had been to get the contingent off the exposed platform and into a transport vehicle as quickly as possible. Two Naboo guards appeared, alert and ready, their blaster rifles presented before them. Typho nodded grimly, glad to see that his soldiers were taking nothing for granted, that they understood the gravity of the situation and their responsibility here in protecting the Senator.

Next came Amidala, in her typical splendor, with her paradoxical beauty, both simple and involved. With her large brown eyes and soft features, Amidala could outshine anyone about her, even if she was dressed in simple peasant's clothing, but in her Senatorial attire, this time a fabulous weave of black and white, and with her hair tied up and exaggerated by a black headdress, she outshone the stars themselves. Her mixture of intelligence and beauty, of innocence and allure, of courage and integrity and yet with a good measure of a child's mischievousness, floored Typho every time he looked upon her.

The captain turned from the descending entourage back to Dolphe across the way, offering a satisfied nod in acknowledgment of the man's point-running work.

And then, suddenly, Typho was lying facedown on the permacrete, thrown to the ground by a tremendous concussion, blinded for a moment by a brilliant flash as an explosion roared behind him. He looked up as his vision returned to see Dolphe sprawled on the ground.

Everything seemed to move in slow motion for Typho at that terrible moment. He heard himself yelling "No!" as he scrambled to his knees and turned about.

Pieces of burning metal spread through the Coruscant sky like fireworks, fanning high and wide from the wreckage. The remaining hulk of the Royal Cruiser burned brightly, and seven figures lay on the ground before it, one wearing the decorated raiments that Typho knew so very well.

Disoriented from the blast, the captain stumbled as he tried to rise. A great lump welled in his throat, for he knew what had happened.

Typho was a veteran warrior, had seen battle, had seen people die violently, and in looking at those bodies, in looking at Amidala's beautiful robes, at their placement about the very still form, he instinctively knew.

The woman's wounds were surely mortal. She was fast dying, if not already dead.

"You reset the coordinates!" Obi-Wan Kenobi said to his young Padawan. Obi-Wan's wheat-colored hair was longer now, hanging loosely about his shoulders, and a beard, somewhat unkempt, adorned his still-young-looking face. His light brown

Jedi traveling clothes, loose fitting and comfortable, seemed to settle on him well. For Obi-Wan had become comfortable, had grown into the skin of Jedi Knight. No longer was he the intense and impulsive Jedi Padawan learner under the training of Qui-Gon Jinn.

His companion at this time, however, appeared quite the opposite. Anakin Skywalker looked as if his tall, thin frame simply could not contain his overabundance of energy. He was dressed similarly to Obi-Wan, but his clothing seemed tighter, crisper, and his muscles under it always seemed taut with readiness. His sandy-blond hair was cropped short now, except for the thin braid indicative of his status as a Jedi Padawan. His blue eyes flashed repeatedly, as if bursts of energy were escaping.

"Just to lengthen our time in hyperspace a bit," he explained. "We'll come out closer to the planet."

Obi-Wan gave a great and resigned sigh and sat down at the console, noting the coordinates Anakin had input. There was little the Jedi could do about it now, of course, for a hyperspace leap couldn't be reset once the jump to lightspeed had already been made. "We cannot exit hyperspace too close to Coruscant's approach lanes. There's too much congestion for a safe flight. I've already explained this to you."

"But—"

"Anakin," Obi-Wan said pointedly, as if he were scolding a pet perootu cat, and he tightened his wide jaw and stared hard at his Padawan.

"Yes, Master," Anakin said, obediently looking down.

Obi-Wan held the glare for just a moment longer. "I know that you're anxious to get there," he conceded. "We have been too long away from home."

Anakin didn't look up, but Obi-Wan could see the edges of his lips curl up in a bit of a smile.

"Never do this again," Obi-Wan warned, and he turned and walked out of the shuttle's bridge.

Anakin flopped down into the pilot's chair, his chin falling into his hand, his eyes set on the control panels. The order had been about as direct as one could get, of course, and so Anakin silently told himself that he would adhere to it. Still, as he considered their current destination, and who awaited them there, he thought the scolding worth it, even if his resetting of the coordinates had bought him only a few extra hours on Coruscant. He was indeed anxious to get there, though not for the reason Obi-Wan had stated. It wasn't the Jedi Temple that beckoned to the Padawan, but rather a rumor he had heard over the comm chatter that a certain Senator, formerly the Queen of Naboo, was on her way to address the Senate.

Padmé Amidala.

The name resonated in young Anakin's heart and soul. He hadn't seen her in a decade, not since he, along with Obi-Wan and Qui-Gon, had helped her in her struggle against the Trade Federation on Naboo. He had only been ten years old at that time, but from the moment he had first laid eyes on Padmé, young Anakin had known that she was the woman he would marry.

Never mind that Padmé was several years older than he was. Never mind that he was just a boy when he had known her, when she had known him. Never mind that Jedi were not allowed to marry.

Anakin had simply known, without question, and the image of beautiful Padmé Amidala had stayed with him, had been burned into his every dream and fantasy, every day since he had left Naboo with Obi-Wan a decade ago. He could still smell the freshness of her hair, could still see the sparkle of intelligence and passion in her wondrous brown eyes, could still hear the melody that was Padmé's voice.

Hardly registering the movement, Anakin let his hands return to the controls of the nav computer. Perhaps he could find a little-used lane through the Coruscant traffic congestion to get them home faster.

Klaxons blared and myriad alarms rent the air all about the area, screaming loudly, drowning out the cries from the astonished onlookers and the wails of the injured.

Typho's companion pilot raced past him, and the captain scrambled to regain his footing and follow. Across the way, Dolphe was up and similarly running toward the fallen form of the Senator.

The female fighter pilot arrived first, dropping to one knee beside the fallen woman. She pulled the helmet from her head and quickly shook her brown tresses free.

"Senator!" Typho yelled. It was indeed Padmé Amidala kneeling beside the dying woman, her decoy. "Come, the danger has not passed!"

But Padmé waved the captain back furiously, then bent low to her fallen friend.

"Cordé," she said quietly, her voice breaking. Cordé was one of her beloved bodyguards, a woman who had been with her, serving her and serving Naboo, for many years. Padmé gathered Cordé up in her arms, hugging her gently.

Cordé opened her eyes, rich brown orbs so similar to

Padmé's own. "I'm sorry, m'Lady," she gasped, struggling for breath with every word. "I'm . . . not sure I . . ." She paused and lay there, staring at Padmé. "I've failed you."

"No!" Padmé insisted, arguing the bodyguard's reasoning, arguing against all of this insanity. "No, no, no!"

Cordé continued to stare at her, or stare past her, it seemed to the grief-stricken young Senator. Looking past her and past everything, Cordé's eyes stared into a far different place.

Padmé felt her relax suddenly, as if her spirit simply leapt from her corporeal form.

"Cordé!" the Senator cried, and she hugged her friend close, rocking back and forth, denying this awful reality.

"M'Lady, you are still in danger!" Typho declared, trying to sound sympathetic, but with a clear sense of urgency in his voice.

Padmé lifted her head from the side of Cordé's face, and took a deep and steadying breath. Looking upon her dead friend, remembering all at once the many times they had spent together, she gently lowered Cordé to the ground. "I shouldn't have come back," she said as she stood up beside the wary Typho, tears streaking her cheeks.

Captain Typho came up out of his ready stance long enough to lock stares with his Senator. "This vote is very important," he reminded her, his tone uncompromising, the voice of a man sworn to duty above all else. So much like his uncle. "You did your duty, Senator, and Cordé did hers. Now come."

He started away, grabbing Padmé's arm, but she shrugged off his grasp and stood there, staring down at her lost friend.

"Senator Amidala! Please!"

Padmé looked over at the man.

"Would you so diminish Cordé's death as to stand here and

risk your own life?" Typho bluntly stated. "What good will her sacrifice be if—"

"Enough, Captain," Padmé interrupted.

Typho motioned for Dolphe to run a defensive perimeter behind them, then he led the stricken Padmé away.

Back over at Padmé's Naboo fighter, R2-D2 beeped and squealed and fell into line behind them.

The Senate Building on Coruscant wasn't one of the tallest buildings in the city. Dome-shaped and relatively low, it did not soar up to the clouds, catching the afternoon sun as the others did in a brilliant display of shining amber. And yet the magnificent structure was not dwarfed by those towering skyscrapers about it, including the various Senate apartment complexes. Centrally located in the complex, and with a design very different from the typical squared skyscraper, the bluish smooth dome provided a welcome relief to the eye of the beholder, a piece of art within a community of simple efficiency.

The interior of the building was no less vast and impressive, its gigantic rotunda encircled, row upon row, by the floating platforms of the many Senators of the Republic, representing the great majority of the galaxy's inhabitable worlds. A significant number of those platforms stood empty now, because of the separatist movement. Several thousand systems had joined in with Count Dooku over the last couple of years to secede from a Republic that had, in their eyes, grown too ponderous to be effective, a claim that even the staunchest supporters of the Republic could not completely dispute.

Still, with this most important vote scheduled, the walls of the circular room echoed, hundreds and hundreds of voices chattering all at once, expressing emotions from anger to regret to determination.

In the middle of the main floor, standing at the stationary dais, the one unmoving speaking platform in the entire building, Supreme Chancellor Palpatine watched and listened, taking in the tumult and wearing an expression that showed deep concern. He was past middle age now, with silver hair and a face creased by deep lines of experience. His term limit had ended several years ago, but a series of crises had allowed him to stay in office well beyond the legal limit. From a distance, one might have thought him frail, but up close there could be no doubt of the strength and fortitude of this accomplished man.

"They are afraid, Supreme Chancellor," Palpatine's aide, Uv Gizen, remarked to him. "Many have heard reports of the demonstrations, even violent activity near this very building. The separatists—"

Palpatine held up his hand to quiet the nervous aide. "They are a troublesome group," he replied. "It would seem that Count Dooku has whipped them into murderous frenzy. Or perhaps," he said with apparent reflection, "their frustrations are mounting despite the effort of that estimable former Jedi to calm them. Either way, the separatists must be taken seriously."

Uv Gizen started to respond again, but Palpatine put a finger to pursed lips to silence him, then nodded to the main podium, where his majordomo, Mas Amedda, was calling for order.

"Order! We shall have order!" the majordomo cried, his

bluish skin brightening with agitation. His lethorn head tentacles, protruding from the back side of his skull and wrapping down over his collar to frame his head like a cowl, twitched anxiously, their brownish-tipped horns bobbing on his chest. And as he turned side to side, his primary horns, standing straight for almost half a meter above his head, rotated like antennae gathering information on the crowd. Mas Amedda was an imposing figure in the Senate, but the chatter, the thousand private conversations, continued.

"Senators, please!" Mas Amedda called loudly. "Indeed, we have much to discuss. Many important issues. But the motion before us at this time, to commission an army to protect the Republic, takes precedence. That is what we will vote on at this time, and that alone! Other business must defer."

A few complaints came back at Mas Amedda, and a few conversations seemed to gather momentum, but then Supreme Chancellor Palpatine stepped up to the podium, staring out over the gathering, and the great hall went silent. Mas Amedda bowed in deference to the great man and stepped aside.

Palpatine placed his hands on the rim of the podium, his shoulders noticeably sagging, his head bowed. The curious posture only heightened the tension, making the cavernous room seem even more silent, if that was possible.

"My esteemed colleagues," he began slowly and deliberately, but even with that effort, his voice wavered and seemed as if it would break apart. Curiosity sent murmurs rumbling throughout the nervous gathering once more. It wasn't often that Supreme Chancellor Palpatine appeared rattled.

"Excuse me," Palpatine said quietly. Then, a moment later, he straightened and inhaled deeply, seeming to gather inner

strength, which was amply reflected in his solid voice as he repeated, "My esteemed colleagues. I have just received some
tragic and disturbing news. Senator Amidala of the Naboo system . . . has been assassinated!"

A shock wave of silence rolled about the crowd; eyes
went wide; mouths, for those who had mouths, hung open in
disbelief.

"This grievous blow is especially personal to me," Palpatine
explained. "Before I became Chancellor, I was a Senator, serving Amidala when she was Queen of Naboo. She was a great
leader who fought for justice. So beloved was she among her
people that she could have been elected Queen for life!" He
gave a great sigh and a helpless chuckle, as if that notion had
been received as purely preposterous by the idealistic Amidala, as indeed it had. "But Senator Amidala believed in term
limits, and she fervently believed in democracy. Her death
is a great loss to us all. We will all mourn her as a relentless champion of freedom." The Supreme Chancellor tilted his
head, his eyes lowering, and he sighed again. "And as a dear
friend."

A few conversations began, but for the most part, the rever-
ential silence held strong, with many Senators nodding their
heads in agreement with Palpatine's eulogy.

But at that critical time, on this most important day, the
grim news could not overwhelm. Palpatine watched, without
surprise, as the volatile Senator of Malastare, Ask Aak, maneuvered his floating platform down from the ranks and into the
center of the arena. His large head rotated slowly about, his
three eyes, protruding on fingerlike stalks, seeming to work in-
dependently, his horizontal ears twitching.

"How many more Senators will die before this civil strife ends?" the Malastarian cried. "We must confront these rebels now, and we need an army to do it!"

That bold statement brought many shouts of assent and dissent from the huge gathering, and several platforms moved all at once. One, bearing a blue-haired, scrunch-faced being, swept down fast beside the platform of Ask Aak. "Why weren't the Jedi able to stop this assassination?" demanded Darsana, the ambassador of Glee Anselm. "How obvious it is that we are no longer safe under the protection of the Jedi!"

Another platform floated in fast on the heels of Darsana's. "The Republic needs more security now!" agreed Twi'lek Senator Orn Free Taa, his thick jowls and long blue lekku head tentacles shaking. "Now! Before it comes to war!"

"Must I remind the Senator from Malastare that negotiations are continuing with the separatists?" Supreme Chancellor Palpatine interjected. "Peace is our objective here. Not war."

"You say this while your friend lies dead, assassinated by those same people with whom you wish to negotiate?" Ask Aak asked, his orange-skinned face a mask of incredulity. All around the central arena, shouts and cries erupted, with Senators arguing vehemently. Many fists and other, more exotic, appendages were waved in the air at that explosive point.

Palpatine, supremely calm through it all, kept his disarming stare on Ask Aak.

"Did you not just name Amidala as your friend?" Ask Aak screamed at him.

Palpatine simply continued to stare at the man, a center of calm, the eye of the storm that was raging all about him.

Palpatine's majordomo rushed to the podium then, taking

the cue that his master must remain above this petulant squabbling if he was to be the voice of reason throughout this ferocious debate.

"Order!" Mas Amedda cried repeatedly. "Senators, please!"

But it went on and on, the screaming, the shouting, the fist waving.

Unnoticed through it all, yet another platform, bearing four people, approached the Senate gallery from the side, moving slowly but deliberately.

Aboard the approaching platform, Senator Padmé Amidala was shaking her head with disgust at the shouting and lack of civility emanating from the huge gallery before them. "This is exactly why Count Dooku was able to convince so many systems to secede," she commented to her handmaiden Dormé, who was standing beside her, with Captain Typho and Jar Jar Binks in front of them, the captain driving the platform.

"There are many who believe that the Republic has become too large and disjointed," Dormé agreed.

They came into the gallery, then moved slowly onto the main, central arena, but the Senators there, and those in the lower rows of the gallery, were too involved with their shouting and arguing to even notice the unexpected appearance.

Standing at the podium, though, Palpatine did see Amidala. His expression was one of blatant shock, for just a moment, but then he shook himself out of it and a smile widened upon his face.

"My noble colleagues," Amidala said loudly, and the sound of her most familiar voice quieted many of the Senators, who turned to regard her. "I concur with the Supreme Chancellor. At all costs, we do not want war!"

Gradually at first, but then more quickly, the Senate Hall went quiet, and then came a thunderous outburst of cheering and applause.

"It is with great surprise and joy that the chair recognizes the Senator from Naboo, Padmé Amidala," Palpatine declared.

Amidala waited for the cheering and clapping to subside, then began slowly and deliberately. "Less than an hour ago, an assassination attempt was made upon my life. One of my bodyguards and six others were ruthlessly and senselessly murdered. I was the target, but, more important, I believe this security measure before you was the target. I have led the opposition to building an army, but there is someone who will stop at nothing to assure its passage."

Cheers became boos from many areas of the gallery as those surprising words registered, and many others shook their heads in confusion. Had Amidala just accused someone in the Senate of trying to assassinate her?

As she stood there, her gaze moving about the vast, circular room, Amidala knew that her words, on the surface, could be seen as an insult to many. In truth, though, she wasn't thinking along those lines concerning the source of the assassination. She had a definite hunch, one that went against the obvious logic. The people who would most logically want her silenced were indeed those in favor of the formation of an army of the Republic, but for some reason she could not put her finger on—some subconscious clues, perhaps, or just a gut feeling—Amidala believed that the source of the attempt was exactly those who would not logically, on the surface, at least, want her silenced. She remembered Panaka's warning about the Trade Federation reportedly joining hands with the separatists.

She took a deep breath, steeling herself against the growing rancor in the audience, and steadfastly went on. "I warn you, if you vote to create this army, war will follow. I have experienced the misery of war firsthand; I do not wish to do so again."

The cheering began to outweigh the booing.

"This is insanity, I say!" Orn Free Taa yelled above it all. "I move that we defer this vote, immediately!" But that suggestion only led to more yelling.

Amidala looked at the Twi'lek Senator, understanding his sudden desire to defer a vote that her mere presence had cast into doubt.

"Wake up, Senators—you must wake up!" she went on, shouting him down. "If we offer the separatists violence, they can only show us violence in return! Many will lose their lives, and all will lose their freedom. This decision could well destroy the very foundation of our great Republic! I pray you do not let fear push you into a disastrous decision. Vote down this security measure, which is nothing less than a declaration of war! Does anyone here want that? I cannot believe they do!"

Ask Aak, Orn Free Taa, and Darsana, on their floating platforms down by the podium, exchanged nervous glances as the cheers and boos echoed about the great hall. The fact that Amidala had just survived an assassination attempt and yet was here begging the Senate to put off raising an army against the likely perpetrators only added strength to her argument, only elevated Amidala higher in the eyes of many—and the former Queen of Naboo, having stood firm against the Trade Federation a decade before, was already held in high esteem by many.

At Ask Aak's nod, Orn Free Taa demanded the floor, and was given it promptly by Palpatine.

"By precedence of order, my motion to defer the vote must be dealt with first," Orn Free Taa demanded. "That is the rule of law!"

Amidala glared at the Twi'lek, her expression both angry and frustrated by the obvious delaying tactic. She turned plaintively to Palpatine, but the Supreme Chancellor, though his responding expression seemed to be sympathetic to her plight, could only shrug. He moved to the podium and held up his hands for order, and when the room was quiet enough, announced, "In view of the lateness of the hour and the seriousness of this motion, we will take up these matters tomorrow. Until then, the Senate stands adjourned."

Traffic clogged the Coruscant sky, flowing slowly about the meandering smoggy haze. The sun was up, giving the sprawling city an amber glow, but many lights were still on, shining behind the windows of the great skyscrapers.

The massive towers of the Republic Executive Building loomed above it all, seeming as if they would reach the very heavens. And that seemed fitting indeed, for inside, even at this early hour, the events and participants took on godlike stature to the trillions of common folk of the Republic.

Supreme Chancellor Palpatine sat behind his desk in his spacious and tasteful office, staring across at his four Jedi Master visitors. Across the room, a pair of red-clad guards flanked the door, imposing, powerful figures, with their great curving helmets and wide, floor-length capes.

"I fear this vote," Palpatine remarked.

"It is unavoidable," replied Mace Windu, a tall and muscular human, bald, and with penetrating eyes, standing next to the even taller Ki-Adi-Mundi.

"And it could unravel the remainder of the Republic," Palpatine said. "Never have I seen the Senators so at odds over any issue."

"Few issues would carry the import of creating a Republic army," Jedi Master Plo Koon remarked. He was a tall, sturdy Kel Dor, his head ridged and ruffled at the sides like the curly hair of a young girl, and with dark, shadowed eyes and a black mask over the lower portion of his face. "The Senators are anxious and afraid, and believe that no vote will ever be more important than this one now before them."

"And this way or that, much mending must you do," said Master Yoda, the smallest in physical stature, but a Jedi Master who stood tall against anyone in the galaxy. Yoda's huge eyes blinked slowly and his tremendous ears swiveled subtly, showing, for those who knew him, that he was deep in thought, giving this situation his utmost attention. "Unseen is much that is here," he said, and he closed his eyes in contemplation.

"I don't know how much longer I can hold off the vote, my friends," Palpatine explained. "And I fear that delay on this definitive issue might well erode the Republic through attrition. More and more star systems are joining the separatists."

Mace Windu, a pillar of strength even among the Jedi, nodded his understanding of the dilemma. "And yet, when the vote is done, if the losers do break away—"

"I will not let this Republic that has stood for a thousand years be split in two!" Palpatine declared, slamming a fist determinedly on his desk. "My negotiations will not fail!"

Mace Windu held his calm, keeping his rich voice even and controlled. "But if they do, you must realize there aren't enough Jedi to protect the Republic. We are keepers of the peace, not soldiers."

Palpatine took a few steadying breaths, trying to digest it all. "Master Yoda," he said, and he waited for the greenish-skinned Jedi to regard him. "Do you really think it will come to war?"

Again Yoda closed his eyes. "Worse than war, I fear," he said. "Much worse."

"What?" an alarmed Palpatine asked.

"Master Yoda, what do you sense?" Mace Windu prompted.

"Impossible to see, the future is," the small Jedi Master replied, his great orbs still looking inward. "The dark side clouds everything. But this I am sure of . . ." He popped open his eyes and stared hard at Palpatine. "Do their duty, the Jedi will."

A brief look of confusion came over the Supreme Chancellor, but before he could begin to respond to Yoda, a hologram appeared on his desk, the image of Dar Wac, one of his aides. "The loyalist committee has arrived, my Lord," said Dar Wac, in Huttese.

"Send them in."

The hologram disappeared and Palpatine rose, along with the seated Jedi, to properly greet the distinguished visitors. They came in two groups, Senator Padmé Amidala walking with Captain Typho, Jar Jar Binks, her handmaiden Dormé, and major-domo Mas Amedda, followed by two other Senators, Bail Organa of Alderaan and Horox Ryyder.

Everyone moved to exchange pleasant greetings, and Yoda pointedly tapped Padmé with his small cane.

"With you, the Force is strong, young Senator," the Jedi

Master told her. "Your tragedy on the landing platform, terrible. To see you alive brings warm feelings to my heart."

"Thank you, Master Yoda," she replied. "Do you have any idea who was behind this attack?"

Her question had everyone in the room turning to regard her and Yoda directly.

Mace Windu cleared his throat and stepped forward. "Senator, we have nothing definitive, but our intelligence points to disgruntled spice miners on the moons of Naboo."

Padmé looked to Captain Typho, who shook his head, having no answers. They had both witnessed the frustration of those spice miners back on Naboo, but those demonstrations seemed a long way from the tragedy that had occurred on the landing platform here on Coruscant. Releasing Typho from her gaze, she stared hard at Mace Windu, wondering if it would be wise to voice her hunch at this time. She knew the controversy she might stir, knew the blatant illogical ring to her claim, but still . . .

"I do not wish to disagree," she said, "but I think that Count Dooku was behind it."

A stir of surprise rippled about the room, and the four Jedi Masters exchanged looks that ranged from astonishment to disapproval.

"You know, M'Lady," Mace said in his resonant and calm voice, "Count Dooku was once a Jedi. He wouldn't assassinate anyone. It's not in his character."

"He is a political idealist," Ki-Adi-Mundi, the fourth of the Jedi contingent, added. "Not a murderer." With his great domed head, the Cerean Jedi Master stood taller than anyone in the room, and the ridged flaps at the side of his pensive face added a measure of introspection to his imposing physical form.

Master Yoda tapped his cane, drawing attention to himself, and that alone exerted a calming influence over the increasingly tense mood. "In dark times, nothing is what it appears to be," the diminutive figure remarked. "But the fact remains, Senator, in grave danger you are."

Supreme Chancellor Palpatine gave a dramatic sigh and walked over to the window, staring out at the Coruscant dawn. "Master Jedi," he said, "may I suggest that the Senator be placed under the protection of your graces?"

"Do you think that a wise use of our limited resources at this stressful time?" Senator Bail Organa was quick to interject, stroking his well-trimmed black goatee. "Thousands of systems have gone over fully to the separatists, and many more may soon join them. The Jedi are our—"

"Chancellor," Padmé interrupted, "if I may comment. I do not believe the—"

"Situation is that serious," Palpatine finished for her. "No, but I do, Senator."

"Chancellor, please!" she pleaded. "I do not want any more guards!"

Palpatine stared at her as would an overprotective father, a look that Padmé might have viewed as condescending from any other man. "I realize all too well that additional security might be disruptive for you," he began, and he paused, and then a look came over him as if he had just struck upon a logical and acceptable compromise. "But perhaps someone you are familiar with, an old friend." Smiling cleverly, Palpatine looked to Mace Windu and Yoda. "Master Kenobi?" he finished with a nod, and his smile only widened when Mace Windu nodded back.

"That's possible," the Jedi confirmed. "He has just returned from a border dispute on Ansion."

"You must remember him, M'Lady," Palpatine said, grinning as if it was a done deal. "He watched over you during the blockade conflict."

"This is not necessary, Chancellor," Padmé said determinedly, but Palpatine didn't relinquish his grin in the least, showing clearly that he knew well how to defeat the independent Senator's argument.

"Do it for me, M'Lady. Please. I will rest easier. We had a big scare today. The thought of losing you is unbearable."

Several times, Amidala started to respond, but how could she possibly say anything to deny the Supreme Chancellor's expressed concern? She gave a great defeated sigh, and the Jedi rose and turned to leave.

"I will have Obi-Wan report to you immediately, M'Lady," Mace Windu informed her.

As he passed, Yoda leaned in close to Padmé and whispered so that only she could hear, "Too little about yourself you worry, Senator, and too much about politics. Be mindful of your danger, Padmé. Accept our help."

They all left the room, and Padmé Amidala stared at the door and the flanking guards for a long while.

Behind her, at the back of his office, Chancellor Palpatine watched them all.

"It troubles me to hear Count Dooku's name mentioned in such a manner, Master," Mace said to Yoda as the Jedi made

their way back to their Council chamber. "And from one as esteemed as Senator Amidala. Any mistrust of Jedi, or even former
Jedi, in times such as these can be disastrous."

"Deny Dooku's involvement in the separatist movement, we
cannot," Yoda reminded him.

"Nor can we deny that he began in that movement because
of ideals," Mace argued. "He was once our friend—that we
must not forget—and to hear him slandered and named as an
assassin—"

"Not named," Yoda said. "But darkness there is, about us
all, and in that darkness, nothing is what it seems."

"But it makes little sense to me that Count Dooku would
make an attempt on the life of Senator Amidala, when she is the
one most adamantly opposed to the creation of an army. Would
the separatists not wish Amidala well in her endeavors? Would they
not believe that she is, however unintentionally, an ally to their
cause? Or are we really to believe that they want war with the
Republic?"

Yoda leaned heavily on his cane, seeming very weary, and his
huge eyes slowly closed. "More is here than we can know," he
said very quietly. "Clouded is the Force. Troubling it is."

Mace dismissed his forthcoming reflexive response, a further
defense of his old friend Dooku. Count Dooku had been among
the most accomplished of the Jedi Masters, respected among the
Council, a student of the older and, some would say, more profound Jedi philosophies and styles, including an arcane lightsaber fighting style that was more front and back, thrust and
riposte, than the typical circular movements currently employed
by most of the Jedi. What a blow it had been to the Jedi Order,
and to Mace Windu, when Dooku had walked away from them,
and for many of the same reasons the separatists were now try-

ing to walk away: the perception that the Republic had grown too ponderous and unresponsive to the needs of the individual, even of individual systems.

It was no less troubling to Mace Windu concerning Dooku, as it was, no doubt, to Amidala and Palpatine concerning the separatists, that some of the arguments against the Republic were not without merit.

As the lights of Coruscant dimmed, gradually replaced by the natural lights of the few twinkling stars that could get through the nearly continual glare, the great and towering city took on a vastly different appearance. Under the dark evening sky, the skyscrapers seemed to become gigantic natural monoliths, and all the supersized structures that so dominated the city, that so marked Coruscant as a monument to the ingenuity of the reasoning species, seemed somehow the mark of folly, of futile pride striving against the vastness and majesty beyond the grasp of any mortal. Even the wind at the higher levels of the structures sounded mournful, almost as a herald to what would eventually, inevitably, become of the great city and the great civilization.

As Obi-Wan Kenobi and Anakin Skywalker stood in the turbolift of the Senate apartment complex, the Jedi Master was indeed pondering such profound universal truths as the subtle change of day to night. Beside him, though, his young Padawan certainly was not. Anakin was about to see Padmé again, the woman who had captured his heart and soul when he was but ten years old and had never let it go.

"You seem a little on edge, Anakin," Obi-Wan noted as the lift continued its climb.

"Not at all," came the unconvincing reply.

"I haven't seen you this nervous since we fell into that nest of gundarks."

"You fell into that nightmare, Master, and I rescued you. Remember?"

Obi-Wan's little distraction seemed to have the desired effect, and the pair shared a much-needed laugh. Coming out of it, though, Anakin remained obviously on edge.

"You're sweating," Obi-Wan noted. "Take a deep breath. Relax."

"I haven't seen her in ten years."

"Anakin, relax," Obi-Wan reiterated. "She's not the Queen anymore."

The lift door slid open and Obi-Wan started away, while Anakin, behind him, muttered under his breath, "That's not why I'm nervous."

As the pair stepped into the corridor, a door across the way slid open and a well-dressed Gungan, wearing fine red and black robes, stepped into the corridor opposite them. The three regarded each other for just a moment, and then the Gungan diplomat, losing all sense of reserve and propriety, began hopping around like a child.

"Obi! Obi! Obi!" Jar Jar Binks cried, tongue and ears flapping. "Mesa so smilen to see'en yousa! Wahoooo!"

Obi-Wan smiled politely, though his glance at Anakin did

show that he was a bit embarrassed, and he patted his hands gently in the air, trying to calm the excitable fellow. "It's good to see you, too, Jar Jar."

Jar Jar continued to hop about for just a moment, then suddenly, and with obvious great effort, calmed down. "And this, mesa guessen, issen yousa apprentice," he went on, and the Gungan seemed to have much more control of himself. For a moment, at least, until he took a good look at the young Padawan, and all pretense melted away. "Noooooooo!" he shrieked, clapping his hands together. "Annie? Noooooooo! Little bitty Annie?" Jar Jar grabbed the Padawan and pulled him forcefully to arm's length, studying him head to toe. "Noooooooo! Yousa so biggen! Yiyiyiyi! Annie! Mesa no believen!"

Now it was Anakin's turn to wear the embarrassed smile. Politely, he offered no resistance as the overexcited Gungan slammed him into a crushing hug, childish hops shaking him violently.

"Hi, Jar Jar," Anakin managed to say, and Jar Jar just continued on, hopping and crying out his name, and issuing a series of strange *yiyi* sounds. It seemed as if it would go on forever, but then Obi-Wan gently but firmly grabbed Jar Jar by the arm. "We have come to speak with Senator Amidala. Could you show us to her?"

Jar Jar stopped bouncing and looked at Obi-Wan intently, his duck-billed face taking on a more serious expression. "Shesa expecting yousa. Annie! Mesa no believen!" His head bobbed a bit more, then he grabbed Anakin by the hand and pulled him along.

The apartment inside was tastefully decorated, with cushiony chairs and a divan set in a circular pattern in the center, and a few, well-placed artworks set about the walls. Dormé and Typho were in the room, standing beside the divan, the captain wearing his typical military garb, blue uniform under a brown leather tunic, with black leather gloves and a stiff cap, its brim and band of black leather. Beside him stood Dormé in one of the elegant, yet understated dresses typical of Padmé's handmaidens.

Anakin, though, didn't see either of them. He focused on the third person in the room, Padmé, and on her alone, and if he had ever held any moments of doubt that she was as beautiful as he remembered her, they were washed away, then and there. His eyes roamed the Senator's small and shapely frame in her black and deep purple robes, taking in every detail. He saw her thick brown hair, drawn up high and far at the back of her head in a basketlike accessory, and wanted to lose himself in it. He saw her eyes and wanted to stare into them for eternity. He saw her lips, and wanted to . . .

Anakin closed his eyes for just a moment and inhaled deeply, and he could smell her again, the scent that had been burned into him as Padmé's.

It took every ounce of willpower he could muster to walk in slowly and respectfully behind Obi-Wan, and not merely rush in and crush Padmé in a hug . . . and yet, paradoxically, it took every bit of his willpower to move his legs, which were suddenly seeming so very weak, and take that first step into the room, that first step toward her.

"Mesa here. Lookie! Lookie!" screeched Jar Jar, hardly the announcement Obi-Wan would have preferred, but one that he knew he had to expect from the emotionally volatile Gungan. "Desa Jedi arriven."

"It's a pleasure to see you again, M'Lady," Obi-Wan said, moving to stand before the beautiful young Senator.

Standing behind his Master, Anakin continued to stare at

the woman, to note her every move. She did glance at him once, though very briefly, and he detected no recognition in her eyes.

Padmé took Obi-Wan's hand in her own. "It has been far too long, Master Kenobi. I'm so glad our paths have crossed again. But I must warn you that I think your presence here is unnecessary."

"I am sure that the members of the Jedi Council have their reasons," Obi-Wan replied.

Padmé wore a resigned, accepting expression at that answer, but a look of curiosity replaced it as she glanced again behind the Jedi Knight, to the young Padawan standing patiently. She took a step to the side, so that she was directly in front of Anakin.

"Annie?" she asked, her expression purely incredulous. Her smile and the flash in her eyes showed that she needed no answer.

For just a flicker, Anakin felt her spirit leap.

"Annie," Padmé said again. "Can it be? My goodness how you've grown!" She looked down and then followed the line of his lean body, tilting her head back to emphasize his height, and he realized that he now towered over her.

That did little to bolster Anakin's confidence, though, so lost was he in the beauty of Padmé. Her smile widened, a clear sign that she was glad to see him, but he missed it, or the implications of it, at least. "So have you," he answered awkwardly, as if he had to force each word from his mouth. "Grown more beautiful, I mean." He cleared his throat and stood taller. "And much shorter," he teased, trying unsuccessfully to sound in control. "For a Senator, I mean."

Anakin noted Obi-Wan's disapproving scowl, but Padmé laughed any tension away and shook her head.

"Oh, Annie, you'll always be that little boy I knew on Tatooine," she said, and if she had taken the lightsaber from his belt and sliced his legs out from under him, she would not have shortened Anakin Skywalker any more.

He looked down, his embarrassment only heightened by the looks he knew that both Obi-Wan and Captain Typho were throwing his way.

"Our presence will be invisible, M'Lady," he heard Obi-Wan assure Padmé.

"I'm very grateful that you're here, Master Kenobi," Captain Typho put in. "The situation is more dangerous than the Senator will admit."

"I don't need any more security," Padmé said, addressing Typho initially, but turning to regard Obi-Wan as she continued. "I need answers. I want to know who is trying to kill me. I believe that there might lie an issue of the utmost importance to the Senate. There is something more here . . ." She stopped as a frown crossed Obi-Wan Kenobi's face.

"We're here to protect you, Senator, not to start an investigation," he said in calm and deliberate tones, but even as he finished, Anakin contradicted him.

"We will find out who's trying to kill you, Padmé," the Padawan insisted. "I promise you."

As soon as he finished, Anakin recognized his error, one that clearly showed on the scowl that Obi-Wan flashed his way. He had been fashioning a response to Padmé in his thoughts, and had hardly even registered his Master's explanation before he had blurted out the obviously errant words. Now he could only bite his lip and lower his gaze.

"We are not going to exceed our mandate, my young Padawan learner!" Obi-Wan said sharply, and Anakin was stung to be so dressed down publicly—especially in front of this particular audience.

"I meant, in the interest of protecting her, Master, of course."

His justification sounded inane even to Anakin.

"We are not going through this exercise again, Anakin," Obi-Wan continued. "You will pay attention to my lead."

Anakin could hardly believe that Obi-Wan was continuing to do this in front of Padmé. "Why?" he asked, turning the question and the debate, trying desperately to regain some footing and credibility.

"What?" Obi-Wan exclaimed, as taken aback as Anakin had ever seen him, and the young Padawan knew that he was pushing too far and too fast.

"Why else do you think we were assigned to her, if not to find the killer?" he asked, trying to bring a measure of calm back to the situation. "Protection is a job for local security, not for Jedi. It's overkill, Master, and so an investigation is implied in our mandate."

"We will do as the Council has instructed," Obi-Wan countered. "And you will learn your place, young one."

"Perhaps with merely your presence about me, the mysteries surrounding this threat will be revealed," offered Padmé, ever the diplomat. She smiled alternately at Anakin and at Obi-Wan, an invitation for civility, and when both leaned back, shoulders visibly relaxing, she added, "Now, if you will excuse me, I will retire."

They all bowed as Padmé and Dormé exited the room, and then Obi-Wan stared hard at his young Padawan again, neither seeming overly pleased with the other.

"Well, I know that I'm glad to have you here," Captain Typho offered, moving closer to the pair. "I don't know what's going on here, but the Senator can't have too much security right now. Your friends on the Jedi Council seem to think that miners have something to do with this, but I can't really agree with that."

"What have you learned?" Anakin asked.

Obi-Wan threw him a look of warning.

"We'll be better prepared to protect the Senator if we have some idea of what we're up against," Anakin explained to his Master, logic he knew that Obi-Wan had to accept as reasonable.

"Not much," Typho admitted. "Senator Amidala leads the opposition to the creation of a Republic army. She's very determined to deal with the separatists through negotiation and not force, but the attempts on her life, even though they've failed, have only strengthened the opposition to her viewpoint in the Senate."

"And since the separatists would not logically wish to see a Republic army formed . . ." Obi-Wan reasoned.

"We're left without a clue," Typho said. "In any such incident, the first questioning eyes turn toward Count Dooku and the separatists." A frown crossed Obi-Wan's face, and Typho quickly added, "Or to some of those loyal to his movement, at least. But why they'd go after Senator Amidala is anyone's guess."

"And we are not here to guess, but merely to protect," Obi-Wan said, in tones that showed he was finished with this particular line of discussion.

Typho bowed, hearing him clearly. "I'll have an officer on every floor, and I'll be at the command center downstairs."

Typho left, then, and Obi-Wan began a search of the room

and adjoining chambers, trying to get a feel for the place. Anakin started to do likewise, but he stopped when he walked by Jar Jar Binks.

"Mesa bustin wit happiness seein yousa again, Annie."

"She didn't even recognize me," Anakin said, staring at the door through which Padmé had departed. He shook his head despondently and turned to the Gungan. "I've thought about her every day since we parted, and she's forgotten me completely."

"Why yousa sayen that?" Jar Jar asked.

"You saw her," Anakin replied.

"Shesa happy," the Gungan assured him. "Happier than mesa see'en her in a longo time. These are bad times, Annie. Bombad times!"

Anakin shook his head and started to repeat his distress, but he noted Obi-Wan moving toward him and wisely held his tongue.

Except that his observant Master had already discerned the conversation.

"You're focusing on the negative again," he said to Anakin. "Be mindful of your thoughts. She was pleased to see us—leave it at that. Now, let's check the security here. We have much to do."

Anakin bowed. "Yes, Master."

He could say the compliant words because he had to, but the young Padawan could not dismiss that which was in his heart and in his thoughts.

Padmé sat at her vanity, brushing her thick brown hair, staring into the mirror but not really seeing anything there. Her thoughts were replaying again and again the image of Anakin, the look he had given her. She heard his words again,

". . . grown more beautiful," and though Padmé was undeniably that, those were not words she was used to hearing. Since she had been a young girl, Padmé had been involved in politics, quickly rising to powerful and influential positions. Most of the men she had come into contact with had been more concerned with what she could bring to them in practical terms than with her beauty, or, for that matter, with any true personal feelings for her. As Queen of Naboo and now as Senator, Padmé was well aware that she was attractive to men in ways deeper than physical attraction, in ways deeper than any emotional bond.

Or perhaps not deeper than the latter, she told herself, for she could not deny the intensity in Anakin's eyes as he had looked at her.

But what did it mean?

She saw him again, in her thoughts. And clearly. Her mental eye roamed over his lean and strong frame, over his face, tight with the intensity that she had always admired, and yet with eyes sparkling with joy, with mischief, with . . .

With longing?

That thought stopped the Senator. Her hands slipped down to her sides, and she sat there, staring at herself, judging her own appearance as Anakin might.

After a few long moments, Padmé shook her head, telling herself that it was crazy. Anakin was a Jedi now. That was their dedication and their oath, and those things, above all else, were things Padmé Amidala admired.

How could he even look at her in such a manner?

So it was all her imagination.

Or was it her fantasy?

Laughing at herself, Padmé lifted her brush to her hair again, but she paused before she had even begun. She was wearing a silky white nightgown, and there were, after all, security cams in her room. Those cams had never really bothered her, since she had always looked at them clinically. Security cams, with guards watching her every move, were a fact of her existence, and so she had learned to go about her daily routines, even the private ones, without a second thought to the intrusive eyes.

But now she realized that a certain young Jedi might be on the other end of those lenses.

Clad in gray armor that was somewhat outdated, burned from countless blaster shots, but still undeniably effective, the bounty hunter stood easily on the ledge, a hundred stories and more up from the Coruscant street. His helmet, too, was gray, except for a blue ridge crossing his eyes and running down from brow to chin. His perch seemed somewhat precarious, considering the wind at this height, but to one as agile and skilled as Jango, and with a penchant for getting himself into and out of difficult places, this was nothing out of the ordinary.

Right on time, a speeder pulled up near the ledge and hovered there. Jango's associate, Zam Wesell, nodded to him and climbed out, stepping lithely onto the ledge in front of a couple of bright advertisement windows. She wore a red veil over the bottom half of her face. This was not a statement of modesty or fashion. Like everything else she wore, from her blaster to her armor to her other concealed and equally deadly weapons, Zam's veil was a practical implement, used to hide her Clawdite features.

Clawdites were not a trusted species, for obvious reasons.

"You know that we failed?" Jango asked, getting right to the point.

"You told me to kill those in the Naboo starship," Zam said. "I hit the ship, but they used a decoy. Those who were aboard are all dead."

Jango fixed her with a smirk, and didn't bother to call her words a dodge. "We'll have to try something more subtle this time. My client is getting impatient. There can be no more mistakes." As he finished, he handed Zam a hollow, transparent tube containing a pair of whitish centipedelike creatures as long as his forearm.

"Kouhuns," he explained. "Very poisonous."

Zam Wesell lifted the tube to examine the marvelous little murderers more closely, her black eyes sparkling with excitement, and her cheekbones lifting as her mouth widened beneath the veil. She looked back at Jango and nodded.

Certain that she understood, Jango nodded and started around the corner toward his waiting speeder. He paused before stepping in, and looked back at his hired assassin.

"There can be no mistakes this time," he said.

The Clawdite saluted, tapping the tube containing the deadly kouhuns to her forehead.

"Tidy yourself up," Jango instructed, and he headed away.

Zam Wesell turned back to her own waiting speeder and pulled off her veil. Even as she lifted the cloth, her features began to morph, her mouth tightening, her black eyes sinking back into shapely sockets, and the ridges on her forehead smoothing. In the time it took her to unhook her veil, she had already assumed a shapely and attractive female human form, with dark and sensuous features. Even her clothing seemed to fit her differently, flowing down gracefully from her face.

Off to the side, Jango nodded approvingly and sped away. As a Clawdite, a changeling, Zam Wesell did bring some advantages to the trade, he had to admit.

The vast Jedi Temple sat on a flat plain. Unlike so many of Coruscant's buildings, monuments of efficiency and spare design, this building itself was a work of art, with many ornate columns and soft, rounded lines that drew in the eye and held it. Bas-reliefs and statues showed in many areas, with lights set at varying angles to distort the shadows into designs of mystery.

Inside, the Temple was no different. This was a place of contemplation, a place whose design invited the mind to wander and to explore, a place whose lines themselves asked for interpretation. Art was as much a part of what it was to be a Jedi Knight as was warrior training. Many of the Jedi, past and present, considered art to be a conscious link to the mysteries of the Force, and so the sculptures and portraits that lined every hall were more than mere replicas—they were artistic interpretations of the great Jedi they represented, saying in form alone what the depicted Masters might speak in words.

Mace Windu and Yoda walked slowly down one polished and decorated corridor, the lights low, but with a brightly illuminated room in the distance before them.

"Why couldn't we see this attack on the Senator?" Mace pondered, shaking his head. "This should have been no surprise to the wary, and easy for us to predict."

"Masking the future is this disturbance in the Force," Yoda replied. The diminutive Jedi seemed tired.

Mace understood well the source of that weariness. "The prophecy is coming true. The dark side is growing."

"And only those who have turned to the dark side can sense the possibilities of the future," Yoda said. "Only by probing the dark side can we see."

Mace spent a moment digesting that remark, for what Yoda referred to was no small thing. Not at all. Journeys to the edges of the dark side were not to be taken lightly. Even more dire, the fact that Master Yoda believed that the disturbance all the Jedi had sensed in the Force was so entrenched in the dark side was truly foreboding.

"It's been ten years and the Sith still have not shown themselves," Mace remarked, daring to say it aloud. The Jedi didn't like to even mention the Sith, their direst of enemies. Many times in the past, the Jedi had dared hope that the Sith had been eradicated, their foul stench cleansed from the galaxy, and so they all would have liked to deny the existence of the mysterious dark Force-users.

But they could not. There could be no doubt and no denying that the being who had slain Qui-Gon Jinn those ten years before on Naboo was a Sith Lord.

"Do you think the Sith are behind this present disturbance?" Mace dared to ask.

"Out there, they are," Yoda said with resignation. "A certainty that is."

Yoda was referring to the prophecy, of course, that the dark side would rise and that one would be born who would bring balance to the Force and to the galaxy. Such a potential chosen one was now known among them, and that, too, brought more than a little trepidation to these hallowed halls.

"Do you think Obi-Wan's learner will be able to bring balance to the Force?" Mace asked.

Yoda stopped walking and slowly turned to regard the other Master, his expression showing a range of emotions that reminded Mace that they didn't know what bringing balance to the Force might truly mean. "Only if he chooses to follow his destiny," Yoda replied, and as with Mace's question, the answer hung in the air between them, a spoken belief that could only lead to more uncertainty.

Both Yoda and Mace Windu understood the places that some of the Jedi, at least, might have to travel to find the true answers, and those places, emotional stops and not physical, could well test all of them to the very limits of their abilities and sensibilities.

They resumed their walk, the only sound the patter of their footsteps. In their ears, though, both Mace and Yoda heard the ominous echo of the diminutive Jedi Master's dire words.

"Only by probing the dark side can we see."

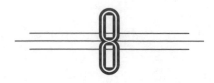

The door chime was not unexpected; somehow, Padmé had known that Anakin would come to speak with her as soon as the opportunity presented itself. She started for the door, but paused, and moved instead to retrieve her robe, aware suddenly that her nightgown was somewhat revealing.

Her movements again struck her as curious, though, for never before had Padmé Amidala harbored any feelings of modesty.

Still, she pulled the robe up tight as she opened the door, finding, predictably, Anakin Skywalker standing before her.

"Hello," he said, and it seemed as if he could hardly draw his breath.

"Is everything all right?"

Anakin stuttered over a response. "Oh yes," he finally managed to say. "Yes, my Master has gone to the lower levels to check on Captain Typho's security measures, but all seems quiet."

"You sound disappointed."

Anakin gave an embarrassed laugh.

"You don't enjoy this," Padmé remarked.

"There is nowhere else in all the galaxy I'd rather be," Anakin blurted, and it was Padmé's turn to give an embarrassed little laugh.

"But this . . . inertia," she reasoned, and Anakin nodded as he caught on.

"We should be more aggressive in our search for the assassin," he insisted. "To sit back and wait is to invite disaster."

"Master Kenobi does not agree."

"Master Kenobi is bound by the letter of the orders," Anakin explained. "He won't take a chance on doing anything that isn't explicitly asked of him by the Jedi Council."

Padmé tilted her head and considered this impetuous young man more carefully. Was not discipline a primary lesson of the Jedi Knights? Were they not bound, strictly so, within the structure of the Order and their Code?

"Master Kenobi is not like his own Master," Anakin said. "Master Qui-Gon understood the need for independent thinking and initiative—otherwise, he would have left me on Tatooine."

"And you are more like Master Qui-Gon?" Padmé asked.

"I accept the duties I am given, but demand the leeway I need to see them to a proper conclusion."

"Demand?"

Anakin smiled and shrugged. "Well, I ask, at least."

"And presume, when you can't get the answers you desire," Padmé said with a knowing grin, though in her heart she was only half teasing.

"I do the best I can with every problem I am given," was the strongest admission Anakin would offer.

"And so sitting around guarding me is not your idea of fun."

"We could be doing better and more exciting things,"

Anakin said, and there was a double edge to his voice, one that intrigued Padmé and made her pull her robe up even tighter.

"If we catch the assassin, we might find the root of these attempts," the Padawan explained, quickly putting the discussion back on a professional level. "Either way, you will be safer, and our duties will be made far easier."

Padmé's mind whirled as she tried to sort out Anakin's thoughts, and his motivations. He was surprising her with every word, considering that he was a Jedi Padawan, and yet, given the fire that she clearly saw burning behind his blue eyes, he was not surprising her. She saw trouble brewing there, in those simmering and too-passionate eyes, but even more than that, she saw excitement and the promise of thrills.

And, perhaps, the promise of finding out who it was that was trying to kill her.

Obi-Wan Kenobi stepped off the turbolift tentatively, warily, glancing left and right. He noted the two posted guards, alert and ready, and he nodded his approval to them. Every corridor had been like this throughout the massive apartment complex, and in this particular area, above, below, and near Amidala's room, the place was locked down tight.

Captain Typho had been given many soldiers at his disposal, and he had situated them well, overseeing as fine a defensive perimeter as Obi-Wan had ever witnessed. The Jedi Master took great comfort in that, of course, and knew that Typho was making his job easier.

But Obi-Wan could not relax. He had heard about the attack on the Naboo cruiser in great detail from Typho, and considering the many precautions that had been taken to protect the vessel—everything from broadcasting false entry lanes to the appointed landing pad to the many shielding fighters, the three accompanying the ship directly, and many more, both Naboo and Republic, covering every conceivable attack lane—these assassins could not be underestimated. They were good and they were well connected, to be sure.

And, likely, they were stubborn.

To get at Senator Amidala through the halls of this building, though, would take an army.

Obi-Wan nodded to the guards and walked a circuit of this lower floor then, satisfied, headed back to the turbolift.

Padmé took a deep breath, her thoughts lost in the last images of Anakin as he had left her room. Images of her sister Sola flitted about her, almost as if she could hear Sola teasing her already.

The Senator shook all of the thoughts, of Sola and particularly of Anakin, away and motioned to R2-D2, the little droid standing impassively against the wall beside the door. "Implement the shutdown," she instructed.

R2-D2 replied with a fearful *"oooo."*

"Go ahead, Artoo. It's all right. We have protection here."

The droid gave another worried call, but extended a probe out to the security panel on the wall beside him.

Padmé looked back to the door, recalling again the last images of Anakin, her tall and lean Jedi protector. She could see his shining blue eyes as surely as if he was standing before her, full of intensity, watching over her more carefully than any security cam ever could.

*   *   *

Anakin stood in the living room of Padmé's apartment, absorbing the silence around him, using the lack of physical noise to bolster his mental connection to that more subtle realm of the Force, feeling the life about him as clearly as if his five physical senses were all attuned to it.

His eyes were closed, but he could see the region about him clearly enough, could sense any disturbance in the Force.

Anakin's eyes popped open wide, his gaze darting about the room, and he pulled his lightsaber from his belt.

Or almost did, stopping fast when the door slid open and Master Kenobi walked into the room.

Obi-Wan looked about curiously, his gaze settling on Anakin. "Captain Typho has more than enough men downstairs," he said. "No assassin will try that way. Any activity up here?"

"Quiet as a tomb," Anakin replied. "I don't like just waiting here for something to happen."

Obi-Wan gave a little shake of his head, a movement showing his resignation concerning Anakin's predictability, and took a view scanner from his belt, checking his screen. His expression, shifting from curious to confused to concerned, spoke volumes to Anakin: He knew that Obi-Wan could see only part of Padmé's bedroom—the door area and R2-D2 standing by the wall, but nothing more.

The Jedi Knight's expression asked the question before he even spoke the words.

"Padmé . . . Senator Amidala, covered the cam," the Padawan explained. "I don't think she liked me watching her."

Obi-Wan's face tensed and he let out a little growl. "What is she thinking? Her security is paramount, and is compromised—"

"She programmed Artoo to warn us if there's an intruder,"

Anakin explained, trying to calm Obi-Wan before his concern could gain any real momentum.

"It's not an intruder I'm worried about," Obi-Wan countered. "Or not merely an intruder. There are many ways to kill a Senator."

"I know, but we also want to catch this assassin," Anakin said, his tone determined, stubborn even. "Don't we, Master?"

"You're using her as bait?" Obi-Wan asked incredulously, his eyes widening with shock and disbelief.

"It was her idea," Anakin protested, but his sharp tone showed clearly that he agreed with the plan. "Don't worry. No harm will come to her. I can sense everything going on in that room. Trust me."

"It's too risky," Obi-Wan scolded. "Besides, your senses aren't that attuned, my young apprentice."

Anakin parsed his words and his tone carefully, trying to sound not defensive, but rather suggestive. "And yours are?"

Obi-Wan could not deny the look of intrigue that crossed his face. "Possibly," he admitted.

Anakin smiled and nodded, and closed his eyes again, falling into the sensations of the Force, following them to Padmé, who was sleeping quietly. He wished that he could see her, could watch the quiet rise and fall of her belly, could hear her soft breathing, could smell the freshness of her hair, could feel the smoothness of her skin, could kiss her and taste the sweetness of her lips.

He had to settle for this, for feeling her life energy in the Force.

A place of warmth, it was.

*　　*　　*

In a different way, Padmé was thinking of Anakin, as well. He was there beside her, in her dreams.

She saw the fighting match that she knew would soon ensue in the Senate, the screaming and fist waving, the threats and the loud objections. How badly it drained her.

Anakin was there.

Her dream became a nightmare, some unseen assassin chasing her, blaster bolts whipping past her, and her feet seemed as if they were stuck in deep mud.

But Anakin rushed past, his lightsaber ignited and waving, deflecting the blaster bolts aside.

Padmé shifted a bit and gave a little groan, on many levels as uncomfortable with the identity of her rescuer as she was with the presence of the assassin. She didn't truly awaken, though, just thrashed a bit and raised her head, opening her eyes only briefly before burying her face in her pillow.

She didn't see the small round droid hovering behind the blinds outside her window. She didn't see the appendages come out of it, attaching to the window, or the sparks arcing about those arms as the droid shut down the security system. She didn't see the larger arm deploy, cutting a hole in the glass, nor did she hear the slight, faint sound as the glass was removed.

Over by the door in Padme's room, R2-D2's lights went on. The droid's domed head swiveled about, scanning the room, and he gave a soft *"wooo"* sound.

But then, apparently detecting nothing amiss, the droid shut back down.

Outside, a small tube came forth from the probe droid, moving to the hole in the window, and crawling through it, into Padmé's room, came a pair of kouhuns, like bloated white maggots with lines of black legs along their sides and nasty mandibles. Dangerous as those mandibles looked, though, the true danger of the kouhuns lay at the other end, the tail stinger, dripping of venom. The vicious kouhuns crawled in through the blinds and started immediately toward the bed and the sleeping woman.

"You look tired," Obi-Wan said to Anakin in the adjoining room.

The Padawan, still standing, opened his eyes and came out of his meditative trance. He took a moment to register the words, and then gave a little shrug, not disagreeing. "I don't sleep well anymore."

That was hardly news to Obi-Wan. "Because of your mother?" he asked.

"I don't know why I keep dreaming about her now," Anakin answered, frustration coming through in his voice. "I haven't seen her since I was little."

"Your love for her was, and remains, deep," Obi-Wan said. "That is hardly reason for despair."

"But these are more than . . ." Anakin started to say, but he stopped and sighed and shook his head. "Are they dreams, or are they visions? Are they images of what has been, or do they tell of something that is yet to be?"

"Or are they just dreams?" Obi-Wan said, his gentle smile showing through his scraggly beard. "Not every dream is a premonition, some vision or some mystical connection. Some dreams are just . . . dreams, and even Jedi have dreams, young Padawan."

Anakin didn't seem very satisfied with that. He just shook his head again.

"Dreams pass in time," Obi-Wan told him.

"I'd rather dream of Padmé," Anakin replied with a sly smile. "Just being around her again is . . . intoxicating."

Obi-Wan's sudden frown erased both his and Anakin's smiles. "Mind your thoughts, Anakin," he scolded in no uncertain tone. "They betray you. You've made a commitment to the Jedi Order, a commitment not easily broken, and the Jedi stand on such relationships is uncompromising. Attachment is forbidden." He gave a little derisive snort and looked toward the sleeping Senator's room. "And don't forget that she's a politician. They're not to be trusted."

"She's not like the others in the Senate, Master," Anakin protested strongly.

Obi-Wan eyed him carefully. "It's been my experience that Senators focus only on pleasing those who fund their campaigns, and they are more than willing to forget the niceties of democracy to get those funds."

"Not another lecture, Master," Anakin said with a profound sigh. He had heard this particular diatribe repeatedly. "At least not on the economics of politics."

Obi-Wan was no fan of the politics of the Republic. He started speaking again, or tried to, but Anakin abruptly interrupted.

"Please, Master," Anakin said emphatically. "Besides, you're generalizing. I know that Padmé—"

"Senator Amidala," Obi-Wan sternly corrected.

"—isn't like that," Anakin finished. "And the Chancellor doesn't seem to be corrupt."

"Palpatine's a politician. I've observed that he is very clever at following the passions and prejudices of the Senators."

"I think he is a good man," Anakin stated. "My instincts are very positive about . . ."

The young Padawan trailed off, his eyes widening, his expression becoming one of shock.

"I sense it, too," Obi-Wan said breathlessly, and the two Jedi exploded into motion.

Inside the bedroom, the kouhuns crawled slowly and deliberately toward the sleeping Padmé's exposed neck and face, their mandibles clicking excitedly.

"Wee oooo!" R2-D2 shrieked, catching on to the threat. The droid tootled a series of alarms and focused a light on the bed, highlighting the centipede invaders perfectly as Obi-Wan and Anakin burst into the room.

Padmé awoke, her eyes going wide, sucking in her breath in terror as the wicked little creatures stood up and hissed, and came at her.

Or would have, except that Anakin was there, his blue lightsaber blade slashing across, just above the bedcovers, once and again, slicing both creatures in half.

"Droid!" Obi-Wan cried, and Anakin and Padmé turned to see him rushing for the window. There, hovering outside, was the remote assassin, its appendages retracting fast.

Obi-Wan leapt into the blinds, taking them with him right through the window, shattering the glass. He reached into the Force as he leapt, using it to extend his jump, to send him far through the air to catch hold of the retreating droid assassin. With his added weight, the floating droid sank considerably, but it compensated and stabilized quickly, leaving the Jedi hanging on to it a hundred stories up.

Off flew the droid, taking Obi-Wan with it.

"Anakin?" Padmé asked, turning to him. When she saw him return the look, and saw the sudden flicker of intensity in his blue eyes, she pulled her nightdress higher about her shoulders.

"Stay here!" Anakin instructed. "Watch her, Artoo!" He rushed for the door, only to stop abruptly as Captain Typho and a pair of guards, along with the handmaiden Dormé, charged in.

"See to her!" was all that Anakin explained as he scrambled past them, running full out for the turbolift.

Not without defensive systems, the probe droid repeatedly sent electrical shocks arcing over its surface, stinging Obi-Wan's hands.

The Jedi Knight gritted through the pain, having no alternative but to hold on. He knew he shouldn't look down, but he did so anyway, to see the city teeming far, far below.

Another shock nearly sent him plummeting toward that distant bustle.

Reflexively, and hardly considering all the implications, the Jedi fumbled with one hand, found a power wire, and pulled it free, ceasing the electrical shocks.

But ending, too, the power that kept the probe droid aloft.

Down they went, falling like stones, the lights of the various floors flashing past them like strobes as they dropped.

"Not good, not good!" Obi-Wan said over and over as he worked frantically to reconnect the wire. Finally, he got it. The probe droid's lights blinked back on, and off the remote soared, with Obi-Wan hanging on desperately. The droid wasted no time in reigniting the series of electrical shocks, stinging the Jedi, but not shaking the stubborn man free.

Anakin was in no mood to wait for a turbolift. Out came his lightsaber, and with a single well-placed thrust the Padawan had the doors open, though the turbolift car was nowhere near his floor. Anakin didn't even pause long enough to discern if it was above him or below, he just leapt into the shaft, catching hold of one of the supporting poles with one arm, propping the side of his foot tight against it, and spinning downward. His mind whirled, trying to remember the layout of the building, and which levels held the various docking bays.

Suddenly that sixth sense, feeling through the Force, alerted him to danger.

"Yikes!" he yelled as he looked down to see the turbolift racing up at him.

Grabbing on tighter to the pole, he held his open palm downward, then sent a tremendous Force push below, not to stop the lift, but to propel himself back up the shaft, keeping him ahead of the lift with sufficient speed for him to reorient himself and land, sprawled, atop the speeding car.

Again, whipping out his lightsaber, he stabbed it through the catch on the lift's top hatch. Ignoring the shrieks from the car's occupants below, Anakin pulled open the hatch, grabbed the edge as he shut off his blade, then somersaulted into the car.

"Docking bay level?" he asked the pair of stunned Senators, a Sullustan and a human.

"Forty-seven!" the human responded at once.

"Too late," the Sullustan added, noting the rolling floor numbers. The diminutive Senator started to add, "Next is sixty-something," but Anakin slammed the brake button, and when that didn't work fast enough for him, he reached into the Force again and grabbed at the braking mechanisms, forcing them even more tightly into place.

All three went off the floor with the sudden stop, the Sullus-tan landing hard.

Anakin banged on the door, yelling for it to open. A hand on his shoulder slowed him, and he turned to see the human Senator step by, one finger held up in a gesture bidding the eager young Jedi to wait.

The Senator pushed a button, clearly marked on the panel, and the turbolift door slid open.

With a shrug and a sheepish smile, Anakin had to fall to his belly and squeeze through the opening to drop to the hallway below. He ran frantically, left and then right, finally spotting a balcony adjacent to the parking garage. Out he ran, then vaulted over a rail, dropping to a line of parked speeders. One yellow, snub-nosed speeder was open, so he jumped in, firing it up and zooming away, off the platform and then up, up, heading for the line of traffic flowing high above.

He tried to get his bearings as he rose. What side of the building was he now on? And which side had Obi-Wan flown away from? And what angle had the fleeing probe droid taken?

As he tried to sort it all out, Anakin realized that only one of two things could possibly put him on Obi-Wan's trail, dumb luck or . . .

The Padawan fell into the Force yet again, searching for the sensation that he could identify as his Jedi Master.

Zam Wesell leaned against the side of her speeder, impatiently tapping her gloved fingers on the roof of the old vehicle. She wore an oversized purple helmet, front-wedged and solid save a small rectangle cut out about her eyes, but while that hid her assumed beauty, her formfitting grav-suit showed every feminine curve.

Zam didn't think much about it at that time, though, for

with this particular mission it was more important that she merely blend in. Often she had taken assignments where her assumed feminine wiles had helped her tremendously, where she had played upon the obvious weakness of a male to get close.

Those wiles weren't going to help her with this assignment, though, and Zam knew it. This time, she was out to kill a woman, a Senator, and one who was very well guarded by beings absolutely devoted to her, as protective of her as a parent might be to a child. Zam wondered what this woman might have done to so invoke the wrath of her employers.

Or at least, she started to wonder, as she had started to wonder several times since Jango had hired her to kill the Senator. The professional assassin never truly let her thoughts travel down that path. It wasn't her business. She was not a moral gauge for anyone, not one to decide the value of her assignment or the justice or injustice involved—she was just a tool, in many ways, a machine. She was the extension of her employers and nothing more.

Jango had bade her to kill Amidala, and so she would kill Amidala, fly back and collect her due, and go on to the next assignment. It was clean and it was simple.

Zam could hardly believe that the explosive charge she had managed to hide on the landing platform had not done the job, but she had taken that lesson to heart, had come to understand that the weaknesses of Senator Amidala were not easily discerned and exploited.

The changeling banged her fist on the roof of the speeder. She hated that she had been forced to go outside for help, to procure a probe droid to do the task that she so relished handling personally.

But now there were Jedi about Amidala, by all the rumors, and Zam had little desire to do battle with one of those troublesome fanatics.

She glanced into the speeder, to the timepiece on the console, and nodded grimly. The job should be completed by now. The poisonous kouhuns had been delivered, likely, and one scratch of a venomous stinger should be more than enough.

Zam stood up straight, sensing something, some sudden feeling of uneasiness.

She heard a cry, of surprise or of fear, and she glanced all about, and then her eyes, within the cut-out rectangle of the helmet, went wide indeed. She watched in blank amazement as the probe droid, her programmed assassin, wove through the towering buildings of Coruscant, with a man, dressed like a Jedi, hanging on to it! Zam's fear lessened and her smile widened, though, as she watched the droid go into defensive action, for this one was well programmed. It smacked against the side of a building, nearly dislodging the Jedi, and when that didn't work, the clever droid dived back into the traffic lane, soaring behind a speeder, just above the vehicle's exhaust.

The Jedi squirmed and tucked and somehow managed to keep himself out of that fiery exhaust, and so the droid swooped off to the side, taking a different tack. It flew in low over the top of one building.

Zam's eyes widened as she watched the spectacle. She was impressed at the way the Jedi did not allow himself to be slammed off, but rather tucked his legs enough to run along the rooftop as the droid skimmed across it. Oh, he was good!

This was truly entertaining to the confident bounty hunter, but enough was enough.

Zam reached into the speeder and pulled out a long blaster rifle, casually lifting and leveling. She fired off a series of shots, and explosions ignited all about the Jedi and the droid.

Zam looked up from her sights, stunned to see that the crafty man had somehow avoided those shots, had dodged, or had, she mused, used his Jedi powers to deflect them.

"Block this," the bounty hunter said, raising the rifle again. Taking aim at the Jedi's chest, she lifted the barrel just a bit and squeezed the trigger.

The probe droid exploded.

The Jedi plummeted from sight.

Zam sighed and shrugged, telling herself that the cost of the probe droid was worth the show. And hopefully the victory. If Senator Amidala lay dead in her room, then that cost would be a minor thing indeed, for this bounty exceeded anything Zam had ever hoped to collect.

The bounty hunter slipped her rifle back into her speeder, then bent low and squeezed in, soaring off into the Coruscant traffic lanes.

Obi-Wan screamed as he dropped . . . ten stories . . . twenty. There was nothing in his Jedi repertoire to save him this time. He looked all about frantically, but there was nothing—no handholds, no platform, no awning of thick and padded cloth.

Nothing. Just another five hundred stories to the ground!

He tried to find his sense of calm, tried to fall into the Force and accept this unwelcomed end.

And then a speeder swooped beside him and he saw that cocky smile of his unruly Padawan, and never in his life had Obi-Wan Kenobi been happier to see anything.

"Hitchhikers usually stand on the platforms," Anakin informed him, and he swooped the speeder near enough for Obi-Wan to grab on. "A novel approach, though. Gets the attention of passing traffic."

Obi-Wan was too busy clawing his way into the passenger seat to offer a retort. He finally settled in next to Anakin.

"I almost lost you there," the Padawan remarked.

"No kidding. What took you so long?"

Anakin eased back in his seat, putting his left arm up on the door of the open speeder and assuming a casual posture. "Oh, you know, Master," he said flippantly. "I couldn't find a speeder I really liked. One with an open cockpit, of course, and with the right speed capabilities to catch your droid scooter. And then, you know, I had to hold out for just the right color—"

"There!" Obi-Wan shouted, pointing up to a closed-in speeder, recognizing it as the one behind the assassin who had been shooting at him. It soared above them, and Anakin cut hard on the wheel and the stick, angling in fast pursuit.

Almost immediately, an arm came out of the lead speeder's open window, holding a blaster pistol, and the bounty hunter squeezed off a series of shots.

"If you'd spend as much time working on your lightsaber skills as you do on your wit, young Padawan, you would rival Master Yoda!" Obi-Wan said, and he ducked, getting jostled about, as Anakin cut a series of evasive turns.

"I thought I already did."

"Only in your mind, my very young Padawan," Obi-Wan retorted. He gave a little cry and ducked reflexively as Anakin dived in and out of traffic, narrowly missing several vehicles. "Careful! Hey, easy! You know I don't like it when you do that!"

"Sorry, I forgot you don't like flying, Master!" Anakin said, his voice rising at the end as he took the speeder down suddenly to avoid another blaster bolt from the stubborn bounty hunter.

"I don't mind flying," Obi-Wan insisted. "But what you're doing is suicide!" His words nearly caught in his throat, along with his stomach, as Anakin cut hard to the right, then dropped suddenly, punched the throttle, pulled back to the left, and lifted the nose, zipping the speeder up through the traffic lane and back in sight of the bounty hunter—only to see another line of blaster bolts coming at them.

Then the bounty hunter dived to the side suddenly, and both Jedi opened their eyes and their mouths wide, their screams drowned out by a commuter train crossing right in front of them.

Obi-Wan tasted bile again, but somehow, Anakin managed to avoid the train, coming out the other side. Obi-Wan looked over to his Padawan, to see him assuming a casual, in-control posture.

"Master, you know I've been flying since before I could walk," Anakin said with a sly grin. "I'm very good at this."

"Just slow down," Obi-Wan instructed, in a voice that suggested the dignified Jedi Knight was about to throw up.

Anakin ignored him, taking the speeder in fast pursuit of the assassin, right into a line of giant trucks. Around and around they went, cutting fast corners through the traffic, over the traffic, under the traffic, and around the buildings, always keeping the assassin's speeder in sight. Anakin took his craft right up on edge, skimming the side of one building.

"He can't lose me," the Padawan boasted. "He's getting desperate."

"Great," Obi-Wan answered dryly.

"Oh wait," Obi-Wan added when the speeder in front dived into a tram tunnel. "Don't go in there!"

But Anakin zoomed right in, and then zoomed right back out, a huge rushing train chasing him, Obi-Wan screaming about as loudly as the train was blowing its horn. "You know I don't like it when you do that!"

"Sorry, Master," Anakin answered unconvincingly. "Don't worry. This guy's gonna kill himself any minute now."

"Well, let him do that alone!" Obi-Wan insisted.

They watched as the assassin zoomed right into traffic, soaring the wrong way down a congested lane.

Anakin went in right behind.

Both speeders zigged and zagged wildly, frantically, the occasional blaster bolt shooting back from the lead one. And then, suddenly, the assassin cut fast, straight up, a tight loop that brought Zam behind the two Jedi.

"Great move," Anakin congratulated. "I got one, too." He slammed on his brakes, reversing thrust, and the assassin's speeder flashed up right beside them.

And there was the assassin, firing point blank at Obi-Wan.

"What are you doing?" Obi-Wan demanded. "He's going to blast me!"

"Right," Anakin agreed, working frantically to maneuver away. "This isn't working."

"Nice of you to notice." Obi-Wan dodged, then lurched as the speeder dropped suddenly, Anakin taking it right under the assassin's.

"He can't shoot us down here," the Padawan congratulated himself, but his smile lasted only the split second it took for their opponent's new tactic to register. The assassin swerved out of the traffic lane and shot straight for a building, coming in at an angle to just skim the rooftop.

Obi-Wan started to shout out Anakin's name, but the word came out as *"Ananananana."* The Padawan was in control, though, and he slowed and lifted his speeder's nose just up over the edge of the rooftop.

Another obstacle showed itself almost immediately, a large craft coming in low and slow.

"It's landing!" Obi-Wan shouted, and when Anakin didn't immediately respond, he added desperately, "On us!"

It came out, *"On uuuuuuuuuuuuus!"* as Anakin brought the speeder up on edge and zipped around a corner, clipping a flagpole and taking its cloth contents free.

"Clear that," the seemingly unshakable Padawan said, nodding down to the torn flag, which had caught itself on one of the speeder's front air scoops.

"What?"

"Clear the flag! We're losing power! Hurry!"

Complaining under his breath with every movement, Obi-Wan crawled out of the cockpit and gingerly onto the front engine. He bent low and tugged the flag free, and the speeder lurched forward, nearly dislodging him.

"Don't do that!" he screamed. "I don't like it when you do that!"

"So sorry, Master."

"He's heading for the power refinery," Obi-Wan said. "But take it easy. It's dangerous near those power couplings."

Anakin zoomed right past one of the couplings, and a huge electrical bolt had the air crackling all about them.

"Slow down!" Obi-Wan ordered. "Slow down! Don't go through there!"

But Anakin did just that, banking left, right, left.

"What are you doing?"

"Sorry, Master!"

More bolts crackled all about them. Right, left, right again, up and over, down and around, and somehow, incredibly, out the other side.

"Oh, that was good," Obi-Wan admitted.

"That was crazy," the rattled Anakin corrected. The older Jedi snapped a glare at him, recognized the greenish color that had suddenly come to the Padawan's face, and then just put his head in his hands and groaned.

"Got him now!" Anakin announced. The assassin was sliding his speeder sidelong around a corner between two buildings up ahead.

Anakin went right around behind, only to find the lead speeder stopped and blocking the alleyway, the assassin leaning out the door, blaster pistol leveled.

"Ah, blast," the Padawan remarked.

"Stop!" Obi-Wan told him, and both ducked as a line of bolts came at them.

"No, we can make it!" Anakin insisted, punching the throttle.

He dived his speeder under the assassin's, barely missing it, then went up on edge, slipping through a small gap in the building. But there were pipes there, and no level of flying could put the speeder safely through them. They bounced sidelong, then flipped end over end, narrowly missing a giant crane and clipping some struts. The damage brought forth a giant fiery gas ball, nearly immolating them, and in the uncontrolled spin that followed, they bounced off yet another building and the speeder stalled out.

Anakin winced, expected a line of curses to come at him, but when he finally looked at Obi-Wan, he saw the Jedi staring straight ahead, eyes wide and unblinking, and saying, "I'm crazy, I'm crazy, I'm crazy . . ." over and over again.

"But it worked," Anakin dared to say. "We made it."

"It didn't work!" Obi-Wan yelled at him. "We've stalled! And you almost got us killed!"

Anakin looked down at his hands and body, and waggled his fingers. "I think we're still alive!" He grinned, trying to disarm his fuming Master, but Obi-Wan seemed as if he was about to explode.

"It was stupid!" Obi-Wan roared.

Anakin worked wildly, trying to restart the speeder. "I could have made it," he protested sheepishly. His confident expression strengthened as the speeder roared back to life.

"But you didn't! And now we've lost him!"

Even as Obi-Wan finished, a barrage of laser bolts rained down around them, setting off explosions that rocked them back and forth. The pair looked up, to see the assassin zooming away.

"No, we didn't," a smiling Anakin said. He took the speeder up, the sudden thrust violently throwing them both back in their seats. They came through the area of smoke and carnage with several small fires burning on their speeder. Obi-Wan slapped at flames on the control panel.

Again they chased the assassin into the main travel lanes, dodging and turning fast about incoming traffic. Up ahead, the assassin cut fast to the left, between two buildings, and Anakin responded, going right and up.

"Where are you going?" a perplexed Obi-Wan asked. "He went down there, the other way."

"This is a shortcut. I think."

"What do you mean, *you think*? What kind of shortcut? He went completely the other way! You've lost him!"

"Master, if we keep this chase going, that creep's gonna end up deep-fried," Anakin tried to explain. "Personally, I'd very much like to find out who he is, and who he's working for."

"Oh," Obi-Wan replied, his voice dripping with sarcasm. "So that's why we're going in the wrong direction."

Anakin took them up and around, finally settling into a hover some fifty stories up from the street.

"Well, you lost him," Obi-Wan said.

"I'm deeply sorry, Master," Anakin replied. Again, he seemed hardly convincing, as if he was saying just what he had to say to keep Obi-Wan from scolding him further. The Jedi Knight looked at him hard, ready to call him on it, when he noticed that Anakin, seemingly deep in concentration, was counting softly.

"Excuse me for a moment," the Padawan said. He stood up and, to Obi-Wan's complete shock, stepped out of the speeder.

Obi-Wan lurched over to the edge and stared down, watching Anakin drop—about five stories, before landing atop the roof of a familiar speeder that was zooming beneath them.

"I hate it when he does that," Obi-Wan muttered incredulously, shaking his head.

*　　*　　*

Zam Wesell skimmed close to the buildings, staying to the side of the main traffic lanes. She didn't know whether the probe droid had successfully completed its mission, but she was feeling pretty good at that moment, having outwitted a pair of Jedi.

Suddenly her speeder shook hard. At first she thought she had been hit by a blaster bolt, but then, surveying for damage, she came to know the truth of the missile, and to know that it—that he—had somehow landed on her speeder.

Zam backed off on the throttle, then slammed it out full, lurching the craft ahead. The force of the sudden acceleration nearly dislodged Anakin, sending him sliding back to the tail, but he hung on stubbornly and, to Zam's dismay, even began crawling back toward the cockpit.

With a sneer, Zam hit the brakes, hard, and Anakin went sliding and bouncing past her.

But the stubborn young Jedi caught one of the twin front forks of the speeder and hung on yet again.

Zam accelerated and reached out her blaster pistol, letting fly a series of bolts in Anakin's general direction. The angle was wrong, though, and she couldn't score any hits. And there he was, crawling back stubbornly toward the roof despite all of Zam's evasive maneuvers. Her Clawdite form came back, suddenly and briefly, as she lost concentration, but she recovered quickly.

The bounty hunter cursed under her breath and swooped back into traffic, trying to formulate some plan for ridding herself of the troublesome Jedi. She went back into her evasive, traffic-dodging maneuvers yet again, entertaining the thought of moving in close to some of the heavier traffic and letting the exhaust plume smoke the fool atop her craft.

She had almost convinced herself to do just that when suddenly a glowing blue blade of energy sheared through the top of her speeder and plunged down beside her. She looked up to see the stubborn young Jedi cutting through the roof.

Swerving all about, she fired off a shot at him, then another. Finally, to her relief, a shot took the lightsaber from his hand, though whether she had taken the hand, as well, or just the weapon, she could not tell.

Obi-Wan had finally caught sight of Zam's speeder, with Anakin scrambling atop it, when the lightsaber tumbled from the Padawan's grasp. Obi-Wan gave a shake of his head and dived his speeder toward the street, angling for an interception.

Anakin's hand plunged through the hole in the roof, and Zam lifted her blaster pistol in his direction. He didn't reach for her, just held his hand there outstretched, and before she could fire, some unseen force yanked the pistol from her hand, throwing it right into the Jedi's grasp. "No!" the bounty hunter yelled, gasping in astonishment. She lurched in her seat, letting go of her speeder's controls to grab the pistol desperately with both hands. The pair struggled over the weapon, the speeder dipping right and left, and then the pistol went off, hitting neither opponent, but blowing a hole in the flooring of Zam's speeder, cutting some control pipes in the process.

The speeder careened out of control, and Zam fell back over the controls, desperately but futilely.

They dived and spun, sidelong and head over. Screaming, both hung on for dear life as they spiraled toward the street.

Finally, at the last possible second, Zam gained some control, enough to turn the impending crash into a spark-throwing skid along the broken permacrete of this seedy section of Coruscant's belly.

The speeder bounced up on edge and slammed to a halt, and Anakin went flying, tumbling along the street for a long, long way. When he finally got control, he saw the assassin leaping from the speeder and running down the street, so he climbed back to his feet and started to follow.

The splash as he stepped in one dirty puddle woke Anakin to the harsh realities about him. This was the underbelly of Coruscant, the smelly and dirty streets. He slowed—the assassin was out of sight anyway—and looked about curiously, noting the many lowlifes, mostly nonhumans of quite a variety of species. Many beings were panhandling up and down the street.

He shook it all away quickly, though, reminding himself of the real reason he was here, and of Padmé and her need for security. Spurred by images of the beautiful Senator from Naboo, the young Jedi sprinted along the broken sidewalk, catching sight of the assassin moving through a crowd of ruffians. Anakin charged right in behind, pushing and shoving, but making little headway against the press.

He spotted the assassin at the last second, before the helmeted killer disappeared through a doorway.

Anakin shoved through, finally, and glanced up to see the glare of the gambling sign above the establishment. Undaunted, he started again for the door, and then stopped as he heard Obi-Wan calling.

A familiar yellow speeder dropped to a resting place on the side of the street.

"Anakin!" Obi-Wan walked toward the young Jedi, point-edly holding Anakin's dropped lightsaber in his hand.

"She went into that club, Master!"

Obi-Wan patted his hand in the air to calm the Padawan, not even registering Anakin's surprising use of the feminine pronoun. "Patience," he said. "Use the Force, Anakin. Think."

"Sorry, Master."

"He went in there to hide, not run," Obi-Wan reasoned.

"Yes, Master."

Obi-Wan held the lightsaber out toward his student. "Next time try not to lose it."

"Sorry, Master."

Obi-Wan pulled the precious weapon back as Anakin reached for it, and held the young Padawan's gaze with his own stern look. "A Jedi's lightsaber is his most precious possession."

"Yes, Master." Again, Anakin reached for the lightsaber, and again Obi-Wan pulled it back, never letting Anakin go from his scrutinizing stare.

"He must keep it with him at all times."

"I know, Master," Anakin replied, a bit of exasperation creeping into his tone.

"This weapon is your life."

"I've heard this lesson before."

Obi-Wan held it out again, finally relinquishing that awful stare, and Anakin took the weapon and replaced it on his belt.

"But you haven't learned anything, Anakin," the Jedi Knight said, turning away.

"I try, Master."

There was sincerity in his tone, Obi-Wan clearly recognized, and a bit of regret, perhaps, and that reminded Obi-Wan of the difficult circumstances under which Anakin had entered the Order. He had been far too old, nearly ten years of age, and Master Qui-Gon had taken him in without permission, without the blessing of the Jedi Council. Master Yoda had seen potential danger in young Anakin Skywalker. No one they had ever encountered had been stronger with the Force, in terms of sheer potential. But the Jedi Order normally required training from the earliest possible age. The Force was too powerful a tool—no, not a tool, and that was the problem. An unwise Jedi might consider the Force a tool, a means to his own ends. But a true Jedi understood that the Force was a partner on a concurrent course, a common pathway to true harmony and understanding.

After Qui-Gon's death at the hands of a Sith Lord, the Jedi Council had rethought their decision about young Anakin, and had allowed his training to go forward, with Obi-Wan fulfilling his promise to Qui-Gon that he would take the talented young boy under his tutelage. The Council had been hesitant, though, and obviously not happy about it. Yoda had seemed almost resigned, as if this path was one that they could not deny, rather than one they would willingly and eagerly walk. For the whispers spoke of Anakin as the chosen one, the one who would bring balance to the Force.

Obi-Wan wasn't sure what that meant, and he was more than a little fearful. He looked up at Anakin, who was standing patiently, properly subdued after the tongue-lashing, and he took comfort in that image, in this incredibly likable, somewhat stubborn, and obviously brash young man.

He hid his smile only because it would not do for Anakin to

understand himself forgiven so easily for his rash actions and the loss of his weapon.

Obi-Wan had to disguise a chuckle as a cough. After all, hadn't he been the one who had leapt out through a window a hundred stories above the streets of Coruscant?

The Jedi Knight led the way into the gambling club. Humans and nonhumans mingled about in the smoky air, sipping drinks of every color and puffing on exotic pipes full of exotic plants. Many robes showed bulges reminiscent of weapons, and in looking around, both Jedi understood that everyone was a potential threat.

"Why do I think that you're going to be the death of me?" Obi-Wan commented above the clamor.

"Don't say that, Master," Anakin replied seriously, and the intensity of his tone surprised Obi-Wan. "You're the closest thing I have to a father. I love you, and I don't want to cause you pain."

"Then why don't you listen to me?"

"I will," Anakin said eagerly. "I'll do better. I promise."

Obi-Wan nodded and glanced all around. "Do you see him?"

"I think he's a she."

"Then be extra careful," Obi-Wan said, and he gave a snort.

"And I think she's a changeling," Anakin added.

Obi-Wan nodded to the crowd ahead of them. "Go and find her." He started the opposite way.

"Where are you going, Master?"

"To get a drink," came the short response.

Anakin blinked in surprise to see his Master heading for the bar. He almost started after, to inquire further, but he recalled the scolding he had just received and his promise to do better, to obey his Master. He turned and started away, milling through the crowd, trying to hold his calm against the wave of faces staring at him, most with obvious suspicion, some even openly hostile.

Over at the bar, Obi-Wan watched him for a bit, out of the corner of his eye. He signaled to the bartender, then watched as a glass was placed in front of him and amber liquid poured in.

"Wanna buy some death sticks?" came a guttural voice from the side.

Obi-Wan didn't even turn to fully regard the speaker, who wore a wild mane of dark hair, with two antennae twirled up from his hair like curly horns.

"Nobody's got better death sticks than Elan Sleazebaggano," the ruffian added with a perfectly evil smile.

"You don't want to sell me death sticks," the Jedi coolly said, waggling his fingers slightly, bringing the weight of the Force into his voice.

"I don't want to sell you death sticks," Elan Sleazebaggano obediently repeated.

Again the Jedi waggled his fingers. "You want to go home and rethink your life."

"I want to go home and rethink my life," Elan readily agreed, and he turned and walked away.

Obi-Wan tossed back his drink and motioned for the bartender to fill it up.

A short distance away, walking among the crowd, Anakin continued his scan. Something didn't seem quite right to him—but of course, how could he expect it to be in this seedy place? Still, some sensation nagged at him, some mounting evil that seemed above the level expected even in here.

He didn't actually see the blaster pistol coming out of the holster, didn't see it rising up toward the apparently unsuspecting Obi-Wan's back.

But he felt . . .

Anakin spun as Obi-Wan spun, to see his Master coming around, lightsaber igniting, in a beautiful and graceful turn with perfect balance. It seemed almost as if in slow motion to Anakin, though of course Obi-Wan was moving with deadly speed and precision, as his blade, blue like Anakin's, cut a short vertical loop and then a second, reaching farther out toward his foe. The would-be assassin—and he could see clearly now that it was a woman, since she had taken off her helmet—shrieked in agony as her arm, still clutching the blaster, fell free to the floor, sheared off above the elbow.

The room exploded into motion, with Anakin rushing to Obi-Wan's side, club patrons leaping up all about them, bristling with nervous energy.

"Easy!" Anakin said loudly, patting his hands in the air, imbuing his voice with the strength of the Force. "Official business. Go back to your drinks."

Gradually, very gradually, the club resumed its previous atmosphere, with conversations beginning again. Seeming hardly concerned, Obi-Wan motioned for Anakin to help him, and together they helped the assassin out to the street.

They lowered her gently to the ground, and she started awake as soon as Obi-Wan began to attend her wounded arm.

She growled ferally and winced in agony, all the while staring up hatefully at the two Jedi.

"Do you know who it was you were trying to kill?" Obi-Wan asked her.

"The Senator from Naboo," Zam Wesell said matter-of-factly, as if it hardly mattered.

"Who hired you?"

Her answer was a glare. "It was just a job."

"Tell us!" Anakin demanded, coming forward threateningly.

The tough bounty hunter didn't even flinch. "The Senator's going to die soon anyway," she said. "It won't end with me. For the price they're offering, there'll be bounty hunters lining up to take the hit. And the next one won't make the same mistake I did."

Tough as she was, she ended with a grunt and a groan.

"This wound's going to need more treatment than I can give it here," an obviously concerned Obi-Wan explained to Anakin, but if the younger man even cared, he didn't show it. His expression angry, he came forward.

"Who hired you?" he asked again, and then he continued, throwing the full weight of the Force into his demand, a strength that surprised Obi-Wan, that came from something more than prudence or dedication to his current job. "Tell us. Tell us now!"

The bounty hunter continued to glare at him, but, lips twitching, she started to answer. "It was a bounty hunter called—"

They heard a puff from above and the bounty hunter twitched and gasped, and simply expired, her human female features twisting grotesquely back into the lumpy form of her true Clawdite nature.

Anakin and Obi-Wan tore their eyes away from the spectacle to look up, and heard the roar as they watched an armored rocket-man lift away into the Coruscant night, disappearing into the sky.

Obi-Wan looked back to the dead creature and pulled a small item from her neck, holding it up for Anakin to see. "Toxic dart."

Anakin sighed and looked away. So they had foiled this attempt and killed one assassin.

But it was clear to him that Senator Amidala—Padmé—remained in grave danger.

Anakin stood quietly in the Jedi Council chamber, encircled by the Masters of the Order. Beside him stood Obi-Wan, his Master, but not one of *the* Masters. Obi-Wan, like the majority of the ten thousand Jedi, was a Knight, but these select few sitting around the edges of this room were Masters, the highest-ranking members of this Order. Anakin had never been comfortable in this esteemed company. He knew that more than half of the Jedi Masters sitting here had expressed grave doubts about allowing him into the Order at the advanced age of ten. He knew that even after Yoda had swayed the vote to allow him to begin studying under Obi-Wan, a few continued to hold those doubts.

"Track down this bounty hunter, you must, Obi-Wan," Master Yoda said as the others passed the toxic dart about.

"Most importantly, find out who he's working for," Mace Windu added.

"What about Senator Amidala?" Obi-Wan asked. "She will still need protecting."

Anakin, anticipating what might be coming, straightened as Yoda turned his gaze his way.

"Handle that, your Padawan will."

Anakin felt his heart soar at Yoda's declaration, both because of the confidence obviously being shown in him, and also because this was one assignment he knew that he would truly enjoy.

"Anakin, escort the Senator back to her home planet of Naboo," Mace added. "She'll be safer there. And don't use registered transport. Travel as refugees."

Anakin nodded as the assignment was explained, but he knew immediately that there would be a few obstacles to such a course. "As the leader of the opposition to the Military Creation Act, it will be very difficult to get Senator Amidala to leave the capital."

"Until caught this killer is, our judgment she must respect," Yoda replied.

Anakin nodded. "But I know how deeply she cares about this upcoming vote, Master," he replied. "She is more concerned with defeating the act than with—"

"Anakin," Mace interrupted, "go to the Senate and ask Chancellor Palpatine to speak with her." The tone of his voice made it clear that they had spent enough time on these issues. The Jedi Knight and his Padawan had their assignments, and Yoda dismissed them with a nod.

Anakin started to say something further, but Obi-Wan had his arm almost immediately, guiding him out of the room.

"I was only going to explain Padmé's passion about this vote," Anakin said when he and Obi-Wan were out in the hall.

"You made Senator Amidala's feelings quite clear," Obi-Wan replied. "That is why Master Windu bade you to have the

Chancellor intervene." The two started walking down the corridor, Anakin biting back any responses that came to him.

"The Jedi Council understands, Anakin," Obi-Wan remarked.

"Yes, Master."

"You must trust in them, Anakin."

"Yes, Master." Anakin's response was automatic. He had already gone past this issue in his thoughts. He knew that Padmé wouldn't be easily convinced to leave the planet before the vote, but in truth, it hardly mattered to him. The important thing was that he would be with her, guarding her. With Obi-Wan off chasing the bounty hunter, Padmé would be his sole responsibility, and that was no small thing to Anakin.

No small thing at all.

Anakin was not nervous in the office of Chancellor Palpatine. Certainly he understood the man's power, and certainly he respected the office itself, but the young Padawan felt very comfortable here, felt as if he was with a friend. He hadn't spent much time with Palpatine, but on those few occasions when he had spoken with the man privately, he had always felt as if the Supreme Chancellor was taking an honest interest in him. In some ways, Anakin felt as if Palpatine was an additional mentor—not as directly as Obi-Wan, of course, but offering solid and important advice.

More than that, though, Anakin always felt as if he was welcome here.

"I will talk to her," Palpatine agreed, upon hearing Anakin's request that he speak with Padmé about leaving Coruscant for the relative safety of Naboo. "Senator Amidala will not refuse an executive order. I know her well enough to assure you of that."

"Thank you, Your Excellency."

"And so, my young Padawan, they have finally given you an assignment," the Chancellor said with a wide and warm smile, the way a father might talk to a son. "Your patience has paid off."

"Your guidance more than my patience," Anakin replied. "I doubt my patience would have held, had it not been for your assurances that my Jedi Masters were watching me, and that they would trust me with some important duties before too long."

Palpatine nodded and smiled. "You don't need guidance, Anakin," he said. "In time you will learn to trust your feelings. Then you will be invincible. I have said it many times, you are the most gifted Jedi I have ever met."

"Thank you, Your Excellency," Anakin replied coolly, though in truth, he had to consciously stop himself from trembling. Hearing such a compliment from one who did not understand— like from his mother—was much different than hearing it from Palpatine, the Supreme Chancellor of the Republic. This was an accomplished man, more accomplished, perhaps, than anyone else in all the galaxy. He was not an underling of Yoda or Mace Windu. Anakin understood that a man like Palpatine would not throw out such compliments if he did not believe them.

"I see you becoming the greatest of all the Jedi, Anakin," Palpatine went on. "Even more powerful than Master Yoda."

Anakin hoped his legs wouldn't simply buckle beneath him. He could hardly believe the words, and yet a part of him did believe them. There was a strength within him, a power beyond the limits the Jedi seemed to place upon him, and upon themselves. Anakin sensed that clearly. He knew that Obi-Wan didn't understand, and that was his biggest frustration with his Master. To Anakin's thinking, Obi-Wan's leash was far too short.

He had no idea of how he might answer Palpatine's continuing compliments, so he just stood in the center of the room and smiled for a bit, while the Chancellor stood by the window, looking out at the endless streams of Coruscant traffic.

After many moments had passed, Anakin worked up the courage to move around the desk and join him following the Supreme Chancellor's gaze up at the traffic lanes.

"I am concerned for my Padawan," Obi-Wan Kenobi said to Yoda and Mace Windu as the three walked along the corridors of the Jedi Temple. "He is not ready to be given this assignment on his own."

"The Council is confident in this decision, Obi-Wan," Yoda said.

"The boy has exceptional skills," Mace agreed.

"But he still has much to learn, Master," Obi-Wan explained. "His skills have made him . . . well, arrogant."

"Yes, yes," Yoda agreed. "It's a flaw more and more common among Jedi. Too sure of themselves, they are. Even the older, more experienced Jedi."

Obi-Wan considered the words with an assenting nod. They certainly rang true, and the current conditions among the Jedi in this time of mounting tension were a bit unsettling, with many off on their own far from Coruscant. And had not arrogance played a major role in Count Dooku's decision to depart the Order, and the Republic?

"Remember, Obi-Wan," Mace remarked, "if the prophecy is true, your apprentice is the only one who can bring the Force into balance."

How could Obi-Wan ever forget that little fact? Qui-Gon had been the first to see it, the first to predict that Anakin would be the one to fulfill the prophecy. What Qui-Gon, or anyone else for that matter, had failed to explain, was exactly what bringing balance to the Force might mean.

"If he follows the right path," the Jedi Knight said to the two Masters, and neither of them corrected him.

"Attend to your own duties, you must," Yoda reminded, drawing Obi-Wan from his distracting contemplation as surely as if he was reading the Jedi's mind. "When solved is this mystery of the assassin, other riddles might be answered."

"Yes, Master," Obi-Wan replied, and he held the small dart he had taken from the dead Clawdite up before his eyes.

With gentle hands, Shmi Skywalker Lars lifted the dull bronze chest piece up to the wiry droid, setting it in place. She smiled at C-3PO, and, though his face could not similarly twist, she could tell that he, too, in that curious droidlike way, was pleased. How often he had complained about the sand blowing into his wiring, chipping away at the silicon coverings, even breaking through and causing jarring jolts on a couple of occasions. And now Shmi was taking care of that problem, was finishing what Anakin had started in building the droid.

"Now?" she managed to ask aloud, through lips caked with dried blood. No, she realized, it was not now. She had covered C-3PO all those days ago—or was it weeks ago, or even years ago?—when Cliegg had taken her to the moisture farm. Yes, there were spare coverings to fit the protocol droid in the garage area, against the wall, under an old workbench.

She remembered that, so clearly, but she had no idea of when it had been.

And now . . . now she was . . . somewhere.

She couldn't open her eyes to look around; she didn't have

the strength at that moment, and the blood on them had dried, making any flutter of her eyelids painful.

She thought it curious that her eyelids were the only place where she actually felt any real pain at that moment. She thought she was injured.

She thought. . .

Shmi heard something behind her. Shuffling footsteps? Then some mumbling. Yes, they were always mumbling.

Her thoughts went back to C-3PO, poor 3PO, who still needed his battered wiry arms covered. *Gently, she lifted the covering . . .*

She heard a sharp sound—or she knew it was a sharp sound, though she heard it only distantly—then felt a brush across her back.

There were no nerves left there to register the bite of the whip any more clearly than that.

Anakin Skywalker and Jar Jar Binks stood at the door separating Padmé's bedroom from the anteroom where Anakin and Obi-Wan had kept watch the night before. Looking through the room to the broken window, the pair watched the Coruscant skyline, the endless lines of traffic.

Padmé and her handmaiden Dormé rushed about the bedroom, throwing the luggage together, and from her sharp movements, both Anakin and Jar Jar knew that they would do well to keep a fair distance from the upset and angry young Senator. As the Jedi had requested, Chancellor Palpatine had intervened to bid Padmé to return to Naboo. She was complying, but that did not mean that she was happy about it.

With a profound sigh, Padmé stood straight, one hand on her lower back, which ached from all the bending. She sighed again and moved before the two observers.

"I'm taking an extended leave of absence," she said to Jar Jar, her voice thick and somber, as if she was hoping to inject some of that gravity into the goofy Gungan. "It will be your responsibility to take my place in the Senate. Representative Binks, I know I can count on you."

"Mesa honored . . ." Jar Jar blurted in reply, standing at attention, except that his head was wagging, and his ears were flopping. One could dress a Gungan up like a dignitary, but such a creature's nature was not so easily changed.

"What?" Padmé's voice was stern and showed more than a little exasperation. She was entrusting something important to Jar Jar, and was obviously not thrilled to hear him acting like his old, goofy self.

Obviously embarrassed, Jar Jar cleared his throat and stood a bit straighter. "Mesa honored to be taken on dissa heavy burden. Mesa accept this with muy . . . muy humility andda—"

"Jar Jar, I don't wish to hold you up," Padmé interrupted. "I'm sure you have a great deal to do."

"Of course, M'Lady." With a great bow, as if trying to use pretense to cover up the fact that he was blushing like a Darellian fire crab, the Gungan turned and left, flashing a bright smile Anakin's way as he passed.

Anakin's eyes followed the retreating Gungan, but any levity or sense of calm he felt from that last exchange was washed away a moment later, when Padmé addressed him in a tone that reminded him that she was not in the best of moods.

"I do not like this idea of hiding," she said emphatically.

"Don't worry. Now that the Council has ordered an investigation, it won't take Master Obi-Wan long to find out who hired that bounty hunter. We should have done that from the beginning. It is better to take the offensive against such a threat, to find out the source rather than try to react to the situation." He meant to go on, to claim credit for asking for such an investigation from the very beginning, to let Padmé know that he had been right all along and that it had taken the Council long enough to come around to his way of thinking. He could see, though, that her eyes were already beginning to glaze over, so he quieted and let her speak.

"And while your Master investigates, I have to hide away."

"That would be most prudent, yes."

Padmé gave a little sigh of frustration. "I haven't worked for a year to defeat the Military Creation Act not to be here when its fate is decided!"

"Sometimes we have to let go of our pride and do what is requested of us," Anakin replied—a rather unconvincing statement, coming from him—and he knew as soon as he spoke the words that he probably shouldn't have phrased things quite like that.

"Pride!" came the roaring response. "Annie, you're young, and you don't have a very firm grip on politics. I suggest you reserve your opinions for some other time."

"Sorry, M'Lady, I was only trying to—"

"Annie! No!"

"Please don't call me that."

"What?"

"Annie. Please don't call me 'Annie.' "

"I've always called you that. It is your name, isn't it?"

"My name is Anakin," the young Jedi said calmly, his jaw firm, his eyes strong. "When you say Annie, it's like I'm still a little boy. And I'm not."

Padmé paused and looked him over, head to toe, nodding as she took the sight of him in completely. He could see sincerity on her face as she nodded her agreement, and her tone, too, became one of more respect. "I'm sorry, Anakin. It's impossible to deny you've . . . that you've grown up."

There was something in the way she said that, Anakin sensed, some suggestion, some recognition from Padmé that he was indeed a man now, and perhaps a handsome one at that. That, combined with the little smile she flashed him, had him a bit flushed and put him back up on his heels. He found an ornament sitting on a shelf to the side, then, and using the Force, picked it up, letting it hover above his fingers, needing the distraction.

Still, he had to clear his throat to cover his embarrassment, for he was afraid that his voice would break apart as he admitted, "Master Obi-Wan manages not to see it. He criticizes my every move, as if I was still a child. He didn't listen to me when I insisted that we go in search of the source of the assassination—"

"Mentors have a way of seeing more of our faults than we would like," Padmé agreed. "It's the only way we grow."

With a thought, Anakin used the Force to lift the little globe ornament higher into the air, manipulating it all about. "Don't get me wrong," he remarked. "Obi-Wan is a great mentor, as wise as Master Yoda and as powerful as Master Windu. I am truly thankful to be his learner. Only . . ." He paused and shook his head, looking for the words. "Only, although I'm a Padawan learner, in some ways—in a lot of ways—I'm ahead of him. I'm ready for the trials. I know I am! He knows it, too. He feels I'm too unpredictable—other Jedi my age have gone through the trials and made it. I know I started my training late, but he won't let me move on."

Padmé's expression grew curious, and Anakin could well understand her puzzlement, for he, too, was surprised at how openly he was speaking, critically, of Obi-Wan. He thought that he should stop right there, and silently berated himself.

But then Padmé said, with all sympathy, "That must be frustrating."

"It's worse!" Anakin cried in response, willingly diving into that warm place. "He's overly critical! He never listens! He just doesn't understand! It's not fair!"

He would have gone on and on, but Padmé began to laugh, and that stopped Anakin as surely as a slap across the face.

"I'm sorry," she said through her giggles. "You sounded exactly like that little boy I once knew, when he didn't get his way."

"I'm not whining! I'm not."

Across the room, Dormé, too, began to chuckle.

"I didn't say it to hurt you," Padmé explained.

Anakin took a deep breath, then blew it all out of him, his shoulders visibly relaxing. "I know."

He seemed so pitiable then, not pitiful, but just like a lost little soul. Padmé couldn't resist. She walked over to him and lifted her hand to gently stroke his cheek. "Anakin."

For the first time since they had been reunited, Padmé truly looked into the blue eyes of the young Padawan, locked stares with him so that they each could see beneath the surface, so that they each could view the other's heart. It was a fleeting moment, made so by Padmé's common sense. She quickly altered the mood with a sincere but lighthearted request. "Don't try to grow up too fast."

"I am grown up," Anakin replied. "You said it yourself." He finished by making his reply into something suggestive, as he looked deeply into Padmé's beautiful brown eyes again, this time even more intensely, more passionately.

"Please don't look at me like that," she said, turning away.

"Why not?"

"Because I can see what you're thinking."

Anakin broke the tension, or tried to, with a laugh. "Oh, so you have Jedi powers, too?"

Padmé looked past the young Padawan for a moment, glimpsing Dormé, who was watching with obvious concern and not even trying to hide her interest anymore. And Padmé understood that concern, given the strange and unexpected road this conversation had taken. She looked squarely at Anakin again and said, with no room for debate, "It makes me feel uncomfortable."

Anakin relented and looked away. "Sorry, M'Lady," he said professionally, and he stepped back, allowing her to resume her packing.

Just the bodyguard again.

But he wasn't, Padmé knew, no matter how much she wished it were true.

On a water-washed, wind-lashed world, far to the most remote edges of the Outer Rim, a father and his son sat on a skirt of shining black metal, watching carefully in the few somewhat calm pools created by the currents swirling about the gigantic caryatid that climbed out of the turbulent ocean. The rain had let up a bit, a rare occasion in this watery place, allowing for some calm surface area, at least, and the pair stared hard, searching for the meter-long dark silhouettes of rollerfish.

They were on the lowest skirt of one of the great pillars that supported Tipoca City, the greatest city on all of Kamino, a place of sleek structures, all rounded to deflect the continual wind, rather than flat-faced to battle against it. Kamino had been designed, or upgraded at least, by many of the best architects the galaxy could offer, who understood well that the best way to battle planetary elements was to subtly dodge them. Towering transparisteel windows looked out from every portal—the father, Jango, often wondered why the Kaminoans, tall and thin, pasty white creatures with huge almond-shaped eyes set in oblong heads on necks as long as his arm, wanted so many windows. What was there to see on this violent world other than rolling waters and nearly constant downpours?

Still, even Kamino had its better moments. It was all relative, Jango supposed. Thus, when he saw that it was not raining very hard, he had taken his boy outside.

Jango tapped his son on the shoulder and nodded toward one of the quiet eddies, and the younger one, his face showing all the exuberance of a ten-year-old boy, lifted his pocker, an ion-burst-powered atlatl, and took deadly aim. He didn't use the laser sighting unit, which automatically adjusted for watery refraction. No, this kill was to be a test of his skill alone.

He exhaled deeply, as his father had taught him, using the technique to go perfectly steady, and then, as the prey turned sidelong, he snapped his arm forward, throwing the missile. Barely a meter from the boy's extended hand, the back of the missile glowed briefly, a sudden and short burst of power that shot it off like a blaster bolt, knifing through the water and taking the fish in the side, its barbed head driving through.

With a shout of joy, the boy twisted the atlatl handle, locking the nearly invisible but tremendously strong line, and then, when the fish squirmed away enough to pull the line taut, the boy slowly and deliberately turned the handle, reeling in his catch.

"Well done," Jango congratulated. "But if you had hit it a centimeter forward, you would have skewered the primary muscle just below the gill and rendered it completely helpless."

The boy nodded, unperturbed that his father, his mentor, could always find fault, even in success. The boy knew that his beloved father did so only because it forced him to strive for perfection. And in a dangerous galaxy, perfection allowed for survival.

The boy loved his father even more for caring enough to criticize.

Jango went tense suddenly, sensing a movement nearby, a footfall, perhaps, or just a smell, something to tell the finely attuned bounty hunter that he and his boy were not alone. There weren't many enemies to be found on Kamino, except far out in the watery wastes, where giant tentacled creatures roamed. Here there was little life above the water, other than the Kaminoans themselves, and so Jango wasn't surprised when he saw that the newcomer was one of them: Taun We, his usual contact with the Kaminoans.

"Greetings, Jango," the tall, lithe creature said, holding up a slim arm and hand in a gesture of peace and friendship.

Jango nodded but didn't smile. Why had Taun We come out here—the Kaminoans were hardly ever out of their city of globes—and why would she interrupt Jango when he was with his son?

"You have been scarce within the sector of late," Taun We remarked.

"Better things to do."

"With your child?"

In response, Jango looked over at the boy, who was lining up another rollerfish. Or at least, he was appearing to, Jango recognized, and the insight brought a knowing nod of satisfaction to the crusty bounty hunter. He had taught his son well the art of deception and deflection, of appearing to do one thing while, in reality, doing something quite different. Like listening in on the conversation, measuring Taun We's every word.

"The tenth anniversary approaches," the Kaminoan explained.

Jango turned back to her with a sour expression. "You think I don't know Boba's birthday?"

If Taun We was fazed at all by the sharp retort, the delicately featured Kaminoan didn't show it. "We are ready to begin again."

Jango looked back at Boba, one of his thousands of children, but the only one who was a perfect clone, an exact replica with no genetic manipulation to make him more obedient. And the only one who hadn't been artificially aged. The group that had been created beside Boba had all reached maturity now, were adult warriors, in perfect health.

Jango had thought that policy of accelerating the aging process a mistake—wasn't experience as much a part of attaining warrior skill as genetics?—but he hadn't complained openly to the Kaminoans about it. He had been hired to do a job, to serve as the source, and questioning the process wasn't in his job description.

Taun We cocked her head a bit to the side, eyes blinking slowly.

Jango recognized her expression as curiosity, and it nearly brought a chuckle bubbling to his lips. The Kaminoans were much more alike than were humans, especially humans from different planets. Perhaps their singular concept, their commonness within their own species, was a part of their typical reproductive process, which now included a fair amount of genetic manipulation, if not outright cloning. As a society, they were practically of one mind and one heart. Taun We seemed genuinely perplexed, and so she was, to see a human with so little apparent regard for other humans, clones or not.

Of course, hadn't the Kaminoans just created an army for

the Republic? There wouldn't be wars without some disagreement, now, would there?

But that, too, held little interest for Jango. He was a solitary bounty hunter, a recluse—or he would have been if not for Boba. Jango didn't care a whit about politics or war or this army of his clones. If every one of them was slaughtered, then so be it. He had no attachment to any.

He looked to the side as he considered that. To any except for Boba, of course.

Other than that, though, this was just a job, well paying and easy enough. Financially, he couldn't have asked for more, but more important, only the Kaminoans could have given him Boba—not just a son, but an exact replica. Boba would give Jango the pleasure of seeing all that he might have become had he grown up with a loving and caring father, a mentor who cared enough to criticize, to force him to perfection. He was as good as it got concerning bounty hunters, concerning warriors, but he had no doubt that Boba, bred and trained for perfection, would far outshine him to become one of the greatest warriors the galaxy had ever known.

This, then, was Jango Fett's greatest reward, right here, sitting with his son, his young replica, sharing quiet moments.

Quiet moments within the tumult that had been Jango Fett's entire life, surviving the trials of the Outer Rim alone practically from the day he learned to walk. Each trial had made him stronger, had made him more perfect, had honed the skills that he would now pass along to Boba. There was no one better in all the galaxy to teach his son. When Jango Fett wanted you caught, you were caught. When Jango Fett wanted you dead, you were dead.

No, not when Jango "wanted" those things. This was never

personal. The hunting, the killing, it was all a job, and among the most valuable of lessons Jango had learned early on was how to become dispassionate. Completely so. That was his greatest weapon.

He looked at Taun We, then turned to grin at his son. Jango could be dispassionate, except for those times when he could spend time alone with Boba. With Boba, there was pride and there was love, and Jango had to work constantly to keep both of those potential weaknesses at a minimum. While he loved his son dearly—*because* he loved his son dearly—Jango had been teaching him those same attributes of dispassion, even callousness, from his earliest days.

"We will commence the process again as soon as you are ready," Taun We remarked, bringing Jango back from his contemplations.

"Don't you have enough of the material to do it without me?"

"Well, since you are here anyway, we would like you to be involved," Taun We said. "The original host is always the best choice."

Jango rolled his eyes at the thought—of the needles and the probing—but he did nod his agreement; this was really an easy job, considering the rewards.

"Whenever you are ready." Taun We bowed and turned and walked away.

If you wait for that, you'll be waiting forever, Jango thought, but he kept quiet, and again he turned to Boba, motioning for the boy to put his atlatl back to work. *Because now I have all that I wanted,* Jango mused, watching Boba's fluid motions, his eyes darting about, searching for the next rollerfish.

*   *   *

The industrial sector of Coruscant held perhaps the greatest freight docks in all the galaxy, with a line of bulky transports coming in continually, huge floating cranes ready to meet them and unload the millions of tons of supplies necessary to keep alive the city-planet, which long ago had become too populous to support itself through its own resources. The efficiency of these docks was nothing short of amazing, and yet the place was still tumultuous, and sometimes gridlocked by the sheer number of docking ships and floating cranes.

This was also a place for living passengers, the peasantry of Coruscant, catching cheap rides on freighters outbound, thousands and thousands of people looking to escape the sheer frenzy that had become the world.

Blended into that throng, Anakin and Padmé walked along, dressed in simple brown tunics and breeches, the garb of Outland refugees. They walked side by side to the shuttle exit as they approached the dock and walkway that would take them to one of the gigantic transports. Captain Typho, Dormé, and Obi-Wan stood waiting for them at that exit door.

"Be safe, M'Lady," Captain Typho said with genuine concern. It was clear that he was not thrilled with allowing Padmé out of his sight and control. He handed a pair of small luggage bags over to Anakin and gave a nod of confidence to the young Jedi.

"Thank you, Captain," Padmé replied, her voice thick with gratitude. "Take good care of Dormé. The threat will be on you two now."

"He'll be safe with me!" Dormé put in quickly.

Padmé smiled, appreciating the small attempt at levity. Then she embraced her handmaiden in a great and tight hug, squeezing all the tighter when she heard Dormé start to weep.

"You'll be fine," Padmé whispered into the other woman's ear.

"It's not me, M'Lady. I worry about you. What if they realize you've left the capital?"

Padmé moved back to arm's length and managed a smile as she looked over to Anakin. "Then my Jedi protector will have to prove how good he is."

Dormé gave a nervous chuckle and wiped a tear from her eye as she smiled and nodded.

Off to the side, Anakin held his smile within, deciding consciously to wear a posture that exuded confidence and control. But inside he was thrilled to hear Padmé's compliments coming his way.

Obi-Wan shattered that warmth, pulling the young Padawan off to the side.

"You stay on Naboo," Obi-Wan said. "Don't attract attention. Do absolutely nothing without checking in with me or the Council."

"Yes, Master," Anakin answered obediently, but inside, he was churning, wanting to lash out at Obi-Wan. Do nothing, absolutely nothing, without checking in, without asking for permission? Hadn't he earned a bit more respect than that? Hadn't he proven himself a bit more resourceful, a Padawan to be trusted?

"I will get to the bottom of this plot quickly, M'Lady," he heard Obi-Wan say to Padmé. Anakin seethed inwardly. Hadn't that been exactly the course he had suggested to his Master when they had first been assigned to watch over the Senator?

"You'll be back here in no time," Obi-Wan assured her.

"I will be most grateful for your speed, Master Jedi."

Anakin didn't appreciate hearing Padmé speak of any gratitude at all toward Obi-Wan. At least, he didn't want Padmé to elevate Obi-Wan's importance in all of this above his own. "Time to go," he said, striding forward.

"I know," Padmé answered him, but she didn't seem pleased.

Anakin reminded himself not to take it personally. Padmé felt that her duty was here. She wasn't thrilled with running offplanet—and she wasn't thrilled with having another of her dear handmaidens stepping into the line of fire in her stead, especially with images of dead Cordé so fresh in her mind.

Padmé and Dormé shared another hug. Anakin took up the luggage and led the way off the speeder bus, onto a landing where R2-D2 waited.

"May the Force be with you," Obi-Wan said.

"May the Force be with you, Master." Anakin meant every word of it. He wanted Obi-Wan to find out who was behind the assassination attempts, to make the galaxy safe for Padmé once again. But he had to admit that he hoped it wouldn't happen too quickly. His duty now put him right beside the woman he loved, and he wouldn't be happy if this assignment proved a short one, if duty pulled him away from her yet again.

"Suddenly I'm afraid," Padmé said to him as they walked away, heading toward the giant star freighter that would take them to Naboo. Behind the pair, R2-D2 rolled along, tootling cheerily.

"This is my first assignment on my own. I am, too." Anakin turned about, taking Padmé's gaze with his own, and grinned widely. "But don't worry. We've got Artoo with us!"

Again, the levity was much needed.

Back at the bus, waiting for it to take them back to the main city, the three left behind watched Anakin, Padmé, and R2-D2 blend into the throng of the vast spaceport.

"I hope he doesn't try anything foolish," Obi-Wan said. The mere fact that he would speak so openly concerning his student showed Captain Typho how much the Jedi Knight had come to trust him.

"I'd be more concerned about *her* doing something than him," Typho replied. He shook his head, his expression serious. "She's not one to follow orders."

"Like-minded traveling companions," Dormé observed.

Obi-Wan and Typho turned to regard her, and Typho shook his head helplessly again. Obi-Wan didn't disagree with Dormé's assessment, however innocently she meant it. Padmé Amidala was a stubborn one indeed, one of strong and independent thinking and more than willing to trust her own judgment above that of others, whatever their position and experience.

But of the pair who had just left the speeder bus, she wasn't the most headstrong.

It was not a comforting thought.

The great Jedi Temple was a place of reflection and of hard training, and it was also a place of information. The Jedi were traditionally the keepers of the peace, and also of knowledge. Beneath their high ceilings, off the main corridor of the Temple, stood the glass cubicles, the analysis rooms, filled with droids of various shapes and sizes, and various purposes.

Obi-Wan Kenobi was thinking of Anakin and Padmé as he made his way through the Temple. He wondered, not for the first time and certainly not for the last, about the wisdom of sending Anakin off with the Senator. The eagerness with which the Padawan had embraced his new duty set off warning bells in Obi-Wan's head, but he had allowed the mission to go forth anyway, mostly because he knew that he'd be too busy following the leads he hoped he could garner here, uncovering the source of Amidala's troubles.

The analysis cubicles were busy this day, as they were nearly every day, with students and Masters alike hard at their studies. Obi-Wan found one open cubicle with an SP-4 analysis droid, the type he needed. He sat down in front of the console and the droid responded immediately, sliding open a tray.

"Place the subject for analysis on the sensor tray, please," the droid's metallic voice said. Obi-Wan was already moving, pulling forth the toxic dart that had killed the subcontracting bounty hunter.

As soon as the tray receded, the screen before Obi-Wan lit up and began scrolling through a series of diagrams and streams of data.

"It's a toxic dart," the Jedi explained to the SP-4. "I need to know where it came from and who made it."

"One moment, please." More diagrams rolled by, more reams of data scrolling, and then the screen paused, showing a somewhat similar dart. But it wasn't a match and the scrolling started again. Images of the dart flashed up before Obi-Wan, superimposed with diagrams of similar objects. Nothing matched.

The screen went blank. The tray slid back out.

"As you can see on your screen, subject weapon does not exist in any known culture," SP-4 explained. "Markings cannot be identified. Probably self-made by a warrior not associated with any known culture. Stand away from the sensor tray, please."

"Excuse me? Could you try again please?" There was no hiding the frustration in Obi-Wan's voice.

"Master Jedi, our records are very thorough. They cover eighty percent of the galaxy. If I can't tell you where it came from, nobody can."

Obi-Wan picked up the dart, looked at the droid, and sighed, not so sure that he agreed with that particular assessment. "Thanks for your assistance," he said. He wondered if SP-4s were equipped to understand the inflections of sarcasm.

"You may not be able to figure this out, but I think I know someone who might."

"The odds do not suggest such a possibility," SP-4 started to reply, and began rolling along with a dissertation about the completeness of its data banks, of its unequaled search capabilities, of . . .

It didn't matter, for Obi-Wan was long gone, walking briskly along the great corridor and out of the Jedi Temple.

He left without a word to anyone, his thoughts turned inward, trying to find some focus. He needed answers, and quickly. He knew that instinctively, but he had a nagging feeling that it wasn't necessarily about Senator Amidala's safety. He sensed that something more might be at stake here, though what it was, he could only guess. Anakin's mind-set? A greater plot against the Republic?

Or perhaps he was just being jumpy because the normally reliable SP-4 droid hadn't been able to help him at all. He needed answers, and conventional methods of attaining them wouldn't suffice, apparently. But Obi-Wan Kenobi was not a conventional Jedi, in many ways. Although he tended to be reserved, especially when dealing with his Padawan, his former Master, Qui-Gon Jinn, had left a mark on Obi-Wan.

He knew where to get his answers.

He took a speeder to the business section of Coco town, far from where he and Anakin had caught the would-be assassin.

Obi-Wan stopped his vehicle and exited to the street. He moved to one small building, its windows foggy, its walls metallic and brightly painted. Lettering above the door named the place, and though he could not read that particular script, Obi-Wan knew well what it said: DEX'S DINER.

He smiled. He hadn't seen Dex in a long time. Far too long, he mused as he entered.

The inside of the diner was fairly typical of the establishments along the lower level, with booths set against the walls and many small freestanding circular tables surrounded by tall stools. There was a counter area, as well, partly lined with stools and partly open, a variety of beings standing and leaning against it, mostly freighter drivers and dockworkers, people who still used their muscles in a galaxy grown soft through technology.

The Jedi moved to one small table, sliding onto its stool as a waitress droid wiped the table down with a rag.

"Can I help ya?" the droid asked.

"I'm looking for Dexter."

The waitress droid made a rather unpleasant sound.

Obi-Wan just smiled. "I do need to speak with Dexter."

"Waddya want him for?"

"He's not in trouble," the Jedi assured her. "It's personal."

The droid stared at him for a short while, sizing him up, then, with a shake of her head, she moved to the open serving hatch behind the counter. "Someone to see ya, honey," she said. "A Jedi, by the looks of him."

A huge head poked through the open hatchway almost immediately, accompanied by a line of grayish steam. A wide smile—on a mouth wide enough to swallow Obi-Wan's head whole—with huge block teeth grew on the immense face as he set his gaze on the visitor. "Obi-Wan!"

"Hey, Dex," Obi-Wan replied, standing and moving to the counter.

"Take a seat, old buddy! Be right with ya!"

Obi-Wan glanced around. The waitress droid had gone

about her business, tending to other customers. He moved to a booth just to the side of the counter.

"You want a cup of ardees?" the droid asked, her demeanor much more accommodating.

"Thank you."

She moved off toward the counter, slipping aside as the infamous Dexter Jettster moved through the counter door, walking with a stiff gait. He was an impressive sort, a neckless mound of flesh, dwarfing most of the toughies who frequented his establishment. His great belly poked out beneath his grimy shirt and breeches. He was bald and sweaty, and though he had seen many years and did not move fluidly any longer, with too many old injuries slowing him, Dexter Jettster was obviously not a creature anyone wanted to fight—especially since he was possessed of four huge arms, each with a massive fist that could fully bust a man's face. Obi-Wan noted the many respectful glances that went his way as he moved to the booth.

"Hey, ol' buddy!"

"Hey, Dex. Long time."

With great effort, Dexter managed to squeeze himself into the seat opposite Obi-Wan. The waitress droid was back by then, setting two steaming mugs of ardees in front of the old friends.

"So, my friend, what can I do for ya?" Dexter asked, and it was obvious to Obi-Wan that Dex genuinely wanted to help. Obi-Wan was hardly surprised. He didn't always approve of Dexter's antics, of the seedy diner and the many fights, but he knew Dex to be among the most loyal of friends that anyone could ever ask for. Dex would crush the life out of an enemy, but would give his own life for someone he cared about. That was the code among the star wanderers, and one that Obi-Wan could truly appreciate. In many, many ways, being here with Dex appealed to the Jedi Knight much more than the time he had to spend among the ruling elite.

"You can tell me what this is," Obi-Wan answered. He put the dart on the table, watching Dex all the time, noting how the being quickly placed his mug back down, his eyes widening as he regarded the curious and distinctive item.

"Well, waddya know," Dex said quietly, as if he could hardly draw breath. He picked up the dart delicately, almost reverently, the weapon nearly disappearing within the folds of his fat fingers. "I ain't seen one of these since I was prospecting on Subterrel beyond the Outer Rim."

"Do you know where it came from?"

Dexter placed the dart down before Obi-Wan. "This baby belongs to them cloners. What you got here is a Kamino saberdart."

"Kamino saberdart?" Obi-Wan echoed. "I wonder why it didn't show up in our analysis archive."

Dex poked down at the dart with a stubby finger. "It's these funny little cuts on the side that give it away," he explained. "Those analysis droids you've got over there only focus on symbols, you know. I should think you Jedi have more respect for the difference between knowledge and wisdom."

"Well, Dex, if droids could think, there'd be none of us here, would there?" Obi-Wan answered with a laugh.

The Jedi Knight sobered quickly, though, remembering the gravity of his mission. "Kamino . . . doesn't sound familiar. Is it part of the Republic?"

"No, it's beyond the Outer Rim. I'd say about twelve parsecs outside the Rishi Maze, toward the south. It should be easy to find, even for those droids in your archive. These Kaminoans keep to themselves, mostly. They're cloners. Good ones, too."

Obi-Wan picked up the dart again, holding it between them, his elbow resting on the table. "Cloners?" he asked. "Are they friendly?"

"It depends."

"On what?" The Jedi looked past the dart as he asked, and the grin on Dexter's face gave him his answer before it was spoken aloud.

"On how good your manners are and how big your pocket-book is."

Obi-Wan looked back at the saberdart, hardly surprised.

Senator Padmé Amidala, formerly Queen Amidala of Naboo, certainly wasn't used to traveling in this manner. The
freighter held one class, steerage, and in truth, it was nothing
more than a cargo ship, with several great open holds more suit-
able to inanimate cargo than to living beings. The lighting was
terrible and the smell was worse, though whether the odor came
from the ship itself or the hordes of emigrants, beings of many,
many species, Padmé did not know. Nor did she care. In some
ways, Padmé was truly enjoying this voyage. She knew that she
should be back on Coruscant, fighting the efforts to create a Republic army, but somehow, she felt relaxed here, felt free.

Free of responsibility. Free to just be Padmé for a while, instead of Senator Amidala. Moments such as these were rare for
her, and had been since she was a child. All of her life, it seemed,
had been spent in public service; all of her focus had always been
for the greater, the public, good, with hardly any time ever being given just to Padmé, to her needs and her desires.

The Senator didn't regret that reality of her life. She was

proud of her accomplishments, but more than that, even, she felt a profound sense of warmth, of community, of belonging to something greater than herself.

Still, these moments when the responsibility was lifted were undeniably enjoyable.

She looked over at Anakin, who was sleeping somewhat restlessly. She could see him now, not as a Jedi Padawan and her protector, but just as a young man. A handsome young man, and one whose actions repeatedly professed his love for her. A dangerous young man, to be sure, a Jedi who was thinking about things he should not. A man who was inevitably following the call of his heart above that of pragmatism and propriety. And all for her. Padmé couldn't deny the attractiveness of that. She and Anakin were on similar roads of public service, she as a Senator, he as a Jedi Padawan, but he was showing rebellion against the present course, or at least, against the Master who was leading him along the present course, as Padmé never had.

But hadn't she wanted to? Hadn't Padmé Amidala wanted to be just Padmé? Once in a while, at least?

She smiled widely and pointedly turned away from Anakin, scanning the gloomy room for signs of her other companion. She finally spotted R2-D2 in a food line, where he stuck out among the throng of living creatures. Just before the droid, servers ladled out bowls of bland-looking mush, and each being who took one inevitably gave out a low groan of disapproval.

Padmé watched with amusement as one of the servers began yelling and waving his hand at R2-D2, motioning for the droid to move along. "No droids in the food line!" the server yelled. "Get out of here!"

R2-D2 started past the counter, but stopped suddenly, and a

hollow tube came forth from his utilitarian body, hovering over the buffet and sucking up some of the mush and placing it in a storage container for transport to his companions.

"Hey, no droids!" the server yelled again.

R2-D2 took another fast gulp of the mush, reached out with a claw arm to grab a piece of bread, then turned and tootled and rushed away, the server shaking his fist and shouting behind him.

The droid came fast across the wide floor, veering to avoid the many sleeping emigrants, making as straight a line as possible toward the beaming Padmé.

"No, no," came a call beside her. It was Anakin. "Mom, no!"

Padmé turned about quickly, to see that her companion was still asleep, but sweating and thrashing, obviously in the throes of some nightmare.

"Anakin?" She gave him a little shake.

"No, Mom!" he cried, pulling away from her, and she looked down to see his feet kicking, as if he was running away from something.

"Anakin," Padmé said again, more forcefully. She shook him again, harder.

His blue eyes blinked open and he looked about curiously before focusing on Padmé. "What?"

"You seemed to be having a nightmare."

Anakin continued to stare at her, his expression ranging from curiosity to concern.

Padmé took a bowl of mush and a piece of bread from R2-D2. "Are you hungry?"

Anakin took the food as he sat up, rubbing a hand through his hair and shaking his head.

"We went to hyperspace a while ago," she explained.

"How long was I asleep?"

Padmé smiled at him, trying to comfort him. "You had a good nap," she answered.

Anakin smoothed the front of his tunic and straightened himself, looking all around, trying to get his bearings. "I look forward to seeing Naboo again," he remarked and he shifted, trying to orient himself. His expression soured as he looked down at the off-white mush, and he crinkled his nose, bending low to sniff it. "Naboo," he said again, looking back to Padmé. "I've thought about it every day since I left. It's by far the most beautiful place I've ever seen."

As he spoke, his eyes bored into her, taking her in deeply, and she blinked and averted her own gaze, unnerved. "It may not be as you remember it. Time changes perception."

"Sometimes it does," Anakin agreed, and when Padmé looked up to see that he was continuing to scrutinize her, she knew what he was talking about. "Sometimes for the better."

"It must be difficult having sworn your life to the Jedi," she said, taking a different tack to pull his gaze off her. "Not being able to visit the places you like. Or do the things you like."

"Or be with the people I love?" Anakin could easily see where she was leading him.

"Are you allowed to love?" Padmé asked bluntly. "I thought it was forbidden for a Jedi."

"Attachment is forbidden," Anakin began, his voice dispassionate, as if he was reciting. "Possession is forbidden. Compassion, which I would define as unconditional love, is central to a Jedi's life, so you might say we're encouraged to love."

"You have changed so much," Padmé heard herself saying, and in a tone that seemed inappropriate to her, seemed to invite. . .

She blinked as Anakin turned her words back on her. "You haven't changed a bit. You're exactly the way I remember you in my dreams. I doubt if Naboo has changed much either."

"It hasn't. . ." Padmé's voice was breathless. They were too close together. She knew that. She knew that she was in dangerous territory here, both for herself and for Anakin. He was a Padawan learner, a Jedi, and Jedi were not allowed . . .

And what about her? What about all that she had worked so hard for all her adult life? What about the Senate, and the all-important vote against the creation of an army? If Padmé got involved with a Jedi, the implications concerning her vote would become huge! The army, if one was created, would be made to stand beside the Jedi and their duties, and yet Padmé would stand against that army, and so . . .

And so?

It was all so complicated, but even more important than that, it was all so dangerous. She thought of her sister then, and their last conversation before Padmé had flown back to Coruscant. She thought of Ryoo and Pooja.

"You were dreaming about your mother earlier," she remarked, needing to change the subject. She sat back, putting some distance between her and Anakin, gaining some margin of safety between them. "Weren't you?"

Anakin leaned back and looked away, nodding slowly. "I left Tatooine so long ago. My memory of her is fading." He snapped his intense gaze back over Padmé. "I don't want to lose that memory. I don't want to stop seeing her face."

She started to say, "I know," and started to lift her hand to stroke his cheek, but she held back and let him continue.

"I've been seeing her in my dreams. Vivid dreams. Scary dreams. I worry about her."

"I'd be disappointed in you if you didn't," Padmé answered him, her voice soft and full of sympathy. "You didn't leave her in the best of circumstances."

Anakin winced, as if those words had hurt him.

"But it was right that you left," Padmé reminded him, taking his arm. She held his gaze with her own. "Your leaving was what your mother wanted for you. What she needed for you. The opportunity that Qui-Gon offered you gave her hope. That's what a parent needs for her child, to know that he, that you, had been given a chance at a better life."

"But the dreams—"

"You can't help but feel a little guilty about leaving, I suppose," Padmé answered, and Anakin was shaking his head, as if she was missing the point. But she didn't believe that to be the case, so she continued. "It's only natural that you'd want your mother off Tatooine, out here with you, perhaps. Or on Naboo, or Coruscant, or someplace that you feel is safer, and more beautiful. Trust me, Anakin," she said softly but intently, and she put her hand on his forearm again. "You did the right thing in going. For yourself, but more importantly, for your mother."

Her expression, so full of compassion, so full of caring, was not one that Anakin Skywalker could argue against.

The great port city of Theed was in many ways akin to Coruscant, with freighters and shuttles coming down from the skies in lines. Unlike Coruscant, though, this city on Naboo was soft in appearance, with few towering, imposing skyscrapers of hard metal and shining transparisteel. The buildings here were of stone and many other materials, with rounded rooflines and delicate colors. Vines of all sorts were everywhere, crawling up the sides of the buildings, adding vibrancy and scents. Adding comfort.

Anakin and Padmé lugged their bags across a familiar square, a place where they had seen battle a decade before against the droids of the Trade Federation. R2-D2 came behind them, rolling along easily, whistling a happy song, as if he were an extension of the comfortable aura of Theed.

Padmé kept covertly glancing at Anakin, noting the serenity on his face, the widening grin.

"If I grew up here, I don't think I'd ever leave," Anakin remarked.

Padmé laughed. "I doubt that."

"No, really. When I started my training, I was very homesick and very lonely. This city and my mom were the only pleasant things I had to think about."

Padmé's expression turned to one of curiosity and confusion. Anakin's time here had been spent, mostly, in deadly battle! Had he so obsessed about her, about Naboo, that even the bad memories paled against his warm feelings?

"The problem was," Anakin went on, "the more I thought about my mom, the worse I felt. But I would feel better if I thought about Naboo and the palace."

He didn't say it outright, but Padmé knew that what he really meant was that he felt better when he thought about her, or at least that he would include her in those pleasant thoughts.

"The way the palace shimmers in the sunlight, the way the air always smells of flowers."

"And the soft sound of the distant waterfalls," Padmé added. She could not deny the sincerity in Anakin's voice and in his words, and she found herself agreeing and embracing that truth of Naboo, despite her resolve to stay away from those feelings. "The first time I saw the capital, I was very young. I'd never seen a waterfall before. I thought they were so beautiful. I never thought that one day I'd live in the palace."

"Well, tell me, did you dream of power and politics when you were a little girl?"

Again Padmé had to laugh aloud. "No, that was the last thing I thought of." She could feel the wistfulness creeping into her, the memories of those long-ago days before her innocence had been shattered by war, and even more so, by the constant deceptions and conniving of politics. She could hardly believe that she was opening up to Anakin like this. "My dream was to work in the Refugee Relief Movement. I never thought of running for elected office. But the more history I studied, the more I realized how much good politicians could do. So when I was eight, I joined the Apprentice Legislators, which is like making a formal announcement that you're entering public service here on Naboo. From there, I went on to become a Senatorial Adviser, and attacked my duties with such a passion that before I knew it, I was elected Queen."

Padmé looked at Anakin and shrugged, trying not to throw all humility away. "Partly because I scored so high on my education certificate," she explained. "But for the most part, my ascent was because of my conviction that reform was possible. The people of Naboo embraced that dream wholeheartedly, so much so that my age was hardly an issue in the campaign. I wasn't the youngest Queen ever elected, but now that I think back on it, I'm not sure I was old enough." She paused and locked stares with Anakin. "I'm not sure I was ready."

"The people you served thought you did a good job," Anakin reminded her. "I heard they tried to amend the constitution so that you could stay in office."

"Popular rule is not democracy, Anakin. It gives the people what they want, not what they need. And truthfully, I was relieved when my two terms were up." Padmé chuckled as she continued, adding emphasis. "So were my parents! They worried about me during the blockade and couldn't wait for it all to be over. Actually, I was hoping to have a family by now. . . "

She turned away a bit, feeling her face flushing. How could she be so open to him, and so quickly? He was not a longtime friend, she reminded herself, but the warning sounded hollow in her thoughts. She looked back at Anakin, and she felt so at ease, so comfortable with him, almost as if they had been friends for all their lives. "My sister has the most amazing, wonderful kids." Her eyes were sparkling, she knew, but she blinked the emotion away, as Padmé had often blinked away her personal desires for the sake of what she perceived to be the greater good. "But when the Queen asked me to serve as Senator, I couldn't refuse her," she explained.

"I agree!" Anakin replied. "I think the Republic needs you. I'm glad you chose to serve—I feel things are going to happen in our generation that will change the galaxy in profound ways."

"A Jedi premonition?" Padmé kidded.

Anakin laughed. "A feeling," he explained, or tried to explain, for it was obvious that he wasn't quite sure what he was trying to say. "It just seems to me as if it's all grown stale, as if something has to happen—"

"I think so, too," Padmé put in sincerely.

They had arrived at the great doors of the palace, and paused to take in the beautiful scene. Unlike most of Coruscant's buildings, which seemed to have been designed with utter efficiency in mind, this structure was more akin to the Jedi Temple, an understanding that aesthetics were important, that form went hand in hand with purpose.

Padmé knew her way about the place, obviously, and she was well known by almost all of the people within, and so the two walked along easily to the throne room, where they were announced at once.

Smiling faces greeted them. Sio Bibble, Padmé's dear friend and her trusted adviser when she was Queen, stood by the throne, flanking Queen Jamillia as he had so often flanked Padmé. He hadn't aged much over the last years, his white hair and beard still distinguished and perfectly coiffed, his eyes still full of that intensity that Padmé so loved.

Beside him, Jamillia looked every bit the part of Queen. She wore a great headdress and flowing embroidered robes, the same type of outfit Padmé had worn for so very long, and the Senator thought that Jamillia looked at least as regal in them as she had.

Handmaidens, advisers, and guards were all about, and Padmé reflected that one of the side effects of being Queen, and not a pleasant one, was that one was never allowed to be alone.

Queen Jamillia, standing perfectly straight so that her headdress did not topple, rose and walked over to take Padmé's hand. "We've been worried about you. I'm so glad you're here, Padmé," she said, her voice rich and with a southeastern accent that made her enunciate the consonants powerfully.

"Thank you, Your Highness. I only wish I could have served you better by staying on Coruscant for the vote."

"Supreme Chancellor Palpatine has explained it all," Sio Bibble interjected. "Returning home was the only real choice you could have made."

Padmé gave him a resigned nod. Still, being sent home to Naboo bothered her; she had worked so very hard against the creation of a Republic army.

"How many systems have joined Count Dooku and the separatists?" Queen Jamillia asked bluntly. She had never been one for small talk.

"Thousands," Padmé answered. "And more are leaving the Republic every day. If the Senate votes to create an army, I'm sure it's going to push us into civil war."

Sio Bibble punched his fist into his open hand. "It's unthinkable!" he said, gnashing his teeth with every word. "There hasn't been a full-scale war since the formation of the Republic."

"Do you see any way, through negotiations, to bring the separatists back into the Republic?" Jamillia asked, staying calm despite Sio Bibble's obvious agitation.

"Not if they feel threatened." It amazed Padmé to realize how secure she was in these estimations. She felt as if she was beginning to fully understand the nuances of her position, as if she could trust her instincts implicitly. And all of her talents would be needed, she knew. "The separatists don't have an army, but if they are provoked, they will move to defend themselves. I'm sure of that. And with no time or money to build an army, my guess is they will turn to the Commerce Guild or the Trade Federation for help."

"The armies of commerce!" Queen Jamillia echoed with

anger and distaste. All on Naboo knew well the problems associated with such free-ranging groups. The Trade Federation had nearly brought Naboo to its knees, and would have had it not been for the heroics of Amidala, a pair of Jedi, a young Anakin, and the brave flying of the dedicated Naboo pilots. Even that would not have been enough, had not Queen Amidala forged an unexpected alliance with the heroic Gungans. "Why has nothing been done in the Senate to restrain them?"

"I'm afraid that, despite the Chancellor's best efforts, there are still many bureaucrats, judges, and even Senators on the payrolls of the guilds," Padmé admitted.

"Then it is true that the guilds have moved closer to the separatists, as we suspected," Queen Jamillia reasoned.

Sio Bibble punched his open palm again, drawing their attention. "It's outrageous!" he said. "It's outrageous that after all those hearings and four trials in the Supreme Court, Nute Gunray is still the viceroy of the Trade Federation. Do those money-mongers control everything?"

"Remember, Counselor, the courts were able to reduce the Trade Federation's armies," Jamillia reminded, again holding her calm and controlled voice. "That's a move in the right direction."

Padmé winced, knowing that she had to report honestly. "There are rumors, Your Highness, that the Federation's army was not reduced as they were ordered."

Clearing his throat, Anakin Skywalker stepped forward. "The Jedi have not been allowed to investigate," he explained. "It would be too dangerous for the economy, we were told."

Queen Jamillia looked to him and nodded, looked back to Padmé, then squared her shoulders and firmed her jawline, looking regal in the ornate raiments—very much the planetary ruler obedient to the Republic. "We must keep our faith in the Republic," she declared. "The day we stop believing democracy can work is the day we lose it."

"Let's pray that day never comes," Padmé quietly answered.

"In the meantime, we must consider your own safety," Queen Jamillia said, and she looked to Sio Bibble, who motioned to the attendants. All of them, advisers, attendants, and hand-maidens, bowed and quickly left the room. Sio Bibble moved near to Anakin, the appointed protector, then paused, waiting for all of the others to be gone. At last he spoke. "What is your sug-gestion, Master Jedi?"

"Anakin's not a Jedi yet, Counselor," Padmé interrupted. "He's still a Padawan learner. I was thinking—"

"Hey, hold on a minute!" Anakin cut her short, his eyes nar-rowed, brow furrowed, obviously agitated and put off by her dismissal.

"Excuse me!" Padmé shot right back, not backing down from Anakin's imposing glare. "I was thinking I would stay in the Lake Country. There are some places up there that are very isolated."

"Excuse me!" Anakin said, giving it right back to her, in words and in tone. "I am in charge of security here, M'Lady."

Padmé started to fight back, but she noted then the ex-change of suspicious looks between Sio Bibble and Queen Jamillia. She and Anakin should not be fighting in this manner in public, she realized, not without making others believe that something might be going on between them. She calmed down and softened her expression and her voice. "Anakin, my life is at risk and this is my home. I know it very well—that is why we're here. I think it would be wise for you to take advantage of my knowledge in this instance."

Anakin looked around at the two onlookers, and then back at Padmé, and the hardness melted from his expression. "Sorry, M'Lady."

"She is right," an obviously amused Sio Bibble said, taking Anakin's arm. "The Lake Country is the most remote part of Naboo. Not many people up there, and a clear view of the surrounding terrain. It would be an excellent choice, a place where you would have a much easier time protecting Senator Amidala."

"Perfect!" Queen Jamillia agreed. "It's settled then."

Padmé could tell from the way Anakin was looking at her that he wasn't overly pleased. She offered an innocent shrug in response.

"Padmé," Queen Jamillia went on, "I had an audience with your father yesterday. I told him what was happening. He hopes you will visit your mother before you leave. Your family's very worried about you."

How could they not be? Padmé thought, and it pained her to consider that the dangers her strong positions were bringing to her were affecting other people whom she loved. *How could they not?* It was a perfect reminder of why family and public service didn't usually mix. Padmé Amidala had made a conscious and definitive choice: public service or family. Some on Naboo juggled the two, but Padmé had always known that such a dual role as wife, perhaps even mother, and Senator would not do well for family or state.

She hadn't been worried about her own safety at all through

these trials, willing to make whatever sacrifices were necessary. But now, suddenly, she had to remember that her choices and positions could affect others on a very personal level, as well.

She wore no smile as she walked with Anakin, Sio Bibble, and Queen Jamillia out of the throne room and down the palace's main staircase.

The largest room in the vast Jedi Temple on Coruscant was the hall of the Archives. Lighted computer panels stretched out in long, long lines of bluish dots along the walls, running so far that a person viewing them from one end of the room would see them converging at the other end. Throughout were the images of Jedi past and present, groups of sculpted busts done in bronze by many of the finest artisans of Coruscant.

Obi-Wan Kenobi stood at one of these busts, studying it, touching it, as if examining the facial features of the person depicted would give him some insight to the man's motivations. There weren't many visitors in the Archives today—there rarely were more than a few—and so the Jedi expected that his call to Madame Jocasta Nu, the Jedi Archivist, would be answered shortly.

He stood patiently, studying the strong features on the bust, the high and proud cheekbones, the meticulous hairstyle, the eyes, wide and alert. Obi-Wan hadn't known this man, this legend, Count Dooku, very well, but he had seen him on occasion and he knew that this bust captured the essence of Dooku perfectly. There was an intensity about the man as palpable as that which had sometimes surrounded Master Qui-Gon, especially when Qui-Gon had found a particularly important cause. Qui-Gon would go against the Jedi Council when he felt that he was right, as he had done with Anakin some ten years earlier, before the Council had agreed to recognize that the boy's special circumstances, the incredible Force potential and the promise that he might be the one spoken of in prophecy.

Yes, Obi-Wan had seen this kind of intensity in Qui-Gon on occasion, but what he knew of Dooku was that, unlike Qui-Gon, the man had never been able to shut it off, had always been stomping around, chewing over an issue. The lights in his eyes were ever-burning fires.

But Dooku had taken it to extremes, and dangerous ones, Obi-Wan realized. He had left the Jedi Order, had walked out on his calling and on his peers. Whatever problems Dooku must have seen, he should have recognized that he could better repair them by remaining within the Jedi family.

"Did you call for assistance?" came a stern voice behind Obi-Wan, drawing him from his thoughts. He turned to see Madame Jocasta Nu standing beside him, her hands folded together before her, practically disappearing within the folds of her Jedi robes. She was a frail-looking creature, quite elderly, and noting that brought a smile to Obi-Wan's face. How many younger and less experienced Jedi had looked upon that facade, the thin and wrinkled face and neck, the white hair tied tight, thinking that they could push the woman around, getting her to do their studying for them, only to encounter the truth that was Jocasta Nu? She was a firebrand, that weak facade hiding her true strength and determination. Jocasta Nu had been the Archivist for many, many years, and this was her place, her domain, her kingdom. Any Jedi coming in here, even the most exalted of Jedi Masters, would play by the rules of Jocasta Nu, or they would surely face her wrath.

"Yes, yes I did," Obi-Wan finally managed to respond, realizing that Jocasta Nu was staring at him inquisitively, awaiting an answer.

The old woman smiled and walked past him to regard the bust of Count Dooku. "He has a powerful face, doesn't he?" she commented, her quiet tone taking the tension out of the meeting. "He was one of the most brilliant Jedi I have had the privilege of knowing."

"I never understood why he quit," Obi-Wan said, following Jocasta Nu's look to the bust. "Only twenty Jedi have ever left the Order."

"The Lost Twenty," Jocasta Nu said with a profound sigh. "And Count Dooku was the most recent and the most painful. No one likes to talk about it. His leaving was a great loss to the Order."

"What happened?"

"Well, one might say he was a bit out of step with the decisions of the Council," the Archivist replied. "Much like your old Master, Qui-Gon."

Even though Obi-Wan had just been thinking the same thing, somewhat, to hear Jocasta Nu speak the words so definitively caught him off guard, and painted Qui-Gon in a more rebellious light than he had ever considered. He knew that his former Master had his moments, of course, the greatest of those being the confrontations concerning Anakin, but he had never thought of Qui-Gon as that much of a rebel. Apparently, Jocasta

Nu, who had her finger as squarely as anyone on the pulse of the
Jedi Temple, did.

"Really?" Obi-Wan prompted, wanting the information about
Dooku, of course, but also hoping to garner some insight into his
old and beloved Master.

"Oh, yes, they were alike in many ways. Very individual
thinkers. Idealists." She stared at the bust intently, and it seemed
to Obi-Wan as if she had suddenly gone far, far away. "He was
always striving to become a more powerful Jedi. He wanted to
be the best. With a lightsaber, in the old style of fencing, he had
no match. His knowledge of the Force was . . . unique. In the
end, I think he left because he lost faith in the Republic. He believed that politics were corrupt . . ."

Jocasta Nu paused for a moment and looked at Obi-Wan, a
very revealing expression that showed she did not think Dooku
as out of step as many of the others apparently did.

"And he felt that the Jedi betrayed themselves by serving the
politicians," the Archivist stated.

Obi-Wan blinked, soaking in the words. He knew that many,
Qui-Gon included—even himself included, at times—often felt
the same way.

"He always had very high expectations of government," Jocasta Nu went on. "He disappeared for nine or ten years, then
just showed up recently as the head of the separatist movement."

"Interesting," Obi-Wan remarked, looking from the bust to
the Archivist. "I'm still not sure I understand."

"None of us does," Jocasta Nu replied, her serious expression melting into a warm smile. "Well, I'm sure you didn't call
me over here for a history lesson. Are you having a problem,
Master Kenobi?"

"Yes, I'm trying to find a planet system called Kamino. It doesn't seem to show up on any of the archive charts."

"Kamino?" Jocasta Nu looked around, as if she was searching for the system right then and there. "It's not a system I'm familiar with. Let me see."

A few steps brought them to the computer screen where Obi-Wan had been searching. She bent low, and pressed a couple of commands. "Are you sure you have the right coordinates?"

"According to my information, it should be in this quadrant somewhere," said Obi-Wan "Just south of the Rishi Maze."

A few more taps of the keyboard brought nothing more than a frown to Jocasta Nu's old and weathered face. "But what are the exact coordinates?"

"I only know the quadrant," Obi-Wan admitted, and Jocasta Nu turned up to regard him.

"No coordinates? It sounds like the sort of directions you'd get from a street tout—some old miner or furbog trader."

"All three, actually," Obi-Wan admitted with a grin.

"Are you sure it exists?"

"Absolutely."

Jocasta Nu sat back and rubbed a hand pensively over her chin. "Let me do a gravitational scan," she said, as much to herself as to Obi-Wan.

The star map hologram of the target quadrant went into motion after a few more keystrokes, and the pair studied the movements. "There are some inconsistencies here," the sharp Archivist noted. "Maybe the planet you're seeking was destroyed."

"Wouldn't that be on record?"

"It ought to be, unless it was very recent," Jocasta Nu replied, but she was shaking her head even as she spoke the words, not even convincing herself. "I hate to say it, but it looks like the system you're searching for doesn't exist."

"That's impossible—perhaps the Archives are incomplete."

"The Archives are comprehensive and totally secure, my young Jedi," came the imposing response, the Archivist stepping back from her familiarity with Obi-Wan and assuming again the demeanor of archive kingdom ruler. "One thing you may be absolutely sure of: If an item does not appear in our records, it does not exist."

The two stared at each other for a long moment, Obi-Wan taking note that there wasn't the slightest tremor of doubt in Jocasta Nu's declaration.

He looked back to the map, perplexed, caught within a seemingly unanswerable question. He knew that no one in the galaxy was more reliable for information that Dexter Jettster, unless that person was Jocasta Nu, and yet the two were obviously at odds here concerning their information. Dexter had seemed every bit as certain of the origins of the saberdart as Jocasta Nu was now. Both couldn't be right.

The puzzle of finding Senator Amidala's would-be assassin would not be easily solved, it seemed, and that troubled Obi-Wan Kenobi for many, many reasons. With Jocasta Nu's permission, the Jedi punched a few buttons on the keyboard, downloading the archive information on that region of the quadrant to a small hologlobe. Then, the item in hand, he left the area.

But not without one long, last look at the imposing bust of Count Dooku.

Later on that day, Obi-Wan turned away from the Archives and the analysis droids and turned within, to his own insights, instead. He found a small, comfortable room along the Temple's grand balcony, one of many such rooms designed for quiet moments of Jedi reflection. A small fountain bubbled off to the side of him as he settled on a soft but firm mat and crossed his legs. The water trickled down to a bed of polished stones, making a delicate sound, a background noise natural in its beauty and in the simplicity of its song.

Before Obi-Wan, a painting of reds, shifting and darkening to a deep crimson and then to black, a liberal representation of a cooling lava field, hung on the wall, inviting him not to look into it, but to surround himself with it, both its image and the soft warmth and hissing sound helping him to fall far away from his corporeal surroundings.

There, in his trance, Obi-Wan Kenobi sought his answers. He focused on the mystery of Kamino first, expecting that Dexter's analysis was correct. But why hadn't the system shown up in the Archives?

Another image invaded Obi-Wan's meditations as he tried to sort through that puzzle, an image of Anakin and Padmé together on Naboo.

The Jedi Knight started, suddenly afraid that this was a premonition, and that some danger would visit his Padawan and the young Senator . . .

But no, he realized, settling back. No danger was about; the two were relaxed and at play.

Obi-Wan's relief lasted only as long as it took him to realize that the continuing scene in his mind might be the most dangerous thing of all. He dismissed it, though, unsure if this was a premonition, an image of reality, or just his own fears playing out before him. Obi-Wan pointedly reminded himself that the sooner he solved the mystery of Kamino, the mystery of who so desperately wanted Amidala dead, the sooner he could return to Anakin and offer the proper guidance.

The Jedi Knight focused again on the bust of Count Dooku, searching for insights, but for some reason, the image of Anakin kept becoming interposed with that of the renegade Count . . .

Soon after, a frustrated and thoroughly bewildered Obi-Wan walked out of the small meditation chamber, shaking his head and no more certain of anything than he had been when he had entered the place.

His patience exhausted into frustration, the Jedi Knight decided to seek a higher authority, one wiser and more experienced. His short trip took him out of the Temple proper and onto the veranda, and there he paused and watched, and in the innocent scene before him found some relief from the frustration.

Master Yoda was leading twenty of the youngest Jedi recruits, children only four or five years old, through their morning training exercises, battling floating training droids with miniature lightsabers.

Obi-Wan recalled his own training. He couldn't see the eyes of the youngsters, for they wore protective full-face helmets, but he could well imagine the range of emotions playing out on their innocent faces. There would be intensity, and then great joy whenever an energy bolt from a training droid was blocked, and that elation would inevitably dissipate in the next instant, when the joy brought distraction and distraction allowed the next energy bolt to slip past and bring a sudden, jolting sting.

And those little bolts did sting, Obi-Wan remembered, as much physically as in pride. There was nothing worse than getting zapped, particularly in the backside. It always caused one to do a little hopping and twisting dance, which naturally made the embarrassment all the worse. Obi-Wan recalled that feeling vividly, recalled thinking that everyone in the courtyard was staring at him.

The training could be humiliating.

But it was also energizing, because with the failures would come the successes, each one building confidence, each one lending insights into the flowing beauty that was the Force, heightening the connection that separated a Jedi from the rest of the galaxy.

To see Yoda leading the training this day, looking exactly as he had when he had led Obi-Wan's training a quarter century before, brought a flush of warmth to the Jedi Knight.

"Don't think . . . feel," Yoda instructed the group. "Be as one with the Force."

Obi-Wan, smiling, mouthed the exact words as Yoda finished, "Help you, it will."

How many times he had heard that!

He was still grinning widely when Yoda turned to him. "Younglings, enough!" the great Jedi Master commanded. "A visitor we have. Welcome him."

Twenty little lightsabers clicked off and the students came to attention together, removing their helmets and tucking them properly under their left arms.

"Master Obi-Wan Kenobi," Yoda said, keeping enough gravity in his voice so that the younglings wouldn't feel mocked.

"Welcome, Master Obi-Wan!" the twenty called out together.

"I am sorry to disturb you, Master," Obi-Wan said with a slight bow.

"What help to you, can I be?"

Obi-Wan considered the question for a moment. He had specifically come out here looking for Yoda, but now, in seeing the diminutive Master at his important work, he wondered if he had let his patience fall away too quickly. Was it his place to ask Yoda to help him with a mission that was his own responsibility? It didn't take long for Obi-Wan to dismiss the question. He was a Jedi Knight, Yoda, a Master, and his responsibilities and Yoda's were ultimately one and the same. He didn't expect that Yoda could help him with this particular problem, but then again, Yoda had always been full of surprises, full of going far beyond any expectations.

"I'm looking for a planet described to me by an old friend," he explained, and he knew that Yoda was absorbing every word. "I trust him and the information he provided, but the system doesn't show up on the archive maps." As he finished, he showed Yoda that he had a hologlobe with him.

"An interesting puzzle," Yoda answered. "Lost a planet, Master Obi-Wan has. How embarrassing . . . how embarrassing. An interesting puzzle. Gather, younglings, around the map reader. Clear your minds and find Obi-Wan's wayward planet, we will try."

They went into a room to the side of the veranda. A narrow shaft was set in the middle, with a hollow depression at the top. Off to the side, Obi-Wan took up the hologlobe, then moved and placed it in the hollow of the shaft. The shades closed as soon as he put it there, darkening the room, and a star map hologram appeared, glittering distinctly.

Obi-Wan paused a moment before presenting his dilemma, allowing the younglings to get past the initial excitement. He watched with amusement as some reached up and tried to touch the projected starlights. Then, when all quieted, he walked into the middle of the projection. "This is where it ought to be," he explained. "Gravity is pulling all the stars in this area inward to this spot. There should be a star here, but there isn't."

"Most interesting," Yoda said. "Gravity's silhouette remains, but the star and all its planets have disappeared. How can this be? Now, younglings, in your mind, what is the first thing you see? An answer? A thought? Anyone?"

Obi-Wan took Yoda's quiet cue and paused then, watching the Jedi Master look over his gathering.

A hand went up, and while Obi-Wan felt the urge to chuckle at the idea of a youngling solving a riddle that had befuddled a trio of accomplished Jedi, including Yoda and Madame Jocasta Nu, he noted that Yoda was quite focused and serious.

Yoda nodded to the student, who answered at once. "Because someone erased it from the archive memory."

"That's right!" another of the children agreed at once. "That's what happened! Someone erased it!"

"If the planet blew up, the gravity would go away," another one of the children called out.

Obi-Wan stared blankly at the excited group, stunned, but Yoda only chuckled.

"Truly wonderful, the mind of a child is," he explained. "Uncluttered. The data must have been erased."

Yoda started out of the room and Obi-Wan moved to follow, flicking his hand as he passed the reader shaft, Force-pulling the hologlobe back to his grasp and instantly dismissing the starry scene.

"To the center of the pull of gravity go, and find your planet you will," Yoda advised him.

"But Master Yoda, who could have erased information from the Archives? That's impossible, isn't it?"

"Dangerous and disturbing this puzzle is," Yoda replied with a frown. "Only a Jedi could have erased those files. But who and why, harder to answer. Meditate on this, I will. May the Force be with you."

A thousand questions filtered through Obi-Wan's mind, but he understood that Yoda had just dismissed him. They each had their riddles, it seemed, but at least now Obi-Wan's path seemed much clearer before him. He gave a deferential bow, but Yoda, already back to his work with the children, didn't seem to notice. Obi-Wan walked away.

Soon after, not wanting to waste a moment, Obi-Wan was out on the landing platform standing beside his readied starfighter, a long and sleek delta-wing fighter, of a triangular design, with the cockpit set far aft. Mace Windu was there beside him, the tall and strong-featured Master regarding Obi-Wan with his typically calm and controlled demeanor. There was something reassuring about Mace Windu, a sense of power and, even more than that, of destiny. Mace Windu had a way of silently assuring all those around him that things would work out as they were supposed to.

"Be wary," he said to Obi-Wan, tilting his head back just a bit as he spoke, a posture that made him seem all the more impressive. "This disturbance in the Force is growing stronger."

Obi-Wan nodded, though in truth, his concerns were more focused and tangible at that moment. "I'm concerned for my Padawan. He is not ready to be on his own."

Mace gave a nod, as if to remind Obi-Wan that they had covered this already. "He has exceptional skills," the Master replied. "The Council is confident in its decision, Obi-Wan. Not all of the questions about him have been answered, of course, but his talents cannot be dismissed, and we are not disappointed in the progress he has made under your tutelage."

Obi-Wan considered the words carefully and nodded again, knowing that he was walking a fine line here. If he overstated his concerns about Anakin's temperament, he might be doing a great disservice to the Jedi and to the galaxy. And yet, if he let the magnitude of his assignment in training Anakin Skywalker bring him to silence on legitimate questions, then was he doing great harm?

"If the prophecy is true, Anakin will be the one to bring balance to the Force," Mace finished.

"But he still has much to learn. His skills have made him . . . well—" Obi-Wan paused, trying to walk that delicate line. "—arrogant. I realize now what you and Master Yoda knew from the beginning. The boy was too old to start the training, and . . ."

The frown spreading on Mace Windu's face signaled Obi-Wan that he might be pushing a bit too hard.

"There's something else," Mace observed.

Obi-Wan took a deep and steadying breath. "Master, Anakin and I should not have been given this assignment. I'm afraid Anakin won't be able to protect the Senator."

"Why?"

"He has a . . . an emotional connection with her. It's been there since he was a boy. Now he's confused, and distracted." As he spoke, Obi-Wan started toward his starfighter. He climbed up the cockpit ladder and into his seat.

"So you have already stated," Mace reminded. "And your concerns were weighed properly, and did not change the decision of the Council. Obi-Wan, you must have faith that Anakin will take the right path."

It made sense, of course. If Anakin was to become a great leader, a creature of prophecy, then surely his character tests must be passed. Anakin was waging one of those tests right now, Obi-Wan knew, off in seclusion on a distant planet with a woman whom he loved too deeply. He had to be strong enough to pass that test; Obi-Wan just hoped that Anakin recognized the trial for what it was.

"Has Master Yoda gained any insight as to whether or not this war will come about?" he asked, somewhat changing the subject, though he felt that it was all very connected. Finding the assassin, making peace with the separatists—all of these things would allow him to focus more closely on Anakin's training and would keep things at a more even keel around the troubled Padawan.

"Probing the dark side is a dangerous process," Mace stated. "I know not when he will choose to begin, but when he does, it is quite possible that he will remain in seclusion for days."

Obi-Wan nodded his agreement and Mace gave him a smile and a wave. "May the Force be with you."

"Set the course to the hyperspace ring, Arfour," Obi-Wan instructed his astromech droid, an R4-P unit that was hardwired into the left wing of the sleek starfighter. Silently, the Jedi Knight added to himself, *Let's get this thing moving.*

It was a scene of simplicity, of children playing and adults sitting quietly under the warm sun, or gossiping across neatly trimmed hedgerows. It was a scene of absolute normalcy for Naboo, but it was nothing like Anakin Skywalker had ever witnessed. On Tatooine, the houses were singular, out in the desert, or they were clustered tightly in cities like Mos Eisley, with its hustle and bustle and bright colors and brighter characters. On Coruscant, there were no streets like this one any longer. There were no hedgerows and trees lining the ground, just permacrete and old buildings and the gray foundations of the towering skyscrapers. People did not gossip, with children running carefree about them, in either place.

To Anakin, it was a scene of simple beauty.

He was back to wearing his Jedi robes, the peasant garb discarded. Padmé walked alongside him in a simple blue dress that only seemed to enhance her beauty. Anakin kept glancing her way, stealing images of her to burn into his mind, to hold forever in a special place. She could be wearing anything, he realized, and still be beautiful.

Anakin smiled as he recalled the ornate outfits Padmé had often worn as Queen of Naboo, huge gowns with intricate embroidery and studded with gemstones, tremendous headpieces of plumes and swirls and curves and twists.

He liked her better like this, he decided. All of the decorations of her Queenly outfits had been beautifully designed, but still could only detract from the more beautifully designed Padmé. Wearing a great headpiece only hid her silken brown hair. Painting her face in whites and bright red only hid her beautiful skin. The embroidery on the great gowns only blurred the perfection of her form.

This was the way Anakin wanted to see her, where her clothing was just a finishing touch.

"There's my house!" Padmé cried suddenly, startling Anakin from his pleasant daydreams.

He followed her gaze to see a simple but tasteful structure, surrounded, like everything on Naboo, by flowers and vines and hedges. Padmé started off immediately for the door, but Anakin didn't follow right away. He studied the house, every line, every detail, trying to see in it the environment that had produced her. She had told him many stories of her childhood in this house during their trip from Coruscant, and he was replaying those tales, seeing them in context now that the yard was in view.

"What?" Padmé asked him from some distance ahead, when she noticed that he was not following. "Don't tell me you're shy!"

"No, but I—" the distracted Anakin started to answer, but

he was interrupted by the squeals of two little girls, running out from the yard toward his companion.

"Aunt Padmé! Aunt Padmé!"

Padmé's smile went as wide as Anakin had ever seen it and she rushed ahead, bending low to scoop the pair, who looked to be no more than a few years old, one a bit taller than the other, into her arms. One had hair short and blond and curly, the other, the older of the two, had hair that resembled Padmé's.

"Ryoo! Pooja!" Padmé cried, hugging them and twirling them about. "I'm so happy to see you!" She kissed them both and set them down, then took them by the hand and led them toward Anakin.

"This is Anakin. Anakin, this is Ryoo and Pooja!"

The blush on the pair as they shyly said hello brought a burst of laughter from Padmé and a smile to Anakin's face, though he was equally ill at ease as the two children.

The girls' shyness lasted only as long as it took for them to notice the little droid rolling behind Anakin, trying to catch up.

"Artoo!" they shouted in unison. Breaking away from Padmé, they rushed to the droid, leaping upon him, hugging him cheek to dome.

And R2-D2 seemed equally thrilled, beeping and whistling as happily as Anakin had ever heard.

Anakin couldn't help but be touched by the scene, a view of innocence that he had never known.

Well, not never, he had to admit. There were times when Shmi had found some way to produce such moments of joy amid the drudgery that was life as a slave on Tatooine. In their own way, in that dusty, dirty, hot, and smelly place, Anakin and his mother had carved out a few instants of innocent beauty.

Here, though, such moments seemed so much more the norm than the memorable exception.

Anakin turned back to Padmé, to see that she was no longer looking his way, but had turned toward the house, where another woman, who looked very much like Padmé, was approaching.

Not exactly like Padmé, Anakin noted. She was a little older, a little heavier, and a little more . . . *worn*, was the only word he could think of. But not in a bad way. Yes, he could see it now, he thought, watching as she and Padmé hugged tightly. This was whom Padmé could become—more settled, more content, perhaps. Considering the amazing resemblance, Anakin was hardly surprised when Padmé introduced the woman as her sister, Sola.

"Mom and Dad will be so happy to see you," Sola said to Padmé. "It's been a difficult few weeks."

Padmé frowned. She knew that word of the attempts on her life would have reached her parents' ears, and that was possibly the most disturbing thing of all to her.

Anakin saw it all on her face, and he understood it well, and he loved her all the more for that generosity. Padmé wasn't really afraid of anything—she could handle the reality of her current situation, the reality of the fact that someone was trying to kill her, with determination and courage. But the one thing about it all that troubled her, aside from the political ramifications of such distractions, the ways they might weaken her position in the Senate, was the effect of such danger upon those she loved. He knew that she didn't want to bring pain to her family.

Anakin, who had left his mother as a slave on Tatooine, could appreciate that.

"Mom's making dinner," Sola explained, noting Padmé's discomfort and generously changing the subject. "As usual, your timing is perfect." She started toward the house. Padmé waited for Anakin to move beside her, then took his hand, looked up, smiled at him, and led him toward the door. R2-D2 rolled along right behind, with Ryoo and Pooja bouncing all about him.

The interior of the house was just as simply wonderful and just as full of life and soft color as was the yard. There were no glaring lights, no beeping consoles or flickering computer screens. The furniture was plush and comfortable; the floors were made of cool stone or covered in soft carpeting.

This was not a building as Anakin had known on Coruscant, and not a hovel, as he had known all too well on Tatooine. No, seeing this place, this street, this yard, this home, made the young Padawan even more convinced of what he had declared to Padmé not so long before: that if he had grown up on Naboo, he would never leave.

The next introductions were a bit more uncomfortable, but only for a moment, as Padmé showed Anakin to Ruwee, her father, a strong-shouldered man with a face that was plain and strong and compassionate all at once. He wore his brown hair short, but still it was a bit out of place, a bit . . . comfortable. Padmé introduced Jobal next, and Anakin knew that the woman was her mother without being told. The moment he met her, he understood where Padmé had gotten her innocent and sincere smile, a look that could disarm a mob of bloodthirsty Gamorrean raiders. Jobal's face had that same comforting quality, that same obvious generosity.

Soon after, Anakin, Padmé, and Ruwee were sitting at the dinner table, comfortably quiet and listening to the bustle in the next room, which included the clanking of stoneware plates and mugs, and Sola repeatedly saying, "Too much, Mom." And every time she said that, Ruwee and Padmé smiled knowingly.

"I doubt they've been starving all the way from Coruscant,"

an exasperated Sola said as she exited the kitchen, glancing back over her shoulder as she spoke. She returned carrying a bowl full of food.

"Enough to feed the town?" Padmé asked Sola quietly as her older sister put the bowl on the table.

"You know Mom," came the answer, and the tone told Anakin that this was not an isolated incident, that Jobal was quite the hostess. Despite the fact that he had eaten recently, the bowl of food looked and smelled temptingly good.

"No one has ever left this house hungry," Sola explained.

"Well, one person did once," Padmé corrected. "But Mom chased him down and dragged him back in."

"To feed him or cook him?" the quick-witted Padawan retorted, and the other three stared at him for just a moment before catching on and bursting out in laughter.

They were still chuckling when Jobal entered the room, holding an even larger bowl of steaming food, which of course only made them laugh all the louder. But then Jobal fixed an imposing stare over her family and the chuckling quieted.

"They arrived just in time for dinner," Jobal said. "I know what that means." She set the plate down near Anakin and put her hand on his shoulder. "I hope you're hungry, Anakin."

"A little." He looked up and gave her a warm smile.

The look of gratitude was not lost on Padmé. She tossed a little wink his way when he looked back at her. "He's being polite, Mom," she said. "We're starving."

Jobal grinned widely and nodded, offering superior glances at Sola and Ruwee, who just laughed again. It was all so comfortable to Anakin, so natural and so . . . so much like what he had always been wanting in his life, though perhaps he had not known it. This would be perfect, absolutely perfect, except that his mother wasn't there.

A brief cloud passed over his face as he thought of his mother on Tatooine, and considered the disturbing dreams that had been finding their way into his sleep of late. He pushed the thoughts away quickly and glanced around, glad that no one seemed to have noticed.

"If you're starving, then you came to the right place at the right time," Ruwee said, looking at Anakin as he finished. "Eat up, son!"

Jobal and Sola took their seats and began passing the food bowls all around. Anakin took a good helping of several different dishes. The food was all unfamiliar, but the smells told him that he wouldn't be disappointed. He sat quietly as he ate, listening with half an ear to the chatter all about him. He was thinking of his mom again, of how he wished he could bring her here, a free woman, to live the life she so deserved.

Some time passed before Anakin tuned back in, cued by the sudden seriousness in Jobal's voice as she said to Padmé, "Honey, it's so good to see you safe. We were so worried."

Anakin looked up just in time to see the intense, disapproving glare that Padmé answered with. Ruwee, obviously trying to dispel the tension before it could really begin, put his hand on Jobal's arm and quietly said, "Dear—"

"I know, I know!" said the suddenly animated Jobal. "But I had to say it. Now it's done."

Sola cleared her throat. "Well, this is exciting," she said, and everyone looked at her. "Do you know, Anakin, you're the first boyfriend my sister ever brought home?"

"Sola!" Padmé exclaimed. She rolled her eyes. "He isn't

my boyfriend! He's a Jedi assigned by the Senate to protect me."

"A bodyguard?" Jobal asked with great concern. "Oh,
Padmé, they didn't tell us it was that serious!"

Padmé's sigh was intermixed with a groan. "It's not, Mom,"
she said. "I promise. Anyway, Anakin's a friend. I've known him
for years. Remember that little boy who was with the Jedi during the blockade crisis?"

A couple of "ahs" of recognition came back in response,
along with nodding heads. Then Padmé smiled at Anakin and
said, with just enough weight to make him recognize that her
previous claims about his place here weren't entirely true, "He's
grown up."

Anakin glanced at Sola and saw that she was staring at him,
scrutinizing him. He shifted uncomfortably in his seat.

"Honey, when are you going to settle down?" Jobal went
on. "Haven't you had enough of that life? I certainly have!"

"Mom, I'm not in any danger," Padmé insisted, taking
Anakin's hand in her own.

"Is she?" Ruwee asked Anakin.

The Padawan stared hard at Padmé's father, recognizing the
honest concern. This man, who obviously loved his daughter so
much, deserved to know the truth. "Yes, I'm afraid she is."

Even as the words left his mouth, Anakin felt Padmé's grip
tighten. "But not much," she added quickly, and she turned to
Anakin, smiling, but in a *you'll-pay-for-that-later* kind of way.
"Anakin," she said quietly, her teeth gritted, locked into that
threatening smile.

"The Senate thought it prudent to give her some time away,
and under the protection of the Jedi," he said, his tone casual,
showing no reflections of the pain he was feeling as Padmé's

fingernails dug into his hand. "My Master, Obi-Wan, is even now seeing to the matter. All should be well soon enough."

His breath came easier as Padmé loosened her grip, and Ruwee, and even Jobal, seemed to relax. Anakin knew that he had done well, but he was surprised to see that Sola was still staring at him, still smiling as if she knew a secret.

He gave her a quizzical look, but she only smiled all the wider.

"Sometimes I wish I'd traveled more," Ruwee admitted to Anakin as the two walked in the garden after dinner. "But I must say, I'm happy here."

"Padmé tells me you teach at the university."

"Yes, and before that I was a builder," Ruwee answered with a nod. "I also worked for the Refugee Relief Movement, when I was very young."

Anakin looked at him curiously, not really surprised. "You seem quite interested in public service," he remarked.

"Naboo is generous," Ruwee explained. "The planet itself, I mean. We have all that we want, all that we could want. Food is plentiful, the climate is comfortable, the surroundings are—"

"Beautiful," Anakin put in.

"Quite so," said Ruwee. "We are a very fortunate people, and we know it. That good fortune should not be taken for granted, and so we try to share and try to help. It is our way of saying that we welcome the friendship of those less fortunate, that we do not think ourselves entitled to that which we have, but rather, that we feel blessed beyond what we deserve. And so we share, and so we work, and in doing so, we become something larger than ourselves, and more fulfilled than one can become from idly enjoying good fortune!"

Anakin considered Ruwee's words for a few moments. "It is the same with the Jedi, I suppose," he said. "We have been given great gifts, and we train hard to make the most of those. And then we use our given powers to try to help the galaxy, to try to make everything a little bit better."

"And to make the things we love a little bit safer?"

Anakin looked at him, catching the meaning, and he smiled and nodded. He saw respect in Ruwee's eyes, and gratitude, and he was glad for both. He could not deny the way Padmé looked at her family, the love that seemed to flow from her whenever any of them entered the room, and he knew that if Ruwee or Jobal or Sola didn't like him, his relationship with Padmé would be hurt.

He was glad, then, that he had come to this place, not only as Padmé's companion, but also as her protector.

Back in the house, Padmé, Sola, and Jobal were working together to clear the dishes and the remaining food. Padmé noted the tension in her mother's movements, and she knew that these latest events—the assassination attempts, the fights in the Senate over an issue that could well lead to war—were weighing heavily on her.

She looked to Sola, too, to see if she might find some clue as to how to help alleviate the tension, but all she found there was an obvious curiosity that set her off her balance more than had her mother's concerned expression.

"Why haven't you told us about him?" Sola asked with a sly grin.

"What's there to talk about?" Padmé replied as casually as she could. "He's just a boy."

"A boy?" Sola repeated with a laugh. "Have you seen the way he looks at you?"

"Sola! Stop it!"

"It's obvious he has feelings for you," Sola went on. "Are you saying, little baby sister, that you haven't noticed?"

"I'm not your baby sister, Sola," Padmé said flatly, her tone turning to true consternation. "Anakin and I are friends. Our relationship is strictly professional."

Sola grinned again.

"Mom, would you tell her to stop it?" Padmé burst out in embarrassed frustration.

Now Sola began laughing out loud. "Well, maybe you *haven't* noticed the way he looks at you. I think you're afraid to."

"Cut it out!"

Jobal stepped between the two and gave Sola a stern look. Then she turned back to Padmé. "Sola's just concerned, dear," she said. But her words sounded to Padmé like condescension, as if her mother was still trying to protect a helpless little girl.

"Oh, Mom, you're impossible," she said with a sigh of surrender. "What I'm doing is important."

"You've done your service, Padmé," Jobal answered. "It's time you had a life of your own. You're missing so much!"

Padmé tilted her head back and closed her eyes, trying to accept the words in the spirit with which they were offered. For a moment, she regretted coming back here, to see the same old sights and hear the same old advice.

For just a moment, though. Truthfully, when she considered it all, Padmé had to admit she was glad to have people who loved her and cared about her so much.

She offered her mother an appeasing smile, and Jobal nodded

and gently tapped Padmé's arm. She turned to Sola next, and saw her sister still grinning.

What did Sola see?

"Now tell me, son, how serious is this thing?" Ruwee asked bluntly as the two neared the door that would take them back into the house. "How much danger is my daughter really in?"

Anakin didn't hesitate, realizing, as he had at dinner, that Padmé's father deserved nothing but honesty from him. "There have been two attempts on her life. Chances are, there'll be more. But I wasn't lying to you and wasn't trying to minimize anything. My Master is tracking down the assassins. I'm sure he'll find out who they are and take care of them. This situation won't last long."

"I don't want anything to happen to her," Ruwee said, with the gravity of a parent concerned over a beloved child.

"I don't either," Anakin assured him, with almost equal weight.

Padmé stared at her older sister until, at last, Sola broke down and asked, "What?"

The two of them were alone together, while Jobal and Ruwee entertained Anakin out in the sitting room.

"Why do you keep saying such things about me and Anakin?"

"Because it's obvious," Sola replied. "You see it—you can't deny it to yourself."

Padmé sighed and sat down on the bed, her posture and expression giving all the confirmation that Sola needed.

"I thought Jedi weren't supposed to think such things," Sola remarked.

"They're not."

"But Anakin does." Sola's words brought Padmé's gaze up to meet hers. "You know I'm right."

Padmé shook her head helplessly, and Sola laughed.

"You think more like a Jedi than he does," she said. "And you shouldn't."

"What do you mean?" Padmé didn't know whether to take offense, having no idea of where her sister was heading with this.

"You're so tied up in your responsibilities that you don't give any weight to your desires," Sola explained. "Even with your own feelings toward Anakin."

"You don't know how I feel about Anakin."

"You probably don't either," Sola said. "Because you won't allow yourself to even think about it. Being a Senator and being a girlfriend aren't mutually exclusive, you know."

"My work is important!"

"Who said it wasn't?" Sola asked, holding her hands up in a gesture of peace. "It's funny, Padmé, because you act as if you're prohibited, and you're not, while Anakin acts as if he's under no such prohibitions, and he is!"

"You're way ahead of everything here," Padmé said. "Anakin and I have only been together for a few days—before that, I hadn't seen him in a decade!"

Sola shrugged. Her look went from that sly grin she had been sporting since dinner to one of more genuine concern for her sister. She sat down on the bed beside Padmé and draped an arm across her shoulders. "I don't know any of the details, and you're right, I don't know how you feel—about any of this. But I know how he feels, and so do you."

Padmé didn't disagree. She just sat there, comfortable in Sola's hug, gazing down at the floor, trying not to think.

"It frightens you," Sola remarked. Surprised, Padmé looked back up.

"What are you afraid of, Sis?" Sola asked sincerely. "Are you afraid of Anakin's feelings and the responsibilities that he cannot dismiss? Or are you afraid of your own feelings?"

She lifted Padmé's chin, so that they were looking at each other directly, their faces only a breath apart. "I don't know how you feel," she admitted again. "But I suspect that it's something new to you. Something scary, but something wonderful."

Padmé said nothing, but she knew that disagreement would not be honest.

"They're a lot to digest, all at once," Padmé said to Anakin later on, when the two were alone in her room. She had barely unpacked her things, and was now throwing clothes into her bag once more. Different clothes this time, though. Less formal than the outfits she had to wear as a representative of Naboo.

"Your mother is a fine cook," Anakin replied, drawing a curious stare from Padmé, until she realized that he was joking and had understood her point perfectly well.

"You're lucky to have such a wonderful family," Anakin said more seriously, and then, with a teasing grin, he added, "Maybe you should give your sister some of your clothes."

Padmé smirked right back at him, but then looked about at the mess and couldn't really disagree. "Don't worry," she assured him. "This won't take long."

"I just want to get there before dark. Wherever *there* is, I mean." Anakin continued to scan the room, surprised at the number of closets, all of them full. "You still live at home," he said, shaking his head. "I didn't expect that."

"I move around so much," Padmé replied. "I've never had the time to even begin to find a place of my own, and I'm not sure I want to. Official residences have no warmth. Not like here. I feel good here. I feel at home."

The simple beauty of her statement gave Anakin pause. "I've never had a real home," he said, speaking more to himself than to Padmé. "Home was always where my mom was." He looked up at her then, and took comfort in her sympathetic smile.

Padmé went back to her packing. "The Lake Country is beautiful," she started to explain, but she stopped when she glanced back at Anakin, to see him holding a holograph and grinning.

"Is this you?" he asked, pointing to the young girl, seven or eight at the most, in the holo, surrounded by dozens of little green smiling creatures, and holding one in her arms.

Padmé laughed, and seemed embarrassed. "That was when I went with a relief group to Shadda-Bi-Boran. Their sun was imploding and the planet was dying. I was helping to relocate the children." She walked over to stand beside Anakin and placed one hand on his shoulder, pointing to the holograph with the other. "See that little one I'm holding? His name was N'a-kee-tula, which means 'sweetheart.' He was so full of life—all those kids were."

"Were?"

"They were never able to adapt," she explained somberly. "They were never able to live off their native planet."

Anakin winced, then quickly picked up another holograph, this one showing Padmé a couple of years later, wearing official robes and standing between two older and similarly robed Legislators. He looked back at the first holo, then to this one, noting that Padmé's expression seemed much more severe here.

"My first day as an Apprentice Legislator," Padmé explained. Then, as if she was reading his mind, she added, "See the difference?"

Anakin studied the holograph a moment longer, then looked up and laughed, seeing Padmé wearing that same long and stern expression. She laughed as well, then squeezed his shoulder and went back to her packing.

Anakin put the holographs down side by side and looked at them for a long, long time. Two sides of the woman he loved.

The water speeder zoomed above the lake, the downthrusters churning only a slight, almost indistinguishable, wake. Every so often, a wave clipped in, and a fine spray broke over the bow. Anakin and Padmé reveled in the cool water and the wind, eyes half closed, Padme's rich brown hair flying out behind her.

Beside them at the wheel, Paddy Accu gave a laugh at every spray, his graying hair spreading out widely. "Always better over the water!" he shouted in his gruff voice, against the wind and the noise of the speeder. "Are you liking it?"

Padmé turned a sincere smile upon him, and the grizzled man leaned in close and backed off the accelerator. "She's even more fun if I put her down," he explained. "You think you'll like that, Senator?"

Both Padmé and Anakin looked at him curiously, neither quite understanding.

"We were going out to the island," Anakin remarked, a note of concern in his voice.

"Oh, I'll get you there!" Paddy Accu said with a wheezing

laugh. He pushed forward a lever—and the speeder dropped into the water.

"Paddy?" Padmé asked.

The man laughed all the harder. "Don't tell me you've forgotten!" he roared, kicking in the accelerator. The speeder jetted off across the water, no longer smooth in flight, but bouncing across the rippling surface.

"Oh, yes!" Padmé said to him. "I do remember!"

After a moment of initial shock, looking from Padmé to Paddy, wondering if the man was up to some dark deception, Anakin caught on, and was also swept away by the bouncing ride.

The spray was nearly continuous, thrown up by the prow and washing over them.

"It's wonderful!" Padmé exclaimed.

Anakin couldn't disagree. "We spend so much time in control," he replied. His mind went back to his younger days, on Tatooine, Podracing along wild courses, skirting disaster. This was somewhat like that, especially when Paddy, in no apparent hurry to reach the island dock, flipped the speeder up and down from one edge to the other, zigzagging his way. It amazed Anakin how this little adjustment, dropping into the water instead of smoothly skimming above it, had changed the perspective of this journey. It was true, he knew, that technology had tamed the galaxy, and while that seemed a good thing in terms of efficiency and comfort, he had to believe that something, too, had been lost: the excitement of living on the edge of disaster. Or the simple tactile feeling of a ride like this, bouncing across the waves, feeling the wind and the cold spray.

At one point, Paddy put the speeder so far up on edge that both Anakin and Padmé thought they would tip over. Anakin almost reached into the Force to secure the craft, but stopped himself in order to enjoy the thrill.

They didn't tip. Paddy was an expert driver who knew how to take his speeder to the very limits without crashing over. It was some time later that he slowed the craft and allowed it to drift in against the island dock.

Padmé grabbed the older man's hand and leaned in to kiss his cheek. "Thank you!"

Anakin was surprised that he could see Paddy's blush through the man's ruddy skin. "It was . . . fun," he admitted.

"If it isn't, then what's the point?" the gruff-looking man replied with a great belly laugh.

While Paddy secured the speeder, Anakin hopped onto the dock. He reached back to take Padmé's hand, helping her stay balanced while she debarked with her suitcase in her other hand.

"I'll bring the bags up for you," Paddy offered, and Padmé looked back and smiled. "You go and see what you can see— don't want to be wasting your time on the little chores!"

"Wasting time," Padmé echoed. There was an unmistakable wistfulness in her voice.

The young couple walked up a long flight of wooden stairs, past flower beds and hanging vines. They came onto a terrace overlooking a beautiful garden, and beyond that, the shimmering lake and the mountains rising behind it, all blue and purple.

Padmé leaned her crossed forearms on the balustrade and stared out at the wondrous view.

"You can see the mountains in the water," Anakin remarked, shaking his head and grinning. The water was still, the light just right, so that the mountains in the lake seemed almost perfect replicas.

"Of course," she agreed without moving.

He gazed at her until she turned to look back at him.

"It seems an obvious thing to you," he said, "but where I grew up, there weren't any lakes. Whenever I see this much water, every detail of it . . ." He ended by shaking his head, obviously overwhelmed.

"Amazes you?"

"And pleases me," he said with a warm smile.

Padmé turned back to the lake. "I guess it's hard to hold on to appreciation for some things," she admitted. "But after all these years, I still see the beauty of the mountains reflected in the water. I could stare at them all day, every day."

Anakin stepped up to the balustrade beside her, leaning in very close. He closed his eyes and inhaled the sweet scent of Padmé, felt the warmth of her skin.

"When I was in Level Three, we used to come here for school retreat," she said. She pointed out across the way, to another island. "See that island? We used to swim there every day. I love the water."

"I do, too. I guess it comes from growing up on a desert planet." He was staring at her again, his eyes soaking in her beauty. He could tell that Padmé sensed his stare, but she pointedly continued to look out over the water.

"We used to lie on the sand and let the sun dry us . . . and try to guess the names of the birds singing."

"I don't like the sand. It's coarse and rough and irritating. And it gets everywhere."

Padmé turned to look back at him

"Not here," Anakin went on. "It's like that on Tatooine—everything's like that on Tatooine. But here, everything's soft, and smooth." As he finished, hardly even aware of the motion, he reached out and stroked Padmé's arm.

He nearly pulled back when he realized what he was doing, but since Padmé didn't object, he let himself stay close to her. She seemed a bit tentative, a bit scared, but she wasn't pulling away.

"There was a very old man who lived on the island," she said. Her brown eyes seemed to be looking far away, across the years. "He used to make glass out of sand—and vases and necklaces out of the glass. They were magical."

Anakin moved a bit closer, staring at her intensely until she turned to face him. "Everything here is magical," he said.

"You could look into the glass and see the water. The way it ripples and moves. It looked so real, but it wasn't."

"Sometimes, when you believe something to be real, it becomes real." It seemed to Anakin as if she wanted to look away. But she didn't. Instead, she was falling deeper into his eyes, and he into hers.

"I used to think if you looked too deeply into the glass, you would lose yourself," she said, her voice barely a whisper.

"I think it's true . . ." He moved forward as he spoke, brushing his lips against hers, and for a moment, she didn't resist, closing her eyes, losing herself. Anakin pressed in closer, a real and deep kiss, sliding his lips across hers slowly. He could lose himself here, could kiss her for hours, forever . . .

But then Padmé pulled back, suddenly, as if waking from a dream. "No, I shouldn't have done that."

"I'm sorry," Anakin said. "When I'm around you, my mind is no longer my own."

He stared at her hard again, beginning that descent into the glass, losing himself in her beauty.

But the moment had passed, and Padmé gathered her arms in close and leaned again on the balustrade, looking out over the water.

As soon as the starlight shrank back from its speed-shift elongation, Obi-Wan Kenobi saw the "missing" planet, exactly where the gravity flux had predicted it would be.

"There it is, Arfour, right where it should be," he said to his astromech droid, who tootled in response from the left wing of the fighter. "Our missing planet, Kamino. Those files *were* altered."

R4 beeped curiously.

"I have no idea who might have done it," Obi-Wan replied. "Maybe we'll find some answers down there."

He ordered R4 to disengage the hyperspace ring, a band encircling the center area of the starfighter, with a pair of powerful hyperdrive engines, one on either side. Then he took the Delta-7 away, gliding in casually, registering information on his various scanners.

As he neared the planet, he saw that it was an ocean world, with no visible landmasses showing behind the nearly solid cloud cover. He checked his sensors, searching for any other ships that might be in the area, not really sure of what he should expect. His computer registered a transmission directed his way, asking for identification, and he flipped his signal beacon on, transferring all the information. A moment later, to his relief, there came a second transmission from Kamino, this one containing approach coordinates to a place called Tipoca City.

"Well, here we go, Arfour. Time to find some answers."

The droid beeped and set the coordinates into the nav computer, and the fighter swooped down at the planet, breaking atmosphere and soaring along over rain-lashed, whitecapped seas. The trip across the stormy sky was rougher than the atmospheric entry, but the fighter held its course perfectly, and soon after, Obi-Wan got his first look at Tipoca City. It was all gleaming domes and angled, gracefully curving walls, built on gigantic stilts rising out of the lashing sea.

Obi-Wan spotted the appropriate landing pad, but did a flyby first, crossing the city and circling about, wanting to observe this spectacular place from all angles. It seemed as much a work of art as a practical and magnificent piece of engineering, the whole of the city reminding him more of the Senate Building and the Jedi Temple on Coruscant. It was brightly lit at all the right places to highlight the domes and curving walls.

"There's so much to see, Arfour," the Jedi lamented. He had visited hundreds of worlds in his life, but viewing a place as strange and beautiful as Tipoca City only reminded him that there were thousands and thousands more yet to see, too many for any one person to visit even if he did nothing else for the entirety of his life.

At last Obi-Wan put his fighter down on the designated landing pad. He pulled his hood up tight over him, then slid back his canopy and scrambled out against the wind and the rain, rushing across the permacrete to a tower across the way. A door slid open before him, spilling out brilliant light, and he went through, crossing into a brightly lit white room.

"Master Jedi, so good to see you," came a melodic voice.

Obi-Wan pushed back his hood, which had offered little protection from the driving rain, and brushed the water from his hair. Wiping his face, he turned to face the speaker, and then he paused, caught by the image of the Kaminoan.

"I am Taun We," she introduced herself.

She was taller than Obi-Wan, pasty white and amazingly slender, with gracefully curving lines, but there was nothing insubstantial about her. Thin, yes, but packed with a solid and powerful presence. Her eyes, huge, almond-shaped, and dark, were sparkling clear, like those of an inquisitive child. Her nose was no more than a pair of vertical slits, connected by a horizontal one, sitting on the bridge above her upper lip. She reached out gracefully toward him with an arm that moved as smoothly as any dancer might.

"The Prime Minister expects you."

The words finally distracted Obi-Wan from his bemused perusal of her strangely beautiful physique. "I'm expected?" he asked, doing little to hide his incredulity. How in the galaxy could these beings possibly have been expecting him?

"Of course." Taun We replied. "Lama Su is anxious to see you. After all these years, we were beginning to think you weren't coming. Now please, this way."

Obi-Wan nodded and tried to play it cool, hiding the million questions buzzing about in his thoughts. *After all these years? They were thinking that I wasn't coming?*

The corridor was nearly as brightly lit as the room, but as his eyes adjusted, Obi-Wan found the light strangely comfortable. They passed many windows, and Obi-Wan could see other Kaminoans busy in side rooms, males—distinguished by a crest atop their heads—and females working about furniture that was highlighted at every edge by shining light, as if that light supported and defined it. He was struck by how clean this place was, everything polished and shining and smooth. He kept his questions to himself, though, as anxious to see this Prime Minister, Lama Su, as Taun We seemed to be in getting him there, judging from the swift pace.

The Kaminoan stopped at one side door and sent it sliding open with a wave of her hand, then motioned for Obi-Wan to enter first.

Another Kaminoan, a bit taller and with the distinctive male crest, greeted them. He looked down at Obi-Wan, blinked his huge eyes, and smiled warmly. With a wave of his hand, he brought an egg-shaped chair gracefully spiraling down from the ceiling.

"May I present Lama Su, Prime Minister of Kamino," Taun We said, then to Lama Su, she added, "This is Master Jedi—"

"Obi-Wan Kenobi," the Jedi finished, nodding his head deferentially.

The Prime Minister indicated the chair, then sat back in his own, but Obi-Wan remained standing, soaking in the scene before him.

"I trust you are going to enjoy your stay," the Prime Minister said. "We are most happy you have arrived at the best part of the season."

"You make me feel most welcome." Obi-Wan didn't add that if the deluge outside was "the best part of the season," he'd hate to see the worst.

"Please . . ." Lama Su indicated the chair once more. When Obi-Wan finally sat down, the Kaminoan continued. "And now to business. You will be delighted to hear we are on schedule. Two hundred thousand units are ready, with another million well on the way."

Obi-Wan's tongue suddenly seemed fat in his mouth, but he fought past the stutter and tucked his questions away, and improvised, "That is good news."

"We thought you would be pleased."

"Of course."

"Please tell your Master Sifo-Dyas that we have every confidence his order will be met, on time and in full. He is well, I hope."

"I'm sorry," the overwhelmed Jedi replied. "Master? . . ."

"Jedi Master Sifo-Dyas. He is still a leading member of the Jedi Council, is he not?"

The name, known to Obi-Wan as that of a former Jedi Master, elicited yet another surge of questions, but again, he put them out of mind and focused on keeping Lama Su talking and giving out potentially valuable information. "I'm afraid to say that Master Sifo-Dyas was killed almost ten years ago."

Lama Su blinked his huge eyes again. "Oh, I'm so sorry to hear that. But I'm sure he would have been proud of the army we've built for him."

"The army?" Obi-Wan asked before he could even think the direction through.

"The army of clones. And I must say, one of the finest we've ever created."

Obi-Wan didn't know how far he could press this. If it was indeed Sifo-Dyas who had commissioned an army of clones, then why hadn't Master Yoda or any of the others said anything about it? Sifo-Dyas had been a powerful Jedi before his untimely death, but would he have acted alone on an issue as important as this? The Jedi studied his two companions, even reaching into the Force to gain a feeling about them. Everything seemed straightforward here, and open, and so he followed his instincts and kept the conversation rolling along. "Tell me, Prime Minister, when my Master first contacted you about the army, did he say who it was for?"

"Of course he did," the Kaminoan offered unsuspiciously. "The army is for the Republic."

Obi-Wan almost blurted out, *The Republic!* but his discipline allowed him to keep his surprise well buried, along with the tumult in his thoughts, a mounting storm as furious as the one that raged outside. What in the galaxy was going on here? An army of clones for the Republic? Commissioned by a Jedi Master? Did the Senate know of this? Did Yoda, or Master Windu?

"You understand the responsibility you incur in creating such an army for the Republic?" he asked, trying to cover his confusion. "We expect, and must have, the very best."

"Of course, Master Kenobi," Lama Su said, seeming supremely confident. "You must be anxious to inspect the units for yourself."

"That's why I'm here," Obi-Wan answered. Taking Lama Su's cue, he rose and followed the Prime Minister and Taun We out of the room.

Lush grasses sprinkled with flowers of all colors and shapes graced the hilly meadow. Beyond its borders, shining waterfalls spilled into the lake, and from this spot, many other lakes could be seen about the distant hills, all the way to the horizon.

Puffballs floated by on the warm breeze, and puffy clouds drifted across the shining blue sky above. It was a place full of life and full of love, full of warmth and full of softness.

To Anakin Skywalker, it was a place perfectly reflective of Padmé Amidala.

A herd of benevolent creatures called shaaks grazed contentedly nearby, seemingly oblivious to the couple. They were curious-looking four-legged beasts, with huge, bloated bodies. Insects buzzed about in the air, too busy with the flowers to take any time to bother either Anakin or Padmé.

Padmé sat on the grass, absently picking flowers, bringing

them up to deeply inhale their scents. Every so often, she glanced over at Anakin, but only briefly, almost afraid to let him notice. She loved the way he was reacting to this place, to all of Naboo, his simple joys forcing her to see things as she had when she was younger, before the real world had pushed her to a place of responsibility. It surprised her that a Jedi Padawan would be so . . .

She couldn't think of the word. *Carefree? Joyous? Spirited?* Some combination of the three?

"Well?" Anakin prompted, forcing Padmé to consider again the question he had just asked her.

"I don't know," she said dismissively, purposely exaggerating her frustration.

"Sure you do! You just don't want to tell me!"

Padmé gave a helpless little laugh. "Are you going to use one of your Jedi mind tricks on me?"

"They only work on the weak-minded," Anakin explained. "You are anything but weak-minded." He ended with an innocent, wide-eyed look that Padmé simply could not resist.

"All right," she surrendered. "I was twelve. His name was Palo. We were both in the Legislative Youth Program. He was a few years older than I . . ." She narrowed her eyes as she finished, teasing Anakin with sudden intensity. "Very cute," she said, her voice taking on a purposeful, suggestive tone. "Dark curly hair . . . dreamy eyes . . ."

"All right, I get the picture!" the Jedi cried, waving his hands in exasperation. He calmed a moment later, though, and settled back more seriously. "Whatever happened to him?"

"I went into public service. He went on to become an artist."

"Maybe he was the smart one."

"You really don't like politicians, do you?" Padmé asked, a

bit of anger creeping in despite the warm wind and the idyllic setting.

"I like two or three," Anakin replied. "But I'm not really sure about one of them." His smile was perfectly disarming and Padmé had to work hard to keep any semblance of a frown against it.

"I don't think the system works," Anakin finished, matter-of-factly.

"Really?" she replied sarcastically. "Well, how would you have it work?"

Anakin stood up, suddenly intense. "We need a system where the politicians sit down and discuss the problem, agree what's in the best interests of the people, and then do it," he said, as if it was perfectly simple and logical.

"Which is exactly what we do," came Padmé's unhesitating reply.

Anakin looked at her doubtfully.

"The trouble is that people don't always agree," she explained. "In fact, they hardly ever do."

"Then they should be made to."

That statement caught Padmé a bit off guard. Was he so convinced that he had the answers that he . . . No, she put that unsettling thought out of her mind. "By whom?" she asked. "Who is going to make them?"

"I don't know," he answered, waving his hands again in obvious frustration. "Someone."

"You?"

"Of course not me!"

"But someone."

"Someone wise."

"That sounds an awful lot like a dictatorship," Padmé said, winning the debate. She watched Anakin as a mischievous little grin began to spread across his face.

"Well," he said calmly, "if it works . . ."

Padmé tried to hide her shock. What was he talking about? How could he believe that? She stared at him, and he returned the severe look—but he couldn't hold it, and burst out laughing.

"You're making fun of me!"

"Oh no," Anakin said, backing away and falling to sit on the soft grass, hands out defensively before him. "I'd be much too frightened to tease a Senator."

"You're so bad!" She reached over, picked up a piece of fruit, and threw it at him, and when he caught it, she threw another, and then another.

"You're always so serious," Anakin scolded, and he began juggling the fruit.

"I'm so serious?" Her incredulity was feigned, because Padmé agreed with the assessment to a great extent. For all her life, she had watched people like Palo go off and follow their hearts, while she had followed the path of duty. She had known great triumph and great joy, to be sure, but all of it had been wrapped up in the extravagant outfits of Naboo's Queen, and now in the endless responsibilities of a Galactic Senator. Maybe she just wanted to take off all those trappings, all those clothes, and dive into the sparkling water, for no better reason than to feel its cool comfort, for no better reason than to laugh.

She grabbed up another piece of fruit and threw it at Anakin, and he caught it and seamlessly put it up with the others. Then another, and another, until too many went his way and he lost control, then tried futilely to duck away from the dropping fruit.

Padmé had to clutch at her belly, she was laughing so hard. Caught up in the whirlwind of the moment, Anakin sprang to his feet and ran off to the side, cutting in front of a shaak and frightening it with his sheer jubilance.

The normally passive grazers gave a snort and took up the chase, with Anakin running in circles and then off over the hill.

Padmé sat back and considered this moment, this day, and her companion. What was happening here? She couldn't dismiss the pangs of guilt that she was out here playing without purpose, while others worked hard to carry on the fight against the Military Creation Act, or while Obi-Wan Kenobi scoured the galaxy in search of those who would see her dead.

She should be out there, somewhere, doing something . . .

Her thoughts fell away in another burst of incredulous laughter as Anakin and the shaak came by once more, this time with the Jedi riding the beast, one hand clenched on a fold of its flesh, the other high and waving behind him for balance. What made it all the more ridiculous was that Anakin was riding backward, facing the shaak's tail!

"Anakin!" she cried in amazement. A bit of trepidation crept into her voice as she repeated the call, for the shaak had broken into a full gallop, and Anakin was trying to stand up on its back.

He almost made it, but then the lumbering creature bucked and he flew away, tumbling to the ground.

Padmé howled with laughter, clutching her stomach.

But Anakin lay very still.

She stopped and stared at him, suddenly frightened. She scrambled up, thinking her whole world had just crashed down around her, and rushed to his side. "Annie! Annie! Are you all right?"

Gently, Padmé turned him over. He seemed serene and still.

And then his face twisted into a perfectly stupid expression and he burst out laughing.

"Oh!" Padmé cried, and she punched out at him. He caught her hand and pulled her in close, and she willingly crashed onto him, wrestling with fury.

Anakin finally managed to roll her over and pin her, and Padmé stopped struggling, suddenly aware of the closeness. She looked into his eyes and felt the press of his body upon hers.

Anakin blushed and let go, rolling away, but then he stood up and very seriously reached his hand out to her.

All self-consciousness was gone now from Padmé. She looked hard into Anakin's blue eyes, finally and silently admitting the truth. She took his hand and followed him to the shaak, which was grazing contentedly once more.

Anakin climbed onto its back and pulled Padmé up behind him, and they rode off across the meadow, with Padmé's arms about his waist, her body pressed up against his, a swirl of emotions and questions spinning about in her mind.

Padmé jumped at the sound of the knock on the door. She knew who it was, and knew she was safe—from everything but her own feelings.

The afternoon at the meadow replayed in her thoughts, particularly the ride on the shaak, when Anakin had taken her back to the lodge. For the minutes of that ride, Padmé had not hidden behind a mask of denial, or behind anything else. Sitting behind Anakin, her arms about his waist, her head resting on the back of his shoulder, she had felt safe and secure, perfectly content and . . .

She had to take a deep breath to keep her hand from trembling as she reached up for the doorknob.

She pulled the door back, and could see nothing but the tall and lean silhouette, backlit by the setting sun.

Anakin shifted just a bit, blocking the rosy glow enough so that Padmé could see his smile. He started to move in, but she held her ground. It wasn't a conscious decision; she was simply entranced, for it seemed to her as if the sun was setting behind Anakin's shoulders and not behind the horizon, as if he was big enough to dismiss the day. Orange flames danced about his silhouette, dulling the distinction between Anakin and eternity.

Padmé had to consciously remember to breathe. She stepped back and Anakin sauntered in, apparently oblivious to the wondrous moment she had just experienced. He was grinning mischievously, and for some reason she felt embarrassed. She wondered for a moment if she should have chosen a different outfit, for the evening dress she was wearing was black and off the shoulder, showing quite a bit of flesh. She wore a black choker, as well, with a line of sheer fabric running down over the front of the dress, barely concealing her cleavage.

She moved to close the door, but paused and looked back over the lake, at the rose-colored tint filtering across the shimmering water.

When she turned back, Anakin was already standing by the table, looking over the bowl of fruit and the settings Padmé had put out. She watched him glance up at one of the floating light globes, its glow growing as the sunlight began to diminish outside. He playfully poked at it, seemingly oblivious that she, or anyone else, was watching him, and his smile nearly reached his ears as the globe bounced away from his touch, elongating the soft sphere of light.

The next few moments of just watching Anakin were quite pleasant for Padmé, but the next few after that, when he started looking back at her, his expression alternately playful and intense, proved more than a bit uncomfortable.

Soon enough, though, the pair had settled in at the table, seated across from each other. Two of the resort waitresses, Nandi and Teckla, served them their meal, while Anakin began recounting some of the adventures he had known over the last ten years, training and flying with Obi-Wan.

Padmé listened attentively, captivated by Anakin's flair for storytelling. She wanted to do more, though. She wanted to talk about what had happened out at the meadow, to try to make some sense of it with Anakin, to share with him the solution as they had shared the out-of-bounds emotions and moments. But she could not begin, and so she just allowed him to ramble on, contenting herself with enjoying his tales.

Dessert was Padmé's favorite, yellow-and-cream-colored shuura fruit, juicy and sweet. She grinned as Nandi put a bowl before her.

"And when I went to them, we went into . . ." Anakin paused, drawing Padmé's full attention, a wry smile on his face. "Aggressive negotiations," he finished, and then he thanked Teckla as she placed some dessert fruit before him.

"Aggressive negotiations? What's that?"

"Uh, well, negotiations with a lightsaber," the Padawan said, still grinning wryly.

"Oh," Padmé said with a laugh, and she eagerly went for her dessert, stabbing with her fork.

The shuura moved and her fork hit the plate. A bit confused, Padmé stabbed at it again.

It moved.

She looked up at Anakin, a bit confused and embarrassed,

but then she saw that he was fighting hard not to laugh, staring down at his own plate a bit too innocently.

"You did that!"

He looked up, his expression wide-eyed. "What?"

Padmé scowled, pointing her fork at him and waving it threateningly. Then, suddenly, she went for the shuura again.

But Anakin was quicker. The fruit slipped out of the way, and she stabbed the plate. Then, before she could scowl at him again, the shuura rose into the air to hover before her.

"That!" Padmé answered. "Now stop it!" She couldn't hold her feigned anger, though, and laughed aloud as she finished. Anakin started laughing, too. Half looking at him, Padmé snapped her hand at the floating fruit.

He waggled his fingers and the fruit looped about her hand. "Anakin!"

"If Master Obi-Wan was here, he'd be very grumpy," the Padawan admitted. He pulled back his hand, and the shuura flew across the table to his waiting grasp. "But he's not here," he added, cutting the fruit into several slices. Reaching for the Force, he made one piece float upward and slide toward Padmé. She bit it right out of the air.

Padmé laughed and so did Anakin. They finished their dessert with many fleeting glances, and then, as Teckla and Nandi returned to clean up the plates, the couple retreated to the sitting area, with its comfortable chairs and sofa, and a huge warm fire blazing in the hearth.

Nandi and Teckla finished and bade the couple good-bye, and then they were alone, completely alone, and the tension returned almost immediately.

She wanted him to kiss her, so desperately, and it was

precisely that out-of-control sensation that had stopped her cold. This was not right—she knew that in her head, despite what her heart might be telling her. They each had bigger responsibilities for the time being; she had to deal with the continuing split of the Republic, and he had to continue his Jedi training.

Anakin settled back into the sofa. "From the moment I met you, all those years ago, a day hasn't gone by when I haven't thought of you." His voice was husky, intense, and the sparkle in his eyes bored right through her. "And now that I'm with you again, I'm in agony. The closer I get to you, the worse it gets. The thought of not being with you makes my stomach turn over, my mouth go dry. I feel dizzy! I can't breathe! I'm haunted by the kiss you never should have given me. My heart is beating, hoping that kiss will not become a scar."

Padmé's hand slowly dropped to her side and she sat listening in amazement at how honestly he was opening up before her, baring his heart though he knew she might tear it asunder with a single word. She was honored by the thought, and truly touched. And afraid.

"You are in my very soul, tormenting me," Anakin went on, not a bit of falseness in his tone. This was no ploy to garner any physical favors; this was honest and straightforward, refreshingly so to the woman who had spent most of her life being attended by handmaidens whose job it was to please and entertaining dignitaries whose agendas were never quite what they seemed.

"What can I do?" he asked softly. "I will do anything you ask."

Padmé looked away, overwhelmed, finding security in the distracting dance of the flames in the hearth. Several moments of silence slipped by uncomfortably.

"If you are suffering as much as I am, tell me," Anakin prompted.

Padmé turned on him, her own frustrations bubbling over. "I can't!" She sat back and struggled to collect herself. "We can't," she said as calmly as she could. "It's just not possible."

"Anything's possible," Anakin replied, leaning forward. "Padmé, please listen—"

"*You* listen," she scolded. Somehow, hearing her own denial brought some strength to her—much-needed strength. "We live in a real world. Come back to it, Anakin. You're studying to become a Jedi Knight. I'm a Senator. If you follow your thoughts through to conclusion, they will take us to a place we cannot go . . . regardless of the way we feel about each other."

"Then you do feel something!"

Padmé swallowed hard. "Jedi aren't allowed to marry," she pointed out, needing to deflect attention away from her feelings at that debilitating moment. "You'd be expelled from the Order. I will not let you give up your future for me."

"You're asking me to be rational," Anakin replied without the slightest hesitation, and his confidence and boldness here caught Padmé a bit by surprise. There was no longer anything of the child in the man before her. She felt her control slip a notch.

"That is something I know I cannot do," he went on. "Believe me, I wish I could wish my feelings away. But I can't."

"I am not going to give in to this," she said with all the conviction she could muster. She finished with her jaw clenched very tightly, knowing that she had to be the strong one here, for Anakin's sake more than for her own. "I have more important things to do than fall in love."

He turned away, looking wounded, and she winced. He

stared into the fire, his face twisting this way and that as he tried to sort through it all. She knew he was trying to find a way around her resolve.

"It wouldn't have to be that way," he said at length. "We could keep it a secret."

"Then we'd be living a lie—one we couldn't keep up even if we wanted to. My sister saw it, so did my mother. I couldn't do that. Could you, Anakin? Could you live like that?"

He stared at her intensely for a moment, then looked back to the fire, seeming defeated.

"No, you're right," he finally admitted. "It would destroy us."

Padmé looked from Anakin to the fire. Which would destroy her—destroy *them*—she had to wonder. The action or the thought?

Wow!" Boba Fett exclaimed, rushing across the landing pad to view the sleek starfighter up close.

"Beautiful ship," Jango agreed, strolling to catch up to his son, studying the craft with every stride. He noted the markings and design, the extra firepower, and, particularly, the astromech droid hardwired into the left wing, tootling happily.

"This is a Delta-Seven," the excited Boba announced, pointing out the rear-cockpit position. Jango nodded, glad that his son had been taking his lessons seriously. These were new ships—so new that they hadn't yet been fitted with hyperdrive engines, Jango realized, and he inadvertently glanced up at the cloudy sky, wondering if parent ships were up there. He shook the thought away, turning back to Boba.

"And what of the droid?" he asked. "Can you identify the unit?"

Boba climbed up the side of the fighter and studied the markings for a moment, then turned back to his father, finger to pursed lips, an intense expression on his face. "It's an Arfour-Pea," he said.

"And is that a common droid for this type of starfighter?"

"No," Boba answered without hesitation. "A Delta-Seven pilot would usually use an Arthree-Dee. It's better at keeping the guns targeted, and the fighter is so maneuverable that handling the laser cannons is tricky. I read that some pilots wind up shooting their own nose cones off in this fighter! They do a snap-roll, coming out over and around, but they haven't compensated the manual swivel . . ." As he spoke, he moved his arms over each other and about, tangling them up in front of him.

Jango was hardly listening to the details, though he was thrilled that Boba had taken to his lessons with such energy. "Suppose the pilot didn't need the extra gunnery skills of an Arthree-Dee?" he asked.

Boba looked at him curiously, as if he didn't understand.

"Would the Arfour-Pea then be a better choice?"

"Yes," came the halting response.

"And what pilot wouldn't need the extra droid gunnery skills?"

Boba stared blankly, but then a smile spread on his face. "You!" he blurted, seeming quite pleased with himself.

Jango took the compliment with an appreciative smile—and it was true enough. Jango could wheel any fighter, and if he ever had the opportunity to fly in a Delta-7, he'd likely choose an R4-P over the R3-D. But that wasn't what he had in mind right now, for he knew of one other type of pilot, pilots with heightened senses, who would similarly choose the better nav, but less weapon-oriented droid.

Jango Fett looked back up at the sky, wondering if a host of Jedi were about to descend upon Tipoca City.

*   *   *

Great racks holding glass spheres stretched across the immense room to the end of Obi-Wan's vision. Each sphere contained an embryo, suspended in fluid, and when the Jedi reached into the Force, he sensed strong waves of life energy.

"The hatchery," he stated more than asked.

"The first phase, obviously," Lama Su replied.

"Very impressive."

"I hoped you would be pleased, Master Jedi," the Prime Minister said. "Clones can think creatively. You'll find that they are immensely superior to droids, and that ours are the best in all the galaxy. Our methods have been perfected over many centuries."

"How many are there?" Obi-Wan asked. "In here, I mean."

"We have several hatcheries throughout the city. This, of course, is the most crucial phase, though with our techniques, we expect a survival rate of over ninety percent. Every so often, an entire batch will develop a . . . an issue, but we expect the clone production to remain steady, and with our accelerated growth methods, these before you will be fully matured and ready for battle in just over a decade."

Two hundred thousand units are ready, with another million well on the way. Lama Su's previous boast echoed ominously in Obi-Wan's thoughts. A production center, supremely efficient, producing a steady stream of superbly trained and conditioned warriors. The implications were staggering.

Obi-Wan stared at the closest embryo, floating contentedly in its fluid, curled and with its little thumb stuck into its mouth. In ten short years, that tiny creature, that tiny man, would be a soldier, killing and, likely, soon enough killed.

He shuddered and looked to his Kaminoan guide.

"Come," Lama Su bade him, walking along the corridor.

Next on the tour was a huge classroom, with desks in neat, orderly rows and with students in neat, orderly rows. They all looked to be about ten years of age. All dressed the same, all with the same haircut, all with exactly the same features and posture and expressions. Obi-Wan reflexively looked at the shining white walls of the huge room, almost expecting to see mirrors there, playing a trick on his eyes to make one boy seem to be many.

The students went about their studies without paying any more heed to the visitors than a quick glance.

Disciplined, Obi-Wan thought. *Much more so than any normal children.*

Another thought grabbed him. "You mentioned growth acceleration—"

"Oh yes, it's essential," the Prime Minister replied. "Otherwise a mature clone would take a lifetime to grow. Now we can do it in half the time. The units you will soon see on the parade ground we started ten years ago, when Sifo-Dyas first placed the order, and they're already mature and quite ready for duty."

"And these were started about five years ago?" the Jedi reasoned, and Lama Su nodded.

"Would you care to inspect the final product now?" the Prime Minister asked, and Obi-Wan could hear excitement in his voice. Clearly he was proud of this accomplishment. "I would like your approval before you take delivery."

The callousness of it all struck Obi-Wan profoundly. *Units. Final product.* These were living beings they were talking about. Living, breathing, and thinking. To create clones for such a singular purpose, under such control, even stealing half their childhood for efficiency, assaulted his sense of right and wrong, and the fact that a Jedi Master had begun all of this was almost too much to digest.

The tour took him through the commissary next, where hundreds of adult clones—all young men Anakin's age—sat in neat rows, all dressed in red, all eating the same food in the same manner.

"You'll find that they are totally obedient," Lama Su was saying, seemingly oblivious to the Jedi's discomfort. "We modified their genetic structure to make them less independent than the original, of course."

"Who was the original?"

"A bounty hunter named Jango Fett," Lama Su offered without any hesitation. "We felt that a Jedi would be the perfect choice, but Sifo-Dyas handpicked Jango himself."

The notion that a Jedi might have been used nearly floored Obi-Wan. An army of clones strong in the Force?

"Where is this bounty hunter now?" he asked.

"He lives here," Lama Su replied. "But he's free to come and go as he pleases." He kept walking as he spoke, leading Obi-Wan along a long corridor filled with narrow transparent tubes.

The Jedi watched with amazement as clones climbed up into those tubes and settled in place, closing their eyes and going to sleep.

"Very disciplined," he remarked.

"That is the key," Lama Su replied. "Disciplined, and yet with the ability to think creatively. It is a mighty combination. Sifo-Dyas explained to us the Jedi aversion to leading droids. He told us Jedi could only command an army of life-forms."

And you wanted a Jedi as host? Obi-Wan thought, but he did not it say aloud. He took a deep breath, wondering how Master Sifo-Dyas, how any Jedi, could have so willingly and unilaterally crossed the line to create *any* army of clones. Obi-Wan realized that he had to suppress his need for a direct answer to that right now, and simply listen and observe, gather as much information as he could so that he and the Jedi Council might sort it out.

"So Jango Fett willingly remains on Kamino?"

"The choice is his alone. Apart from his pay, which is considerable, I assure you, Fett demanded only one thing—an unaltered clone for himself. Curious, isn't it?"

"Unaltered?"

"Pure genetic replication," the Prime Minister explained. "No tampering with the structure to make it more docile. And no growth acceleration."

"I would very much like to meet this Jango Fett," Obi-Wan said, as much to himself as to Lama Su. He was intrigued. Who was this man selected by Sifo-Dyas as the perfect source for a clone army?

Lama Su looked to Taun We, who nodded and said, "I would be most happy to arrange it for you."

She left them, then, as the tour continued, with Lama Su taking Obi-Wan along the areas that showed him pretty much the entire routine of the clones at every level of their development. The culmination came later on, when Taun We rejoined the pair on a balcony, sheltered from the brutal wind and rain and overlooking a huge parade ground. Below them, thousands and thousands of clone troopers, dressed in white armor and wearing full-face helmets, marched and drilled with all the precision of programmed droids. Entire formations, each made up of hundreds of soldiers, moved as one.

"Magnificent, aren't they?" Lama Su said.

Obi-Wan looked up at the Kaminoan, to see his eyes glowing with pride as he looked out upon his creation. There were no ethical dilemmas as far as Lama Su was concerned, Obi-Wan knew immediately. Perhaps that was why the Kaminoans were so good at cloning: their consciences never got in the way.

Lama Su looked down at him, smiling widely, prompting a response, and Obi-Wan offered a silent nod.

Yes, they were magnificent, and the Jedi could only imagine the brutal efficiency this group would exhibit in battle, in the arena for which they were grown.

Once again, a shudder coursed down Obi-Wan Kenobi's spine. For the first time, he appreciated Senator Amidala's crusade to stop the creation of an Army of the Republic, and the inevitable consequence: war!

A Jedi Knight here on Kamino. The thought was more than a little unsettling to Jango Fett.

The bounty hunter fell back in his seat and tightened his face in frustration—such were the problems with working for the Trade Federation. They were masters at weaving deception within deception, and they were up to so much right now that there was no single focus Jango could determine.

He looked across the room at Boba, who was hard at work poring over the schematics and capabilities of a Delta-7 starfighter, and matching them up against the known strengths and weaknesses of an R4-P unit.

Life was so simple for the boy, Jango thought with a touch of envy. For Boba, there was the love of and for his father, and his studies. Other than those two givens, the only real challenge before the boy was in finding enjoyable things to do at those times when Jango was away or busy with the Kaminoans.

At that moment, looking at his son, Jango Fett felt vulnerable, so very vulnerable, and it was not an emotion with which he was the least bit comfortable. He almost told Boba to go and pack, then and there, so they could blast away from Kamino, but he recognized the danger of that course. He would be leaving without learning anything about his potential enemy, this Jedi Knight who had arrived unexpectedly. His boss would want that information.

And Jango would need that information. If he took off now, after receiving a note from Taun We telling him that he would be receiving a visitor later that same day, it would be fairly obvious that he was fleeing.

Then he'd have a Jedi Knight on his tail, and one about whom he knew practically nothing.

Jango continued to stare at Boba, at the only thing that really mattered.

"Play it cool," he whispered to himself. "You're nothing more than a clone source, well paid enough to want to know nothing about why you're being cloned."

That was his litany, that was his plan. And it had to work.

For Boba's sake.

A wave of Taun We's hand brought forth the chime of an unseen bell, reminding Obi-Wan yet again of how foreign this world of Kamino, this city of Tipoca, really was. He didn't give it much thought, though, for he was focused on the locking mechanism on the door before him, an elaborate electronic clasp and bolt. Quite a bit of security, it seemed to him, given the supposedly genteel nature of Jango Fett's relationship with the

Kaminoans, and the obvious control the cloners held over their city. Was the locking mechanism designed to keep people out, or to keep Jango in?

Likely the former, he reasoned. Jango was a bounty hunter, after all. Perhaps he had made more than a few dangerous enemies.

He was still studying the device when the door suddenly opened, revealing a young boy, an exact replica of those Obi-Wan had been viewing all day.

The identical one that Jango had demanded, only this one was *actually* ten years old.

"Boba," Taun We said with great familiarity, "is your father home?"

Boba Fett stood staring at the human visitor for a long moment. "Yep."

"May we see him?"

"Sure," Boba answered. He stepped back, but his eyes never left Obi-Wan as the Jedi and Taun We stepped across the threshold.

"Dad!" Boba yelled.

The title struck Obi-Wan as curious, given that this was a clone and not a natural son. Was there a connection here? A real one? Had Jango wanted the exact replica not for any professional gain but simply because he had wanted a son?

"Dad!" the boy shouted again. "Taun We's here!"

Jango Fett walked in, dressed in simple shirt and trousers. Obi-Wan recognized him immediately, though he was many years older than the oldest clone, his face scarred and pitted, and unshaven. His body had thickened with age, but he was still physically imposing, much like many of the old gutter dwellers Obi-Wan encountered in far-flung places. A few extra pounds, sure, but those covered muscles hardened by years of tough living. Tattoos crossed both of Jango's muscular forearms, of a strange design that Obi-Wan did not recognize.

As he glanced up, he recognized the clear suspicion with which Jango was eyeing him. The man was on edge here, dangerously so, Obi-Wan understood.

"Welcome back, Jango," Taun We remarked. "Was your trip productive?"

Obi-Wan studied the bounty hunter intensely. Back from where? But Jango was a professional, and his expression revealed not the slightest tic or wince.

"Fairly," the man casually offered. He continued to size up Obi-Wan as he spoke, his eyes narrowing in an almost open threat.

"This is Jedi Master Obi-Wan Kenobi," Taun We said, her tone lighter, obviously an attempt to relieve some of the palpable tension. "He's come to check on our progress."

"That right?" If Jango cared, his tone didn't show it.

"Your clones are very impressive," Obi-Wan said. "You must be very proud."

"I'm just a simple man trying to make my way in the universe, Master Jedi."

"Aren't we all?" Obi-Wan finally broke eye contact with Jango as he spoke, scanning the room, looking for clues. He focused on the half-open door through which Jango had appeared, and thought he saw pieces of body armor in there, battered and stained, much like that worn by a rocket-man after delivering a toxic dart into the changeling Zam Wesell. And he saw a curving bluish line, like the goggle and breather area of the helmet he had seen back on Coruscant. Before he could scrutinize the sight any more closely, though, Jango walked in front of him, pointedly blocking his view.

"Ever make your way as far into the interior as Coruscant?" Obi-Wan asked, rather bluntly.

"Once or twice."

"Recently?"

Again the bounty hunter's gaze became obviously suspicious. "Possibly . . ."

"Then you must know Master Sifo-Dyas," Obi-Wan remarked, not out of any logical follow-up reasoning, but simply to gauge the man's reaction.

There was none, nor did Jango Fett move a centimeter out of Obi-Wan's line of sight, and when the Jedi tried to subtly alter his angle to gain a view, Jango said, in a coded language, "Boba, close the door."

Not until that bedroom door shut did Jango Fett move to the side, and then it seemed to Obi-Wan as if the man was stalking him. "Master who?" Jango asked.

"Sifo-Dyas. Isn't he the one who hired you for this job?"

"Never heard of him," Jango replied, and if there was a lie in his words, Obi-Wan could not detect it.

"Really?"

"I was recruited by a man called Tyranus on one of the moons of Bogden," Jango explained, and again it seemed to Obi-Wan as if he was speaking truthfully.

"Curious . . ." Obi-Wan muttered. He glanced down, surprised and at a loss as to what all of this might mean.

"Do you like your army?" Jango Fett asked him.

"I look forward to seeing them in action," the Jedi replied.

Jango continued to stare at him, to try to see the intent behind his words, Obi-Wan knew. And then, as if it hardly mattered, the bounty hunter gave a toothy smile. "They'll do their job well. I'll guarantee that."

"Like their source?"

Jango Fett continued to smile.

"Thanks for your time, Jango," Obi-Wan said against that uncompromising stare. Then he turned to Taun We and started for the door.

"Always a pleasure to meet a Jedi," came the reply. It was heavy with double meaning, almost like a veiled threat.

But Obi-Wan wasn't about to call him on it. Jango Fett was clearly a dangerous man, streetwise and cunning, and likely better than most with any weapon handy. Before he pushed things any further, Obi-Wan realized that he should relay all that he had learned thus far back to Coruscant and the Jedi Council. This discovery of a clone army was nothing short of amazing, and more than a little unsettling, and none of it made much sense.

And *was* Jango the rocket-man Obi-Wan had seen in Coruscant that night when Padmé Amidala had been attacked?

Obi-Wan's gut told him that Jango was, but how did that jibe with the man also being the host for a clone army supposedly commissioned by a former Jedi Master?

With Taun We beside him, the Jedi left the apartment, and the door slid closed behind him. Obi-Wan paused and focused his senses back, even reaching out with the Force.

The door lock quietly secured.

"It was his starfighter, wasn't it, Dad?" Boba Fett asked. "He's a Jedi Knight, so he can use the Arfour-Pea."

Jango gave his son an absent nod.

"I knew it!" Boba squealed, but then Jango abruptly stole the moment.

Jango fixed Boba with a no-nonsense look that the young boy had learned well not to ignore.

"What is it, Dad?"

"Pack your things. We're leaving."

Boba started to reply, but—

"Now," the bounty hunter said, and Boba practically tripped over himself, scrambling for his bedroom.

Jango Fett shook his head. He didn't need this aggravation. Not at this time. Not for the first time, the bounty hunter questioned his decision to take the contract against Padmé Amidala. He had been surprised when the Trade Federation had approached him with the offer. They had been adamant, explaining only that the death of the Senator was critical to securing necessary allies, and they had made an offer too lucrative for Jango to refuse, one that would set him and Boba up forever on a planet of their choosing.

Little had Jango known, though, that taking the contract on Senator Amidala would put him in the crosshairs of the Jedi Knights.

He looked across the way to Boba.

That was not a place he wanted to be at this time. Not at all.

Padmé awoke suddenly, her senses immediately tuning in to her surroundings. Something was wrong, she knew instinctively, and she jumped up, scrambling about out of fear that another of those centipede creatures was upon her.

But her room was quiet, with nothing out of place.

Something had awakened her, but not something in here.

"No!" came a cry from the adjoining bedroom, where Anakin was sleeping. "No! Mom! No, don't!"

Padmé slipped out of bed and ran to the door, not even bothering to grab a robe, not even caring or noticing that she was wearing a revealing silken shift. At the door, she paused and listened. Hearing cries from within, followed by more jumbled yelling, she realized that there was no immediate danger, that this was another of Anakin's nightmares, like the one that had gripped him on the shuttle ride to Naboo. She opened the door and looked in on him.

He was thrashing about on the bed, yelling "Mom!" repeatedly. Unsure, Padmé started in.

But then Anakin calmed and rolled back over, the dream, the vision, apparently past.

Then Padmé did become aware of her revealing dress. She moved back through the door, shutting it gently, then waited for a long while. When she heard no further screaming or tossing, she went back to her bed.

She lay awake in the dark for a long, long while, thinking of Anakin, thinking that she wanted to be in there beside him, holding him, helping him through his troubled dreams. She tried to dismiss the notion—they had already covered this dangerous ground and had come to an understanding of what must be. And that agreement did not include her climbing into bed beside Anakin.

The next morning, she found him on the east balcony of the lodge, overlooking the lake and the budding sunrise. He was standing by the balustrade, so deep in thought that he did not notice her approach.

She moved up slowly, not wanting to disturb him, for as she neared, she realized that he was doing more than thinking here, that he was actually deep in meditation. Recognizing this as a private time for Anakin, she turned and started away, as quietly as she could.

"Don't go," Anakin said to her.

"I don't want to disturb you," she told him, surprised.

"Your presence is soothing."

Padmé considered those words for a bit, taking pleasure in hearing them, then scolding herself for taking that pleasure. But still, as she stood there looking upon him, his face now serene, she couldn't deny the attraction. He seemed to her like a young hero, a budding Jedi—and she had no doubt that he would be among the greatest that great Order had ever known.

And at the same time, he seemed to her to be the same little kid she had known during the war with the Trade Federation, inquisitive and impetuous, aggravating and charming all at once.

"You had a nightmare again last night," she said quietly, when Anakin at last opened his blue eyes.

"Jedi don't have nightmares," came the defiant reply.

"I heard you," Padmé was quick to answer.

Anakin turned to regard her. There was no compromise in her expression—she knew perfectly well that his claim was ludicrous, and she let him know that she knew it.

"I saw my mother," he admitted, lowering his gaze. "I saw her as clearly as I see you now. She is suffering, Padmé. They're killing her! She is in pain!"

"Who?" Padmé asked, moving toward him, putting a hand on his shoulder. When she looked at him more closely, she noted a determination so solid that it took her by surprise.

"I know I'm disobeying my mandate to protect you," Anakin tried to explain. "I know I will be punished and possibly thrown out of the Jedi Order, but I have to go."

"Go?"

"I have to help her! I'm sorry, Padmé," he said. She saw from his expression that he meant it, that leaving her was the last thing he ever wanted to do. "I don't have a choice."

"Of course you don't. Not if your mother is in trouble."

Anakin gave her an appreciative nod.

"I'll go with you," she decided.

Anakin's eyes widened. He started to reply, ready to argue, but Padmé's smile held his words in check.

"That way, you can continue to protect me," she reasoned.

Somehow she made it sound perfectly logical. "And you won't be disobeying your mandate."

"I don't think this is what the Jedi Council had in mind. I fear that I'm walking into danger, and to take you with me—"

"Walking into danger," Padmé echoed, and she laughed aloud. "A place I've never been before."

Anakin stared at her, hardly believing what he was hearing. He couldn't resist, though, and his smile, too, began to widen. For some reason he did not quite understand, the Padawan found a good measure of justification in his abandoning the letter of his orders now that Padmé was in on, and agreeing with, the plan.

Neither Padmé nor Anakin could miss the stark contrast when they took her sleek starship out of hyperspace and saw the brown planet of Tatooine looming before them. How different it was from Naboo, a place of green grasses and deep blue water, with cloud patterns swirling all across it. Tatooine was just a ball of brown hanging in space, as barren as Naboo was alive.

"Home again, home again, to go to rest," Anakin recited, a common children's rhyme.

"By hearth and heart, house and nest," Padmé added.

Anakin looked over at her, pleasantly surprised. "You know it?"

"Doesn't everyone?"

"I don't know," Anakin said. "I mean, I wasn't sure if anyone else . . . I thought it was a rhyme my mother made up for me."

"Oh, I'm sorry," Padmé said. "Maybe she did—maybe hers was different than the one my mother used to tell me."

Anakin shook his head doubtfully, but he wasn't bothered by the possibility. In a strange way, he was glad that Padmé knew the rhyme, glad that it was a common gift from mothers to their children.

And glad, especially, that he and Padmé had yet another thing in common.

"They haven't signaled any coordinates yet," she noted.

"They probably won't, unless we ask," Anakin replied. "Things aren't very strict here, usually. Just find a place and park it, then hope no one steals it while you go about your business."

"As lovely as I remember it."

Anakin looked at her and nodded. How different things were now than that decade before when Padmé had been forced to land on Tatooine with Obi-Wan and Qui-Gon in order to effect repairs on their ship. He tried to manage a smile, but the edge of his nervousness kept it from appearing genuine. Too many disturbing thoughts assaulted him. Was his mother all right? Was his dream a premonition of what was to come, or a replay of something that had already happened?

He brought the ship down fast, breaking through the atmosphere and soaring across the sky. "Mos Espa," he explained when the skyscape of the city came into sight against the horizon.

He went in hard, and some protests did squeal over the comlink. But Anakin knew his way around this place as surely as if he had never left. He did a flyby over the edge of the city, then put the starship down in a large landing bay amid a jumble of vessels of all merchant and mercenary classes.

"Yous can't just drop in uninvited!" barked the dock officer, a stout creature with a piggish face and spikes running down the length of his back and tail.

"It's a good thing you invited us, then," Anakin said calmly, with a slight wave of his hand.

"Yes, it's a good thing I invited you then!" the officer happily replied, and Anakin and Padmé walked past.

"Anakin, you're bad," Padmé said as they exited onto the dusty street.

"It's not like there are dozens of ships lined up to fill the bay," Anakin replied, feeling pretty good about himself and the ease with which he had Force-convinced the piggish officer. He waved down a floating rickshaw pulled by an ES-PSA droid, a short and thin creature with a wheel where its legs should have been.

Anakin gave it the address and off it went, pulling them behind in the floating rickshaw, charging along the streets of Mos Espa, expertly zigging and zagging to avoid the heavy traffic, and blasting forth a shrill sound whenever someone didn't get out of the way.

"Do you think he was involved?" Padmé asked Anakin.

"Watto?"

"Yes, that was his name, right? Your former master?"

"If Watto has hurt my mother in any way, I will pluck his wings from his back," he promised, meaning every word. He wasn't sure how he would feel about seeing the slaver, even if Watto had nothing to do with bringing any harm to Shmi. Watto had treated him better than most in Mos Espa treated their slaves, and hadn't beaten him too often, but still, it hung in Anakin's thoughts that Watto had not let Shmi go with him when Obi-Wan and Qui-Gon had bought out his slave debt.

Anakin understood that he was probably just deflecting some of his own guilt about leaving his mother with Watto, who was a businessman, after all.

"Here, Espasa," Anakin said to the droid, and the rickshaw glided to a stop in front of a shop all too familiar to Anakin Skywalker. There, sitting on a stool near the door, fiddling with an electronic driver on a broken piece of equipment that looked like a droid component, was a rounded, winged Toydarian with a long snout. A black round hat adorned his head, and a small vest was pulled as far as it would go about his girth. Anakin recognized him immediately.

He paused for so long in just staring at Watto that Padmé got out before him and held her hand to help him.

"Wait here," she instructed the droid. "Please."

"No chuba da wanga, da wanga!" Watto yelled at the broken component, and at a trio of pit droids who were scrambling all about, trying to help.

"Huttese," Anakin explained to Padmé.

"No, not that one—that one!" she replied, and at Anakin's expression of surprise that she knew the strange language, she added, "You think it's easy being the Queen?"

Anakin shook his head and looked back to Watto, then glanced at Padmé once or twice as they neared. *"Chut chut, Watto,"* he greeted.

"Ke booda?" came the surprised response.

"Di nova, chut chut," Anakin reiterated, his words barely audible above the clamoring pit droids.

"Go ana bopa!" Watto yelled at the trio, and on his command, they immediately shut down and snapped back into their storage position.

"*Ding mi chasa hopa,*" Anakin offered, taking the piece of the broken droid from Watto, and manipulating it expertly. Watto watched him for a moment, his buglike eyes growing even larger in surprise.

"*Ke booda?*" he asked. "*Yo baan pee hota. No wega mi condorta. Kin chasa du Jedi. No bata tu tu.*"

"He doesn't know you," Padmé whispered to Anakin, trying to hold back her laughter at Watto's last statement, which translated to "Whatever it is, I didn't do it."

"*Mi boska di Shmi Skywalker,*" Anakin bluntly stated.

Watto's eyes narrowed suspiciously. Who would be looking for his old slave? The Toydarian's gaze went from Anakin to Padmé, then back to Anakin.

"Annie?" he asked in Basic. "Little Annie? Naaah!"

Anakin's answer came with a deft twist of his hands, and the sound of the little piece of equipment whirring to life. Smiling widely, he handed it back to Watto.

There weren't many around who could work such magic on broken droid parts.

"You *are* Annie!" the Toydarian cried. "It *is* you!" His wings started beating furiously, lifting him from the stool to hover in the air. "Ya sure sprouted!"

"Hello, Watto."

"Weehoo!" the Toydarian cried. "A Jedi! Waddya know? Hey, maybe you couldda help wit some deadbeats who owe me a lot of money—"

"My mother—" Anakin prompted.

"Oh yeah, Shmi. She's not mine no more. I sold her."

"Sold her?" Anakin felt Padmé squeeze his forearm.

"Years ago," Watto explained. "Sorry, Annie, but you know,

business is business. Sold her to a moisture farmer named Lars.
Least I think it was Lars. Believe it or not, I heard he freed her
and married her. Can ya beat that?"

Anakin just shook his head, trying hard to digest it all. "Do
you know where they are?"

"Long way from here. Someplace over on the other side of
Mos Eisley, I think."

"Could you narrow it down?"

Watto thought about it for a moment, then just shrugged.

"I'd like to know," Anakin said, his tone and expression
grim and determined, even threatening. The way Watto's features seemed to tighten showed that he got the hint that Anakin
wasn't fooling around.

"Yeah, sure," he said. "Absolutely. Let's go look at my
records."

The three went into the shop, and seeing the place brought
memories swirling back to Anakin. How many hours, years, he
had toiled in here, fixing everything Watto threw his way. And
out back, where he had put all the spare parts he could find, so
that he could build a Podracer. Not all of the memories were
bad, he had to admit, but the good ones did not overcome the
reality that he had been a slave. Watto's slave.

Fortunately for Watto, his records gave a location for the
moisture farm of one Cliegg Lars.

"Stay a while, Annie," the Toydarian offered after sharing
the information on Shmi's new owner—or was it her husband?

Without a word, Anakin turned about and walked away.
This was the last time he would look at Watto and the shop, he
decided. Unless of course, he found out that Watto was lying
to him about Shmi's fate, or that Watto had somehow hurt his
mother.

"Back to the lot, Espasa," he said to the droid as he and Padmé rushed back to the rickshaw. "Fast."

"Ya sure I can't get ya something to drink?" Watto called to them from the door of his shop, but they were already rushing away, kicking up dust in their wake.

"Annie du Jedi," Watto remarked, and he waved both his hands dismissively at the departing rickshaw. "Waddya know."

Anakin took the starship out even more furiously than he had brought it in, blasting away from the lot and nearly colliding with a small freighter as it maneuvered to put down. Calls of protest came into him from Mos Espa control, but he just switched off the comm and zoomed off across the city. Soon after, they passed over the race grounds where the younger Anakin had often raced in his Pods, but he barely glanced at it as he put the ship out straight over the desert, heading for Mos Eisley. When that port came into view, he veered to the north and crossed past it, moving higher in the sky.

They spotted one moisture farm, and then another, and then the third, almost in a direct line from the city.

"That one," Padmé said. Anakin nodded grimly, and brought the ship down on a bluff overlooking the homestead.

"I'm really going to see her again," he breathed, shutting down the engines.

Padmé squeezed his arm and offered him a comforting smile.

"You don't know what it's like, to leave your mother like that," he said.

"I leave my family all the time," she replied. "But you're right. It's not the same. I can't imagine what it's like to be a slave, Anakin."

"It's worse to know that your mother is one."

Padmé nodded, conceding the point. "Stay with the ship, Artoo," she instructed the droid, who beeped in reply.

The first form that came into view as they walked toward the homestead was that of a very thin droid, dull gray in color, with weatherbeaten metal coverings. Obviously in need of a good oil bath, he bent stiffly and worked on some sort of fence sensor. Then he rose with a jerky motion, seeing their approach. "Oh, hello," he greeted. "How might I be of service? I am See—"

"Threepio?" Anakin said breathlessly, hardly believing his eyes.

"Oh my!" the droid exclaimed, and he began to shake violently. "Oh, my maker! Master Anakin! I knew you would return! I knew you would! And this must be Miss Padmé!"

"Hello, Threepio," Padmé said.

"Oh, my circuits! I'm so pleased to see you both!"

"I've come to see my mother," Anakin explained. The droid turned sharply up toward him, then seemed to shrink back.

"I think . . . I think," C-3PO stuttered. "Perhaps we'd better go indoors." He turned toward the homestead, motioning with his hand for the couple to follow.

Anakin and Padmé exchanged nervous glances. Anakin could not shake the feeling of doom that lingered long after the imagery of his nightmares had faded . . .

By the time they caught up to the droid, he was in the courtyard, shouting, "Master Cliegg! Master Owen! Might I present two important visitors?"

A young man and woman came rushing out of the house almost immediately, but slowed at the site of Padmé and Anakin.

"I'm Anakin Skywalker," Anakin said at once.

"Anakin?" the man echoed, his eyes going wide. "Anakin!"

The woman at his side brought her hand up to cover her mouth. "Anakin the Jedi," she whispered breathlessly.

"You know of me? Shmi Skywalker is my mother."

"Mine, too," said the man. "Not my real mom," he added at Anakin's obviously puzzled look, "but as real a mom as I've ever known." He extended his hand. "Owen Lars. This is my girlfriend, Beru Whitesun."

Beru nodded and said, "Hello."

Padmé, after giving up on Anakin ever remembering to introduce her, came forward. "I'm Padmé."

"I guess I'm your stepbrother," Owen said, his eyes never leaving the young Jedi of whom he had heard so very much. "I had a feeling you might show up."

"Is my mother here?"

"No, she's not," came a gruff answer from behind Owen and Beru, from the shadows of the house door. All four turned to see a heavyset man glide out on a hoverchair. One of his legs was heavily bandaged, the other, missing, and Anakin knew at once that these were fairly recent wounds. His heart seemed to leap into his throat.

"Cliegg Lars," the man said, moving in close and extending his hand. "Shmi is my wife. We should go inside. We have a lot to talk about."

Anakin followed as if in a dream, a very horrible dream.

"It was just before dawn," Cliegg was saying, gliding toward the table in the homestead kitchen with Owen beside him, while Beru peeled off to gather some food and drinks for the guests.

"They came out of nowhere," Owen added.

"A band of Tusken Raiders," Cliegg explained.

A sinking feeling nearly buckled Anakin's knees and he slumped into a seat across from Owen. He'd had some experience with Tusken Raiders, but on a very limited basis. Once he had tended the wound of one gravely injured Raider, and when the Tusken's friends showed up, they had let him go—something unheard of among the more civilized species of Tatooine. But still, despite that one anomaly, Anakin didn't like hearing the name of Shmi spoken in the same breath as the grim words, *Tusken Raiders.*

"Your mother had gone out early, like she always did, to pick mushrooms that grow on the vaporators," Cliegg explained. "From the tracks, she was about halfway home when they took her. Those Tuskens walk like men, but they're vicious, mindless monsters."

"We'd seen many signs that they were about," Owen piped in. "She shouldn't have gone out!"

"We can't live huddled in fear!" Cliegg scolded, but he calmed at once and turned back to Anakin. "All signs were that we'd chased the Tuskens away. We didn't know how strong this raiding band was—stronger than anything any of us have ever seen. Thirty of us went out after Shmi. Four of us came back."

He grimaced and rubbed his leg, and Anakin felt the man's pain clearly.

"I'd still be out there, only . . . after I lost my leg . . . " Cliegg nearly broke down, and it struck Anakin how much the man loved Shmi.

"I just can't ride anymore," Cliegg went on. "Until I heal."

The proud man drew in a deep breath and forcibly steadied himself, squaring his broad shoulders. "This isn't the way I wanted to meet you, son," he said. "This isn't how your mother and I planned it. I don't want to give up on her, but she's been gone a month. There's little hope she's lasted this long."

The words hit Anakin like a stinging slap, and he retreated from them, back into himself, back into the Force. He reached out, using his bond with his mother to try to somehow feel her presence in the Force.

Then he shot to his feet.

"Where are you going?" Owen asked.

"To find my mother," came the grim reply.

"No, Anakin!" Padmé cried out, rising to grab his forearm.

"Your mother's dead, Son," the resigned Cliegg added. "Accept it."

Anakin glowered at him, at them all. "I can feel her pain," he said, his jaw clenched, teeth gritted. "Continuing pain. And I will find her."

A moment of silence ensued, and then Owen offered, "Take my speeder bike." He jumped up from his seat and strode by Anakin.

"I know she's alive," Anakin said, turning to face Padmé. "I *know* it."

Padmé winced but said nothing, and she let go of Anakin's arm as he moved to follow Owen.

"I wish he'd have come a bit earlier," Cliegg lamented.

Padmé looked over at him, and at Beru, who was standing over the tearful man, hugging him.

Then, having no words to offer, Padmé turned and rushed out to join Anakin and Owen. By the time she caught up, Owen was heading back for the house and Anakin was standing near the speeder, staring out over the empty desert.

"You're going to have to stay here," Anakin said to her

as she hurried to his side. "These are good people. You'll be safe."

"Anakin . . ."

"I know she's alive," he said, still staring out at the dunes.

Padmé hugged him tightly. "Find her," she whispered.

"I won't be long," he promised. He straddled the speeder bike, kicked it to life, and rocketed away across the dunes.

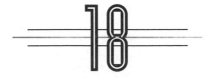

When the call beamed into the Jedi Temple on Coruscant, using scramble code 5 and in care of "the old folks home," Mace Windu and Yoda knew that it was important. Extremely important.

They took the call in Yoda's apartment, after Mace checked the corridor both ways, then pointedly closed the door.

The hologram of Obi-Wan Kenobi appeared before them. The man was obviously on edge, glancing repeatedly over his shoulder.

"Masters, I have successfully made contact with Lama Su, the Prime Minister of Kamino."

"Ah, good it is that your planet you have found," Yoda said.

"Right where your students predicted," Obi-Wan replied. "These Kaminoans are cloners—best in the galaxy I've been told, and from what I've seen, I don't doubt the claims."

Both Jedi Masters frowned.

"They are using a bounty hunter named Jango Fett to create a clone army."

"An army?" Mace repeated.

"For the Republic," came Obi-Wan's startling answer. "What's more, I have a strong feeling that this bounty hunter is behind the plot to assassinate Senator Amidala."

"Do you think these cloners are involved in that, as well?"

"No, Master, there appears to be no motive."

"Do not assume anything, Obi-Wan," Yoda advised. "Clear, your mind must be if you are to discover the real villain behind this plot."

"Yes, Master," Obi-Wan said. "Prime Minister Lama Su has informed me that the first battalion of clone troopers are ready for delivery. He also wanted me to remind you that if we require more—and they've another million well on the way to completion—it will take more time to grow them."

"A million clone warriors?" Mace Windu asked in disbelief.

"Yes, Master. They say Master Sifo-Dyas placed the order for the clone army almost ten years ago. I was under the impression he was killed before that. Did the Council ever authorize the creation of a clone army?"

"No," Mace answered without hesitation, and without even looking to Yoda for confirmation. "Whoever placed that order did not have the authorization of the Jedi Council."

"Then how? And why?"

"The mystery deepens," Mace said. "And it is one that needs unraveling, for more reasons than the safety of Senator Amidala."

"The clones are impressive, Master," Obi-Wan explained. "They have been created and trained for one purpose alone."

"Into custody, take this Jango Fett," Yoda instructed. "Bring him here. Question him, we will."

"Yes, Master. I will report back when I have him." Obi-Wan glanced over his shoulder again and abruptly instructed R4 to cut the transmission.

"A clone army," Mace remarked, alone with Yoda once again, the hologram gone. "Why would Sifo-Dyas—"

"When placed, this order was, may provide insight," Yoda said, and Mace nodded. If the timing of the order was correct, then Sifo-Dyas must have placed it right before he died.

"If this Jango Fett was involved in trying to kill the Senator, and just happened to be chosen as the source for a clone army, created for the Republic . . . " Mace Windu stopped and shook his head. The coincidence was too great for those two items to be simple chance. But how could one tie in with the other? Was it possible that whoever decided to create the clone army was afraid that Senator Amidala would be a strong enough voice to prevent that army from being used?

The Jedi Master rubbed a hand over his forehead and looked to Yoda, who sat with his eyes closed. Probably contemplating the same riddles as he was, Mace knew. And equally troubled, if not more so.

"Blind we are, if the development of this clone army we could not see," Yoda remarked.

"I think it is time to inform the Senate that our ability to use the Force has diminished."

"Only the Dark Lords of the Sith know of our weakness," Yoda replied. "If informed the Senate is, multiply our adversaries will."

For the two Jedi Masters, this surprising development was troubling on several different levels.

*　　*　　*

Obi-Wan moved along the corridor carefully. He knew nothing of Jango Fett's accomplishments, but he figured they must be considerable, given the selection of the man as the prototype for a clone army. Pausing, he closed his eyes and reached out to the Force, searching for hidden enemies. A moment later, convinced that Jango wasn't in the immediate area, he approached the door. Gently, he ran his fingers along the frame, sensing for potential traps, then finally touched the locking mechanism. Holding one hand there, he tried the door.

It didn't budge.

Obi-Wan reached for his lightsaber thinking to shear through the portal, but he changed his mind, preferring subtlety. He closed his eyes and sent his strength through his outstretched hand and into the lock, manipulating the mechanism easily. Then, one hand going to his lightsaber, he tried the door again, and it slid open.

As soon as he viewed the room inside, he knew that he wouldn't be needing his weapon. The apartment was in complete disorder. The drawers of every cabinet hung open, some lay on the floor, and the chairs were knocked all askew.

To the side, the bedroom door was open, and it, too, was a wreck. All the signs within pointed to a hurried departure.

Obi-Wan glanced all about, looking for some clue, and his gaze finally settled on a thin computer screen set on a counter in the main living area. Rushing to it, he turned it on and recognized it at once as a security network, tied in to various cams set about the immediate area. Obi-Wan scrolled from view to view, noting the corridor he had just traversed and various angles of the apartment itself. An outside view of the area showed the apartment's rain-lashed roof—and he could see himself through the transparisteel window.

He continued his scroll, widening the lens and zooming in on anything suspicious.

Then he got a shot of a nearby landing pad and an odd-looking ship with a wide, flat base, narrowed to a point on the closest end and thinning as it climbed to a small compartment, perhaps large enough for two or three men.

Rushing about the parked craft was a familiar figure, either Boba Fett or another clone.

Obi-Wan nodded and smiled knowingly as he followed the boy's movements, recognizing from the fluidity and randomness of some small actions that this was indeed Boba and not a perfectly controlled and conditioned clone.

Obi-Wan's grin didn't hold, though, as another familiar figure came into view. It was Jango, dressed in the armor and rocket pack the Jedi had seen before, on the streets of Coruscant. If Obi-Wan had had any doubts that Jango was the man who had hired Zam Wesell, those doubts were now gone. He bolted from the apartment and ran down the corridor, looking for a way out.

"Yeah, I'll let you fly it," Jango said to Boba.

Boba punched a fist into the air in triumph, thrilled that his father was going to let him get behind the controls of *Slave I*. It had been a long time, months, since Boba had been allowed to sit behind the controls.

"Not to take her out, through," Jango added, somewhat dimming the boy's jubilance. "We're going out hot, son, but we'll take her back out of lightspeed early so you can get some time working her about."

"Can I put her down?"

"We'll see."

Boba knew that his father really meant "no," but he didn't press the point. He understood that something big and dangerous was going on around him, and so he decided to take whatever his dad offered, and be happy with that. He hoisted another bag and climbed up the ramp to the small storage hold. He looked back at Jango as he did so, then looked past Jango, to a human form rushing out of the tower's turbolift and toward them through the driving rain.

"Dad! Look!"

As Jango swung about, Boba's eyes went wider still. The running figure was their Jedi visitor—and he was drawing his lightsaber and igniting a blue blade that hissed in the downpour.

"Get on board!" Jango called to him, but Boba hesitated, watching his father pull out his blaster and fire off a bolt at the charging Jedi. With amazing reflexes, Obi-Wan snapped his lightsaber about, deflecting the bolt harmlessly wide.

"Boba!" Jango yelled, and the boy came out of his trance and scrambled up the ramp and into *Slave I*.

Obi-Wan launched himself through the air at the bounty hunter. Another blaster shot followed, then another, and the Jedi easily picked them both off, deflecting one and turning the other back at Jango. But as the bolt ricocheted toward him, the bounty hunter leapt away, his rocket pack flaring to life, sending him up to the top of the nearby tower.

Obi-Wan tumbled headlong, turning while he rolled to come around as Jango fired again. Without even thinking of the movement, letting the Force guide his hand, the Jedi brought his lightsaber to the left and down, knocking the energy bolt aside.

"You're coming with me, Jango," he called.

The man answered with a series of shots, a line of bolts coming at the Jedi. The lightsaber went alternately left then right, picking off each one, and when Jango altered the pattern, left, right, left, right, then right again, the Force guided Obi-Wan's hand true.

"Jango!" he started to call out. But then he realized that the bounty hunter's latest shot was not a bolt but an explosive pack, and the next moment he was diving, enhancing his leap with the Force.

All of *Slave I* recoiled from the explosion outside, and the jolt sent Boba tumbling to the side. "Dad!" he cried. He scrambled to the viewscreen, flicking it on and orienting the cam on the scene below.

He saw his father immediately, and burst out in tears of relief. He calmed himself quickly, though, scanning the area for the enemy Jedi, and saw Obi-Wan coming over from a roll, back to his feet—and blocking another series of bolts with seeming ease.

Boba scanned the panel, trying to remember all his lessons about *Slave I*, glad that he had been so diligent in his studies. With a wicked grin that would have made his father proud, Boba fired up the energy packs and clicked off the locking mechanism of the main laser.

"Block this, Jedi," he whispered. He took a bead on Obi-Wan and pulled the trigger.

"You have a lot to answer!" Obi-Wan called to Jango, his voice sounding thin in the thunderous downpour and lashing wind. "It'll go easier on you, and on your son, if—"

He stopped suddenly, registering the report of a heavy laser somewhere in his subconscious. The Force had him moving instinctively before he even understood what was happening, leaping and flying across the air in a double somersault.

He landed to find the ground shaking violently under his feet, quaking from the thunder of *Slave I*'s heavy laser cannon, which swung around to follow him.

Obi-Wan had to dive again, but this time the bouncing report sent him sprawling to the ground, his lightsaber skidding from his grasp across the rain-slickened surface.

Fortunately, *Slave I*'s cannon went quiet, the energy pack depleted for the moment, and Obi-Wan wasted no time leaping to his feet and charging at Jango Fett, who was coming hard his way.

A blaster bolt led the bounty hunter in, but Obi-Wan leapt above the streaking line of energy, flying forward and spinning around to snap-kick the weapon from Jango's hand.

The bounty hunter didn't flinch. He charged right into the Jedi as Obi-Wan landed, looping his arms over Obi-Wan's and bearing him backward.

He tried to wrestle Obi-Wan to the ground, but the Jedi's feet were too quick for that, setting him in perfect balance almost immediately. He slid one leg between the bounty hunter's feet and started to twist to the side, weakening Jango's hold on his arms.

Jango smiled wickedly and snapped his forehead into Obi-Wan's face, dazing him for a moment. The bounty hunter pulled a hand free and launched a heavy punch, but realized his mistake immediately as the Jedi ducked the blow and did a tight, stationary somersault right under the swinging arm, double-kicking out as he came over, his feet slamming Jango in the chest and throwing him backward.

Now Obi-Wan had gained the initiative and he used it with a fierce charge, slamming into the stumbling bounty hunter, thinking to bring him down to the ground beneath him, where the encumbering armor the man wore would work against him.

But Jango showed the Jedi why he had been chosen as the basis for the clones. He went with the flow of the tackle for a moment, then suddenly reversed his footing and his momentum, stopping Obi-Wan's progress cold.

Jango launched a left hook. Obi-Wan ducked and snapped out a straight right in response. Jango slipped his head to the side so that the blow barely grazed him. A short rocket burst had him in the air and spinning a circle kick out at Obi-Wan, who dropped to his knees and ducked it, then came up high in a leap, over the second kick as Jango came around again.

Now Obi-Wan snapped off a kick of his own, but Jango accepted the blow against his lowered hip and snapped his left arm down across the Jedi's shin, locking the leg long enough for him to drive a right cross into Obi-Wan's inner thigh.

The Jedi threw his head and torso back, lying flat out and lifting his left leg as he did, kicking Jango under the side of his ribs. A sudden scissor-twist, right leg going down and across, left leg shooting across the other way above it, had Jango and Obi-Wan spinning sidelong. Obi-Wan caught himself with extended arms as he turned facedown, broke his feet from their hold on Jango, and mule-kicked the falling man backward. Then, going down to the platform to launch himself right back up to his feet, he turned about and rushed forward, gaining an advantage on the off-balance and struggling Jango.

A right cross smashed the bounty hunter across the face, followed by a looping left hook that should have laid the man low. But again, with brilliant reflexes, Jango ducked the brunt of that blow and caught the surprised Obi-Wan with a sudden and short, but heavy, left and right in the gut.

The Jedi's right hand waved across between his face and Jango's, and he used a quick Force shove to throw the man back a step until he could straighten and find a defensive posture once more.

Jango came right back in, fiercely, wildly, kicking and punching with abandon.

Obi-Wan's hands worked vertically before him, hardly moving, amazingly precise, turning blow after blow harmlessly aside. He turned one hand in and down suddenly, taking the momentum from a heavy kick, then came right back up to lift Jango's jabbing fist up high. Then he snapped his hand straight out, his stiffened fingers smashing against a seam in the bounty hunter's armor. Jango winced and fell back. Obi-Wan launched himself forward, diving onto the man, going for the victory.

But Jango had an answer, firing his rockets and lifting both himself and the grappling Jedi up into the air. A burst of a side-thruster sent the pair out past the landing pad proper to the sloping skirt of the structure.

Jango's hands worked almost imperceptibly, twisting in and about the Jedi's arms and hands, expertly loosening Obi-Wan's grip. Then he fired his thrusters, left and right, causing a sudden and repeated jerk that broke him free of Obi-Wan's grasp.

Obi-Wan hit the deck hard and slid perilously close to the edge—close enough to hear the great waves breaking against the platform's stilts below him. He caught a hold and reached into the Force, using it to grab his lightsaber, recognizing that he was suddenly vulnerable.

He heard a shot from the side, not the screech of a blaster bolt, but a *pfizzt* sound, and rolled as far as he could.

But not far enough. He lost his concentration, along with his grasp on his lightsaber, as a thin wire slid under his wrists, then wrapped about them, securing him tightly.

And then he was sliding, back up the sloping skirt and across the platform, towed by the rocket-man. With reflexes honed by years of intensive training, and with the Force-strength of a Jedi Master, Obi-Wan snap-rolled his body forward, back up over his outstretched arms, tumbling to his feet, then leaping out to the side as the towline again went taut, jerking him along. He rolled about a pylon and came back to his feet again, now having the leverage of the metal pole helping to hold him there.

Reaching deeply in the Force once more, he grounded himself, becoming, for an instant, almost as one with the platform.

Immovable.

The wire snapped tightly, but Obi-Wan didn't budge.

He felt the angle of the pull change dramatically as the rocket-man plunged to the deck, his pack breaking away.

Obi-Wan started around the pole, but stopped and shielded his eyes as Jango Fett's rocket pack exploded with a burst of light and a tremendous concussion.

"Dad!" Boba Fett cried as the rocket pack blew apart, his face coming right to the viewscreen. But then he saw Jango, off to the side and apparently unharmed, though tugging frantically against the pull of the wire—that was now being controlled by the Jedi.

Boba slapped one hand helplessly against the screen, mouthing "Dad" again, and then he winced as the Jedi slammed into his father, kicking and butting him, and both of them, locked together, went rolling off the back edge of the landing pad, sliding fast down the skirt and toward the raging ocean.

Obi-Wan kicked and tried to find his way back to the Force, but Jango punched him repeatedly. He could hardly believe that the bounty hunter would waste the effort, with certain death awaiting them both at the end of the slide and fall. He managed to pull back somewhat and saw Jango lift one forearm, a strange smile on his face. The bounty hunter clenched his fist, and a line of claws popped forth from the armor.

Obi-Wan instinctively recoiled as Jango lifted that arm higher, but then the bounty hunter slammed it down, not on Obi-Wan, but on the platform skirt. At the same time, Jango worked his other hand, releasing the locking mechanism of the wire-launching bracelet, and it slid free of his arm.

He screeched to a halt, and Obi-Wan slid past him.

"Catch a rollerfish for me," the Jedi heard Jango say, and then he was falling, over the lip and down toward the raging whitecaps.

"Dad! Oh, Dad!" Boba Fett cried in relief as he spotted his father clambering back over the skirt lip and onto the platform. Jango climbed to his feet and stumbled toward *Slave I*, and Boba rushed to the hatch, sliding it open and reaching down to help his father aboard.

"Get us out of here," the dazed and battered Jango said, and Boba grinned and rushed to the control panel, firing up the engines.

"I'll put her right to lightspeed!"

"Just break atmosphere and take her straight out!" Jango ordered, and his words came out with a growl of pain as he held his bruised side. Then he noticed his son's wounded look. "Get the nav computer on line and have it set the coordinates for the jump," he conceded.

Boba's smile beamed brighter than ever. "Liftoff!" he shouted.

Obi-Wan used the Force to grab the trailing, loose end of the wire that still held him by the wrists, and he threw that end out, looping it over a crossbeam in the platform structure. His descent stopped with a sudden jerk.

He glanced around, then began to swing, back and forth, gaining momentum until he was far enough out to pull himself free of the bond and drop lightly onto a small service platform, barely above the lashing waves.

He took only a moment to catch his breath, and then opened the door of the service turbolift with a wave of his hand. Even before the door opened at the landing platform, he heard the engines of the bounty hunter's ship roar to life.

He came over the lip, spotting his lightsaber immediately and calling it in to him with the Force.

But he was too late. The ship was already shuddering, ready to blast away.

Obi-Wan pulled a small transmitter from his belt and threw it out long and far at *Slave I*. The magnetic lock of the tracking device grasped on to the ship's hull just in time.

Rain and steam pouring all about him, Obi-Wan Kenobi stood there for a long while until *Slave I* disappeared from view.

He looked around at the platform, replaying the battle in his head, his respect for this bounty hunter, Jango Fett, growing considerably. He understood now why Jango had been selected by Sifo-Dyas, or Tyranus, or whoever it was that selected him. The man was good, full of tricks and full of skill.

He had taken Obi-Wan Kenobi, a Jedi Knight, the man who had defeated the Sith Lord Darth Maul, to the very precipice of disaster.

But Obi-Wan was still pleased at the way it had played out. He would track Jango now. Perhaps at the end of the coming journey, he would finally get some answers instead of even more riddles.

Boba sat quietly, sensing the tension, as *Slave I* blasted away from Kamino. He wanted to talk about his shot with the laser cannon, about how he had knocked the Jedi down and sent his lightsaber flying away. But this wasn't the time, he knew, for Jango wore an intense expression that Boba recognized all too well, one that told him clearly that now was not the time for him to speak.

The boy rested back against the wall farthest from his father as Jango worked the controls, setting the coordinates for the jump to hyperspace. "Come on, come on," Jango said repeatedly, rocking back and forth as if urging the ship on, and glancing over at the sensors every few seconds as if he expected a fleet of starships to be chasing them away.

Then he gave a shout of victory and punched the hyperdrive, and Boba went back against the wall, watching the stars elongate.

Jango Fett slumped back in his seat and breathed a sigh of

relief, his expression softening almost immediately. "Well, that was a bit too close," he said with a laugh.

"You smashed him good," Boba replied, his excitement beginning to bubble up again. "He never had a chance against you, Dad!"

Jango smiled and nodded. "To tell the truth, Son, he had me in real trouble there," he admitted. "After he dodged that explosive pack, I'd about run out of tricks."

Boba frowned at first, wanting to argue against anyone ever getting the upper hand on his father, but then, as he considered the moment Jango had mentioned, his frown became a wide smile. "I got him good with the laser cannon!"

"You did great," Jango replied. "You fired at just the right time, and were right there, ready to help me in when it was time for us to go. You're learning well, Boba. Better than I ever believed possible."

"That's because I'm a little you," the boy reasoned, but Jango was shaking his head.

"You're better than I was at your age, and by a long way. And if you keep working hard, you'll be the best bounty hunter this galaxy's ever seen."

"Which was your plan from the beginning with the Kaminoans, right, Dad? That's why you wanted me!"

Jango Fett moved over and lifted one hand to tousle Boba's hair. "That and a lot of other reasons," he said quietly, reverently. "And in every regard, in every hope and dream, you've done better than I ever expected."

There was nothing that anyone in all the galaxy could ever have said to young Boba Fett to make him feel better than those words from his father.

Jango took *Slave I* out of hyperspace a bit early, so that Boba could have some time piloting the ship on the approach to Geonosis. For Boba, sitting in the chair beside his father, working the controls deftly, even showing off a bit, there could be no greater moment, and the boy was saddened by the sight of the red planet, Geonosis, and the asteroid belts that ringed it.

"Security's tight here," Jango explained, taking the helm. "It'll be better if I put her down."

Boba sat back in the chair without complaint. He knew his father was right, and even if he had disagreed, he wouldn't have done so openly.

He turned his attention to the scan screens, showing the composition of the asteroid field nearby, and some distant traffic around the other side of the planet.

He noted one blip in particular, disengaging from the asteroid belt and moving out behind *Slave I*. He didn't think too much of it at first, until a second blip appeared, right behind *Slave I*, though nothing substantial enough to be a separate ship.

"Nearly there, Son," Jango remarked.

"Dad, I think we're being tracked," Boba told him. "Look at the scan screen. Isn't that a cloaking shadow of our own ship?"

Jango looked at him doubtfully, then turned that skeptical expression upon the scan screen. Boba watched with mounting excitement as his father's gaze turned intense and he slowly began to nod.

"That Jedi must have put a tracking device on our hull before we left Kamino," he agreed. "But how? I thought he was dead."

"Someone's following us," Boba observed.

"We'll fix that," Jango assured him. "Hang on, son! Watch

me put us into that asteroid field—he won't be able to follow us there." He looked over at Boba and winked. "And if he does, we'll leave him a couple of surprises."

Jango opened a side panel and pulled a lever, releasing an electric charge along his hull that was designed to destroy just such tracking devices. A quick look at the scan screen showed that the cloaking shadow had disappeared.

"Here we go," Jango said, and he dived *Slave I* into the asteroid field, pulling a fast circuit over and around a nearby rock, then diving out fast to the side, rolling about a spinning boulder, and cutting fast between another pair. In and around he wove, with no apparent pattern, and a few moments later, Boba, who was still studying the scanner, announced, "He's gone."

"Maybe he's smarter than I thought and headed on toward the planet surface," Jango said with a grin and another wink.

Even as he finished, though, the scanner beeped.

"Look, Dad!" Boba cried, pointing out the blip, now inside the asteroid field, as well. "He's back!"

"Hang on!" Jango said, and he put *Slave I* through a wild series of dips, climbs, and turns, then finished with a straight-out run, while uncapping a firing trigger and squeezing the plunger. "Seismic charge," he explained to Boba, who grinned.

But then the boy was screaming a warning as the forward viewscreen filled up with an asteroid.

Jango was already on it, turning the amazingly maneuverable *Slave I* up on its end and running up over the giant space rock.

"Stay calm, son," he assured Boba. "We'll be fine. That Jedi won't be able to follow us through this."

IIis declaration was accentuated by a sudden flash and a jarring buck as the sonic charge detonated far behind them.

"He got through it!" Boba cried a moment later, seeing the Jedi's ship reappear on the scan screen.

"This guy can't take a hint," said Jango, who remained unrattled. "Well, if we can't lose him, we'll have to finish him."

Boba cried out again, but his father was in complete control. He put the ship down a narrow tunnel creasing one of the larger asteroids. He had to slow a bit to maneuver, and when *Slave I* came out the other end, Jango and Boba saw the Jedi starfighter stream over and past them. The hunted had suddenly become the hunters.

"Get him, Dad!" Boba cried out. "Get him! Fire!"

Laser bolts burst out of *Slave I*, tracing lines all about the starfighter, which cut a snap-roll to the right and down.

Jango stayed with him, trying to line up another shot, but the Jedi was good, snap-rolling one after another, each time coming out near an asteroid and sliding behind it for cover.

Boba continued to urge his father on, but Jango kept his patience, figuring that sooner or later, the Jedi was going to run out of hiding places.

A fast dive, then a sudden turn back up, then a sudden roll and bank to the right had the Jedi moving behind yet another asteroid, but this time, instead of following, Jango cut in short of the rock and fired blindly past it.

Out came the Jedi's starfighter, right into the line of fire, and the ship bucked, pieces flying, as a laser bolt clipped it.

"You got him!" Boba yelled in victory.

"And now we just have to finish him," the ever-cool Jango explained. "There'll be no more dodging." He pushed a series of buttons, arming a torpedo and sliding open the tube, then moved to punch the red trigger. He paused, though, and smiled, and nodded for Boba to move closer.

Boba could hardly breathe as his father slid his hand onto the smooth trigger grip, then looked down at him and nodded.

The boy punched the trigger and *Slave I* jolted as the torpedo slid away, diving at the Jedi starfighter and taking up the chase as the starfighter bolted and tried to evade.

A few brief moments later, *Slave I*'s viewscreen lit up in the light of a tremendous explosion, forcing Boba and Jango to shield their eyes with their arms. When they recovered and looked back, they were greeted by pieces of wreckage and torn chunks of metal. The scan screen was clear.

"Got him!" Boba shouted. "Yeahhhh!"

"Nice shot, kid," Jango said, and he tousled Boba's hair again. "You earned that one. We won't see him again."

A few deft turns had *Slave I* out of the asteroids and speeding down toward Geonosis, and despite his earlier reasoning, Jango Fett allowed Boba to guide the craft down. Truly, this was no flight for a boy to pilot, but Boba Fett was so far above any ordinary boy.

Anakin traveled through great canyons of multicolored stone, across dunes of blowing and shifting sand, and along an ancient, long-dry riverbed. His only guide was the sensation of Shmi, of her pain. But it was not a definitive homing beacon, and though he suspected he was moving in the general direction, the landscape of Tatooine was vast and empty, and none knew how to hide among the sand and stones better than the Tusken Raiders.

On a high bluff, Anakin paused and scanned the horizon.

Off to the south, he noted a huge vehicle, resembling a gigantic tilting box, plodding along on a single huge track. Nodding with recognition of the Jawas, and well aware that no one knew the movements of all creatures among the desert better than they, he kicked his speeder bike away.

He caught up to them soon after, riding into a group of the brown- and black-robed creatures, their inquisitive red eyes poking out at him from the shadows of huge cowls, their ceaseless chatter humming like strange music all about him.

It took him a long time to convince the Jawas that he wasn't interested in purchasing any droids, and a longer time to get them to understand that he was merely looking for information about any Tusken Raiders.

The Jawas talked excitedly among themselves, pointing this way and that, hopping all about. Jawas were no friends of Tuskens, who preyed on them as they preyed on anyone else they found vulnerable. Even worse to the Jawa salesman mentality, Tuskens never purchased any droids!

The group eventually came to agreement, and pointed as one to the east. With a nod, Anakin sped away. The lack of monetary compensation seemed to aggravate the Jawas, but Anakin had no time to care.

The asteroids rolled along their silent way, undisturbed, seemingly unshaken from the explosions and zigzagging vessels.

In a deep depression on the back side of one such rock huddled a small starfighter, its definitive outline and consistent colors showing stark contrast to the rough-edged and bleeding, broken mineral streaks of the asteroid.

"Blast. This is why I hate flying," Obi-Wan said to R4, and

the droid's responding beeps showed that he was in complete agreement. Few things could rattle the Jedi Knight, but engaging in a space battle with a pilot as obviously skilled as Jango Fett was surely one of them. Unlike many of his Jedi associates, Obi-Wan Kenobi had never much enjoyed space travel, let alone piloting.

He winced as his asteroid came over and around, showing him again a glowing piece of torn metal that had taken up orbit within the belt. His ship was wounded from the laser blast—nothing substantial, just a thruster-angler—and he had understood that he could not hope to outmaneuver the clever torpedo. So he had ordered R4 to eject all the spare parts canisters, and fortunately, that had been enough to detonate the missile. Despite the success, between the shock of that blast and landing hard and fast on the asteroid to complete the ruse, Obi-Wan was relieved to see that his ship had remained intact.

He wanted no further space fights with Jango and his strange, and supremely efficient, ship, though, and so he had sat here as the minutes slipped past.

"Have you got their last trajectory logged?" he asked the droid, then nodded as R4 assured him that he did. "Well, I think we've waited long enough. Let's go." Obi-Wan paused for a moment, trying to digest all the amazing things he had seen on the trail of Jango Fett. "This mystery gets more wound up all the time, Arfour. Think maybe we'll finally get some answers?"

R4 gave a sound that Obi-Wan could only think of as a verbal shrug.

Following the path taken by *Slave I*, Obi-Wan was not surprised that it led straight for the red planet, Geonosis. What did surprise him, though, was that they were not alone up there. A series of beeps and whistles from R4 alerted him, and Obi-Wan adjusted his scan screen accordingly, locking on to a huge fleet of vessels, settled on the other side of the asteroid belt.

"Trade Federation ships," he mused aloud as he angled to get a better view. "So many?" He shook his head in confusion, noting several of the great battleships among the group; their unique design made them hard to miss—a sphere surrounded by a nearly enclosed ring. If the clone army was for the Republic, commissioned by a Jedi Master, and Jango Fett was the basis for the clones, then what ties would Jango have to the Trade Federation? And if Jango was indeed behind the assassination attempts on Senator Amidala, the leading voice of opposition to creating a Republic army, then why would the Trade Federation approve?

It occurred to Obi-Wan that he might have misjudged Jango, or misjudged his motivations, at least. Maybe Jango, like Obi-Wan and Anakin, had been chasing the bounty hunter who had tried to kill Amidala. Maybe the toxic dart had been fired not to silence the would-be assassin, but as punishment for the attempt on Amidala's life.

The Jedi couldn't convince himself of that, though. He still believed that Jango was the man behind the assassination attempt, and that he had killed the changeling so that she could not give him up. But why the clone army? And why the Trade Federation ties? There was no apparent logic to it.

He knew that he would get no answers up here, so he took his ship down toward Geonosis, keeping the asteroid belt between him and the Trade Federation fleet.

He went down low as soon as he broke Geonosis' atmosphere, ducking below any tracking systems that might be in place, skimming the red plains and broken stones, weaving around the buttes and mesas. The whole of the planet seemed a barren and arid red plain, but his scanners did pick up some activity in the distance. Obi-Wan skimmed that way, climbing one mesa and running low to its far end. He slid his ship under a rocky overhang and put her down, then climbed out and walked to the mesa edge.

The night air had a curious metallic taste to it, and the temperature was comfortable. A strong breeze blew in Obi-Wan's face, carrying that metallic taste and odor, and the occasional strange cry.

"I'll be back, Arfour."

The droid gave a long *"ooooo."*

"You'll be fine," Obi-Wan assured him. "And I won't be long." Glad to be back on the ground once again, Obi-Wan checked his bearings, measured against the area where he had noted the activity, and started off, moving along a rocky trail.

The hours were unbearable for Padmé. Owen and Beru were friendly enough, and Cliegg was obviously glad for the added company in his time of great concern and profound grief, but she could hardly speak to them, so worried was she for Anakin. She had never seen him in a mood like the one that had taken him from the moisture farm, his determination so palpable, so consuming, that it seemed almost destructive. She had felt Anakin's power in that parting, an inner strength beyond anything she had ever known.

If his mother was indeed alive, and she believed that Shmi was, since Anakin had said so, Padmé knew that no army would be strong enough to keep the young Jedi from her.

She didn't sleep that night, rising often from her bed and

pacing all about the compound. She wandered into the garage area, alone with her thoughts—or so she believed.

"Hello, Miss Padmé," came a chipper voice, and as soon as Padmé got over the initial shock, she recognized the speaker.

"You can't sleep?" C-3PO asked.

"No, I have too many things on my mind, I guess."

"Are you worried about your work in the Senate?"

"No, I'm just concerned about Anakin. I said things . . . I'm afraid I might have hurt him. I don't know. Maybe I only hurt myself. For the first time in my life, I'm confused."

"I'm not sure it will make you feel any better, Miss Padmé, but I don't think there's been a time in my life when I haven't been confused."

"I want him to know that I care about him, Threepio," Padmé said quietly. "I do care about him. And now he's out there, and in danger—"

"Don't worry about Master Annie," the droid assured her, moving over to pat her shoulder. "He can take care of himself. Even in this awful place."

"Awful?" Padmé asked. "You're not happy here?"

C-3PO stepped back and held his hands out wide, showing his battered coverings and the chipped insulation in those areas where some of his wiring showed. Padmé moved forward, bending to see, and noticed sand clinging in many of the droid's joints.

"Well, this is a very harsh environment, I'm afraid," the droid explained. "And when Master Annie made me, he never quite found the time to give me any outer coverings. Mistress Shmi did well in finishing me, but even with the coverings, the wind and the sand are quite harsh. It gets in under my coverings, and it's quite . . . itchy."

"Itchy?" Padmé echoed with a laugh—a much-needed laugh.

"I do not know how else to describe it, Miss Padmé. And I fear that the sand is doing damage to my wiring."

Padmé looked all around, her gaze settling on a chain hoist over an open tub of dark liquid. "You need an oil bath," she said.

"Oh, I would welcome a bath!"

Glad for the distraction, Padmé moved to the oil tub and began sorting out the hoist chain. In a short while she had C-3PO secured and everything in place, and she gently lowered the droid into the oil.

"Oooh!" the droid cried. "That tickles!"

"Tickles? You're sure it's not an itch?"

"I do know the difference between a tickle and an itch," C-3PO answered. Padmé giggled and forgot, for a while, all of her troubles.

As soon as he came upon the grisly scene, Anakin knew that it was the work of Tuskens. Three farmers, likely some of those whom Cliegg had been with before being forced to return home, lay dead about a campfire, their bodies battered and torn. A pair of eopies, long-legged dromedaries with big padded feet and equine faces that showed little intelligence, stood tethered nearby, lowing mournfully, and beyond them hung the smoking remains of a speeder.

Anakin ran his fingers through his short hair. "Calm down," he told himself. "Find her." He fell within himself then, within the Force, and sent his senses out far and wide, needing the confirmation that his mother had not yet met a similar fate.

A stab of pain assaulted him, and a cry that was both hopeful and helpless entered his mind.

"Mom," he mouthed breathlessly, and he knew that time was running out, that Shmi was in terrible pain and was barely holding on.

He didn't have the time to bury the poor farmers, but he did resolve to come back for them. He jumped astride the speeder bike and put it flat out, rushing across the dark desert landscape, following Shmi's call.

The trail was narrow and steep, but at least Obi-Wan was back on solid footing.

Or almost solid, he realized, as a shrill shrick split the air, startling him. His foot slipped. He nearly tumbled but caught his balance, as a bunch of stones fell loose, bouncing down the side of the mesa.

The Jedi drew out his lightsaber but did not ignite it. He moved along cautiously, down and around a bend in the rocky path.

He saw the large, lizardlike creature coming for him, its huge fangs dripping lines of drool. It stood on strong hind legs, its little forelegs twitching eagerly. The lightsaber hummed to life and Obi-Wan dived down to the side, slashing back as he fell, opening the creature's side from foreleg to hind. The creature landed and tried to turn, but as it spasmed in pain, it over-balanced and fell off the trail, plummeting hundreds of feet and shrieking all the way.

Obi-Wan had no time to watch the descent, though, for another of the beasts appeared, coming at him fast, its toothy maw open wide.

The Jedi filled that maw with lightsaber, shearing through teeth and gums, driving the blade right through the back of the creature's head. He pulled hard to the side, the energy blade tearing right through the beast's skull, and turned to face yet another leaping beast. Falling back and down, he let the lizard fly past, then he came up immediately and started to pursue. But abruptly he stopped, reversed his grip, and stabbed out behind him, impaling a fourth creature. He spun about, flipping the weapon from his right hand to his left, then slashed it out the side of the dying beast as he completed his circuit, coming right around to face the one that had leapt past.

The creature circled slowly, seemingly sizing him up, and Obi-Wan turned with it, but kept his eyes and ears scanning the area.

He tried to scare the creature off, and with two of its companions lying dead on the rocks and a third having gone over the cliff, he fully expected it to flee.

But not this fierce beast. It charged suddenly, jaws snapping.

A sidestep, forward step, and overhand slash had the creature's head rolling free on the ground.

"Fun place," the Jedi remarked after a while, when he was confident that no more of the creatures were about. He put his weapon away and moved along, and soon after rounded the corner of the mesa.

A great plain spread out wide before him with many tall shapes in the far distance, indistinguishable in the darkness. Obi-Wan took out his electrobinoculars and peered across the plain. He saw a cluster of great towers—not natural stalagmites like those he had seen dotting the landscape, but shaped structures. A roll of his finger increased the magnification, of both size and available light, and he scanned slowly to the side.

Trade Federation starships, scores of them, lined the region, settled on platforms. The Jedi watched in amazement as another platform rose beside one ship and thousands of Battle Droids stepped off it and into the vessel, which then lifted away.

And was quickly replaced by another starship, settling down on the platform.

Another platform rose to the side, and again, thousands of droids stepped off to board the waiting starship, and that one, now filled with droid soldiers, lifted away.

"Unbelievable," the Jedi muttered and he looked to the eastern horizon, trying to gauge the amount of time he had before dawn, wondering if he could make the run before the light found him.

Not if he had to slowly work his way down the mesa, he realized, and so he shrugged and stepped ahead, closing his eyes and finding his power in the Force. Then he leapt out, lifting himself with the Force to ease his descent. He hit a bluff many feet down, but sprang away and fell again, and again, half bouncing, half flying his way down to the dark plain.

The sun was still below the eastern rim, though the land was beginning to lighten around him, when he reached the grandest tower of the complex. The entryway was heavily guarded by battle droids, but Obi-Wan had no intention of going anywhere near that area. Using the Force and his own conditioning, the Jedi scaled the tower, until he came to a small window.

He slipped in silently and moved from shadow to shadow, then ducked behind a wind curtain as he heard the approach of a pair of strange-looking creatures—Geonosians, he supposed. They wore little clothing, and their skin was reddish, like the air about them, with flaps hanging in rolls in many places about their slender frames. Leathery wings showed behind their bony shoulders. Their heads were large and elongated, their skulls ridged top and side, and they had thick-lidded, bulbous eyes. Their expressions seemed to be locked in a perpetual scowl.

"Too many sentients," he heard one of them say.

"It is not your place to question Archduke Poggle the Lesser," the other scolded, and grumbling, the pair wandered away.

Obi-Wan moved out behind them, going the opposite way. He slipped from shadow to shadow along a narrow corridor lined with pillars. He couldn't help but see the contrast between this place and Tipoca City. Where Tipoca City was a work of art, all rounded and smooth, all glass and light, this place was rough-edged, all sharp corners and utilitarian features.

The Jedi moved along, coming to an open vent, sharp noises and pounding echoing up from it. He dropped to the ground and looked all about, then crawled and peered over the edge.

A factory, a huge alignment of conveyor belts and pounding machines, lay below, in a wide-open area. Obi-Wan watched in blank amazement as many, many Geonosians—these without wings like the pair that had walked past him—worked at various stations assembling droids. At the far end of the conveyor, completed droids stepped off under their own power, walking away down a distant corridor.

To platforms that would lift them to waiting Trade Federation starships, the Jedi realized.

With a shake of his head, Obi-Wan ran along, and then he sensed something, fleeting but definite. He followed his instincts along the maze of corridors, at last coming to a vast underground chamber, with huge vaulted ceilings and rough-styled arches. He started across, moving pillar to pillar, sensing that something or someone was near.

He heard their voices before he saw them, and he fell flat against the stone.

A group of six figures walked past him, four in front and two behind. Two Geonosians were in that front row, along with a Neimoidian viceroy whom Obi-Wan knew all too well and a man whose features were also recognizable from busts the Jedi had seen in the Temple on Coruscant.

"Now we must persuade the Commerce Guild and the Corporate Alliance to sign the treaty," that former Jedi, Count Dooku, was saying. The man was tall and regal, with perfect posture and a graceful gait. His hair was silver and perfectly trimmed and his elegant features, strong jaw, and piercing eyes completed the look of a man who had once been among the greatest of the Jedi. He wore a black cape, clipped at his neck by a silver chain, and a black shirt and pants of the finest materials. In looking at him, in feeling his presence, Obi-Wan understood that nothing less would ever suit this one.

"What about the Senator from Naboo?" asked the Neimoidian, Nute Gunray, his beady eyes and thin features seeming smaller still beneath the tripronged headdress he always wore. "Is she dead yet? I'm not signing your treaty until I have her head on my desk."

Obi-Wan nodded, huge pieces of the puzzle starting to fall into place. It made sense to him that Nute Gunray would want Amidala dead, even if her voice of opposition to an army of the Republic was working in his favor. Amidala had embarrassed the Neimoidian badly in the Battle of Naboo, after all.

"I am a man of my word, Viceroy," one of the separatists answered.

"With these new battle droids we've built for you, Viceroy,

you'll have the finest army in the galaxy," said the Geonosian whom Obi-Wan believed to be Poggle the Lesser. He didn't look much like the winged commoners and workers Obi-Wan had seen. His skin was lighter, more a grayish tan than red-tinted, and his head was huge, his large scowling mouth protruding just a bit, giving him a fierce appearance; an elongated chin that seemed more a long beard hung halfway down his torso.

They continued their banter, but had moved out of earshot by then, and Obi-Wan didn't dare step out to follow. They moved across the way, through an archway and up a flight of stairs.

After a short pause to make sure they were well along, Obi-Wan rushed out, peeking through to the stairs, then crept up them, coming to a narrow archway overlooking a smaller room. Inside, he saw the six who had passed, along with several others, notably three opposition Senators the Jedi recognized. First came Po Nudo of Ando, an Aqualish who looked as if he was wearing a helmet with great goggles, but was not, of course. Beside him sat neckless Toonebuck Toora of Sy Myrth, with her rodentlike head and wide mouth, and the Quarren Senator Tessek, his face tentacles waggling anxiously. Obi-Wan had met this trio before, back on Coruscant.

Yes, he realized, it seemed he had walked into the center of the hive.

"You have met Shu Mai?" Count Dooku, seated at the head of the table, asked the three Senators. "Representing the Commerce Guild." Across the way, Shu Mai nodded deferentially. Her delicate and gray, wrinkled head was set on a long neck and her most striking feature, aside from long and pointy horizontal ears, was a hairstyle that looked much like a skin-covered horn, protruding out the back of her skull, rising up and curving forward.

"And this is San Hill, distinguished member of the Inter-Galactic Banking Clan," Dooku went on, indicating a creature with the longest and narrowest face Obi-Wan had ever seen.

Those gathered about the table murmured their greetings, nodded to each other, for many moments, and then they went silent, all eyes settling on Count Dooku, who seemed to Obi-Wan in complete control here, even above the Archduke of the planet.

"As I explained to you earlier, I'm quite convinced that ten thousand more systems will rally to our cause with your support," the Count said. "And let me remind you of our absolute commitment to capitalism . . . to the lower taxes, the reduced tariffs, and the eventual abolition of all trade barriers. Signing this treaty will bring you profits beyond your wildest imagination. What we are proposing is complete free trade." He looked to Nute Gunray, who nodded.

"Our friends in the Trade Federation have pledged their support," Count Dooku went on. "When their battle droids are combined with yours, we shall have an army greater than anything in the galaxy. The Republic will be overwhelmed."

"If I may, Count," said one of the others, one of the two who had trailed Dooku to the room.

"Yes, Passel Argente," Count Dooku said. "We are always interested in hearing from the Corporate Alliance."

The huddled and nervous man offered a slight bow to Dooku. "I am authorized by the Corporate Alliance to sign the treaty."

"We are most grateful for your cooperation, Magistrate," Dooku said.

Obi-Wan recognized that exchange for what it was, a play for the benefit of the other, less enthusiastic, people at the table. Count Dooku was trying to build some momentum.

That momentum hit a bit of a bump a moment later, though, when Shu Mai piped in. "The Commerce Guild at this time does not wish to become openly involved." However, she smoothed it over immediately. "But we shall support you in secret, and look forward to doing business with you."

Several chuckles erupted about the table, and Count Dooku only smiled. "That is all we ask," he assured Shu Mai. Then he looked to the distinguished member of the Banking Clan, and all the other gazes settled on San Hill, as well.

"The InterGalactic Banking Clan will support you wholeheartedly, Count Dooku," San Hill declared. "But only in a nonexclusive arrangement."

Obi-Wan settled back, trying to sort out the implications of it all. Count Dooku had it all falling together here, a threat beyond anything the Republic had expected. With the money of the bankers and the commercial and trade guilds behind him, and this factory—and likely many others like it—churning out armies of battle droids, the potential danger was staggering.

Was that why Sifo-Dyas had commissioned the clone army? Had the Master sensed this growing danger, perhaps? But if that was true, then what was the tie between Jango Fett and this group on Geonosis? Was it mere coincidence that the man chosen as source for the clone army to defend the Republic had been hired by the Trade Federation to kill Senator Amidala?

It seemed too much a coincidence to Obi-Wan, but he had little else to go on. He wanted to hang around and listen in some more, but he knew then that he had to get out of there, had to return to his ship and R4, and get a warning out across the galaxy to the Jedi Council.

Over the last hours, Obi-Wan had seen nothing but armies, clone and droid, and he knew that it would all be coming together very quickly in an explosion beyond anything the galaxy had seen in many, many centuries.

She wasn't seeing much with her eyes. Caked with blood and swollen from the beatings, they would hardly open. She wasn't hearing much with her ears, for the sounds around her were harsh and threatening, relentlessly so. And she wasn't feeling with her body, for there was nothing there but pain.

No, Shmi had fallen inside herself, reliving those moments long ago, when she and Anakin had lived their lives as Watto's slaves. It was not an easy life, but she had her Annie with her, and given that, Shmi could remember those times fondly. Only now, with the prospects for ever seeing her son again so distant, did she truly appreciate how much she had missed the boy over the last ten years. All those times staring up at the night sky, she had thought of him, had imagined him soaring across the galaxy, rescuing the downtrodden, saving planets from ravaging monsters and evil tyrants. But she had always expected to see her Annie again, had always expected him to walk onto the moisture farm one day, that impish smile of his, the one that could light up a room, greeting her as if they had never been apart.

Shmi had loved Cliegg and Owen. Truly she had. Cliegg was her rescuer, her dashing knight, and Owen had been like the son she had lost, always compassionate, always happy to listen to her endless stories of Anakin's exploits. And Shmi was growing to love Beru, too. Who could not? Beru was that special combination of compassion and quiet inner strength.

But despite the good fortune that had brought those three into her life, improving her lot a millionfold, Shmi Skywalker had always kept a special place in her heart reserved for her Annie, her son, her hero. And so now, as it seemed the end of her life was imminent, Shmi's thoughts focused on those memories she had of Anakin, while at the same time, she reached out to him with her heart. He was always different with such feelings, always so attuned to that mysterious Force. The Jedi who had come to Tatooine had seen it in him clearly.

Perhaps, then, Annie would feel her love for him now. She needed that, needed to complete the cycle, to let her son recognize that through it all, through the missing years and the great distances between them, she had loved him unconditionally and had thought of him constantly.

Annie was her comfort, her place to hide from the pain the Tuskens had, and were, exacting upon her battered body. Every day they came in and tortured her a bit more, prodding her with sharp spears or beating her with the blunt shafts and short whips. It was more than a desire to inflict pain, Shmi realized, though she didn't speak their croaking language. This was the Tusken way of measuring their enemies, and from the nods and the tone of their voices, she realized that her resilience had impressed them.

They didn't know that her resilience was wrought of a mother's love. Without the memories of Annie and the hope that he would feel her love for him, she would surely have given up long ago and allowed herself to die.

Under the pale light of a full moon, Anakin Skywalker pulled the speeder bike to the ridge of a high dune and peered across the desert wastes of Tatooine. Not too far below him, he saw an encampment spread about a small oasis, and he knew at once, even before spotting a figure, that it was a Tusken camp. He could sense his mother down there, could feel her pain.

He crept closer, studying the straw and skin huts for any anomalies that might clue him in to their respective purposes. One especially sturdy hut at the edge of the oasis caught and held his attention: It seemed less tended than the others, yet more solidly constructed. As he came around a bit more, he grew even more intrigued, noting that only one hut was guarded, by a pair of Tuskens flanking the entrance.

"Oh, Mom," Anakin whispered.

Silent as a shadow, the Padawan slipped through the encampment, moving hut to hut, flat against walls and belly-crawling across open spaces, working his way gradually toward the hut he felt held his mother. He came against its side at last, and put his hands against the soft skin wall, feeling the emotions and pain of the person within. A quick glance around the front showed him the two Tusken guards, sitting a short distance in front of the door.

Anakin drew and ignited his lightsaber, then crouched low, shielding the glow as much as he could. He slid the energy blade through the wall and easily cut the material away, then, without even pausing to see if any Tuskens were inside, he crawled through.

"Mom," he breathed again, and his legs weakened beneath

him. The room was lit by dozens of candles, and by a shaft of pale moonlight, streaming through a hole in the roof, illuminating the figure of Shmi, tied facing against a rack to the side of the tent. Her arms were outstretched, bound at bloodied wrists, and her face, when she turned to the side, showed the weeks of beatings.

Anakin quickly cut her free and gently lowered her from the perch, into his arms and then down to the floor.

"Mom . . . Mom . . . Mom," he whispered softly. Anakin knew that she was alive, though she did not immediately respond and had come down so pitifully limp. He could feel her in the Force, though she was a thin, thin sensation.

He cradled her head and kept repeating her name softly, and finally, Shmi's eyelids fluttered open as much as she could manage through the swelling and the dried blood.

"Annie?" she whispered back. He could feel her wheezing as she tried to speak, and knew that many of her ribs had been crushed. "Annie? Is it you?"

Gradually her eyes began to focus upon him, and he could see a thin smile of recognition coming to her battered face.

"I'm here, Mom," he told her. "You're safe now. Hang on. I'm going to get you out of here."

"Annie? Annie?" Shmi replied, and she tilted her head, the way she often had when Anakin was a boy, seeming quite amused by him. "You look so handsome."

"Save your strength, Mom," he said, trying to calm her. "We've got to get away from here."

"My son," Shmi went on, and she seemed to be in a different place than Anakin, a safer place. "My grown-up son. I knew you'd come back to me. I knew it all along."

Anakin tried again to tell her to lie still and save her strength, but the words simply wouldn't come out of his mouth.

"I'm so proud of you, Annie. So proud. I missed you so much."

"I missed you, too, Mom, but we can talk later . . ."

"Now I am complete," Shmi announced then, and she looked straight up, past Anakin, past the hole in the ceiling, to the shining moon, it seemed.

Somewhere deep inside, Anakin understood. "Just stay with me, Mom," he pleaded, and he had to work very hard to keep the desperation out of his voice. "I'm going to make you well again. Everything's . . . going to be fine."

"I love . . ." Shmi started to say, but then she went very still, and Anakin saw the light leave her eyes.

Anakin could hardly draw his breath. Wide-eyed with disbelief, he lifted Shmi to his breast and rocked her there for a long time. She couldn't be gone! She just couldn't! He pulled her back again, staring into her eyes, silently pleading with her to answer him. But there was no light there, no flicker of life. He hugged her close, rocking her.

Then he laid her back to the floor and gently closed her eyes.

Anakin didn't know what to do. He sat motionless, staring at his dead mother, then looked up, his blue eyes blazing with hatred and rage. He replayed all of the recent events of his life in his head, wondering what he might have done differently, done better, to keep Shmi alive. He should never have left her here in the first place, he realized, should never have let Qui-Gon take him away from Tatooine without bringing his mother along, as well. She said she was proud of him, but how could he deserve her pride if he could not even save her?

He wanted Shmi to be proud of him, wanted to tell his mom all about the things that had come into his life, his Jedi training, all the good work he had already done, and most of all, about Padmé. Oh how he had wanted his mom to get to know Padmé! She would have loved her. How could she not? And Padmé would have loved her.

Now what was he going to do?

The minutes slipped past and Anakin just sat there, immobilized by his confusion, by a budding rage and the most profound sense of emptiness he had ever known. Only when the pale light began to grow around him, making the low-burning candles seem even thinner, did he even remember where he was.

He looked about, wondering how he might get his mother's body out of there—for he certainly wasn't going to leave it to the Tusken Raiders. He could hardly move, though. There seemed a profound pointlessness to it all, a series of motions without meaning.

At that time, the only meaning, the only purpose, that Anakin could fathom was that of the rage building within him, an anger at losing someone he did not wish to give up.

Some small part of him warned him not to give in to that anger, warned him that such emotions were of the dark side.

Then he looked at Shmi lying there, so still, seeming at peace but covered with the clear evidence of all the pain that had been inflicted upon her poor body these last days.

The Jedi Padawan climbed to his feet and took up his lightsaber, then boldly strode through the door.

The two Tusken guards gave a yelp and lifted their staves, rushing for him, but the blue-glowing blade ignited, and in a flash of killing light, Anakin took them down, left and right.

The rage was not sated.

Deep in his meditations, peering through the dark side, Master Yoda felt a sudden surge of anger, of outrage beyond control.

The diminutive Master's eyes popped open wide at the overwhelming strength of that rage.

And then he heard a voice, a familiar voice, crying, "No, Anakin! No! Don't! No!"

It was Qui-Gon. Yoda knew that it was Qui-Gon. But Qui-Gon was dead, had become one with the Force! One could not retain consciousness and sense of self in that state; one could not speak from beyond the grave.

But Yoda had heard the ghostly call, and in his deep meditative state, his thoughts focused as precisely as they had ever been, the Jedi Master knew that he had not been mistaken.

He wanted to focus on that, then, perhaps to try to follow that call back to the ghostly source, but he could not, overwhelmed again by the surge of rage and pain and . . . power.

He made a noise and lurched forward, then came out of his trance as his door opened and Mace Windu rushed in.

"What is it?" Mace asked.

"Pain. Suffering. Death! I fear something terrible has happened. Young Skywalker is in pain. Terrible pain."

He didn't tell Mace the rest of it, that somehow Anakin's rush of agony manifesting in the Force had tapped into the spirit of the dead Jedi Master who had discovered him. Too much was happening here.

That disembodied familiar voice hung profoundly in Yoda's thoughts. For if it was true, if he had heard what he was sure he had heard . . .

Anakin, too, had heard the voice of Qui-Gon, imploring him to restrain himself, to deny the rage. He hadn't recognized it, though, for he was too full of pain and anger. He spotted a Tusken woman to the side, in front of another of the tents, carrying a pail of dirty water, and saw a Tusken child in the shadows of another nearby hut, staring at him with an incredulous expression.

Then he was moving, though he was hardly aware of his actions. His blade flashed and he ran on. The Tusken woman screamed, and was impaled.

Now all the camp seemed in motion, Tuskens rushing out of every hut, many with weapons in hand. But Anakin was into the dance of death then, into the energy of the Force. He leapt far and long, clearing one hut and coming down before another, his blade flashing even before he landed, even before the two Tuskens recognized that he had jumped between them.

A third came at him, thrusting forth a spear, but Anakin lifted an empty hand and set up a wall of Force energy as solid as stone. Then he shoved out with that hand, and the Tusken spearman flew away, fully thirty meters, smashing through the wall of yet another hut.

Anakin was off and running, off and leaping, his blade spinning left and right in a blur, every stab taking a Tusken down, writhing to the ground, every slash putting a piece of a Tusken on the ground.

Soon none were standing against him, all trying to flee, but Anakin would have none of that. He saw one group rush into a hut and reached out across the way, to a large boulder in the distance. It flew to his call, soaring across the sand, smashing one fleeing Tusken down and flying on.

Anakin dropped it on the hut full of Tuskens, crushing them all.

And then he was running, his strides enhanced by the Force, overcoming the fleeing creatures, slaughtering them, every one.

He didn't feel empty any longer. He felt a surge of energy

and strength beyond anything he had ever known, felt full of the Force, full of power, full of life.

And then it was over, suddenly, it seemed, and Anakin stood among the ruins of the encampment, dozens and dozens of dead Tusken Raiders all about him, and only a single hut still standing.

He put his lightsaber away and walked back to that hut, where he gently and reverently scooped his mother's body into his arms.

There!" Padmé announced, as she hoisted C-3PO back out of the oil bath. She had to fight hard to keep from giggling, for she had inadvertently lowered the droid too far, and now he was waving his arms about crazily, yelling that he was blind.

Padmé yanked him over to the side and found a cloth to wipe the excess oil off of his face. That done, she set the droid down on the floor and unhitched him.

"Better?" she asked.

"Oh, much better, Miss Padmé." C-3PO waved his arms about and seemed quite pleased.

"No itches?" Padmé asked, inspecting her work.

"No itches," C-3PO confirmed.

"Well, good," she said with a smile. But her smile faltered as she realized that she was done. She had used her work with the droid to shield her from her fears over the last hours—she had hardly even realized that the sun had risen—and now those fears for Anakin were already coming back to her.

She was running out of places to hide.

"Oh, Miss Padmé, thank you! Thank you!" said C-3PO. He came forward, his arms outstretched to hug her, but then he moved back suddenly, seeming to remember himself and his sudden lack of protocol.

"Thank you," he said again, with a little more dignity. "Thank you very much."

Owen Lars entered the garage area. "Well, there you are," he said to Padmé. "We've been looking all over for you."

"I was out here all the time, giving Threepio a much-needed bath."

"Well, Padmé," Owen said, and when she turned to regard him, Padmé saw that he was grinning widely. "I'm returning this droid to Anakin. I know that's what my mom would want."

Padmé smiled and nodded.

"He's back! He's back!" came Beru's call from outside the garage. Smiles gone, Padmé and Owen turned and rushed out.

They caught up with Beru outside, and Cliegg soon joined them, his hoverchair banging and clunking against furniture and doorways as he glided out of the house.

"Where?" Padmé asked.

Beru pointed across the desert.

Squinting and shielding her eyes from the glare of the suns, Padmé finally marked the black dot that was Anakin, rushing toward them. As the speck grew into a distinguishable form, she realized that he was not alone, that there was someone tied over the back of the speeder.

"Oh, Shmi," Cliegg Lars said breathlessly. He was trembling visibly.

Beru sniffled and struggled to keep from sobbing. Owen

stood beside her, his hand draped across her shoulders, and when Padmé looked over at them, she noticed a tear sliding down Owen's cheek.

Anakin crossed into the compound a few moments later, pulling up short of the stunned group. Without a word, he dismounted and moved to unstrap his dead mother, lifting her and cradling her in his arms. He walked up to Cliegg and paused there for a bit, two men sharing a moment of grief.

Then, still without speaking, Anakin walked past the man and into the house.

All that time, the thing that struck Padmé the most was the look upon Anakin's face, an expression unlike anything she had ever seen on the Padawan: part rage, part grief, part guilt, and part resignation, even defeat. She knew that Anakin would need her, and soon.

But she had no idea of what she might do for him.

There wasn't much talking in the Lars homestead the rest of that day. Everyone just went about their chores, any chores, obviously trying to avoid the outpouring of grief that they all knew would inevitably come.

At work preparing a meal for Anakin, Padmé was surprised when Beru came up to help her, and even more surprised when the woman started some small talk with her.

"What's it like there?" Beru asked.

Padmé looked at her curiously. "I'm sorry?"

"On Naboo. What's it like?"

Padmé could hardly even register the question, for her thoughts remained with Anakin. It took her a long time to respond, but finally she managed to say, "Oh, it's very . . . very green. You know, with lots of water, and trees and plants every-where. It's not like here at all." She turned away as soon as she finished, and knew she was being a bit rude. But all she wanted was to be with Anakin, and so she started loading the food tray.

"I think I like it here better," Beru remarked.

"Maybe you'll come and see it someday," Padmé said, more to be polite than anything else.

But Beru answered seriously. "I don't think so. I don't like to travel."

Padmé picked up the tray and turned to go. "Thanks, Beru," she said with as much of a smile as she could muster.

She found Anakin standing at a workbench in the garage, working on a part from the speeder bike.

"I brought you something to eat."

Anakin glanced at her, but immediately went back to his work. She noted that he was exaggerating every movement, ob-viously frustrated, obviously distracted from the task at hand. "The shifter broke," he explained, too intently. "Life seems so much simpler when you're fixing things. I'm good at fixing things. I always was. But I . . ."

Finally he slammed down the wrench he was using and just stood there, head bowed.

Padmé recognized that he was on the verge of collapse.

"Why did she have to die?" he mouthed quietly. Padmé slid the tray down on the workbench and moved behind him, putting her arms about his waist and resting her head comfort-ingly on his back.

"Why couldn't I save her?" Anakin asked. "I know I could have!"

"Annie, you tried." She squeezed him a bit tighter. "Some-times there are things no one can fix. You're not all-powerful."

He stiffened at her words and pulled away from her suddenly—and angrily, she realized. "But I should be!" he growled, and then he looked at her, his face a mask of grim determination. "And someday I will be!"

"Anakin, don't say such things," Padmé replied fearfully, but he didn't even seem to hear her.

"I'll be the most powerful Jedi ever!" he railed on. "I promise you! I will even learn to stop people from dying!"

"Anakin—"

"It's all Obi-Wan's fault!" He stormed across the room and slammed his fist onto the workbench again, nearly dislodging the plate of food. "He put me out of the way."

"To guard me," she said quietly.

"I should have been out with him, hunting the assassins! I'd have had them a long time ago, and would've gotten here in time and my mother would still be alive!"

"You can't know—"

"He's jealous of me," Anakin rambled on, paying no attention to her at all. He wasn't talking to her, she realized, but was just playing it all out verbally for himself. She could hardly believe what she was hearing. "He put me out of the way because he knows that I'm already more powerful than he is. He's holding me back!"

He finished by picking up his wrench and throwing it across the garage, where it smashed against a far wall and clattered down among some spare parts.

"Anakin, what's wrong?" she cried at him.

Her volume and tone finally got his attention. "I just told you!"

"No!" Padmé yelled back at him. "No. What's *really* wrong?"

Anakin just stared at her, and she knew that she was on to something.

"I know it hurts, Anakin. But this is more than that. What's really wrong?"

He just stared at her.

"Annie?"

His body seemed to shrink then, and slump forward just a bit. "I . . . I killed them," he admitted, and if Padmé hadn't run to him and grabbed him close, he would have fallen over. "I killed them all," he admitted. "They're dead. Every single one of them."

He looked at her then, and it seemed to her as if he had suddenly returned to her from somewhere far, far away.

"You did battle . . ." she started to reason.

He ignored her. "Not just the men," he went on. "And the men are the only fighters among the Tuskens. No, not just them. The women and the children, too." His face contorted, as if he was teetering between anger and guilt. "They're like animals!" he said suddenly. "And I slaughtered them like animals! I hate them!"

Padmé sat back a bit, too stunned to respond. She knew that Anakin needed her to say something or do something, but she was paralyzed. He wasn't even looking at her—he was just staring off into the distance. But then he lowered his head and began to sob, his lean, strong shoulders shaking.

Padmé pulled him in and hugged him close, never wanting to let go. She still didn't know what to say.

"Why do I hate them?" Anakin asked her.

"Do you hate them, or do you hate what they did to your mother?"

"I hate them!" he insisted.

"And they earned your anger, Anakin."

He looked up at her, his eyes wet with tears. "But it was more than that," he started to say, and then he shook his head and buried his face against the softness of her breast.

A moment later, he looked back up, his expression showing that he was determined to explain. "I didn't . . . I couldn't . . ." He held one hand up outstretched, then clenched it into a fist. "I couldn't control myself," he admitted. "I . . . I don't want to hate them—I know that there is no place for hatred. But I just can't forgive them!"

"To be angry is to be human," Padmé assured him.

"To control your anger is to be a Jedi," Anakin was quick to reply, and he pulled away from her and stood up, turning to face the open door and the desert beyond.

Padmé was right there beside him, draping her arms about him. "Shhh," she said softly. She kissed him gently on the cheek. "You're human."

"No, I'm a Jedi. I know I'm better than this." He looked at her directly, shaking his head. "I'm sorry. I'm so sorry."

"You're like everybody else," Padmé said. She tried to draw closer, but Anakin held himself back from her.

He couldn't hold the pose of defiance for long, though, before he broke down again in sobs.

Padmé was there to hold him and rock him and tell him that everything would be all right.

Obi-Wan Kenobi slumped back in the seat of his starfighter, shaking his head in frustration. It had taken him a long while to extract himself safely from the factory city, and when he had at last found his starfighter, he had thought the adventure over. But not so.

"The transmitter is working," he told R4, who tootled his agreement. "But we're not receiving a return signal. Coruscant's too far." He spun to face the droid. "Can you boost the power?"

The beeps that came back at him were not comforting.

"Okay, then we'll have to try something else." Obi-Wan looked around for an answer. He didn't want to lift off from the planet and risk detection, but so far out and within the heavy and metallic Geonosian atmosphere, he had no chance of reaching distant Coruscant.

"Naboo is closer," he said suddenly, and R4 beeped. "Maybe we can contact Anakin and get the information relayed."

R4 replied with enthusiasm and Obi-Wan climbed back out of the cockpit to repeat the message with the changes for Anakin.

A few moments later, though, the droid signaled him that something was wrong.

With a frustrated growl, the Jedi climbed back up into the cockpit.

"How can he not be on Naboo?" he asked, and R4 gave an "*oooo.*" Rather than argue with a droid, Obi-Wan checked the instruments himself. Sure enough, Anakin's signal was not to be found coming from Naboo.

"Anakin? Anakin? Do you copy? This is Obi-Wan Kenobi?" he said, lifting his ship comm directly and shooting the call out toward the general area of Naboo.

After several minutes with no response, the Jedi put the comm back down and turned to R4. "He's not on Naboo, Arfour. I'm going to try to widen the search. I hope nothing's happened to him."

He sat back as the minutes slipped past. He knew that he was losing precious time, but his choices were limited. He couldn't head back to the city and risk capture, not with so much vital news to relay to the Jedi Council, nor did he want to blast away, for the same reasons. He still had so much to learn here.

So he waited, and finally, some time later, R4 tootled emphatically. Obi-Wan moved to the controls, his eyes widening as he got the confirmation. "That's Anakin's tracking signal all right, but it's coming from Tatooine! What in the blazes is he doing there? I told him to stay on Naboo!"

R4 gave another *"oooo."*

"All right, we're all set—we'll get these answers later." He climbed back out of the cockpit and jumped to the ground. "Transmit, Arfour. We haven't much time."

The droid locked on to him immediately.

"Anakin?" Obi-Wan asked. "Anakin, do you copy? This is Obi-Wan Kenobi."

R4 relayed the response, a series of beeps and whistles that the R4-P didn't normally use, but ones quite familiar to Obi-Wan.

"Artoo? Good, are you reading me clearly?"

The whistle came back affirmative.

"Record this message and take it to the Jedi Skywalker," Obi-Wan instructed the distant droid.

Another affirmative beep.

"Anakin, my long-range transmitter is knocked out. Retransmit this message to Coruscant."

The Jedi began to tell his tale then. He didn't know that the Geonosians had picked up his signal broadcasts and had triangulated those receptions to locate his starfighter. Wound up in his tale, he didn't notice the approach of the armed droidekas, rolling up near to him, then unrolling to their attack posture.

*   *   *

Even the two blazing Tatooine suns could not brighten the somber mood, the tangible grayness permeating the air, around the new grave outside the Lars compound. Two old headstones marked the ground next to the new one, a poignant reminder of the difficulties of life on the harsh world of Tatooine. The five of them—Cliegg, Anakin, Padmé, Owen, and Beru—had gathered, along with C-3PO, to bid farewell to Shmi.

"I know wherever you are, it's become a better place," Cliegg Lars said, and he took a handful of sand and tossed it on the new grave. "You were the most loving partner a man could ever have. Good-bye, my darling wife. And thank you."

He glanced briefly at Anakin, then lowered his head and fought back tears.

Anakin stepped forward and knelt before the marker. He picked up a handful of sand and let it slip through his fingers.

"I wasn't strong enough to save you, Mom," the young man said, suddenly feeling more like a boy. His shoulders bobbed once or twice, but he fought to regain control, and took a deep and determined breath. "I wasn't strong enough. But I promise I won't fail again." His breathing came in short rasps as another wave of grief nearly toppled him. But the young Padawan squared his shoulders and determinedly stood up. "I miss you so much."

Padmé came forward and put her hand on Anakin's shoulder, and all of them stood silent before the grave.

The moment held only briefly, though, broken by a series of urgent beeps and whistles. They turned as one to see R2-D2 rolling their way.

"Artoo, what are you doing here?" Padmé asked.

The droid whistled frantically.

"It seems that he is carrying a message from someone

named Obi-Wan Kenobi," C-3PO quickly translated. "Does that mean anything to you, Master Anakin?"

Anakin squared his shoulders. "What is it?"

R2-D2 beeped and whistled.

"Retransmit?" Anakin asked. "Why, what's wrong?"

"He says it's quite important," C-3PO observed.

With a look to Cliegg and the other two, silently seeking their permission, Anakin, Padmé, and C-3PO followed the excited droid back to the Naboo ship. As soon as they got inside, R2 beeped and spun, and projected an image of Obi-Wan in front of them.

"Anakin, my long-range transmitter has been knocked out," the Jedi's hologram explained. "Retransmit this message to Coruscant." R2 stopped the message there, with Obi-Wan seeming to freeze in place.

Anakin looked at Padmé. "Patch it through to the Jedi Council chamber."

Padmé stepped over and flipped a button, then waited for confirmation that the signal was getting through. She nodded to Anakin, who turned back to R2.

"Go ahead, Artoo."

The droid gave a beep, and Obi-Wan's hologram began to move once more. "I have tracked the bounty hunter Jango Fett to the droid foundries of Geonosis. The Trade Federation is to take delivery of a droid army here and it is clear that Viceroy Gunray is behind the assassination attempts on Senator Amidala."

Anakin and Padmé exchanged knowing glances, neither of them very surprised by that information. Padmé thought back to her meeting with Typho and Panaka on Naboo, before she had left for Coruscant, secretly escorting the doomed starship.

"The Commerce Guild and Corporate Alliance have both pledged their armies to Count Dooku and are forming an—"

The hologram swung about. "Wait! Wait!"

Anakin and Padmé cringed as droidekas appeared in the hologram along with Obi-Wan, grabbing at him and restraining him. The hologram flickered, then broke apart.

Anakin jumped up and rushed at R2-D2, but pulled up short, realizing that there was nothing he could do.

Nothing at all.

On distant Coruscant, Yoda and Mace Windu and the other members of the Jedi Council watched the hologram transmission with trepidation and great sadness.

"He is alive," Yoda announced, after yet another viewing. "I feel him in the Force."

"But they have taken him," Mace put in. "And the wheels have begun to spin more dangerously."

"More happening on Geonosis, I feel, than has been revealed."

"I agree," Mace said. "We must not sit idly by." He looked at Yoda, as did everyone else in the room, and the little Jedi Master closed his eyes, seemingly very weary and very pained by it all.

"The dark side, I feel," he said. "And all is cloudy."

Mace nodded and turned a grim expression on the others. "Assemble," he ordered, a command that had not been given to the Jedi Council in many, many years.

"We will deal with Count Dooku," Mace said through the comlink to Anakin. "The most important thing for you, Anakin, is to stay where you are. Protect the Senator at all costs. That is your first priority."

"Understood, Master," Anakin replied.

His tone, so full of resignation and defeat, struck Padmé profoundly. It galled the fiery Senator to think that Anakin would be stuck here looking over her, when his Master was in obvious danger.

As the hologram switched off, she moved to the ship's console and began flicking switches and checking coordinates, confirming what she already knew. "They have to come halfway across the galaxy," she said, turning to Anakin, who seemed not to care. "They'll never get there in time to save him."

Still no response.

"Look, Geonosis is less than a parsec away!" Padmé announced, flipping a few more controls to show the flight line on the viewscreen. "Anakin?"

"You heard him."

"They can't get from Coruscant in time to save him!" Padmé reiterated, her voice rising. She started flicking the switches on the panel, preparing the engines for firing, but Anakin gently put his hand over hers, stopping her.

"If he's still alive," the young Jedi answered somberly.

Padmé stared at him hard, and he turned away and walked off.

"Anakin, are you just going to sit here and let him die?" she cried, chasing across the bridge to grab him roughly by the arm. "He's your friend! Your mentor!"

"He's like my father!" Anakin shot back at her. "But you heard Master Windu. He gave me strict orders to stay here."

Padmé understood what was happening. Anakin was doubting himself. He felt himself a failure because of his inability to save his mother, and, perhaps for the first time in his life, he was truly doubting his inner voice, his instincts. She had to find a way around that now, for Anakin's sake as much as for Obi-Wan's. If they stayed here and did nothing, Padmé believed that she would lose two friends: Obi-Wan to the Geonosians, and Anakin to his guilt.

"He gave you strict orders to stay here only so that you could protect me," Padmé corrected with a grin, hoping to remind him clearly that his previous orders, which he had ignored, had demanded that he stay on Naboo. She pulled back away from him, returning to the console, and flicked a few more switches. The engines roared to life.

"Padmé!"

"He gave you strict orders to protect me," she said again. "And I'm going to save Obi-Wan. So if you plan to protect me, you'll have to come along."

Anakin stared at her for a few moments, and she held his gaze, her head tilted, hair loose and cascading across half her face, but hardly dimming the brightness of her determination.

Anakin knew that they were acting outside the orders of Mace Windu, whatever Padmé's justification. He knew that this was not what was expected of him as a Jedi Padawan.

When had that ever stopped him?

Matching Padmé's determination, he went to the controls, and a few moments later, the Naboo starship roared up into the Tatooine sky.

The calm beauty of the Republic Executive Building on Coruscant, with its streaming fountains and reflecting pools, ridged columns and flowing statues, masked the turmoil within. The word had passed, from Obi-Wan to Yoda and the Jedi Council, and now from them to the Chancellor and leaders of the Senate, that the Republic was crumbling. The mood inside Chancellor Palpatine's office was both somber and frantic, everyone overwhelmed by a sense of despair and a need to act, frustrated by the apparent lack of options.

Yoda, Mace Windu, and Ki-Adi-Mundi represented the Jedi, lending an air of calm against the nervous energy of Senators Bail Organa and Ask Aak, and Representative Jar Jar Binks. Behind his great desk, Palpatine listened to it all with apparent despair, his aide, Mas Amedda, standing beside him, seeming on the verge of tears.

Silence hung in the room for several long moments after Mace Windu had finished his recounting of the message from Geonosis.

Yoda, leaning on his small cane, glanced at Bail Organa, always a reliable and competent man, and gave a slight nod. Catching the cue, the Senator from Alderaan began the discussion. "The Commerce Guild is preparing for war," he said. "Given the report of Jedi Obi-Wan Kenobi, there can be no doubt of that."

"If the report is accurate," the fiery Ask Aak promptly responded.

"It is, Senator," Mace Windu assured him, and Ask Aak, a Senator of action, accepted that. Indeed, Yoda understood that Ask Aak had only made the remark because he had wanted the Jedi to openly support the report, to impress upon all the others that the situation was on the verge of catastrophe.

"Count Dooku must have made a treaty with them," Chancellor Palpatine reasoned.

"We must stop them before they're ready," Bail Organa said.

Jar Jar Binks moved front and center, trembling a bit but keeping his tongue in his mouth, at least. "Excueeze me, yousa honorable Supreme Chancellor, sir," the Gungan began. "Maybe dissen Jedi stoppen the rebel army."

"Thank you, Jar Jar," Palpatine politely replied, and turned to Yoda. "Master Yoda, how many Jedi are available to go to Geonosis?"

"Throughout the galaxy, thousands of Jedi there are," the diminutive Jedi Master replied. "To send on a special mission, only two hundred are available."

"With all due respect to the Jedi Order, that doesn't sound like enough," Bail Organa said.

"Through negotiation the Jedi maintain peace," Yoda replied. "To start a war, we do not intend."

His continued calm only seemed to push the frantic Ask Aak over the edge. "The debate is over!" he cried. "Now we need that clone army."

Yoda closed his eyes slowly, pained by the weight of reason behind the dreaded words.

"Unfortunately, the debate is not over," Bail Organa said. "The Senate will never approve the use of the army before the separatists attack. And by then, it will likely be too late."

"This is a crisis," Mas Amedda dared interject. "The Senate must vote the Chancellor emergency powers! He could then approve the use of the clones."

Palpatine rocked back at the suggestion, seeming profoundly shaken. "But what Senator would have the courage to propose such a radical amendment?" he asked hesitantly.

"I will!" Ask Aak declared.

Beside him, Bail Organa gave a helpless chuckle and shook his head. "They will not listen to you, I fear. Nor to me," he added quickly, when Ask Aak snapped a glare at him. "We have spent too much of our political capital debating the philosophies of the separatists and arguing for action. The Senate will not see our call as anything more than overly alarmist. We need a voice of reason, one willing to reverse position, even, given the gravity of the current situation."

"If only Senator Amidala was here," Mas Amedda reasoned.

Without hesitation, Jar Jar Binks stepped forward again. "Mesa mosto Supreme Chancellor," the Gungan said, squaring his sloping shoulders as much as possible. "Mesa gusto pallos," he said deferentially to all the others. "Mesa proud to proposing the motion to give Yousa Honor emergency powers."

Palpatine looked from the trembling Gungan to Bail Organa.

"He speaks for Amidala," the Senator from Alderaan said. "By all understanding within the Senate, Jar Jar Binks's words are a reflection of Senator Amidala's desires."

Palpatine nodded grimly, and Yoda sensed a strong fear from the man, as if he knew that he was about to be thrust forward in the most dangerous position he and the Republic had ever known.

Twisting slowly in the force field, restrained by crackling bolts of blue energy, Obi-Wan Kenobi could only watch helplessly as Count Dooku strode into the room. Wearing an expression that showed great sympathy, but one that Obi-Wan certainly did not trust, the regal man walked up right before the Jedi.

"Traitor," Obi-Wan said.

"Hello, my friend," Dooku replied. "This is a mistake. A terrible mistake. They've gone too far. This is madness!"

"I thought you were their leader here, Dooku," Obi-Wan replied, holding his voice as steady as possible.

"This had nothing to do with me, I assure you," the former Jedi insisted. He seemed almost hurt by the accusation. "I promise you that I will petition immediately to have you set free."

"Well, I hope it doesn't take too long. I have work to do." Obi-Wan noted a slight crack in Dooku's remorseful expression, a slight twinge of . . . anger?

"May I ask why a Jedi Knight is all the way out here on Geonosis?"

After a moment's reflection, Obi-Wan decided that he had little to lose here, and he wanted to continue to press Dooku, that he might gauge the truth. "I've been tracking a bounty hunter named Jango Fett. Do you know him?"

"There are no bounty hunters here that I'm aware of. Geonosians don't trust them."

Trust. There was a good word, Obi-Wan thought. "Well, who can blame them?" came his disarming reply. "But he is here, I assure you."

Count Dooku paused for a moment, then nodded, apparently conceding the point. "It's a great pity that our paths have never crossed before, Obi-Wan," he said, his voice warm and inviting. "Qui-Gon always spoke very highly of you. I wish he was still alive—I could use his help right now."

"Qui-Gon Jinn would never join you."

"Don't be so sure, my young Jedi," Count Dooku immediately replied, an offsetting smile on his face, one of confidence and calm. "You forget that Qui-Gon was once my apprentice just as you were once his."

"You believe that brings loyalty above his loyalty to the Jedi Council and the Republic?"

"He knew all about the corruption in the Senate," Dooku went on without missing a beat. "They all do, of course. Yoda and Mace Windu. But Qui-Gon would never have gone along with the status quo, with that corruption, if he had known the truth as I have." The pause was dramatic, demanding a prompt from Obi-Wan.

"The truth?"

"The truth," said a confident Dooku. "What if I told you that the Republic was now under the control of the Dark Lords of the Sith?"

That hit Obi-Wan as profoundly as any of the electric bolts holding him ever could. "No! That's not possible." His mind whirled, needing a denial. He alone among the living Jedi had battled a Sith Lord, and that contest had cost his beloved Master Qui-Gon his life. "The Jedi would be aware of it."

"The dark side of the Force has clouded their vision, my friend," Dooku calmly explained. "Hundreds of Senators are now under the influence of a Sith Lord called Darth Sidious."

"I don't believe you," Obi-Wan said flatly. He only wished he held that truth as solidly as he had just proclaimed.

"The viceroy of the Trade Federation was once in league with this Darth Sidious," Dooku explained, and given the events of a decade before, it seemed a reasonable claim. "But he was betrayed ten years ago by the Dark Lord. He came to me for help. He told me everything. The Jedi Council would not believe him. I tried many times to warn them, but they wouldn't listen to me. Once they sense the Dark Lord's presence and realize their error, it will be too late. You must join with me, Obi-Wan, and together we will destroy the Sith."

It all seemed so reasonable, so logical, so attuned to the legend of Count Dooku as Obi-Wan had learned it. But beneath the silken words and tone was a feeling Obi-Wan had that flew in the face of that logic.

"I will never join you, Dooku!"

The cultured and regal man gave a great and disappointed sigh, then turned to leave. "It may be difficult to secure your release," he tossed back at Obi-Wan as he exited the room.

Approaching Geonosis, Anakin employed the same techniques as Obi-Wan had, using the asteroid ring near Geonosis to hide the Naboo starship from the lurking Trade Federation fleet. And like his mentor, the Padawan recognized the unusual and threatening posture of the unexpected fleet.

Breaking atmosphere, Anakin brought the ship down low, skimming the surface, weaving through valleys and around towering rock formations, circling mesas. Padmé stood next to him, watching the skyline for some signs.

"See those columns of steam straight ahead?" she asked, pointing. "They're exhaust vents of some type."

"That'll do," agreed Anakin, and he banked the starship, zooming in at the distant lines of rising white steam. He brought the ship right into one steam cloud and slid her down, gently, through the vent.

When they had settled on firm ground, he and Padmé prepared to leave the ship.

"Look, whatever happens out there, follow my lead," Padmé told him. "I'm not interested in getting into a war here. As a member of the Senate, maybe I can find a diplomatic solution to this mess."

For Anakin, who had so recently used the diplomacy of the lightsaber, and to devastating effect, the words rang true—painfully so.

"Trust me on this?" Padmé added, and he knew that she had recognized the pain on his face.

"Don't worry," he said, and he made himself grin. "I've given up trying to argue with you."

Behind them as they headed for the landing ramp, R2 gave a plaintive wail.

"Stay with the ship," Padmé instructed both droids. Then she and Anakin went out into the underground complex, and recognized almost immediately that they had entered a huge droid factory.

*　　*　　*

Soon after the pair had departed, R2-D2's legs extended, lifting him off the securing platform, and he began rolling immediately for the ship exit.

"My sad little friend, if they had needed our help, they would have asked for it," C-3PO explained to him. "You have a lot to learn about humans."

R2 tootled back at him and continued to roll.

"For a mechanic, you seem to do an excessive amount of thinking," C3-PO countered. "I'm programmed to understand humans."

R2's responding question came as a burst of short and curt beeps.

"What does that mean?" C-3PO echoed. "That means, I'm in charge here!"

R2 didn't even respond. He just started rolling for the landing ramp, moving right out of the ship.

"Wait!" C-3PO cried. "Where are you going? Don't you have any sense at all?"

The replying beep was quite discordant.

"How rude!"

R2 just gained speed and rolled away.

"Please wait!" C-3PO cried. "Do you know where you're going?"

While the reply was far from confident, the last thing C-3PO wanted at that moment was to be left alone. He rushed to catch up to R2, and followed behind, fussing nervously.

Anakin and Padmé slipped along the vast, pillared corridors of the factory city, their footfalls dulled by the humming and banging noises of the many machines in use in the great halls below them. The place seemed deserted—too much so, Anakin believed.

"Where is everyone?" Padmé whispered, unconsciously echoing his thoughts.

Anakin held his hand up to silence her, and he tilted his head, sensing . . . something.

"Wait," he said.

Anakin moved his hand higher and continued to listen, not with his ears, but with his sensitivity to the Force. There was something here, something close. His instincts turned his eyes up toward the ceiling, and he watched in amazement and horror as the crossbeams above seemed to pulse, as if they were alive.

"Anakin!" Padmé cried, watching, too, as several winged forms seemed to grow right out of the pillars, detaching and dropping down. They were tall and lean, sinewy strong and not skinny, with orange-tinted skin.

Anakin's lightsaber flashed. Turning fast, on pure instinct and reflex, he slashed out, severing part of a wing from one creature swooping in at him. The creature tumbled past, bouncing along the ground, but another took its place, and then another, heading in boldly for the Padawan.

Anakin stabbed out to the right, retracted the blade immediately from the smoking flesh, then brought it spinning about above his head, slashing out to the left. Two more creatures went tumbling. "Run!" he shouted to Padmé, but she was already moving, along the corridor and toward a distant doorway. Waving his lightsaber to keep more of the stubborn creatures at bay, Anakin ran. He darted through the doorway behind her— and nearly fell over the end of a small walkway that extended out over a deep crevasse.

"Back," Padmé started to say, but even as she and Anakin began to turn, the door slammed closed behind them, leaving them trapped on the precarious perch. More of the winged creatures appeared above them, and even worse, the walkway began to retract.

Padmé didn't hesitate. She leapt out for the shortest fall, onto a conveyor belt below.

"Padmé!" Anakin cried frantically. He leapt down, too, landing behind her on the moving conveyor. And then the winged Geonosians were all about him, swarming and swooping, and he had to work his lightsaber desperately to keep them at bay.

"Oh my goodness," C-3PO said, turning all about as he scanned the immense factory. He and R2-D2 came onto a high ledge, overlooking the main area. "Machines creating machines. How perverse!"

R2 gave him an emphatic beep.

"Calm down," C-3PO said. "What are you talking about? I'm not in your way!"

R2 didn't bother to argue. He rolled forward, bumping 3PO off the ledge. The screaming droid bounced onto one unfortunate flying conveyor droid, then crashed down on a conveyor to the side. R2 went off the ledge next, willingly, his little jets igniting to carry him fast across the way to some distant consoles.

"Oh, blast you, Artoo!" C-3PO cried, trying hard to sort himself out. "You might have warned me, or told me of your plan." As he spoke, he finally managed to stand—just in time to rise before a horizontal slicer.

C-3PO gave a single scream for help before the spinning blade lopped his head from his shoulders, his body crumpling down onto the belt, his head bouncing away to land on yet another conveyor, this one bearing lines of other heads, those of battle droids.

One welder stop later, and C-3PO found his head grafted onto a battle droid body. "How ugly!" he exclaimed. "Why would one build such unattractive droids?" He managed to glance to the side, to see his still-standing body rolling into the line with the other droids, where a Battle Droid head got welded onto it.

"I'm so confused," the poor C-3PO wailed.

Above it all, R2-D2 wasn't watching his mechanical friend. He had spied his Mistress Padmé and went in fast pursuit.

Padmé flailed and rolled about the belt, scrambling to her feet, then diving back down low. She backpedaled, then rushed ahead suddenly to scramble under thumping pile drivers, machines slamming metal molds down hard enough to shape the parts of a heavy gauge droid. She dived under one stamper, then scrambled back to her feet right before another, backpedaling furiously, waiting for the precise moment as the heavy head went back up along the guide poles.

And then a winged Geonosian swooped upon her, grabbing at her and throwing her off balance. She used just enough of her attention to free herself momentarily, then hoped she had estimated right and burst forward suddenly, diving and crawling fast, and came out the other side just as the pile driver thundered down.

Right onto the head of the pursuing Geonosian, stamping it flat.

Padmé, facing yet another stamper, didn't even see it. She managed to roll through safely, but just as she emerged, a winged creature reared up right in front of her, wrapping her in its leathery wings and grabbing at her with strong arms.

Padmé wrestled valiantly, but the creature was too strong. It flew off to the side of the conveyor and then unceremoniously dropped her. Padmé landed hard inside a large empty vat. She recovered quickly and tried to scramble out, but the vat was deep and without handholds and she couldn't extract herself.

Anakin, battling furiously with a swarm of winged Geonosians, and all the while scrambling to avoid the deadly stamping machines, still managed somehow to see it all. "Padmé!" he cried as he came through a stamper to see disaster looming. There was no way he could get to her, he realized immediately, and the vat into which she had fallen was fast moving toward a pour of molten metal. "Padmé!"

And then he was fighting again, slashing aside yet another of the winged creatures, watching all the while in horror as his love neared her doom.

He fought wildly, beating the creatures away, scrambling desperately for Padmé and calling out to her. He crashed through another assembly line, sending droid parts everywhere, then leapt another belt, crossing the factory room toward Padmé, who was still struggling helplessly, as she moved ever closer to the pouring molten metal. He thought he might get to her, might leap with the Force, but then he passed too close to another machine and a vise closed over his arm, mechanically moving it into position before a programmed cutting machine.

Anakin kicked out, both feet slamming a winged creature that had pursued him in, knocking the Geonosian away. He struggled mightily against the unyielding grip of the machine and managed to turn enough, just in time, to avoid the cutting blade—with his arm, at least. He could only watch in horror as the machine sliced his lightsaber in half.

And then he looked back, realizing that in a moment, the lightsaber would be the least of his losses.

"Padmé!" he cried.

Across the way, R2-D2 had landed near Padmé's vat. He worked frantically, slipping his controller arm onto the computer access plug, then scrolling through the files.

R2-D2 coolly continued his work, trying to put aside his understanding that Padmé was about to become encased in molten metal.

At last he succeeded in shutting down the correct conveyor. It stopped short, Padmé less than a meter from the metal pour. She barely had time to register relief—a group of winged creatures swooped down upon her and gathered her up in strong grabbing arms.

Anakin, kicking away another of the creatures, continued to struggle with the machine gripping his arm. He could only watch in dismay as a group of deadly droidekas rolled up and unfolded into position around him.

And then an armored rocket-man dropped before him, with blaster leveled his way. "Don't move, Jedi!" the man ordered.

Senator Amidala sat on one side of the large conference table, with Anakin standing protectively behind her. Across the way sat Count Dooku, Jango Fett positioned behind him. It was hardly a balanced meeting, though, for Jango Fett was armed where Anakin was not, and the room was lined by Geonosian guards.

"You are holding a Jedi Knight, Obi-Wan Kenobi," Padmé said calmly, using the tone that had gotten her through so many Senatorial negotiations. "I am formally requesting you turn him over to me now."

"He has been convicted of espionage, Senator, and will be executed. In just a few hours, I believe."

"He is an officer of the Republic," she said, her voice rising a bit. "You can't do that."

"We don't recognize the Republic here," Dooku said. "However, if Naboo were to join our alliance, I could easily hear your plea for clemency."

"And if I don't join your rebellion, I assume this Jedi with me will also die."

"I don't wish to make you join our cause against your will, Senator, but you are a rational, honest representative of your people, and I assume you want to do what's in their best interest. Aren't they fed up with the corruption, the bureaucrats, the hypocrisy of it all? Aren't you? Be honest, Senator."

His words stung her, because she knew there was some truth in them. Just enough to give him a modicum of credibility, enough for Dooku to entice so many systems to join in his alliance. And of course, the reality of the situation around her stung her even more deeply. She knew that she was right, that her ideals meant something, but how did that measure up against the fact that she would be executed for holding them? And even more than that, how did her precious ideals hold up against the fact that Anakin would die for them, as well? She knew in that moment just how much she loved the Padawan, but knew, too, that she could not deny all that she had believed for all of her life, not even for his life and hers. "The ideals are still alive, Count, even if the institution is failing."

"You believe in the same ideals we believe in!" Dooku replied at once, seizing the apparent opening. "The same ideals we are striving to make prominent."

"If what you say is true, you should stay in the Republic and help Chancellor Palpatine put things right."

"The Chancellor means well, M'Lady, but he is incompetent," Dooku said. "He has promised to cut the bureaucracy, but the bureaucrats are stronger than ever. The Republic cannot be fixed, M'Lady. It is time to start over. The democratic process in the Republic is a sham. A game played on the voters. The time will come when that cult of greed called the Republic will lose even the pretext of democracy and freedom."

Padmé firmed her jaw against the assault, consciously reminding herself that he was exaggerating, playing things all in a light to give himself credibility. All she had to do to see through the lies, to see the fangs beneath the tempting sway of the serpent, was remind herself that he had taken Obi-Wan prisoner and meant to execute him. Would the Republic have taken such a prisoner and set him up for execution? Would she?

"I cannot believe that," she said with renewed determination. "I know of your treaties with the Trade Federation, the Commerce Guild, and the others, Count. What is happening here is not government that has been bought out by business, it's business becoming government! I will not forsake all that I have honored and worked for, and betray the Republic."

"Then you will betray your Jedi friends? Without your cooperation, I can do nothing to stop their execution."

"And in that statement lies the truth of your proposed improvement," she said flatly, her words holding firm against the turmoil and agony that was wracking her. In the silence that followed, Dooku's staring expression went from that of a polite dignitary to an angry enemy, for just a flash, before reverting to his usual calm and regal demeanor.

"And what about me?" Padmé continued. "Am I to be executed also?"

"I wouldn't think of such an offense," Dooku said. "But there are individuals who have a strong interest in your demise, M'Lady. It has nothing to do with politics, I'm afraid. It's purely personal, and they have already paid great sums to have you assassinated. I'm sure they will push hard to have you included in the executions. I'm sorry, but if you are not going to cooperate, I must turn you over to the Geonosians for justice. Without your cooperation, I've done all I can for you."

"Justice," Padmé echoed incredulously, with a shake of her head and a knowing smirk. And then there was silence.

Dooku waited patiently for a few moments, then turned and nodded to Jango Fett.

"Take them away!" the bounty hunter ordered.

Much to his dismay, C-3PO found out exactly what the Geonosian had meant when he had said, "Put him in the line!"

He was in group of drilling battle droids, a dozen lines of twenty in a rectangular formation, going through the extensive programming testing before being herded onto great landing pads·to be scooped up by Trade Federation warships.

So flustered was the out-of-place protocol droid, and so unfamiliar with his new body, that when the Geonosian ordered, "Left face," he turned to the right, and when the drill leader then commanded, "March," the battle droid now facing him stomped right into him, bearing him backward, following its orders to a T without the ability to improvise.

"Oh, do stop!" C-3PO pleaded. "You are scratching me! Oh, I do beg you to stop!"

No response followed, because the droids had been programmed to respond only to the drill leader.

"Oh, do stop!" C-3PO begged again, fearful that he was going to be knocked over and trampled by the battle droid, and the four others marching behind it. His sensors, tied in to his new torso, showed him an effective solution to his problem. Without even realizing what he was doing, C-3PO fired his right-arm laser, point blank, into the pushing battle droid's chest, blasting the thing apart.

"Oh my!" C-3PO cried.

"Halt!" the Geonosian drill leader screamed, and all the droids immediately froze in place. Except for poor C-3PO, who stood there positively flummoxed, his torso rotating side to side as he tried to figure out what to do next. He heard the drill leader call out to "take four-dot-seven back for more training," and when he considered his position in the ranks, he knew the Geonosian was talking about him.

"Wait, no, it is a mistake," he cried as a pair of burly maintenance droids rolled over and scooped him up in their vise-grip arms. "Oh, but this is all wrong. I am programmed in over three million languages, not for marching!"

Even before he reached the end of the corridor, Mace Windu sensed Yoda's great sadness. The Master was sitting on a balcony overlooking the Galactic Senate. Below, chaos reigned. Uproar and screaming, loud opinions and counteropinions—the turmoil struck a profound chord in Mace Windu, who understood Yoda's sadness, and shared it. This was the government that he and his proud Order were sworn to protect, though right now many of the Senators hardly seemed worthy of that protection.

Right there and then, all the faults of the Republic were laid bare to Mace Windu, and to Master Yoda, all of the bureaucratic nonsense that seemed to inevitably get in the way of true progress. This was the chaos that had spawned Count Dooku and the separatist movement. This was the nonsense that gave credence to otherwise outlandish claims, and allowed the greedy special interests, like the Trade Federation, to exploit the galaxy.

The tall Jedi Master moved to the end of the corridor and

sat down beside Yoda. He said nothing, because there was nothing to say. Their place was to observe and to fight in defense of
the Republic.

However ridiculous many of the representatives of that body
now appeared below them.

Mace and Yoda watched the Senators screaming furiously at
each other, fists and other appendages waving in the air. At the
podium across the way, Mas Amedda stood anxiously, glancing
about and calling for order.

Finally, after many long minutes, the screaming died away.

"Order! Order!" Mas Amedda repeated many times, obviously trying to ensure that things did not spiral out of control
once again.

Chancellor Palpatine moved front and center, and cast his
gaze all about the amphitheater, meeting many eyes and trying
hard to convey the gravity of the moment.

"In the regrettable absence of Senator Amidala," he said at
length, speaking slowly and distinctly, "the chair recognizes the
Senior Representative of Naboo, Jar Jar Binks."

Mace looked at Yoda, who closed his eyes against the ensu-
ing onslaught of cheers and boos, seemingly equal in strength.
Everyone in the Senate knew what was coming, and the weight
of it threatened to rip the body politic apart.

Mace looked back at the floor and finally spotted Jar Jar,
floating out before the podium on his platform, flanked by Gungan aides.

"Senators!" Jar Jar called. "Dellow felegates—"

The laughter was almost as deafening as the arguing, but the
humor was lost quickly, as jeers erupted once more.

"Stay strong, Jar Jar," Mace quietly mouthed, looking down

at the Gungan, whose face and ears were now bright red from embarrassment.

"Order!" Mas Amedda shouted from the podium. "The Senate will accord the Representative the courtesy of a hearing!"

The floor quieted, and Mas Amedda signaled to Jar Jar, who was by this time gripping the front of his platform tightly.

"In response to the direct threat to the Republic," the Gungan began, speaking clearly and directly, "mesa propose that the Senate give immediate emergency powers to the Supreme Chancellor."

There came a brief silence as everyone turned to look at everyone else. Gradually, a clapping began, and when the jeers erupted from opposing factions, the cheering grew even louder, soon drowning out the opposition. Though she wasn't even present, it was Amidala who had done this, Mace understood. All the years she had worked to win the trust of others had led to this crucial victory. If anyone other than a Representative of Naboo, a voice speaking for Amidala, had suggested such a drastic measure, then the debate would never have been so cleanly decided. But since she had apparently thrown in with the other side on the debate for the creation of an army, so, too, did many of those who had originally followed her lead in opposing that army.

The noise went on for many minutes, and while the jeering died away, the cheering only gained momentum. Finally, Chancellor Palpatine held up his hands, asking for quiet.

"It is with great reluctance that I have agreed to this calling," Palpatine began. "I love democracy—I love the Republic. I am mild by nature and do not desire to see the destruction of democracy. The power you give me I will lay down when this crisis has abated. I promise you. And as my first act with this new authority, I will create a grand army of the Republic to counter the increasing threats of the separatists."

"It is done, then," Mace said to Yoda, and the diminutive Jedi Master nodded grimly. "I will take what Jedi we have left and go to Geonosis to help Obi-Wan."

"And visit, I will, the cloners of Kamino and see this army they have created for the Republic," Yoda said.

Together, the two Jedi walked away from the Senate Hall.

It looked like many of the courtrooms scattered about the galaxy, a round room sectioned by curving railings and tall boxed-off areas, with rows of seats behind the main area for interested onlookers. But the makeup of the principals told Padmé that the resemblance to a hall of justice ended right there. Poggle the Lesser, the Archduke of Geonosis, presided over the gathering, helped by his Geonosian aide, Sun Fac, but clearly there would be no possibility of open-mindedness. Padmé recognized the others as separatist Senators, dignitaries of the various commercial guilds and the InterGalactic Banking Clan.

She watched them carefully, noting the visceral hatred in their eyes. This was no hearing, no trial. It was a proclamation of hatred, and nothing more.

And so Padmé was hardly surprised when Sun Fac stepped forward and announced, "You have been charged and found guilty of espionage."

So much for evidence, Padmé thought.

"Do you have anything to say before your sentence is carried out?" Archduke Poggle the Lesser asked.

Unshaken, the cool Senator stared the Geonosian straight in

the eye. "You are committing an act of war, Archduke. I hope you are prepared for the consequences."

The Geonosian chuckled. "We build weapons, Senator. That is our business! Of course we're prepared!"

"Get on with it!" came the voice of Nute Gunray from the side. "Carry out the sentence. I want to see her suffer."

Padmé only shook her head. All this because she had foiled the Neimoidian's plans to exploit her planet when she was Queen. All this because she hadn't rolled over before the power of Gunray and his followers. And to think that she had agreed to mercy for the Neimoidians after their defeat on Naboo!

"Your other Jedi friend is waiting for you, Senator," Archduke Poggle the Lesser announced, and he waved to the guards. "Take them to the arena!"

At the back of the hall, the young boy soaked it all in and looked up at his father, a perfect older-version replica of himself. "Are they going to feed them to the beasts?" Boba Fett asked.

Jango Fett looked down at his eager son and chuckled. "Yes, Boba." He had many times told Boba stories of the Geonosian arena.

"Oh, I hope they use an acklay," said Boba matter-of-factly. "I want to see if it's as powerful as I've read."

Jango just smiled and nodded, amused that his son was already so interested in such things, and glad for the dispassion in his tone. Boba was being strictly pragmatic here, even in the face of the executions of three people. He was taking in the entire scenario with the cool and collected pragmatism that would allow him to survive in the harsh galaxy.

He was a good learner.

*   *   *

The jumble of information they were downloading into C-3PO would surely have overwhelmed the droid, conditioning him as intended, had his circuits not already been filled to near capacity with linguistic information. C-3PO engaged in multiple translations of each instruction pattern, and in doing so, managed to water them down enough so that they lost any real effect.

His subtlety seemed lost on the brutes programming him, and after a few short hours, they led him out of the room and across the large assembly hall.

It was there that C-3PO heard a plaintive and familiar whine.

"Artoo!" he called, swiveling his head. There was his dome-shaped companion, working at a console. R2-D2 swiveled his head and gave another *"oooo."*

"Oh, Artoo!" C-3PO wailed, and before he could even consider the action, he brought a laser sight up before his eyes, focusing on the restraining bolt set into his friend.

A single blast flew out, skimming the bolt from R2-D2, then ricocheting about the room.

"Hey!" cried one of the instructor droids, moving fast to C-3PO's side.

"Looks like this one needs more programming," another said.

The chief maintenance droid looked about the room and shook his dome. "Nah," he said. "No damage done. Get this one out to the yard and out of here!"

They led C-3PO away.

Soon after they were gone, R2-D2 rolled away from his console without notice. Since all of the relatively benign droids working in here were restrained by bolts, there were no real guards in the room.

The little droid was out and free soon after.

*   *   *

The tunnel was dark and fittingly gloomy, and quiet, except for the occasional echo of cheering from the huge crowd gathered in the arena stands beyond. A single cart was in there, an open oval with a sloping front end that somewhat resembled an insect's head with the top half cut away. Anakin and Padmé were unceremoniously thrown into it, then strapped in place against the framework, facing each other.

Both of them jerked as the cart started into motion, gliding along the dark tunnel.

"Don't be afraid," Anakin whispered.

Padmé smiled at him, her expression one of genuine calm. "I'm not afraid to die," she replied, her voice thick and soft. "I've been dying a little bit each day since you came back into my life."

"What are you talking about?"

Then she said it, and it was real and genuine and warm. "I love you."

"You love me?" he asked, overwhelmed. "You love me! I thought we decided not to fall in love. That we would be forced to live a lie. That it would destroy our lives." But her words had brought a wash of contentment over him.

"I think our lives are about to be destroyed anyway," Padmé replied. "My love for you is a puzzle, Annie, for which I have no answers. I can't control it—and now I don't care. I truly, deeply love you, and before we die, I want you to know."

Padmé leaned against her restraints and craned her head forward, and Anakin did likewise, the two coming close enough for their lips to meet in a soft and gentle kiss, one that lingered and deepened, one that said everything they both realized they should have spoken to each other before. One that, to them, mocked their false heroics in denying the feelings they'd had for each other all along.

The sweet moment was just that, though, a moment, for a crack of the driver's whip had the cart jerking out of the tunnel and into the blinding daylight, rolling onto the floor of a great stadium filled with Geonosian spectators.

Four sturdy posts, a meter in diameter, were centered on the arena floor, each set with chains, and one holding a familiar figure.

"Obi-Wan!" Anakin cried as he was pulled down from the cart, dragged over, and chained to the post beside his Master.

"I was beginning to wonder if you had gotten my message," Obi-Wan replied. Both he and Anakin winced as Padmé was similarly, roughly dragged over to the post next to Anakin, and roughly chained up. They saw her curl a bit, defensively, in what seemed a futile resistance. What they didn't see, though, was the resourceful Padmé managing to slip out a wire she had hidden in her belt.

"I retransmitted your message just as you requested, Master," Anakin explained. "Then we decided to come and rescue you."

"Good job!" came Obi-Wan's quick and sarcastic reply. He ended with a grunt as his arms were pulled up above his head, locking him helplessly in place. Anakin and Padmé were receiving similar treatment. They could turn a bit side to side, though, and so all three were able to watch the arrival of the dignitaries, the masters of ceremony—faces they had come to know all too well.

"The felons before you have been convicted of espionage against the Sovereign System of Geonosis," announced the lackey, Sun Fac. "Their sentence of death is to be carried out in this arena immediately!"

The wild cheering deafened the doomed trio.

"They like their executions," Obi-Wan said dryly.

At the dignitary box, Sun Fac gave way to Archduke Poggle the Lesser, who patted his hands in the air, calling for quiet. "I have decided on an especially entertaining contest this day," he announced, to more appreciative roaring. "Which of our pets would be most suited to carry out the executions of such distinguished criminals? I asked myself this over and over, and for many hours, could find no answer.

"And finally, I chose—" He paused dramatically and the crowd hushed. "—the reek!" At the side of the arena, a gate was lifted and out stepped a huge quadruped with massive shoulders, an elongated face, and three deadly horns, one sticking up from its snout and the other two protruding forward from either side of its wide mouth. The reek stood as tall as a Wookiee, as wide as a human male was tall, and more than four meters long. It was prodded forward into the arena by a line of picadors carrying long spears and riding creatures that were bovine in size, with elongated snouts.

After the cheering died away, Poggle surprised the crowd by announcing, "The nexu!" A second gate rose, revealing a large feline creature. Its head was an extraordinary thing, half the size of its body and with a fang-filled mouth that could open wide enough to bite a large human in half. A ridge of fur stood straight in a line from head to rump, ending right before its whipping, felinoid tail.

Before the surprised crowd could erupt again, Poggle shouted, "And the acklay!" and a third gate rose and the most hideous creature of all rushed in. It moved spiderlike on four legs, each ending in huge elongated claws. Other arms waved menacingly, similarly topped with claws that snapped in the air. Its head, crested by a long and wavy horn, was more than two meters above the ground, glancing about hungrily, and while the other two creatures seemed to need the prodding of the picadors, this one surely did not.

This last one, the acklay, seemed to be the true crowd-pleaser, especially to the young boy, Jango Fett's cloned son, sitting with the dignitaries. Boba grinned and began reciting all that he had read of the deadly beast's exploits.

"Well, this should be fun—for them, at least," lamented Obi-Wan, watching the frenzy mounting around him.

"What?" Anakin asked.

"Never mind," Obi-Wan replied. "You ready for the fight?"

"The fight?" Anakin asked skeptically, looking up at his chained wrists, then back at the three monsters, which had been milling about, and only now seemed to take note that lunch had been served.

"You want to give the crowd its money's worth, don't you?" Obi-Wan asked. "You take the one on the right. I'll take the one on the left."

"What about Padmé?" The two turned to discover that their clever companion had already used the concealed wire to pick the lock on one of her shackles, and had turned her body about, facing the post. She climbed right up the chain to the top of that post, then went to work on the other shackle.

"She seems to be on top of things," Obi-Wan commented wryly.

Anakin looked back just in time to react to the charge of the reek. Acting purely on reflex, the young Jedi leapt straight up, and the beast plowed into the pole beneath him. Seeing an opportunity, Anakin dropped upon the beast's back and wrapped his chain about its strong horn. The reek bucked and tugged, tearing the chain free of the post, and they were off, the reek bucking and Anakin holding on for dear life. He slapped the free end of the chain at the side of the reek's head, and the vicious beast bit it and held on, its stubbornness providing Anakin a makeshift bridle.

After downloading the schematics, R2-D2 had little trouble navigating the huge factory complex. The small droid rolled along, whistling casually to deflect any suspicion on the part of the many Geonosians milling about.

None of them seemed interested in him, anyway, though, and R2 thought he knew why. He had learned of a huge event taking place, a triple execution. He could easily enough guess the identities of the unfortunate prisoners.

He wandered along a meandering course through the complex, avoiding as many Geonosians as possible, passing those he could not with an air of detachment, trying not to look out of place.

He knew that it would get more crowded as he neared the arena, though, and could only hope that the Geonosians there would be too distracted by the thrilling events to bother with a little astromech droid.

Obi-Wan quickly came to learn why the acklay was such a crowd-pleaser. The creature reared up high and came straight in at him. When Obi-Wan rushed behind the pole, the acklay took a more direct route, crashing into the pole, its gigantic claws snapping the wood and the chain. Freed by the beast's fury, Obi-Wan turned and ran, sprinting right at the nearest picador, the acklay in fast pursuit. The Geonosian lowered his spear at the Jedi, but Obi-Wan dodged inside and grabbed it. A sudden tug pulled it free, and Obi-Wan snapped it against the picador's mount, causing the creature to rear. Hardly slowing, Obi-Wan planted the butt of the lance in the ground and leapt, pole-vaulting the picador and his mount.

Again the acklay took the more direct route, slamming into rider and mount, sending the Geonosian tumbling to the sand. Grabbing the picador up in the snap of a claw, the monster crunched the life from him.

Atop her post, Padmé worked frantically to free the chain. But already the felinelike nexu was leaping up to swipe at her with its deadly claws. She dodged, but the nexu came on again.

Padmé whipped it with the chain.

The beast didn't stop, its claws tearing into the pole as it climbed. Then, with a sudden burst, it leapt up to the top and reared before Padmé issuing a victorious roar.

The crowd hushed, sensing the first kill.

As the nexu slashed, Padmé turned in a circle the other way, and while the claws tore her shirt and superficially raked her back, she came around hard, delivering a solid blow across the beast's face with the free-flying end of the chain. The nexu fell back off the pole. Padmé leapt out and back, away from the creature and to the side, and let the chain tug her back, sending her in a spin about the pole. She tucked her legs as she spun, then double-kicked out, knocking the nexu to the ground.

Hardly pausing to consider her handiwork, she scrambled back up the pole, working furiously to free herself completely.

*   *   *

The crowd gasped as one.

"Foul!" cried Nute Gunray in the dignitary box. "She can't do that! Shoot her or something!"

"Wow!" Boba Fett yelled in obvious admiration. Jango put his hand on his son's shoulder, enjoying the show every bit as much as Boba.

"The nexu will have her, Viceroy," Poggle the Lesser assured the trembling Neimoidian.

Gunray remained standing, as did everyone else in the box, as did everyone else in the stadium. The crowd gasped again as Obi-Wan ran around behind the picador's fallen mount, then launched the stolen spear into the neck of the furious acklay. The beast screeched in pain and slapped the struggling orray mount aside.

Across the way, Padmé continued to work the chain as the nexu regained its balance and began to stalk back toward the pole. Finally, she was free.

But the nexu was right below her, looking up, drool spilling from its oversized maw, death in its eyes. It crouched, ready to spring.

And got trampled into the ground by Anakin and his reek mount.

"You okay?" he called.

"Sure."

"Jump on!" Anakin cried, and Padmé was already moving, leaping down from the pole to fall into place right behind Anakin.

They passed the wounded and furious acklay next, and Obi-Wan was quick to take Padmé's hand and vault into place behind her.

Boba Fett yelped in glee again, as did many of the Geonosians.

Nute Gunray, though, wasn't quite so pleased. "This isn't how it's supposed to be!" he yelled at Count Dooku. "She's supposed to be dead by now!"

"Patience," the calm Count replied.

"No!" Nute Gunray shouted back at him. "Jango, finish her off!"

Jango turned an amused expression Nute Gunray's way, and nodded knowingly as Count Dooku motioned for him to stay put.

"Patience, Viceroy," Dooku said to the fuming Gunray. "She will die."

Even as he spoke, even as Gunray seemed about to explode with rage, the Count motioned back to the arena, and the Neimoidian turned to see a group of droidekas roll out from the side paddock. They surrounded the reek and the three prisoners and opened and unfolded into their battle position, giving Anakin no choice but to pull back hard on the makeshift rein and halt the creature.

"You see?" Dooku calmly asked.

The Count's expression changed, though, just for a moment, as a familiar hum began right behind him. He glanced to his right quickly, to see a purple lightsaber blade right beside Jango Fett's neck, then turned slowly to regard the wielder.

"Master Windu," he said with his typical charm. "How pleasant of you to join us! You're just in time for the moment of truth. I would think these two boys of yours could use a little more training."

"Sorry to disappoint you, Dooku," Mace coolly replied. "This party's over." With that, the Jedi Master gave a quick salute with his glowing lightsaber, the prearranged signal, and then brought the blade back in close to Jango Fett.

All about the stadium came a sudden and synchronized flash of lights as a hundred Jedi Knights ignited their lightsabers.

The crowd went perfectly silent.

After a moment's reflection, Count Dooku turned about just a bit, looking back at Mace Windu out of the corner of his eye. "Brave, but foolish, my old Jedi friend. You're impossibly outnumbered."

"I don't think so," Mace countered. "The Geonosians aren't warriors. One Jedi has to be worth a hundred Geonosians."

Count Dooku glanced about the stadium, his smile widening. "It wasn't the Geonosians I was thinking about. How well do you think one Jedi will match up against a thousand battle droids?"

He had timed it perfectly. Just as he finished, a line of battle droids came down the corridor behind Mace Windu, their lasers firing. The Jedi reacted at once, spinning about and flashing his lightsaber to deflect the many bolts, turning them back on his attackers. He knew that these few droids were the least of his troubles, though, for as he glanced around he saw the source of Dooku's confidence: thousands of battle droids rolling along every ramp, in the stands and out into the arena below.

The fight began immediately, the whole stadium filling with screaming laser bolts, Jedi leaping and spinning, trying to close into tight defensive groups, their lightsabers deflecting the bolts wildly. Geonosians scrambled all about, some trying to attack the Jedi—and dying for their trouble—others just scrambling to get out of the way of the wild fire.

Mace Windu spun about, recognizing that his most dangerous enemies were behind him. He faced Jango Fett—and found himself looking down the barrel of a stout flamethrower.

A burst of flames reached out for the Jedi Master, igniting his flowing robes. With both Dooku and the bounty hunter so close, and in such a vulnerable position, Mace just leapt away, lifting himself with the Force to fly out from the box and land in the arena. He pulled the burning robe from his back, throwing it aside.

All around him, the fight intensified, with Jedi battling scores of Geonosians in the stands, and many other Jedi rushing down to the arena floor to join the battle against the largest concentrations of Battle Droids. Mace winced when he spotted Obi-Wan, Anakin, and Padmé sent flying into the air by the terrified and bucking reek. He motioned to other Jedi, but needn't have, for those closest were already rushing toward their vulnerable companions, throwing lightsabers to Anakin and Obi-Wan.

When those two ignited their blades, Anakin's green and Obi-Wan's blue, and Padmé came up between them, a discarded blaster pistol in hand, Mace breathed a bit easier.

But only for a moment. Then the Jedi Master was a blur of motion once more, working his blade furiously to turn back the storm of laser bolts screaming at him from the multitude of battle droids. He joined Obi-Wan near the center of the arena soon after, and back-to-back, they went into action, moving into a crowd of droids, taking down several with deflected bolts, then slashing through, turning in unison as they went. Obi-Wan went at one droid with his lightsaber up high, but when that droid lifted its defenses appropriately, the two Jedi turned about, Mace coming around with his lightsaber down low, shearing the droid in half.

Behind Mace Windu and Obi-Wan, Anakin and Padmé fought in a similar back-to-back posture, with Anakin working in a mostly defensive manner, deflecting all the bolts coming at him and at Padmé, while she picked her shots carefully, taking down droid after droid after Geonosian.

But despite all the gallant efforts, despite the mounds of slaughtered enemies, Geonosian and droid alike, the outcome was beginning to show clearly, as the Jedi were being pushed back by sheer numbers. The general retreat flowed toward the arena, though that area would provide little respite. In addition to the droids and Jedi, the two monsters rushed about crazily, destroying everything in their path.

Into this maelstrom marched C-3PO, his body at least, with the head of a battle droid fixed firmly upon it. Shortly, however, this motley droid caught a blaster bolt in the neck. Down it went, the battle droid head bouncing free of the torso.

Across the arena, in a tunnel and marching toward daylight, 3PO's head, attached to a battle droid body, felt the sensation, but distantly.

"My legs aren't moving!" he cried, though of course his present legs certainly were. "I must need oil."

It was a time for improvisation, too wild a scene for coordinated and predetermined movements.

Just the kind of fight in which Padmé excelled. Firing a blaster with every step, she rushed to the same execution cart that had brought her and Anakin into the arena and scrambled atop the confused orray pulling it.

Right behind her came Anakin, his lightsaber a blur of motion, turning laser shots back at the battle droids. He leapt into the cart and Padmé kicked the orray away.

They charged the circuit, bouncing across the fallen droids and Geonosians, Padmé firing shot after shot and Anakin sending an even greater line of destruction out by turning aside all shots coming their way.

"You call this diplomacy?" said Anakin, deflecting blasts.

Padmé grinned and shouted back, "No, I call it 'aggressive negotiations'!"

C-3PO entered the maelstrom, and if his eye sockets would have allowed him to widen his eyes in surprise and terror, he surely would have.

"Where are we?" he cried. "A battle! Oh no! I'm just a protocol droid. I'm not made for this. I can't do it! I don't want to be destroyed!"

This mixed-up droid lasted about as long as his other half had, across the way. He came around to face the Jedi Master Kit Fisto, who slammed him hard with a Force shove, knocking him to the ground. Next, the agile Jedi did a pirouette movement and with a vicious slice of his lightsaber, took down the battle droid that had been in line right beside C-3PO. It collapsed on top of C-3PO's prone form.

"Help! I'm trapped! I can't get up!" C-3PO wailed, a call that caught the attention of none.

Save one.

R2-D2 rolled into the arena and wove his way about the carnage and danger.

No number of battle droids could hope to separate Mace and Obi-Wan, so perfect were their movements, so attuned were they to each other. But the sheer bulk of the reek was too much even for a pair of lightsabers, and when the furious beast charged at the two Jedi, they had no choice but to dive apart.

The reek followed Mace, and he had to slash wildly to fend it off. He did manage to drive it back, but was butted and lost his lightsaber in the process. He came up facing the reek, and figured that he could outmaneuver it to get his weapon back easily enough, but then an armored rocket-man flew down in his path, blaster leveled.

Mace reached out with the Force and brought his lightsaber flying to his hand, moving like lightning to parry Jango's first shot. With the second shot, Mace was more in control, and his parry sent the bolt right back at the bounty hunter. But Jango was already in motion, diving sidelong and coming around ready to launch a series of shots the Jedi's way.

He was stopped by the reek. Unable to distinguish friend from foe, the reek bore down on Jango. He scored a couple of hits, but they hardly slowed the beast, and he was tossed away. The reek charged him, trying to stomp him as he rolled about desperately. Jango was fast, though. Every time he came around, he fired again, and again, his bolts burrowing into the furious reek's belly.

Finally, the huge bullish creature swayed, and Jango wisely rolled out the far side, opposite Mace, as the beast collapsed.

The Jedi was on him immediately, lightsaber weaving through the air. Jango dodged and lifted into the air with his rockets, trying to keep one step ahead of that deadly blade and to occasionally fire a bolt at Mace.

The man was good, Mace had to admit. Very good, and more than once the Jedi had to parry desperately to turn a bolt aside. He kept up his offensive flurry, though, keeping Jango on the defensive with sudden stabs and slashing cuts.

One misstep . . .

And then it happened, all of a sudden. Mace started to slash to the left, cut it short and stabbed straight out, then reversed his grip and sent the lightsaber slashing across, left to right. He spun a complete circuit, coming around to parry a blaster shot, but there was no shot forthcoming.

That left to right reversal had cleanly landed. Jango Fett's head flew free of his shoulders and fell out of his helmet, to settle in the dirt.

"Straight ahead," Obi-Wan told himself as the acklay came at him, its huge claws snapping in the air.

He went left, then right, then rolled forward at the beast, between the mighty arms and snapping claws, coming around and over with his borrowed lightsaber stabbing straight ahead, burning a hole in the creature's chest.

The acklay dived forward, trying to crush him under its bulk, and the Jedi leapt straight up as he connected. He came down on its back, landing lightly and stabbing repeatedly, before leaping away once more.

"Straight ahead," he told himself again as the enraged beast charged yet again.

Obi-Wan noted the blaster bolt coming at him from the side at the very last second, and turned his lightsaber down and under, deflecting the bolt right into the acklay's face.

The creature hardly slowed and the Jedi had to throw himself to the ground to dodge a swiping, snapping claw.

He rolled out to the side, to avoid a stomping leg, and managed to slash out again, cutting a deep gash.

The acklay howled and came on, and more blaster bolts came at the Jedi.

His lightsaber worked furiously, brilliantly, turning one bolt after another right into the charging beast, finally slowing it and stunning it.

Obi-Wan rushed in and leapt and stabbed, right in the face. He caught his foot on the creature's shoulder and ran right past it. He heard it fall behind him, thrashing in its death throes, but he knew that battle was done and went back to work on the battle droids.

That larger fight seemed far from won, and far from winnable. Mace Windu had finished with Jango Fett by then, and to the other side, Anakin and Padmé continued their perfect teamwork behind the overturned execution cart. Anakin turned all shots aimed at either of them, and Padmé picked off droid after droid. But even with that, even with all of the remaining Jedi fighting brilliantly in the arena, the droids continued to press in, herding them all together in a hopeless position.

"Artoo, what are you doing here?" C-3PO asked when his little friend rolled past his trapped body.

In response, R2-D2 fired a suction cup grapnel from a compartment, attaching it firmly to C-3PO's head.

"Wait!" C-3PO cried as R2-D2 began to tug. "No! How dare you? You're pulling too hard! Stop dragging me, you leadhead!" He felt the sparking as his head tore free of the Battle Droid body, and then R2-D2 pulled C-3PO's head over to its rightful body. R2-D2 extracted his welding arm and began reattaching the protocol droid's head.

"Artoo, be careful! You might burn my circuits. Are you sure my head's on straight?"

*   *   *

More Jedi went down under the sheer weight of the laser barrage. Less than half of them were still standing.

"Limited choices," Ki-Adi-Mundi said to the exhausted and bloody Mace Windu.

Soon they were down to just over twenty, all herded together, and in the stadium all about them stood rank after rank of battle droid, weapons leveled.

And then all movement stopped suddenly.

"Master Windu!" Count Dooku cried from the dignitary box. His expression showed that he had truly enjoyed the spectacle of the battle. "You have fought gallantly. Worthy of recognition in the Archives of the Jedi. Now it is finished." He paused and looked all about, leading the gazes of the trapped Jedi to the rows and rows of enemies still poised to destroy them.

"Surrender," Dooku ordered, "and your lives will be spared."

"We will not become hostages for you to use as barter, Dooku," Mace said without the slightest hesitation.

"Then I'm sorry, old friend," Count Dooku said, in a tone that didn't sound at all sorry. "You will have to be destroyed." He raised his hand and looked to his assembled army, prepared to give the signal.

But then Padmé, exhausted, dirty, and bloody, raised her head to the sky above and shouted, "Look!" All eyes turned up to see half a dozen gunships fast descending upon the arena, screaming down in a dusty cloud about the Jedi, clone troopers rushing out their open sides as they touched down.

A hailstorm of laserfire blasted the new arrivals, but the gunships had their shields up, covering the debarkation of their warriors.

Amid the sudden confusion and flashing laserfire, Master

Yoda appeared in the dropdoor of one of the gunships, offering a salute to Mace and the others.

"Jedi, move!" Mace cried, and the survivors rushed to the nearest gunships, scrambling aboard. Mace climbed in right beside Yoda, and their ship lifted away immediately, cannons blaring, shattering and scattering battle droids as it soared up out of the arena.

Mace could hardly believe the incredible sight unfolding before him, as thousands of Republic ships rushed down on the assembled fleet of the Trade Federation, dropping tens of thousands of clone troopers to the surface of the planet. Behind him, Yoda continued to orchestrate the battle. "More battalions to the left," he instructed his signaler, who relayed it out to the field commanders. "Encircle them, we must, then divide."

After many minutes of a glow so bright that it hurt C-3PO's eyes, R2-D2 retracted his welding arm and tootled that the job was finished—C-3PO's head was back where it belonged.

"Oh, Artoo, you've put me back together!" C-3PO cried, and with some effort, he managed to stand upright. He realized then, from the hailstorm of fire outside the arena tunnel, and with many of those bolts ricocheting inside, that he was far from safe, and so he turned and began to amble away. Unfortunately for him, though, R2-D2 had not yet disengaged the sucker projectile from his forehead. The cord went taut, and C-3PO tumbled backward to the ground.

R2-D2 gave an apologetic whistle as he rolled by, disengaging and retracting the sucker as he went.

"I won't forget this!" C-3PO cried indignantly, and he scrambled up again and shuffled off after his infuriating friend.

*　　*　　*

With the gunships flying off and the battle droids in pursuit, Boba Fett finally found the opportunity to slip down onto the arena floor. He called for his father repeatedly, rushing from pile of carnage to pile of carnage. He passed the dead acklay, and then the reek, calling for Jango, but knowing what had happened, simply because his father, who was always there, wasn't there.

And then he saw the helmet.

"Dad," the boy breathed. His legs giving out beneath him, he fell to his knees beside Jango Fett's empty helmet.

Archduke Poggle the Lesser led Dooku and the others into the Geonosian command center, a huge room with a large circular viewscreen in its center and many other monitors about the walls, where Geonosian soldiers could monitor and direct the widening battle.

Poggle rushed to the side to confer with an army commander, then came back to Dooku and Nute Gunray, his expression fierce. "All of our communications have been jammed!" he informed them. "We are under attack, on land and from above!"

"The Jedi have amassed a huge army!" Nute Gunray cried.

"Where did they get them?" Dooku asked, sounding perplexed. "That doesn't seem possible. How did the Jedi come up with an army so quickly?"

"We must send all available droids into battle," Nute Gunray demanded.

But Dooku, staring at the myriad of scenes, at the many battles and explosions all about the region, was shaking his head before the Neimoidian could begin to argue his reasoning. "There are too many," the Count said, his voice full of resignation. "They will soon have us surrounded."

Even as he spoke, the three winced as the central screen flashed, showing the explosive destruction of a major Geonosian defensive position.

"This is not going well at all," Nute Gunray admitted.

"Order a retreat," said Poggle, and he was trembling so forcefully that it seemed as if he might just fall over. "I am sending all my warriors deep into the catacombs to hide!" He nodded to several of his commanders as he finished, and they turned back to their comlinks, relaying the orders.

"We must get the cores of our ships back into space!" one of Nute Gunray's associates cried, and Gunray was nodding as he considered the words and the devastating scenes of battle flashing across the viewscreens.

"I'm going to Coruscant," Dooku announced. "My Master will not let the Republic get away with this treachery."

Poggle the Lesser rushed across the room to a console and punched in some codes, bringing up a holographic schematic of a planet-sized weapon. With a few keystrokes, he downloaded the schematic onto a cartridge and pulled it from the drive, turning to Dooku. "The Jedi must not find our designs," the Archduke insisted. "If they have any idea of what we are planning to create, we are doomed."

Dooku took the cartridge. "I will take the designs with me," he agreed. "The plans will be much safer with my Master."

With a curt bow, the Count swept from the room.

Obi-Wan, Anakin, and Padmé crouched in the open side of a gunship as it sped across the expanding battlefield outside the arena, its laser cannons blaring, its shields turning back the responding fire from the droids.

Below them, clone troopers rushed across the battlefield on speeder bikes, weaving their way and firing all the while.

"They're good," Obi-Wan remarked, and Anakin nodded.

Their attention went right back to their own situation, then, as the gunship approached a huge Techno Union starship and opened fire. Its laser cannons slammed away at the giant, but seemed to be having little effect.

"Aim right above the fuel cells!" Anakin cried to the gunner. With a slight adjustment, the gunner let fly his next burst.

Huge explosions rocked the starship and it began to tilt ominously to the side. The gunship, and others rushing in nearby, swerved aside as the great craft toppled.

"Good call!" Obi-Wan congratulated his Padawan, then he shouted to the crew, "Those Trade Federation starships are taking off! Target them quickly!"

"They're too big, Master," Anakin replied. "The ground-troopers will have to take them out."

The gunship roared across the widening battlefield, lasers blasting away, explosions erupting all about it, a scene of spectacular destruction and frenzy. Mace Windu shook his head and looked to Yoda.

"Capture Dooku, we must," Yoda said, his calm and steady voice as strong an anchor as Mace could have asked for in that momentous moment. "If escape he does, he will rally more systems to his cause."

Mace looked to the diminutive Master and nodded grimly. "Captain, land at that assembly point ahead," he ordered the clone driving his gunship, and the obedient pilot fast settled the craft. Mace, Ki-Adi-Mundi, and a host of clone troopers jumped out, but Yoda did not follow.

"To the forward command center, take me," he instructed, and the gunship lifted away.

As soon as they put down at the relative safety of the position that had been secured as the command center, the clone commander rushed to the open gunship dropdoor. "Master Yoda, all forward positions are advancing."

"Very good, very good," Yoda said. "Concentrate all your fire on the nearest starship."

"Yes, sir!"

The clone commander ran off, organizing his leaders as he went. Soon after, the forward groups began picking their targets in a more coordinated manner, and the concentrated fire succeeded where sporadic bursts could not, taking down one starship after another.

The gunship slowed and banked suddenly, circling a droid gun emplacement, coming too fast around the back for the stationary system to swivel. A furious barrage destroyed the defensive position completely, but it did manage a single shot the gunship's way, rocking the craft hard.

"Hold on!" Obi-Wan cried, grabbing the edge of the open dropdoor.

"Can't think of a better choice!" Padmé yelled back at him.

Obi-Wan turned a smirk her way, or started to, but then he saw a Geonosian speeder soaring away, an unmistakable figure in the open cockpit. Two fighters flanked the speeder, the trio heading fast away from the main fighting. "Look! Over there!"

"It's Dooku!" Anakin cried. "Shoot him down!"

"We're out of ordnance, sir," the clone captain replied.

"Follow him!" Anakin ordered.

The pilot put the ship up on its side, banking fast to turn into a straight run for the fleeing Count.

"We're going to need some help," Padmé remarked.

"No, there's no time," said Obi-Wan. "Anakin and I can handle this."

As the gunship began to close, the fighters flanking Dooku banked away suddenly, veering off left and right, turning to engage. The clone pilot of the gunship was up to the task, weaving his way through their fire, but then another blast rocked the ship, and with the vehicle up on edge, Obi-Wan and Anakin had to hold on tight and scramble to stay in.

Padmé wasn't so fortunate.

One moment, she was beside Anakin, and then she was gone, tumbling out the open dropdoor.

"Padmé!" Anakin screamed. Everything seemed to be happening in slow motion, and he couldn't catch her, couldn't reach out fast enough.

She tumbled down and hit the ground hard, and lay very still.

"Padmé!" Anakin cried again, and then he yelled to the clone pilot, "Put the ship down!"

Obi-Wan stood before him, his hands on Anakin's shoulders, holding him steady and firm. "Don't let your personal feelings get in the way," he reminded his Padawan. He turned to the pilot. "Follow that speeder."

Anakin pushed to the side, peering over his Master's shoulder, and growled, "Lower the ship!"

Obi-Wan turned to face him again, and this time, his look was not so sympathetic. "Anakin," he said flatly, showing that there was no room for debate. "I can't take Dooku alone. If we catch him, we can end this war right now. We have a job to do."

"I don't care!" Anakin yelled at him. He pushed out to the side again and yelled at the pilot, "Put the ship down!"

"You'll be expelled from the Jedi Order," Obi-Wan said, his grim look showing no room for any argument.

The blunt statement hit Anakin hard. "I can't leave her," he said, his voice suddenly little more than a whisper.

"Come to your senses," said the uncompromising Obi-Wan. "What do you think Padmé would do if she were in your position?"

Anakin's shoulders slumped. "She would do her duty," he admitted. He turned and looked back toward where Padmé had fallen, but they were now too far off, and there was too much dust.

Gunships screamed left and right, trading fire with laser cannon emplacements. On the ground, thousands of clone troopers battled the droids, and it was already becoming apparent that these new soldiers were indeed superior. One against one, a battle droid was nearly a match for a clone trooper, and a super battle droid even more than a match. But in groups and formations, the improvisation of the clone troopers, reacting to the fast-changing battleground and following the relayed orders of their Jedi commander, was quickly giving them all of the best vantage points, all the high ground and the most defensible positions.

The battle soon extended far overhead, as well, as Republic warships engaged those Trade Federation ships that had managed to get offplanet, and those that had not yet landed. Most of those Trade Federation ships inside the asteroid belt and immediately within the perimeter of the battle were troop carriers rather than battleships, and so the Republic was fast gaining the upper hand there, as well.

Over at the command center, an exhausted and dirty Mace Windu joined Master Yoda, the two sharing looks that combined hope for the present and fear for the future.

"You decided to bring them," Mace stated.

"Troubling, it is," Yoda replied, his large eyes slowly blinking. "Two paths were there open, and this one alone offered the return of so many Jedi."

Mace Windu nodded his approval of that choice, but Yoda only looked at the turmoil and destruction raging about him and blinked his large eyes once more.

Obi-Wan pushed past Anakin, moving toward the pilot. "Follow that speeder!"

The gunship did just that, zooming low. They found the speeder soon enough, parked outside a large tower. The gunship skimmed to a stop, moving a bit lower, and Anakin and Obi-Wan leapt out, rushing to the tower door. Hardly pausing, Anakin burst through, lightsaber in hand, entering a huge hangar, with cranes and control panels, tug-ships and workbenches.

They found Count Dooku inside, standing at a control panel, working some instruments. A small interstellar sail ship sat nearby, a graceful, shining craft with a circular pod set on two lander legs, the retracted sails sweeping out to narrowing points behind it, like folded wings.

"You're going to pay for all the Jedi you killed today, Dooku!"

Anakin yelled at him, moving in determinedly. Again he felt the tug of a determined Obi-Wan, holding him back.

"We move in together," Obi-Wan explained. "You slowly on the—"

"No! I'm taking him now!" And Anakin pulled away and charged ahead.

"Anakin, no!"

Like a charging reek, the young Jedi came on, his green lightsaber ready to cut Dooku in half. The Count looked at him out of the corner of his eye, smiling as if truly amused.

Anakin didn't catch the cue. His rage moved him along, as it had with the Tusken Raiders.

But this was no simple warrior enemy. Dooku's hand shot out toward the charging Jedi, sending forth a Force push as solid as any stone wall, and a burst of blue Force lightning, unknown to Jedi, charged all about the trapped and lifted Jedi Padawan.

Anakin managed to hold onto his lightsaber as he went up into the air, held there by the power of the Count. With a wave of his hand, Dooku sent Anakin flying across the room, to crash into a distant wall, where he slumped down, dazed.

"As you can see, my Jedi powers are far beyond yours," Dooku said with complete confidence and calm.

"I don't think so," Obi-Wan countered, moving toward him in a more measured and defensive manner, his borrowed blue lightsaber held across his body diagonally, up over one shoulder.

Dooku smiled and ignited a red-glowing blade.

Obi-Wan stepped slowly at first, then came on in a sudden rush, his blue blade coming in hard, right to left.

But with only a slight movement, the red blade stabbed

under the blue, then lifted up, and Obi-Wan's blade went flying harmlessly high of the mark. With a slight reversal of his wrist, Dooku stabbed straight ahead, and Obi-Wan had to throw himself backward. He brought his lightsaber across as he did, trying to parry, but Dooku had already retracted his blade by then and had settled back into perfect defensive posture.

Against that posture, Obi-Wan's sudden flurry of attacks seemed exaggerated and inefficient, for Dooku defeated each, one after another, with a slight parry or dodge, seeming barely to move. For while Obi-Wan and most of the Jedi were sword fighters, Count Dooku was a fencer, following an older fighting style, one more effective against weapons like lightsabers than against projectile weapons like blasters. The Jedi on the whole had abandoned that old fighting style, considering it almost irrelevant against the enemies of the present galaxy, but Dooku had always held stubbornly to it, considering it among the highest of fighting disciplines.

Now, as the battle played out between the Count and Obi-Wan, the older way showed its brilliance. Obi-Wan leapt and spun, slashing side to side, chopping and thrusting, but all of Dooku's movements seemed far more efficient. He followed a single line, front and back, his feet shifting to keep him constantly in perfect balance as he retreated and came on suddenly with devastating thrusts that had Obi-Wan stumbling backward.

"Master Kenobi, you disappoint me," the Count taunted. "Yoda holds you in such high esteem."

His words spurred Obi-Wan forward with another series of slashes and chops, but Dooku's red blade angled left and then right, then up just enough to send Obi-Wan's descending blade slipping off to the side. Obi-Wan had to retreat soon after, gasping for breath.

"Come, come, Master Kenobi," Dooku said, his lips curled in a wicked smile. "Put me out of my misery."

Obi-Wan steadied himself and shifted his lightsaber from hand to hand, getting a better grip on it. Then he exploded into motion, coming on again fiercely, his blue lightsaber flashing all about. He kept a better measure of his cuts this time, though, reversing his angle often, turning a wide slash into a sudden thrust, and he soon had Dooku backing, the red blade working furiously to keep Obi-Wan at bay.

Obi-Wan pressed forward more forcefully, but Dooku continued to fend off the strikes, and then his momentum played out. He was too far forward, while Dooku remained in perfect balance, ready for a counterstrike.

And then it was Dooku suddenly pressing the attack, his red blade stabbing and retracting so quickly that most of Obi-Wan's cutting parries hit nothing but air. Obi-Wan had to jump back, and then back again, and again, as those thrusts moved ever closer to hitting home.

Dooku stepped forward suddenly, stabbing low for Obi-Wan's thigh. Down went the blue blade to intercept, but to Obi-Wan's horror, Dooku retracted his weapon and thrust it right back out, up high and across the other way. Obi-Wan couldn't get his weapon back to block, nor could he slide back fast enough.

Dooku's red blade stabbed hard into his left shoulder, and as he lurched back, Dooku retracted the blade and stabbed along its original course, digging into Obi-Wan's right thigh. The Jedi stumbled backward, tripping and crashing hard against the wall, but even as he fell, Dooku was there, his red blade rolling over and inside Obi-Wan's blade, and with a sudden jerk, he sent Obi-Wan's lightsaber bouncing across the floor.

"And so it ends," Dooku said to the helpless Obi-Wan. With

a shrug, the elegant Count lifted his red blade up high, then brought it down hard at Obi-Wan's head.

A green blade cut in under it, stopping it with a shower of sparks.

The Count reacted immediately, backpedaling and turning to face Anakin. "That's brave of you, boy, but foolish. I would've thought you'd have learned your lesson."

"I'm a slow learner," Anakin replied coolly, and he came on then, so suddenly, so powerfully, his green blade whirling with such speed that he seemed almost encased in green light.

For the first time, Count Dooku lost his little confident smile. He had to work furiously to keep Anakin's blade at bay, dodging more than parrying. He tried to step out to the side, but stopped as if he had hit a wall, and his eyes widened a bit when he realized that this young Padawan, in the midst of that assault, had used the Force to block his exit.

"You have unusual powers, young Padawan," he sincerely congratulated. His little grin returned, and gradually Dooku put himself back on even footing with Anakin, trading thrust for slash and forcing Anakin to dodge and parry as often as he tried to strike.

"Unusual," Dooku said again. "But not enough to save you this time!" He came on hard, thinking to drive Anakin back and off balance as he had driven Obi-Wan back. But Anakin held his ground stubbornly, his green blade flashing left, right, and down so forcefully and precisely that none of Dooku's attacks got through.

Off to the side, Obi-Wan understood that it couldn't hold. Anakin was expending many times the energy of the efficient Dooku, and as soon as he tired . . .

Obi-Wan knew that he had to do something. He tried to come forward, but winced and fell back, in too much pain. As he collected his thoughts, he reached out with the Force instead, grabbing at his lightsaber and pulling it in to his grasp. "Anakin!" he called, and he tossed the young Padawan the blade. Anakin caught it without ever breaking the flow of his fighting, turning it under and igniting it immediately, putting it into the swirling flow.

Obi-Wan watched in admiration as Anakin worked the two blades in perfect harmony, spinning them over and about with blinding speed and precision.

And he watched with similar feelings the working of Count Dooku's red lightsaber, flashing ahead and back with equal precision, picking off attack after attack and even countering once or twice to interrupt the flow of Anakin's barrage.

Obi-Wan's heart leapt in hope as Anakin charged forward suddenly, bringing his green blade over his shoulder and across, down at the Count. Obi-Wan understood immediately, even before he noted Anakin's blue blade coming up and over the other way—the green blade would push the Count's lightsaber out of the way, clearing the path for the victorious strike!

But Dooku retracted impossibly fast, and Anakin's down-cutting green blade hit nothing but air.

Dooku stabbed straight ahead, intercepting the blue blade. The Count's hand worked up inside and over, then back around with a sudden twist, launching the blue lightsaber from Anakin's grasp. Dooku went on the offensive immediately, driving the surprised and off-balance Anakin back.

Anakin fought hard to regain his fighting posture, but Dooku was relentless, thrusting repeatedly, keeping the young Padawan stumbling backward.

And then he stopped, suddenly, and almost on reflex, Anakin turned back on him, roaring and slashing hard.

"No!" Obi-Wan cried.

Dooku stabbed ahead and slashed out suddenly, intercepting not Anakin's green blade, but the Padawan's arm, at the elbow. Half of Anakin's arm flew to the side, his hand still gripping the lightsaber.

Anakin dropped to the ground, grabbing his severed arm in agony.

Dooku gave another of his resigned shrugs. "And so it ends," he said for the second time.

Even as he spoke, though, the great hangar doors of the tower slid open, smoke from the battle outside pouring in. And through that smoke came a diminutive figure, but one seeming taller than all of them at that moment.

"Master Yoda," Dooku breathed.

"Count Dooku," said Yoda.

Dooku's eyes widened and he stepped back, turning to face Yoda directly. He brought his lightsaber up to his face, shut down the blade, then snapped it to the side in formal salute. "You have interfered with our plans for the last time."

A wave of Dooku's free hand sent a piece of machinery flying at the diminutive Jedi Master, seeming as if it would surely crush him.

But Yoda was ready, waving his own hand, Force-pushing the flying machinery harmlessly aside.

Dooku clutched up at the ceiling, breaking free great blocks that tumbled down at Yoda.

But small hands waved and the boulders dropped to the sides, bouncing across the floor all about the untouched Master Yoda.

Dooku gave a little growl and thrust forth his hand, loosing a line of blue lightning at the diminutive Master.

Yoda caught it in his own hand and turned it aside, but far from easily.

"Powerful you have become, Dooku," Yoda admitted, and the Count grinned—but Yoda promptly took that grin away by adding, "The dark side I sense in you."

"I have become more powerful than any Jedi," Dooku countered. "Even you, my old Master!"

More lightning poured forth from Dooku's hand, but Yoda continued to catch it and turn it, and seemed to become even more settled in his defensive posture.

"Much to learn you still have," Yoda remarked.

Dooku disengaged the futile lightning assault. "It is obvious this contest will not be decided by our knowledge of the Force, but by our skills with a lightsaber."

Yoda reverently drew out his lightsaber, its green blade humming to life.

Dooku gave a crisp salute, igniting his own red blade, but then, formalities over, he leapt at Yoda, a sudden and devastating thrust.

But one that never got close to hitting. With hardly a movement, Yoda turned the blade aside.

Dooku went into a wild flurry then, the likes of which he had not shown against Obi-Wan or Anakin, raining blows at the diminutive Master. But Yoda didn't even seem to move. He didn't step back or to the side, yet his subtle dodges and precision parries kept Dooku's blade slashing and stabbing harmlessly wide.

It went on and on for many moments, but eventually Dooku's

flurry began to slow, and the Count, recognizing the futility of this attempt to overwhelm, stepped back fast.

Not fast enough.

With a sudden burst of sheer power, Master Yoda flew forward, his blade working so mightily that its residual glow outshone even those of both of Anakin's lightsabers when he was at the peak of his dance. Dooku held strong, though, his red blade parrying brilliantly, each block backed by the power of the Force, or else Yoda's strikes would have driven right through.

Just as he was about to launch a counter, though, Yoda was gone, leaping high and turning a somersault to land right behind Dooku, in perfect balance, striking hard.

Dooku reversed his grip and stabbed out behind him, intercepting the blow. He let go of his weapon altogether, tossing it just a bit, and spun about, catching it before it had even disengaged from Yoda's blade.

With a growl of rage, Dooku reached more deeply into the Force, letting it flow through him as if his physical form was a mere conduit for its power. His tempo increased suddenly and dramatically, three steps forward, two back, perfectly balanced all the while. His fighting style was one based on balance, on the back-and-forth charges, thrusts and sudden retreats, and now he came at Yoda with a series of cunning stabs, angled left and right.

Never could he strike low, though, for never did Yoda seem to be on the ground, leaping and spinning, flying all about, parrying each blow and offering cunning counters that had Dooku skipping backward desperately.

Dooku stabbed up high, turning the angle of his lightsaber in anticipation that Yoda would dodge left. But Yoda, as if in complete anticipation of the movement, veered neither left nor right, but rather, dropped to the ground. The Count had already retracted the missed thrust, and began a second stab, this time down low, but Yoda had anticipated that, too, and went right back up behind the stabbing blade.

A sudden stab by Yoda had Dooku quick-stepping back even more off-balance, for the first time, and then Yoda flew away, up and back.

The furious Dooku pursued, thrusting hard for Yoda's head. And in his rage when his stab missed yet again, he reverted to a slashing attack.

Yoda's green blade caught the blow, holding the red lightsaber at bay, locking the two in a contest of strength, physical and of the Force.

"Fought well, you have, my old Padawan," Yoda congratulated, and his lightsaber began to move out, just a bit, forcing Dooku back.

"The battle is far from over!" Dooku stubbornly argued. "This is just the beginning!" Reaching into the Force, he took hold of one of the huge cranes within the hangar and threw it down at Obi-Wan and Anakin.

"Anakin!" Obi-Wan cried. He grabbed at the plummeting crane with the Force, and Anakin, startled awake, did so, as well. Even working together, they hadn't the strength left to stop its crushing descent.

But Yoda did.

Yoda grabbed the crane and held it fast, but in doing so, he had to release Dooku. The Count wasted no time, sprinting away, leaping up the ramp to his sail ship. As Yoda began to move the fallen crane harmlessly aside, the sail ship's engine roared to life, and all three Jedi watched helplessly as Count Dooku blasted away.

As Anakin and Obi-Wan walked over to the exhausted Yoda, Padmé rushed in, running to Anakin and wrapping the sorely wounded young man in a tight, desperate hug.

"A dark day, it is," Yoda said quietly.

EPILOGUE

In the gutters of lower Coruscant, a graceful sail ship glided down, its wings folding delicately as it went to its more conventional drives, settling easily inside the broken pavement of a seemingly abandoned building.

Count Dooku climbed out of his ship, walking to the shadows at the side of the secret landing ramp, where a hooded figure waited. He moved before the shadowy figure and bowed reverently.

"The Force is with us, Master Sidious."

"Welcome home, Lord Tyranus," the Sith Lord replied. "You have done well."

"I bring you good news, my lord. The war has begun."

"Excellent," Sidious said, his gravelly voice hinting at a hiss. From underneath the dark shadows of his huge cowl, the Dark Lord's smile widened. "Everything is going as planned."

Across the city, in the somber Jedi Temple, so many lamented the loss of friends and colleagues. Obi-Wan and Mace

Windu stood staring out the window of Master Yoda's apartment while the diminutive Master sat in a chair across the way, contemplating the troubling events.

"Do you believe what Count Dooku said about Sidious controlling the Senate?" Obi-Wan asked, breaking the contemplative silence. "It doesn't feel right."

Mace started to respond, but Yoda interjected, "Become unreliable, Dooku has. Joined the dark side. Lies, deceit, creating mistrust are his ways now."

"Nevertheless, I feel we should keep a closer eye on the Senate," Mace put in, and Yoda agreed.

After some more quiet contemplation, Mace turned a curious gaze upon Obi-Wan. "Where is your apprentice?"

"On his way to Naboo," Obi-Wan answered. "Escorting Senator Amidala home."

Mace nodded, and Obi-Wan caught a glimmer of concern in his dark eyes—concern that Obi-Wan shared about Anakin and Padmé. They let it go at that time, though, for there seemed greater problems at hand. Again, it was Obi-Wan who broke the silence.

"I have to admit, without the clones, it would not have been a victory."

"Victory?" Yoda echoed with great skepticism. "Victory, you say?"

Obi-Wan and Mace Windu turned as one to the great Jedi Master, catching clearly the profound sadness in his tone.

"Master Obi-Wan, not victory," Yoda went on. "The shroud of the dark side has fallen. Begun, this Clone War has!"

His words hung in the air about them, thick with emotion and concern, as dire a prediction as anyone in the Jedi Council had ever heard uttered.

*   *   *

Senator Bail Organa and Mas Amedda flanked Supreme Chancellor Palpatine as he stood on the balcony, overlooking the deployment of the Republic army. Below them, tens of thousands of clone troopers marched about in tight formations, an orderly procession that brought them in files ascending the landing ramps of the huge military assault ships.

A deep sadness marked the handsome features of Bail Organa, but when he looked over at the Supreme Chancellor, he saw there a grim determination.

On distant Naboo, in a rose-covered arbor overlooking the sparkling lake, Anakin and Padmé stood hand in hand, Anakin in his formal Jedi robes and Padmé in a beautiful white gown with flowered trim. Anakin's new mechanical arm hung at his side, the fingers clenching and opening in reflexive movements.

Before them stood a Naboo holy man, his hands raised above their heads as he recited the ancient texts of marriage.

And when the proclamation was made, R2-D2 and C-3PO, bearing witness to the union, whistled and clapped.

And Anakin Skywalker and Padmé Amidala shared their first kiss as husband and wife.